THE MARK OF DAI-NĒ

THE TALES OF DAI-NĒ

BOOK 1

I. N. KNIGHT

Published by I. N. Knight in the United States of America

First Printing, 2024

DEDICATION

Though it's not the first book I've published, this is the first book I've ever started writing and there are a lot of people to thank for that.

To Savannah: for inviting me to the makeshift writing group of three in high school where I started this book.

To Daytona: for naming Blemwick and asking "Is there going to be any magic?" because that broadened my mind on where I was taking this story and spawned all this mess.

To Haley: for always reading what we wrote in the mornings even though it was awful and begging for more. You boosted my confidence where I would have failed otherwise.

To Uncle Tony: for sharing his writing with me and inspiring me.

To my sister, Julia: for reading my trashed stories and saying she wanted to know how it ended because I had her hooked. Even though I got mad at you for reading something I thought was awful, you were one of my first fans.

To Samantha: for getting me into writing in the first place. If it weren't for you, I never would have found my passion in life.

CONTENTS

PROLOGUE

Sixteen Years Prior.

Breathing hard, the woman ducked into a downtown alleyway. She had been expecting an attack once they got to the portal, or after they reached the other side of the Veil. But she had not been expecting their pursuers to anticipate their movements and isolate them from one another before even reaching the other side.

The Akhekhu mount - a reptilian creature that preferred desert regions, but could survive most anywhere, even in certain cold climates - was a terrifying beast to be on the wrong side of. Used by bounty hunters to track down their prey, it had the ability to taste a scent in the air and follow it anywhere. All it needed was something with the scent on it, and it could track anything across country. Even through water. Though it was nearly impossible to lose an Akhekhu once it picked up the trail, it was possible to confuse its sense of smell by masking the target's with a much stronger one.

There were few people that had access to these creatures, let alone the ability to train them. And she had one on her tail.

The guardian made her way through the late night stragglers of the small city, not glancing up at any of them as she went. Scanning the alleys and streets ahead and behind, she watched for any sign of the creature and its rider. The farther she traveled the more frequent the buildings were - towers of glistening metal that seemed to reach for the very stars in the sky, however few there were. Though the night grew later, the stars refused to show their faces, for the lights of the city kept them at bay and kept this strange world aglow for them. It was vastly different from the living cities - some carved out of ancient trees, others formed from the earth, and others still that were a combination of the inhabitants' work and the natural growth of the city. This place felt lifeless. Cold.

Unwelcoming.

Before long the woman stumbled across a patch of wooded area. There was a paved trail that wound around and through the trees with benches alongside it. She stopped and hid behind one of the benches in the shrubbery. Her breath came in short ragged bursts and hung thick in the cold night air.

Snap-

Her head shot around toward the noise. She held her breath as the sound of scuffling and a low hiss like an intake of breath reached her ears.

The sounds were closer now. The woman reached inside her long coat and pulled out a serrated blade. Gripping the handle of the dagger tightly, ready for an attack, she clutched the child in her other arm to her chest.

From behind the trees came a pale skinned stranger shuffling along the paved walkway drowsily. He stepped on a twig and stumbled, his feet scraping the pavement. He was mostly clean shaven, neatly dressed in a coat of thin material, and a white undershirt that had a long dark strip of cloth hanging loosely from his neck. His dark hair was short - barely a few inches long - and somewhat disheveled. The tension in the guardian's shoulders ebbed slightly.

Idiot, she silently scolded herself. *Jumping at the slightest sound will get us both killed.*

She glanced down at the child asleep in her arms. There was a spell on each of the Dai-Nē to sleep until the next sunrise. By then each of them should be well out of the way of danger - it wouldn't do to have the child awakened while trying to hide and create a ruckus, crying.

It also wouldn't do any good to have her heart leaping at every single twig snap either. She briefly closed her eyes and took a deep breath. She let it out slowly, the tension with it, though the grip on her knife stayed tight. The guardian eyed the stranger again as he sniffled to himself, unaware he was being watched. His face was wet from crying.

The Akhekhu lunged from the underbrush behind the guardian, surprising her. With a grunt of exertion, she slashed at the creature as it came down on her, nearly going down with it. The feral hiss it let out as it snapped at her face sent a chill creeping into her gut. It had a good whiff of her now. There would be no escaping it if she didn't think quickly.

The worst thing about Akhekhu mounts were their ability to go for days without rest, tracking their prey until they gave up or passed out from exhaustion. Once it had a scent good and solidified in its senses there was nothing that could get between it and its prey. Except perhaps a damn good fighter.

The woman dug the knife deeper and twisted the handle, making the blade crunch against bone as it snapped a piece off. The Akhekhu shrieked, injured, and dove away, but not before scoring a slash on the guardian's shoulder with one of its razor sharp talons, narrowly missing its target in her arms. She let out a growl of pain as she stumbled out of the bushes and into the open where the sniffling stranger caught sight of her, and yelped in surprise.

The Dai-Nē's guardian glanced briefly at the stranger, then back over her shoulder for the creature which was nowhere in sight. Swearing under her breath, she grabbed the confused stranger's arm and ran. She couldn't very well leave the man as bait, but he could also prove useful. Taking an uncertain step backward and giving a shout of surprise when approached, the stranger stumbled heavily, barely keeping up with the guardian who dragged him along by the wrist.

"I- I don't have any money!" he stammered, trying to free himself from this dark-skinned stranger in a trench coat and hooded cloak who smelled of sweat and pine.

The guardian shushed him, ducking behind a tree and dragging him with her. She checked over the shrubs to see if the Akhekhu was following them, but ducked back down almost immediately when she saw the creature not far behind sniffing the air. The rider was gone. And that meant only one thing: ambush. The stranger disrupted her panicked thoughts, begging and pleading hoarsely to spare his life, going on and on about his terrible luck.

"Please-" he whimpered. "My wife just died a few weeks ago, my car was stolen yesterday, and now I think I'm going to get laid off from my job because it made me late again....! I really don't have any-"

Wordlessly, the guardian pressed her hand over the stranger's mouth, the knife still tucked in her grip. The sight of the blood covered blade made the stranger turn as pale as a ghost, eyes bulging in fear. The guardian shushed him again and the stranger nodded fervently. A growl sounded behind them and they both froze. The guardian shook her head at the stranger to not make a noise as she removed her hand.

What was that? the stranger mouthed when he realized they were hiding from something. He tried to crane his neck to see, but the guardian handed him the bundle in her arms and pushed him back against the tree.

"Run," the guardian breathed, barely audible. "I will find you again, but I may have a different face. You will know me by this stone," she added, pulling out the two bands around her neck. Each held a stone; one glowing yellow, the other a bright pulsing blue. "I will explain then. For now, run."

It was a risky move, leaving the child with a stranger, but with the rider gone, this was the only way she could buy some time: to confuse their trail. Without another word she disappeared into the shrubs. Silence fell over the area as the stranger sat in shock, barely daring to breathe as he listened for a sound. The bundle in his arms shifted and he nearly threw it. Cautiously, he pulled back the cloth to see what it was, and revealed a small child. Sleeping.

His mind reeled and tried to piece things together - why did she just hand him her child? Why did she have a huge knife covered in blood? Who or what was supposedly after them? - but his thoughts were interrupted by a noise. A reptilian shriek followed by a low growl and feral hiss came from the direction in which the woman in the trench coat had disappeared.

He chanced a look over the bushes, and his eyes went wide, the very sight tearing a scream from his lips. A creature that looked like a mix between a six foot tall velociraptor with its jagged teeth and head shape, and a komodo dragon with its length and the broadness of its back and tail; reared up, striking at the dark skinned woman with vicious claws. There was a saddle on its back and a bridle around its face, but that didn't hinder it from snapping at the woman. She thrust out her knife to parry the blow, cutting the creature across its limbs. When the stranger holding the child screamed, both the creature and the guardian turned their heads to look in unison, locking eyes on him. The creature took advantage of its opponent's distraction and lunged for the bushes where the stranger knelt, the familiar scent it was hunting emanating from the bundle he held.

"No!" the guardian shouted, leaping after the creature. She jumped forward just as the creature reached the bushes and stabbed down on its shoulder, using her own weight to hold it down. She knew it wouldn't last long for something used to carrying a rider, but the knife in the creature's shoulder was enough to send it crumbling to the ground, its tail lashing about and an uninjured arm scrabbling for a grip in the soil.

"Run!" she yelled at the stranger in the bushes. "Protect the child!" she called, struggling to hold back the creature as it shrieked and flailed in anger. The stranger was already on his feet and running away with everything he had.

He stumbled but kept running, fear pumping his heart faster than he thought possible. Adrenaline rushed through his veins and pushed him onward. His mind was in too much turmoil and cold fear to think. He had to get away, and he had to protect the child from that thing. That's all he knew. Why? He didn't have the capacity to consider that. Run or die? That he understood. He tore out of the park and down the street, not slowing until he realized he could hear something behind him running on the pavement.

The sound of the footsteps behind him set a pounding rhythm that was a little quicker than his own against the cement, getting louder by the minute. He chanced a glance over his shoulder to find a huge figure following him and gaining quickly. A scream tore from his throat and he found his feet could go even faster when properly motivated. Under the streetlight he had seen the glint of steel in various places. This person was a walking armory and whoever they were, he didn't want to meet them. He glanced back over his shoulder to see how close his pursuer was, and saw them draw a weapon. He could hear the *shink* of steel as it slid out of its holster. With another, more high pitched scream, the man's head shot back forward, his eyes searching desperately for somewhere to go, his feet trying to run faster, but physically incapable of doing so.

The police station! he thought. It was around the next corner! They may think he was a lunatic for running in there in the middle of the night, screeching like a madman, but he didn't care. He tore around the corner and onto the next street, the figure behind him getting closer and closer. His blood ran cold when he realized he could hear them grunting with the effort to catch up with him. Having sighted the police station, he screamed for help as he bolted through the set of doors, slipping on the slick, freshly mopped floor up front that sent him sliding past the counter. Startled, the police dispatcher stood up abruptly, and a policeman behind the counter went for his gun.

"He's trying to kill me!" the man on the floor screamed in sheer terror, clutching the bundle to his chest. The policeman snapped his gaze back at the doors to see a shadowed figure standing outside, breathing heavily, but not entering. He ordered the dispatchers to get down behind the counter and watched carefully.

"Any available unit, hostile in the lobby," the dispatcher's voice echoed over the radio, a vague description of the subject following.

"Police! Drop the weapon! Hands where I can see them!" demanded the cop. The man in the doorway turned and disappeared into the street. "Call 127," the policeman instructed the dispatcher, followed by a set of orders to give them. The dispatcher was already a step ahead. Another officer came through a side door and followed the armed figure, hand on the gun at his hip. Three others were right behind him as the dispatcher's voice gave out more information over the radio and the officers answered back. Once that was taken care of, the officer behind the counter looked at the man on the floor, shaking in the corner, clutching a bundle to his chest. "What's that?" he demanded. The man held up one hand to show he meant no harm, then carefully pulled back the cloth and showed him the child. The officer relaxed slightly, and looked surprised.

"Damn I wish I could sleep like that," he muttered. "Do either of you need medical attention?"

The man shook his head, completely unsure of anything, and shifted the bundle in his arms. The child stirred slightly, but still slept.

"Why don't you come to the back where you can answer a few questions?" The officer took the man to the back, and set him down. For the longest, he couldn't find his voice, trying to wrap his mind around everything he just saw, but after he caught his breath, the words seemed to come more easily.

"What's your name?" the cop asked again now that the subject could form words properly.

"J-James," he replied at last. "James Ephraim."

CHAPTER 1
ELEMENT

Present Day

The taillights of the vehicle dimmed as the driver pressed the gas, turning out of the gated enclosure and leaving Amara behind. Her throat had gone dry as reality settled on her. He was really leaving her here. He was really making her go to this boarding school, all because his new girlfriend didn't get along with her.

At least, that's who Amara blamed. Liz had been the one whispering it when she didn't think Amara could hear. Or maybe she just waited until Amara was within earshot to say it, hoping to instigate another fight to prove it was a good idea. That Amara needed more socializing than she'd received with homeschooling, although she was already socialized in some of the weekly programs she did.

"That your social worker?"

Amara blinked out of her thoughts to glance at the gate-keeper who had just finished printing off a piece of paper he was handing her. Thin, white hair barely covered his head, and he sported a thick, wild mustache that stuck out oddly from under his nose. She glanced at his name tag and saw the well-worn letters that spelled 'Bill'.

"No," she replied softly, taking the paper and examining the map of the school grounds with all the ramp entrances and emergency exits highlighted and fire escapes marked. "My dad..."

"Well," Bill said, the subtle twitch of his eyebrow the only sign of his surprise. "The upside is you don't have to deal with parents as much here." His attempt to lighten the mood fell short. A lot short.

She looked past the guard shack and into the grounds. The school was a good three stories high, and the dorms on either side were four stories high each. She hoped most of her classes were on the lower levels. Though, with her luck, they wouldn't be. There was a wide grassy area on either side and behind it - from what she could tell, anyway. There was also a very large sandstone-colored wall surrounding it, topped with red clay shingles and the occasional wrought iron decoration that looked to double as perimeter lights, and neatly trimmed bushes out front and a set of woods behind it, but she couldn't tell if the trees were within school grounds or not. It felt almost like a tiny college campus, with three large, connected buildings containing the campus and dorms.

Bill patted her on the shoulder. "You ready to go, Hot Wheels?"

Amara resisted the urge to snap at him for the nickname. "I can find my way, thanks."

"Sure you don't need help with the umbrella or the doors?" he asked.

"I'll manage," she replied, pushing her chair forward. If one more person called her Hot Wheels today, she was going to strangle them. She didn't want any company at the moment anyhow. She felt like someone had betrayed her, but also like she had been an idiot. They had already moved her things here to prepare for her departure, but there was still a part of her that believed she could talk her father out of it. But here she was - rolling up the side ramp to the school, her pants and shoes getting wet in the rain. No one ever seemed to think making covered ramps would be a good plan when you had to steer a wheelchair and hold an umbrella and a bag and a map at the same time.

Then again, she had just been the one to turn down help. Too irritated to care and letting her anger fuel her refusal to ask for any help, she pried her way through the front doors. After getting buzzed through, she slowed to a stop on the doormat to fold away her umbrella and settle. Inside was just as nice - if not nicer - than the outside. It was clean and well-kept, not showing signs of age, as if it were a newer building. The halls were eerily quiet, empty of any signs of intelligent life anywhere, though that probably wouldn't change when people started filing through.

Things had felt pretty normal when Liz first came along and started dating her dad, but the more she'd interacted with Amara, the more Amara disliked her. Mistrusted her. Yet her dad just shrugged it off, asking for patience and under-standing. And she had tried. Oh, how she had tried, but when the suggestion of boarding school had come up, Amara had given up the niceties and the claws had come out. The fights between her and Liz went from once or twice a week to several times a day.

She never even considered she'd actually lose that battle.

Her fire felt snuffed out as she looked at the map again, tracing her finger across the lines to find the path to the office.

One thing at a time. Right now, she needed to procure her room key and unpack a bit. And by unpacking, she meant lay on the bed and morph into a blob with no defining shape, and pretend like she didn't exist for a while.

Did they even have Wi-Fi here? She groaned at the thought, pulling out her phone and glancing at it. It was just past eleven, but the lock screen image of her and her dad smiling together made her stop, a sharp pain running through her chest. Her hand shook, her vision blurring as she felt something tickle her cheek. Furiously wiping away the unwanted tear, she sniffed and stowed away her phone.

Office, she reminded herself forcefully. *Office, office! Focus on positive things, like finding that one familiar face you're looking forward to seeing.* Tursanay had been Amara's best friend since kindergarten and she'd been going to Blemwick for a few years now. When Amara found out it was the same school, it had been the only saving grace of the whole situation. She wouldn't be completely alone.

She took a breath and glanced down at the map to make sure she was headed in the right direction. As she turned the corner to enter the hallway, she passed a janitor pushing a cart with a trash can and various cleaning items resting on it, headed in her direction. He eyed her a moment, suspiciously, but they wordlessly passed each other. Something about his eyes made her feel uneasy, but she tried to shake it off. It was probably just her nerves anyhow.

The door to the office swung open right as she reached for the handle and the janitor that she had just passed was staring her in the face. She jerked her hand back in surprise, sitting back in her chair. Glancing down the hallway to check and see if there was a place he could have taken a shortcut, she found only an empty stretch of hall and the entrance to the lobby on the left.

"Well, howdy there, Hot Wheels!" the janitor said, beaming. She blinked up at him, too stunned to be pissed at the name. "Come on in, I'll get out of your way," he said in a rather friendly tone. His eyes were different, but his smile was a bit too large for his face and his teeth were a little too sinister to match the cheer in his voice.

Silently and as quickly as she could, she moved past him and into the office.

The janitor nodded to the lady at the desk. "I'll check on it and let you know, Ms. Weatherwax." And with that, he ducked out the door.

Ms. Weatherwax smiled at her from across the desk, the bright red lipstick against her dark skin a pleasant contrast. She had her hair done up in intricate braids on top of her head, with not a strand out of place. Her nails had dark pink polish with little cherry blossoms painted on them. She had broad shoulders and a welcoming energy that emanated from them.

"You must be our new student," she smiled. "I've got all your papers right here. Your schedule, room key, and some things you'll need for class." She handed a thick-looking tan folder to Amara, who flipped through it. "Your books should be here in a day or so. We had the first chapter in all of them scanned so you could follow along in class until then. Your uniforms should be in by Friday. You'll start class tomorrow, and if you need anything at all, don't hesitate to stop by. You've got a map of all your classes, the dorms, and we have marked all the wheelchair access points. Any questions?"

Not that you can answer. Amara shook her head.

"Remember to have your dorm key on you at all times.

The door locks behind you automatically. You'll have a room-mate who has a key as well, but you don't need to rely on that all the time in case they're in class and you need some-thing out of your room, okay?"

Amara nodded.

"Do you need any help unpacking?" she asked.

Amara shook her head again.

"Cat got your tongue?" she teased.

Amara started to shake her head again, but caught herself. "I'm good," she said at last, her throat feeling dry. "I'll be fine."

Ms. Weatherwax smiled softly. "Welcome to Blemwick, honey. I'm sure you'll settle in quickly." She held the door open for Amara and pointed her in the right direction for good measure.

In less than ten minutes, Amara was sitting in front of the dorm room, too hesitant to knock. There was an accessible symbol on the door just below the number, and she wondered if it would live up to its promise. She also really hoped her roommate wasn't in, and that said roommate was female. And that they didn't have bunk beds. And that they had a shower she could go into without difficulty. But those were questions she hadn't thought to ask when she was in the office.

Naturally.

Then again, if it was accessible, then maybe - just maybe - things wouldn't be so bad. Taking a deep breath, she knocked, but no answer came. Testing out the key, she let herself in. On the right side of the room - the bare side - were her boxes and things next to her bed, which was thankfully a single level. On the left side of the room, there was an explo-sion of personality, from rows of books overloading the poor bookshelf at the foot of the bed to posters and art supplies. Hair products and other personal hygiene items dotted the small dresser, as well as various trinkets and jewelry. The bathroom was on the same wall that her bed rested flush against, and directly in the center of the back wall, across the room from the door, was a single window. Setting her things on the bed, she dug through the boxes until she found a dry pair of clothes to change into. Slipping into the bathroom, she was delighted to find the shower area did not differ from the rest, and the only thing separating it from the rest of the room was a curtain. In the corner was a shower chair. It would be easy to get in and out and still have room to maneuver her chair. She stripped down, dried off, and dressed in a pair of blue jeans and a long sleeve shirt to help her warm up.

Since when were schools this accommodating? Too tired to think about it, she rubbed her face, trying to banish her loud thoughts. Coming back out of the shower and into the room, she sidled over to the bed and crawled into it. It wasn't as soft as her mattress back at home. It was thin and, in a way, it was proof in her mind that this place wasn't as great as it was cracked up to be. She lay face down on the mattress, willing the blankets to smother her, but her face grew too hot and she rolled over in frustration. Too many thoughts going through her head. Circular patterns of thinking. All wanting to blame Liz. Wanting to yell at her dad, knowing it wouldn't get her anywhere. She wanted to scream at everything, but more than anything, she just wanted to not be stuck in her own head.

Getting back up with a sigh and grabbing the map out of her folder, she made her way towards the door and set out, stopping every so often to study the map. There was no point in sulking, she supposed. She paused in a hallway lined with lockers and classroom doors, and she could hear the faint murmur of a teacher saying something from behind one of them. She checked the map again and blinked. Which hall was she in again?

A cold feeling settled in the pit of her stomach. She didn't enjoy being alone like this in a new place. The silence made her skin crawl, and every horror movie she'd ever watched flash through her mind. Things that would seem peaceful and innocent would often have some kind of dark history behind them that often ended up torturing the poor souls that wandered into their paths unknowingly. Things like paranormal beings, creatures of myth and legend, man-made or disease-inspired monsters that were once ordinary people or animals turned into gruesome figures. The ideas made this place unnecessarily scary.

Stop thinking about horror movies, she mentally scolded herself, trying to stay rational. It was probably because of that creepy janitor scaring her earlier...

A bell rang directly above her, and Amara's heart nearly leapt out of her throat. In moments, the classroom doors opened and people began pouring out. Not wanting to be caught in the middle of everything, she struggled to park next to a row of lockers, hoping for all the world not to attract too much attention. But even as she forcibly made her eyes focus on the map, she could feel the stares as people passed. The noise of the crowd and the bustling of students caused her heart rate to pulse in her ears. Now, more than ever, her throat felt like it was sticking together, but she couldn't even swallow, too afraid to move.

The thoughts of horror movies still plagued her mind and part of her—the scared, childish part of her brain that common sense couldn't reason with—was afraid to look at the faces around her. She was afraid there would be something about their demeanor that she would see, that would give a clue to a darker side that their human facades were trying so desperately to hide behind. Some dark evil secret that she didn't want to stir up. And if she dared make eye contact, they'd be able to sense a weakness in her which they could exploit later.

When the crowd thinned, the locker door beside her slammed shut, startling her back into reality with a yelp.

The boy beside her hopped back and lurched away, apparently not having noticed her before. He had Asian features, medium tan skin, and his hair was short and messy, sticking out everywhere. Putting his hand over his chest and patting it as if that would help it calm down, he held up a finger, motioning for Amara to hold on for just a moment. He reached up and put something around his ear and tapped it slightly, then nodded.

"Sorry," he apologized. "I didn't hear you come up. I took this out in class so I wouldn't have to listen to the video," he explained.

"Sorry," Amara apologized, realizing they were hearing aids. Maybe that's why some areas in this school were so nice. There were more disabled people here than just her. At least she wouldn't feel like the odd person out. "I was just-" her throat caught, and she had to cough to speak properly again.

"Do you need some water?" he asked. "I can show you to the cafeteria?" He pointed over his shoulder. "I mean, it's lunchtime anyway."

"Oh, um," Amara managed. "Sure?"

He smiled and nodded, motioning for her to follow.

"Thanks..."

"No problem," he replied, falling in stride beside her. "First day?"

Amara nodded.

"A little overwhelming?"

Amara took a slow, deep breath and nodded again. "Yeah," she breathed. "Little bit."

"I get that," he half smiled as if remembering first coming to this school, too. "What grade are you?" he asked.

"I'm in my junior year," she replied.

"Oh, cool - me too," he noted. "We should have some classes in common if you need some help finding them." Then a thought occurred to him. "Oh! I'm Rodney, by the way."

"Amara," she replied with a polite smile. She wasn't exactly good at conversing with strangers. Thankfully, he was doing most of the talking.

"I'm going to ask you that like twenty more times because I suck at remembering names," he said, earning a small smile from Amara.

It was honestly the first time she'd smiled in probably a month. He rambled as he took a turn, pointing out little things that helped him remember where to turn and go. Landmarks. Landmarks she could remember. It made her feel relieved to have them, making the halls less confusing and endless.

When they reached the cafeteria, Rodney got her a tray, and they went through the line, getting some food, and found a table off to the side to sit at and talk. Amara had grabbed two water bottles and downed the first one in just a few minutes.

"I haven't seen someone that thirsty since I tried begging

for extra credit in history class, so I'd pass," Rodney commented.

Amara nearly choked on her second bottle of water.

"I mean, it worked, but I had to grovel."

"Just to get extra credit?" Amara asked.

"I'd maxed out and needed one more good grade to scrape by," he replied with an exaggerated shrug and a raise of his eyebrows. "He took pity on me."

"Ooh," Amara said.

"Yeah, unfortunately I have two more years to scrape by with, and for someone who is really fantastically bad with names and dates," he added with a grimace. "Let's just say I don't think my calling is going to be a historian."

"I don't know what I want to be," Amara replied. "I'm just worried about surviving high school."

"Where'd you go before here?" Rodney asked.

"I was homeschooled for the most part. I mean, I went to kindergarten, but after that, my dad homeschooled me since he worked from home anyhow."

"Oh cool," he nodded. "I was sort of bounced around from place to place until my social worker landed me here. Let me tell you, it's got its issues, but it's not so bad. I kind of like it. I'm just hoping I can graduate and get a job before someone tries to adopt me."

"They can do that here?" she asked. She looked around wildly, and asked in a hushed voice, "Is this like an... orphanage? Or...?"

"No," he began, then amended. "Well, I mean there are some kids here with no parents and they have the chance to be adopted through foster care, but there are some who still have parents who simply want them to go through boarding school for whatever reason," he began, then amended. "I mean, it's a wonderful school. There are a lot of different programs here that help with learning disabilities and whatnot. Sometimes, students who have been separated from their families come here so they can live a normal life until a better home can be found for them. You get some messed up kids sometimes. But overall, they just try to help."

Amara let that sink in as she nibbled at her lunch.

"Granted, there are some teachers that you just get so tired of. Mr. Higgins? In my next class? Don't sit near the front if you can help it. Man spits worse than a llama with a mouth full of chewing tobacco."

"Oh, I did not need that mental image," Amara grimaced.

They talked amicably for a while, about things they were interested in, interesting stories that came to mind, and Rodney told jokes that had Amara laughing for the first time in forever. The bell rang, signaling for Rodney to head back to class, and Amara bid him goodbye before throwing away her trash and heading back toward the dorm rooms. Now that Rodney had showed her around a bit, she had a better vision of the map in her head.

Amara made her way back to the dorms, slowly counting down the room numbers until she reached hers. But when she tried to open the door, she found it locked and wanted to panic again. She'd left her key on the bed with her other things. How was she going to get back in the room? Wait until her roommate got back? How many hours would that be? Would she have to just sit here until then? She sighed.

"Idiot," she grumbled.

The door swung open to reveal a brown-skinned girl with a lot of hair that fell to the middle of her shoulders with pencil-sized curls. Patches of freckles framed her earth-colored eyes across the bridge of her nose, and when they fell on Amara, they lit up in surprise.

"Tursanay?" Amara blinked. Tursanay and Amara had lived in the same neighborhood for about eight years growing up, and had been inseparable until Tursanay had to move away to live with her grandmother, when her dad went MIA overseas, assumed dead. They had stayed in contact via messaging and social media..

"HEY!" Tursanay exclaimed, leaning over and hugging her with her only arm. She'd been born without the other one. "What are you doing here? That's a cute print!" She reached out and touched the coarse fabric covering Amara's hair.

"Thanks!" she stammered, not sure where to begin. "I told you I was changing schools to here, remember? You said you hoped I was in some of your classes."

"Oh, I meant what are you doing at my room?" Tursanay said before things clicked. "Shut up," Tursanay gasped. "You're my new roommate?"

Amara's grin broadened into a smile. "That extended sleepover we always wanted to do can happen now." She nodded.

Tursanay squealed with a giggle of excitement. "My day just got a lot better." She stepped aside to let Amara in.

"Mine too because I'm about to throw some salt," she replied, referring to her displeasure about being sent here in the first place despite the perks she was finding. Heading into the room, Tursanay let the door swing shut behind them.

"Well, you have come to the right place." Tursanay grinned. "I am all about some salt."

The girls talked for an hour, catching up, sharing news, and rambling like they hadn't been able to in a long time.

Tursanay asked if Amara had met anyone at the school besides the staff, and she mentioned Rodney. Tursanay nodded, saying she was vaguely aware of who Amara was talking about. She had him in a few classes, but knew little about him since they never really hung out and he kept to himself.

At last, Tursanay had to go back to class, explaining it was her study period. Since she didn't have any homework to do, she had come up to the room to read. Much to Amara's good fortune.

"Make yourself a necklace out of your key. Makes it so much easier to keep up with," Tursanay advised, showing her own.

As they made plans to meet up at supper in the cafeteria, the girls said goodbye, leaving Amara alone once more with her thoughts. With all that had happened today, she felt she could brave trying to unpack a bit. After getting a good portion of the things unpacked, put away, and some boxes consolidated, then stored under her bed, Amara laid on her bare mattress and stared up at the ceiling. The move, the shock, and the stress of all that had occurred in just the last few days, along with the excitement of meeting good friends, wore her out. The food in her stomach was lulling her into an extremely sleepy state. Deciding just to close her eyes for a minute before getting back up, Amara relaxed her muscles and in moments had drifted off to sleep.

The scent of the forest was rich, earthy, and smelled strongly of pine and oak. The air was pleasantly warm, as she floated through the air as if swimming through water. Even her hair moved as if underwater, but the air felt light and not restrictive, like water. The bramble was thick and difficult to move through, and it was impossible to go two feet at a time without having to push a branch or thicket of leaves from a bush out of the way.

As Amara looked around curiously, she came across a small clearing in the trees. Inside, there was a boy about her age, with brownish-red hair that fell to his chin. He couldn't see her, it seemed, even though he searched the woods frantically for something. His eyes were the purest green she'd ever seen. Beautiful. Striking. And wide with worry.

Feeling compelled to come forward, Amara broke into the clearing and the boy's eyes fell on her, causing her to pause with a gasp. Suddenly, meeting him face to face made her nervous. She was never good at socializing. What on earth had possessed her to go to him? But even though she was nervous, the feeling that compelled her to swim forward again lingered.

First, his brows pulled together as he stared at her, confused. Then recognition crossed the boy's face, and words tumbled out of his mouth in a rapid fire, the look on his face serious. Except... there was no sound. Everything suddenly became muted, as if someone had turned off the sound. The forest, the smells, the sounds of wildlife. It felt like the world acknowledged the absurdity of swimming in the air and tried to fill the void with water, but she couldn't even hear the rushing in her ears as she felt like she was dunked in a stream. Confusion crossed her face and Amara pantomimed she couldn't hear him, but he mirrored the look of confusion. She spoke out loud, but even as she gestured again, she couldn't hear her own voice. Slowly, the world seemed like it was tilting, a pressure behind her eyes making her dizzy.

Understanding dawned on the boy's face, and he looked around for something. He fled from the clearing, winking out of existence. The second he disappeared, everything turned into a spinning chaos of color and blurred shapes. A shockwave pulsed through the air, causing Amara's stomach to flip as everything in her field of vision lurched. She doubled over, wrapping her arms around her stomach, and shook her head, trying and failing to clear it. There was a hazy feel to the air, as if everything was just a little out of focus. The world seemed to spin on its heel, a whirlwind sweeping her up into its vortex and tossing her about like food in a blender. She struggled to take a breath as the wind ripped it from her lungs, transforming the misty air into water instead. Though she fought to move and free herself from this prison of torment and hell, she couldn't. It was hard to tell what was going on around her.

A faint, distant sound reached her ears. It was just as garbled as everything else, but the closer it got, the clearer it became.

"Ee-dee mwah!"

The foreign sounds reached her ears and made no sense. She tried to look up, and in doing so, caught a brief glimpse of the boy's face. He was back in the clearing, which seemed to get farther and farther away, as if it were being pulled away through a tunnel. She couldn't quite focus on his face, but he was running toward her frantically, screaming the same words repeatedly as he reached out to her.

The world suddenly lurched again and Amara awoke to laying on the floor beside her bed, partially across some of her boxes that she had yet to unpack. There was a throbbing pain in her elbow that had bounced off her wheelchair, and she rolled over, hissing in pain and rubbing the spot. Everything hurt. She glanced around when she had blinked through the tears and caught sight of Tursanay's alarm clock. It was three minutes before the bell would ring, signaling time for supper.

"Ah!" she sat up and scrambled to climb herself out of the floor and back in her chair. It took a good bit of maneuvering, but she sat righted again as the dinner hour struck. Grabbing her key, she headed out the door and tried to note landmarks that would help her memorize this route without carrying the map with her everywhere. When class let out the first time, the halls were crowded, but they had become less desolate compared to when she first arrived. It looked less like a ghost town and felt much more welcoming.

Rodney found her first as she was stuck at a hallway intersection, unsure which hall to take.

"When in doubt," he said, coming up beside her and pointing to the bulletin board with a green background in the hall to their left. "Food is green sometimes if you like that sort of thing, but if it smells funny," he said, pointing down the opposite way. "It's probably the gym class's feet."

"I take it the gym is that way?" Amara laughed.

"Yee," Rodney agreed with an awkward grin.

"Amara!" came a familiar voice. Looking over her shoulder, she saw Tursanay headed her way. A shoulder bag hung diagonally across her torso for easy access.

"Oh, hey!" Amara called. "This is my roommate, Tursanay," she introduced.

"Oh cool," Rodney smiled, though it seemed a little strained, as if he felt uncomfortable suddenly.

"Tursanay, this is who I was telling you about - Rodney," she added. Tursanay greeted him with a smile and a wave.

"Well," Rodney began awkwardly. "I guess I'll leave you

to it." He smiled and nodded as if to dismiss himself, but Amara objected.

"No, come sit with us!" she said, and Tursanay agreed.

"Yeah, it'll be fun!" she piped up.

"O-oh," he said, looking surprised. "Okay, sure." A small smile was tugging at his lips, making him look almost relieved. As they got their trays and sat down, Tursanay noticed the bruise on Amara's elbow and asked her about it. She recounted the weird dream and how she fell.

"Oh, I hate it when that happens," Rodney said. "I did that on the top of a bunk bed once and brought the whole thing down on me when I woke up mid- roll and tried to claw my way back up."

The girls laughed.

"Yeah, my bunkmate didn't think it was too funny," he added.

The conversation moved toward what classes they had—Amara shared every class with at least one or both of them, and was excited that she wouldn't be completely alone. Rodney had history class without either of them and groaned. The one class he would have liked to have help in and he didn't have anyone to help him study. Tursanay, however, volunteered because history was one of her favorite subjects, and the class he was taking she'd already passed.

"If you help me with chemistry," she said. "I will gladly help you with history."

"Freaking deal, man!" agreed Rodney. "I love Chem."

"It makes me want to rip my hair out," Tursanay groaned.

"Careful," Amara warned him. "That's a lot of hair. She could end up strangling someone with it."

"As long as it ain't me, I'm cool," he said, holding up his hands.

The topic turned to how long Rodney and Tursanay had been there and what classes they'd taken—Rodney having been at the school for three years, and Tursanay only two—and trickled down to things they shared in common like interests, hobbies, and what they each wanted to do when they graduated. Amara was even asking if they had a swim team because she loved the water, but a very unwelcome voice interrupted them before they could answer.

"Apparently, Asians are as good at math as they say."

A blond boy with a cleft chin and an out-of-state sports team jacket over his uniform sidled up to the table and patted Rodney on the back rather forcefully.

"How'd you get twice the amount of girls to hang out with you in less than a day? How'd you get actual people to hang out with you, for that matter?" Then he looked at the girls and made a face. "What, were there slim pickings at the petting zoo or something?"

Amara scowled. This guy had been speaking for less than a breath and she already hated him. He must have been one of those students that were passed off here by their wealthy parents and just didn't give a crap. Just because he had family issues didn't mean he had to pick on them.

"Go away, Trenton," Tursanay dismissed. "The glint of fluorescent light off your pale skin is blinding me." She shaded her eyes. "It's almost as blinding as your stupidity."

Amara glanced at Rodney, who had paled as his eyes got the size of dinner plates. He shoveled three heaps of mashed potatoes in his mouth and kept his head down.

"No see," Trenton continued, putting his arm around Rodney's shoulders. Rodney froze, swallowing hard, the look on his face saying the potatoes were trying to stick in his throat. "Roberts here owes me. If it weren't for him yesterday,

I wouldn't have gotten a demerit. And if I hadn't gotten a demerit, I wouldn't have gotten a detention."

"School's only been in for two weeks. How do you already have ten demerits?" Tursanay snorted in disbelief. "That's a demerit a day, excluding weekends. Even the strictest teachers aren't that relentless."

Amara's brows shot up in surprise, but she stayed quiet. If this guy got a demerit a day - which from Tursanay's reaction sounded like an extreme occurrence - this was definitely not good. Her gut was screaming he was going to start something, but she wasn't sure how to avoid it.

"I've got issues with people bossing me around and thinking they can tell me what to do," Trenton replied. His eyes widened as he smiled, giving his features a very sinister appearance. "Besides," he said, turning his attention back to Rodney. "I don't think it's fair that I'm the only one that got a detention."

"Rodney hasn't gotten ten demerits in two weeks," Tursanay replied. Amara glanced at her nervously, but Tursanay seemed relaxed still. "I don't think anyone in this school has gotten ten demerits in two weeks, so congrats for being a trendsetter. Downside to being a trendsetter, though, is going at it alone."

"See, I disagree. I think it'd be a lot more fair if he joined me," Trenton replied. "I mean, if Roberts here doesn't join me, how am I gonna clean the toilets? He has the perfect head of hair for that. You won't even be able to tell it has crap in it."

Again, Amara glanced at Tursanay: there was still no change in her demeanor, but Amara was grinding her teeth.

"How do you hide yours?" Tursanay asked.

"My what?" Trenton asked, almost daring her to give him a reason to start something.

Amara glanced back at Trenton. Her anxiety was skyrocketing between the two of them. Please don't fight. Please don't fight. I don't need to see violence on my first day here. I've already got enough going on, she mentally pleaded.

"You're so full of it, I'm legitimately shocked your eyes haven't turned brown," Tursanay replied.

Amara remembered Tursanay's dad using that line once. Except he put it in a much less nice way. At least she was holding back a bit, Amara thought. She seemed to have a better grip on her temper than the last time they'd been together. She never got angry over simple stuff. Just people that didn't know how to treat others with respect. One reason her gut screamed that something was about to happen was that Tursanay was always the one geared up and ready to fight. Here, though, her posture was still relaxed, and she rarely looked at Trenton directly, not really seeming to care what he had to say. She was lazily eating a French fry.

"If I didn't know any better, Valterri," Trenton scoffed. "I'd say you were trying to start something."

"Honestly, I could beat you with one arm tied behind my back," Tursanay smiled.

Trenton straightened, the humor gone from his face. He sized her up, and Tursanay's gaze suddenly fixated on his face, her hand casually resting on her drink. Amara felt ice churn in her stomach as she mentally willed Tursanay not to start a fight, but she felt like it was a losing battle. Hand on the cup meant she was getting ready to sling it at him if he came towards her. She'd seen her do that once in the mall when a guy wouldn't take no for an answer and leave her alone. Except then it was scalding hot coffee.

"What? You and rolling squatty potty over here gonna stand up for Ching Cheong?" Trenton asked, pushing

Rodney's face into his mashed potatoes. "Hold up, Roberts. Looks like my math was off earlier," he added. "There's like one and a half people at your table now."

"Funny," Tursanay faked a laugh, though the humor was gone from her face now too.

Amara could see the tension in her shoulders.

"I'd say the same about your balls, but they haven't dropped yet."

"You thinkin' about my balls, Valterri?" Trenton countered.

"Does castration count?" Tursanay fired back.

Amara glanced at Rodney, who looked like he either wanted to crawl under the table or throw up. Perhaps both. *Honestly, same,* Amara thought. But after seeing him shove Rodney's face into his food, she almost wanted Tursanay to go off on him. She wanted to say something now, anything, but her voice wouldn't work. When Tursanay's grip on her drink tightened, Amara steeled herself for the blow.

"Trenton!"

The blond boy straightened abruptly, and all eyes turned to an imposing figure. He stood easily over six and a half feet tall and had dark skin, a neatly trimmed goatee, and a shiny bald head. His shoulders were broad and commanding, and his very presence made one sit up taller without realizing it. He seemed stern. Unyielding. But his most striking features were his pale blue eyes. They pierced right through whomever they gazed upon.

"What have I told you about that kind of language? It's inappropriate. That's a demerit."

"What!" Trenton argued. "Mr. Asher, that's not fair! She started it!"

"I will deal with Ms. Valterri. You don't need to worry

about her. Worry about yourself. Next time someone tries to instigate, walk away. Do you understand?" he commanded.

"Yes, sir," Trenton grumbled to himself. Amara exchanged glances with Rodney, who looked just as wide eyed as she did, though he looked less surprised and more terrified.

"Good." Mr. Asher nodded once. "Now walk away." He motioned Trenton away with one finger.

And without even hesitating, Trenton cast one last glare at the trio, then shuffled away. Whoever this man was - obviously a staff member - he was good at commanding respect. And a bit of fear. He cleared his throat.

"Ms. Valterri."

Tursanay sighed, throwing her head back with the effort. "I know."

"You seemed to have a little trouble following through with the concept," Asher replied. "I'd like to reduce conflict in this school, not cultivate it."

"I'm not just going to let someone disrespect me and my friends like that. He is ableist and racist," Tursanay complained.

"Allowing him to get a rise out of you only makes matters worse," Asher said.

"Taking the high road and not letting him get a rise out of me is the same as giving him permission to say those things and worse, without the fear of repercussions," Tursanay countered.

"I see you've been learning some things from the debate team. Good," Asher approved with a nod. "I recommended you to the coach for a reason. You don't have to let Trenton get away with what he's saying and doing. You can use the knowledge and skills you have in you to turn the argument back on him without resorting to violence or name calling. Challenge him. Challenge yourself."

Tursanay grumbled, not looking at him. "It shouldn't be my job to educate him."

"No, it shouldn't," Asher agreed. "That's not your burden to bear. What you need to worry about is using your mind to the best of its abilities. Understand?"

"No," she snapped. She glared for a second, then rolled her eyes. "I'm getting a demerit too, aren't I?"

"I can't give him a demerit and not you, when you both said things you shouldn't have," Asher replied. When Tursanay grumbled, he added, "I don't play favorites." He turned his attention to Amara, who felt like her toes were curling in on themselves. "I take it you're settling in alright, Ms. Ephraim?"

Amara nodded, unsure of how to speak at the moment.

"Oh yeah, she's rooming with me," Tursanay chimed in. "We straight." She grinned to herself, as if enjoying a joke.

"Good." He nodded. "Then I'll leave you to continue eating. If you need anything at all, please feel free to ask." And with that, he left, leaving the trio in an awkward silence.

"How do you talk to him like it's no big deal?" Rodney whispered at last, breaking said silence. His face still had mashed potatoes on it, and Amara handed him a napkin. "He's terrifying."

"What, Trenton?" Tursanay scoffed. She was obviously unimpressed by the bully.

"No- well yes, him too," Rodney amended. "But Mr. Asher - he is like the scariest person I've ever seen."

"Oh - that? Is that because of the rumors that go around about him?" Tursanay laughed. Then she added, "You know he doesn't actually keep an eyeball in a jar on his desk, right?"

"Oh thank God, that used to give me nightmares," Rodney shuddered.

"A what?" Amara asked, eyebrows raised, blinking in disbelief.

"Mr. Asher is completely normal," Tursanay explained. "He's just got that military vibe. I think he was a Lieutenant Colonel or something?"

"Oh, now that makes sense," Amara realized, looking at Rodney. "Her dad was in the military, so she's used to it."

"Reasons I found you terrifying to begin with," Rodney concluded, looking at the other girl as he wiped the potatoes off his face. "I was sure I was about to witness a murder and I was trying to eat my potatoes as fast as I could because they don't get this kind of good quality starch in prison."

Tursanay laughed and made jokes as she flexed her arm to show off her muscles. The other two relaxed a bit, Amara feeling her anxiety ebb, though it still buzzed in her chest a bit. The trio finished their supper and when the evening bell rang; they trickled off to their separate dorms and turned in for the night.

Unfortunately, that was the most peace she would have for a while.

CHAPTER 2
HINDSIGHT

16 Years Prior.

Sendew bustled with merchant tents and vendors bartering and calling out to potential customers that wandered alongside the tall reflective buildings. The mirrored surfaces had panels in various places, situated so they bounced the setting sunlight through the streets, making it glimmer with a warm ambience as the lanterns flickered to life and glow.

Centaurs were making their rounds, collecting garbage from the various businesses and loading it onto a cart that they pulled behind them. The last of the diurnal creatures were trickling back out to their homes as the nocturnal crowd was waking up and moving into the streets to go about their night. Those of dusk and dawn moved indoors, preferring mirror travel to avoid the worst of the sun and starlight.

The smells from the witches' breweries—the baked goods, the strong-scented teas and coffees and other concoctions that were brewing—filled the air. A fresh batch for a fresh group.

Plus, most of the nocturnal crowd needed their blood teas to help them wake up enough to function.

In the back of a merchant tent at the center of the street, a small wood nymph child played idly with her soft, plush toy, not particularly wanting to stay here with her mother while she finished selling enchanted fruits, nuts, berries, and other health products and overpriced spell ingredients before closing up for the night. This one to give you a boost of confidence for your job interview, that one to boost your memory for a test. These to accentuate your best features once you bit into them. Touristy things.

Stretching her legs and sneaking out the back of the tent, the nymph cast one last glance back at her mother haggling with a customer before slipping off to chase her reflection on the buildings. She giggled as she splashed through the recent rain puddles, alternating between racing her reflection and dancing with it behind the safety of the tents where no one could see.

As she passed by a florist tent, she paused, enjoying the scent of the sleepy lilies that were closing up for the night, and the rich scent of pine and basil coming from inside. It almost made her mouth water. Poking her head into a back corner of the tent, she looked around at the nearby pottery, snatching off a leaf before darting back out unseen and skittering further down the street. When she had gone far enough not to be caught, she paused and admired the leaf. It was the basil she had smelled before. Grinning, she held it up for her hair to tangle it into a braid, then admired her reflection in the building, wishing it was an actual playmate and not just a mirror image.

A chorus of giggles sounded nearby and she twisted to see where they came from, but found she was alone. The laughter had seemed like many people and one person all at once, and echoing as if in an enormous cavern but close at the same time. She frowned. Who was watching her? She pulled back a few tent flaps to check, but found no one paying her any attention. The laughter sounded again behind her this time, but when she turned, she only found her reflection. The nymph's reflection blinked as she did, a smile creeping across its face as it waved shyly.

Only she hadn't waved or smiled.

Curiosity lit a smile across her face to rival that of the reflection as she took a step forward. If she could actually play with her reflection, the fun was just beginning. How did that work? What magic was this? Had it been the basil? Food that was enchanted to grant you a wish? That would be a booth she'd be visiting again soon if so.

"Hello," she beamed at her reflection.

The reflection didn't answer, but she could hear its laughter again.

"How are you doing that?" she asked, tilting her head curiously.

Come on, the same voice said, though the reflection's lips hadn't moved. *I can show you.* It motioned for her to follow, and she grinned, obliging. Chasing after her reflection and skipping along, she turned the corner into one of the alleyways and slowed. The street lights didn't reach down the alley and her reflection moved into the darkness. She was more comfortable in the light than the dark despite being adaptable to both, but the darkness ahead made her hair wriggle in protest. She smoothed her hand over the leaves and vines to calm them.

"It's dark down there," she called after her reflection, who she could just make out in the building's shadows.

The eyes seemed different now. A glint of red from some unseen light source seemed to shine in them.

There's light on the other side, it whispered with its unmoving lips. The voice seemed just as close as it had before, despite her reflection being so far away. *Come on, I'll show you. Just touch the glass.* Her reflection put its hand against the glass and beckoned her closer.

Curiously, she moved forward and, as she did, it seemed to move in rhythm with her once again.

Just touch the glass, it repeated when she stopped before her reflection, inches away. The sounds of the market had died away, the lovely scents of baked goods, fruits, and flowers with it. All she could smell here was the decay of fall leaves, an alluringly sweet scent. If there were beds of fallen leaves on the other side, she would wriggle her toes into the earth there and lay down for a nap. Suddenly, exhaustion overwhelmed her. It had been a long day, after all...

She moved her hand in unison with her reflection and gently touched the glass. She was expecting the cold, solid surface to meet her hand, but the reflection's hand had grabbed her own. And now it was pulling. She reflexively tried to pull back, but found it was like trying to move a wall.

A shock of fear coursed through her, erasing all sense of weariness from her and filling her ears with her own cries as she tried and failed to pull away. She dropped her toy and tried to dig her heels into the cobbled stone and use her free hand to grasp onto anything that could save her.

She shrieked for someone to help her, but her cries seemed lost in the night's bustle market. Tears streamed down her face and her throat grew raw from the effort to get anyone's attention, but to no avail. She looked back as she felt her ankle being grabbed and realized her foot had slipped through the glass's surface. Two more sets of solid red eyes appeared above and below her own reflection's eyes, and the smile revealed jagged teeth. She clawed at the ground, begging for the city or anyone to help her.

Come to us, become a part of us, and we will become like you.

"No!" she shrieked.

She looked back to the mouth of the alley, sight blurred with tears as she called for her mother, and saw a small figure not much taller than her standing and watching with silent horror. In a moment of panic, she reached out to the brown-haired boy, screaming for help, and lost her grip on the stonework. Her reflection pulled her in swiftly, her screams abruptly cut off as a ripple went through the glass and they both disappeared in a blur of color.

The echoes of laughter chased the boy down the alley and back out into the street. He screamed for someone the little girl didn't know and ran for all he was worth, away from that sound and the sight of her being attacked by her reflection.

The echoes in the alley faded, and the darkness ebbed away. The only signs anyone had gone down that alley in weeks were the small, soft plush toy lying on the ground soaked by the rain, and a small, crumpled basil leaf.

Present.

As the detectives arrived on the scene, they finally quieted the wailing sounds of the lost child. The moon was just beginning to rise over the tops of the buildings, and the soft glow of the lanterns along the walkways illuminated the streets. It was bright enough to keep one from stumbling, but soft enough to prevent those who could see perfectly in the dark from having their vision bombarded with a flood of light. After gathering all possible information from the area, they cleared the mirror travel station for travel again.

Away from all the detectives, sitting on the back of a medical vehicle, was a young Aziza with his knees tucked into his chest and a blanket wrapped around him securely. He swirled his finger through the thick hair on his feet, his thoughts a million miles away from the look in his eyes. Unable to shake the images from his mind, he had all but given up trying to get the detectives to believe him when someone sat down beside him. He didn't look up at first, too tired to care anymore.

"When I was a boy," said the deep voice beside him. "I remember playing hide and seek with my sister in a market place while our mother was bartering. I saw a young wood nymph skipping into an alley and thought it would be fun to have more players and followed her to ask her to play with me."

The young aziza furrowed his brow as if wondering what this story had to do with him, but said nothing.

"Only when I rounded the corner," the man beside him added, lowering his voice. "I saw her reflection come to life and snatch her through the glass."

The aziza boy glanced up then, uncertain if this was a trick or the truth, and met the man's eye. He wasn't one of the werewolf detectives, despite the gruff beginnings of a dark beard on his chin. His eyes weren't the same wolf like golden, just a warm brown. The knot in the boy's stomach eased, and a queasiness replaced it. The look said, if this stranger was telling the truth, then he really wasn't crazy.

"I believe you," he said softly, then added, "I've not mirror traveled since."

"And a lot of time it's wasted you," came a female voice from the boy's other side.

He twisted to see a lovely woman with her hair pulled back into a braid, the same eyes as the man - if not similar features. She was smiling at them as she sat next to him. "What's your name?" she asked. "I'm Ilarys. And this is my idiot brother, Keir. Don't let him scare you. He's completely harmless." She gave the boy a wink.

"It's true," the aziza boy mumbled. "My father was taken by his reflection. They don't believe me, but they've checked both sides of the mirror. They can smell him going in on this side, but there's no trace of him at the other station. But they still don't believe me." He tucked his face into his knees, disappearing further into the blanket. His toes were curled in so hard they were paling.

"Werewolves can smell almost anything and determine what it is," Ilarys began. "But sometimes they can't see what's right under their noses."

"The reflection that took your father," Keir said. "Was there anything strange about its eyes?" There was a pause before the boy nodded.

"They were red," came the muffled reply.

Keir looked at Ilarys pointedly. Ilarys looked away, trying to hide her frustration at being wrong.

"And there were more than there were supposed to be," the boy added.

"A pair above and below," Keir supplied.

The boy looked up then, wide eyed. He said nothing at first, stunned the man knew what he was talking about. He seemed to have been doubting until now.

"The girl you saw?" he asked quietly. "Did you ever find her?"

A growl from the detectives spared Keir from giving the answer that none of them wanted to hear voiced. They all glanced up to see the werewolf flanked by two cynocephali. The dog headed apes barked orders at them to show some identification. In a moment of panic, the boy between them retreated, stumbling to his feet and taking flight with a cry, his moth-like wings fluttering for all they were worth to escape the scary-looking trio.

"Hey! Someone get that kid. We still need his statement!" barked the detective. One of the cynocephali ran after the boy whilst the other stayed with the detective, growling at the intruders. "Who are you and what are you doing here?" the detective demanded. Keir held up his hands as a gesture of peace, but the werewolf only sniffed experimentally—either to commit their scent to memory or to sense if they had any magic on them, Keir wasn't sure. Either way, they questioned their trustworthiness.

"We are from the OOR," he stated. "We were in the area and heard some reports. The details seemed similar to a case we were working with and we came to investigate."

"The Order of Rynon doesn't have jurisdiction to investigate a domestic crime scene," the detective growled.

"We're not so sure it is," Keir replied.

"Once we compare notes, we should be able to see whether this interest to the Order," Ilarys stepped in. "If not, we can get out of your hair."

"Identification," replied the werewolf firmly.

Keir sighed, reaching to pat his pockets slowly so as not to set the cynocephalus off. Only when he had patted all of his pockets, he frowned.

"Problem?" the detective spat.

"My sachet," Keir said. He looked at Ilarys, who had the same concerned look.

"Mine too." They turned and looked back at where they had sat next to the boy and the way he had fled. "That little-"

Keir looked back at the werewolf hesitantly. "So... about that identification..."

The sound of the cell door clanking shut echoed in their ears like the sound of their doom. The captain of the guard had seen to locking them up himself, lest they try another ridiculous escape attempt that nearly took out several of his men. They'd be in recovery for weeks. He glared at the duo in their separate cages. They didn't look worse for wear, and that made him even more irritated. He could definitely see the family resemblance in their faces. This kind of behavior was in the blood, he surmised.

"You'll be glad to know," he said firmly. "That your precious Order will be informed of your reckless behavior and illegalities, but not until morning and I see just how injured my men are so I can tell them just how injured you will be."

"Sir," the one who had identified herself as Ilarys, stepped forward pleadingly. She was a rather shapely specimen and her big brown eyes caught him off guard as she pressed her face against the bars.

Criminals rarely looked so convincingly innocent. They tried. But he could smell their faux pas a mile away. It was one reason he'd gotten to where he was. Being able to smell intentions was useful.

"Please, just hear me out," she said.

The captain hesitated a moment, the pleading look on her face potent enough to melt anyone's heart, and intentions free of trickery.

"We were looking for the mirror people. We believe they took that boy's father, and it is imperative that an investigation be-"

The mention of mirror people instantly wiped the look of interest off the captain's face and replaced it with a look that questioned her sanity. He held up his hand to make her stop talking. Even the pretty ones could be crazy, his look said. And she believed every word she was saying.

"First, you entered a crime scene without authorization, spoke to a key witness also without authorization, terrified said witness into running away-"

"We weren't the ones that-" she began, but the captain cut her off as he barreled onward.

"-then accused said witness of conveniently stealing your sachets right as the detectives demanded your identification for entering a restricted area. Second, you want me to believe the boy's father went missing because of mirror people? Did the runaway witness tell you that before he supposedly stole your identification?" he retorted. "You have completely and utterly lost your minds."

"It's true you know," Keir spoke up. The captain looked at him with a glower. He'd been stubborn in giving his name, but the female had given it for him. "If you'd let me show you my research, I could show you several accounts of people coming up missing after mirror travel. We've been researching it extensively. We're not madmen, captain, we're researchers."

"And I suppose you think mortal kind exists too," the

captain mocked. Truthfully, this man made his stomach turn. As someone who could sense intentions, the captain couldn't get a read on this man. His intentions never took a shape or form. It was as if they changed with each spoken word and each passing instant. As if he were constantly changing and shifting his thoughts and actions. But it wasn't like the shift of someone that had the gift of foresight. He didn't always make the choice that turned out the best in the situation. Sometimes he seemed to go for the worst solution. Sometimes, he was just quiet. It was unnerving.

"I'm not concerned with other conspiracy theories. I'm concerned with missing people," Keir replied.

"Says the man that lost us a key witness," the captain argued. Again, with the inconsistencies.

"That aziza would not have flown away had your were-wolf not growled at him-" Ilarys balked.

"My detectives were trying to keep you two away from the child! You two, who mauled seven of my men, I might add," the captain continued, ignoring her. "and took one hostage-"

"No, no, I was the hostage," Ilarys argued yet again. The captain's jaw muscle was pulsing as he ground his teeth in anger.

"That's true as well," Keir agreed. "Because I'm the one that took her hostage to get them to stop fighting long enough to listen to reason." The captain cut him a look. "And yes, I fought with the... cynocephali-" he said, gesturing to his own face to mimic the muzzle of a dog. "My point is-"

"I don't care which part of it's true or what point you're trying to make," the captain snapped. "The fact remains, seven of my men are in the healer's tent, and you two are the reason for all the commotion. So, until I get more information about their condition in the morning, you're going to sit in that cell and be silent. Understand?"

"So, you will not take the time to check out my research?" Keir asked.

"You better hope I don't find it because at this rate, I'm burning it!" the captain bristled, turning on heel and leaving the prisoners to talk amongst themselves.

"That would be destruction of the Order's case records!" Keir called after him, ending with a half shout so the guard could hear him the further away he got. When no response came other than the slamming of a door, he tsked.

"I know I said I would support you no matter how ridiculous this case got, but a dungeon?" Ilarys sighed. "This is what I get for listening to you again."

"It will work out," Keir replied.

"How could it possibly work out from here? We could be disbanded from the Order at this rate," Ilarys argued. "How are you still optimistic?" Keir let out a low curse. "What?"

"Well, turns out if we had just put a protective arm around the aziza when we were talking to him, we would have discovered that he had our sachets, and could have made him agree to call us friends of the family and we'd have avoided going to the dungeon all together."

Ilarys cut him a rather rude look. "You're bringing that up *now*?" she growled. "Don't you think it's a little *late* for that?!"

"I can't help when I get predictions," Keir said with a shrug. "You know that."

"Yet you can get an almost perfect step by step of what is going to happen next in a fight and come out unscathed!" she argued, throwing her hands up in frustration.

"One step at a time, not several times in a row," Keir replied. "That's cheating."

"Cheating?" Ilarys yelled. *"It's called surviving and not going to the dungeon!"*

"Silence!" came a voice from Keir's direction. Possibly another prisoner.

"You know, last time I trusted you, that tiyanak almost ate us. The time before that, they kicked us out of a gambling hall because you attempted to cheat in a place that specifically had wards against that kind of magic, and now THIS."

"It was worth a shot," he said with a shrug. "Besides-"

"Besides nothing, Keir! You are the worst Seer I've ever met," she argued, derailing his excuse. "Your power is spotty at best. And you thought-"

"Ilarys-" Keir sighed, trying to interrupt before she could get on a tangent.

"-that it would be a good idea-" she continued, already on it.

"Ilarys-" he tried again, louder. "I'm not here to coddle you. I'm here to get to find out what happened to those people-"

"Quiet!" called the voice again.

"-to punch an already angry werewolf-" she said, speaking over him, each word getting louder.

"Look, once we get back to the Order we can straighten this out and-" he retorted, trying to outshout her. She always found something to complain about, but he was too invested in this case to go back now. She could. He'd see to it. But he was sticking around.

"-in the light of a full moon no less!" she finished. Or so he'd thought. Foolishly hoped. "I thought sight was supposed to make you smarter by showing you what was ahead. Not give you the confidence to be stupid!"

"Quiet!"

"I predicted you were going to say that," he grumbled. "I don't see that far ahead, more of how changing my choices can benefit me in the future. You know this!"

"When I get out of here, I am going to choke you!" Ilarys growled. "I've tried not to berate you about this, brother. I honestly have, but I have reached my limits. You were terrified by something when we were children, I know. But we have grown! It's time you dropped your ridiculous childhood fear and moved on!" A growl sounded in the next cell over.

"I-Ilarys-" Keir began when he heard it. However, Ilarys would not stop.

"If you weren't so obsessed with this ridiculous fear of mirrors and reflections, we might actually get some actual work done! Instead, you go gallivanting off at the first sign of strange occurrences and immediately think it's your mysterious 'mirror world species' that no one else even seems to have ever heard of, let alone believe in! Do you know how many countless hours we waste traveling across the country when we could literally step through a mirror station and be there instantaneously?"

"Ilarys - hold on - there's something growling in the cell next to me. I think it wants you to keep it down-" Keir tried. But Ilarys was already gearing up for a fight.

"*Tell me to keep quiet one more time, brother,*" Ilarys roared. "*And there will be death!*"

"*Then perish!*" came a guttural growl that had Ilarys's attention now, too. For with the last word, it kicked the wall for emphasis and a brick came flying out and sailed past Keir's face, narrowly missing him. By the grace of his sight, he barely moved just enough to keep himself from dying. It had made an indent in the wall of Ilarys's cell and made her realize her brother had not been the one telling her to keep quiet the whole while.

There was a pregnant pause.

"Who-" Ilarys began, having to swallow before continuing. "Who are you?"

"Who wants to know?" the prisoner snipped.

"The person who just watched you kick a hole into a brick wall and would be very interested in working together to make an escape attempt," Keir replied, trying to not press himself into the bars of his cell to get away. A derisive snort came as an answer.

"What about your precious Order?" the prisoner laughed.

"They will not find out we're here before those guards beat us senseless," Ilarys replied.

"Then file a complaint with the Council," the prisoner said.

"You mean the Council whose guards we just mauled and pissed off?" Keir piped up. "Yes, that'll go brilliantly. Like the Council of Dai-Nē listens to anyone that talks negatively about their golden children anyhow."

"Not a fan of the Council?" the prisoner asked sarcastically. The voice was like thunder rumbling in the distance. "I thought the Council and the Order were allies."

"If you call entertaining a spoiled, tantrum-throwing child with a lot of really dangerous weapons so they don't use them on us or our allies, then sure, I guess," Ilarys quipped. There was a long pause, followed by laughter from the other cell. The very sound was like a thunderclap.

"I feel as if I have misjudged you," the prisoner chuckled. "I am called Kapena."

"I am called Ilarys. And this is my idiot brother," she added. "He is called Keir. But he answers to-"

"No, I don't. I only answer to Keir," he interjected over his sister. There was no need to start that fight again. "Keir and Keir only."

"So, you want to plan an escape, Keir and Keir only?" Kapena said. "Pray tell what's in it for me."

"You get out too?" Keir offered.

"To be betrayed later? Something more substantial," Kapena denied.

"We could... see if the Order can grant you immunity? What are you in for?" Keir asked.

"Piracy," Kapena replied. "Amongst a few other things."

Keir pressed his face to the bars of his cell so that he could see Ilarys. He mouthed the word pirate with a wary look.

Ilarys nodded back, mouthing, I know. After all, she was standing right there and could hear everything Keir could hear. Plus, she was trying not to think of how impossible that charge would be to drop.

What do we do? Keir asked silently.

Think of something, Ilarys mouthed back.

I'm trying! Keir replied, his facial expressions getting more and more exaggerated.

"Problems?" Kapena asked. There seemed to be a bit of amusement in the question's tone.

"No, no problem at all," Keir replied a little too quickly.

"We could pay you," Ilarys offered. "To help us get out of here," she clarified.

"How much?" Kapena asked, intrigued.

There was another moment of silence as the siblings exchanged looks.

How much do you have? Keir asked.

Seven gold, three silver, five copper, Ilarys replied. You?

Three silver, two copper, Keir replied.

Ilarys glowered at him. He'd gambled the rest of the twenty gold he'd started out with away.

"We have five gold and four silver," Ilarys lied. "We can give you half now and half when we get clear of this place."

There was a pause, and a scuffle as Kapena seemed to stand up. A sigh and grunt - sounds of stretching - followed by a jingle of metal and a creaking of the cell door opening. A black scaled taniwha - a reptilian creature with far too many teeth standing nearly seven feet tall - wearing tattered, sea weathered clothes strolled out in front of their cells holding the ring of keys in hand.

"If you had that the whole time, why were you just sitting in that cell?" Keir asked suspiciously.

"I stole them while you were distracting the captain," Kapena replied. "I was going to take a nap before leaving, but plans have changed."

Keir shared a look with his sister. It was no longer scared, but intrigued. This could be interesting.

"What would you say to maybe joining the Order? Could really use someone of your skills later," Keir offered as Kapena opened his cell door.

Kapena laughed. "And what would the Order want with a pirate?"

"Depends on if you will join us," Keir prompted.

"I'm not much one for following someone else's rules," Kapena replied.

"Oh, good, you'll fit right in," Keir commented, earning a smack from his sister once she was free.

"You agreed to help us after you found out we disliked the Council," Ilarys noted.

"Was there a question in there?" Kapena asked, motioning for them to follow. The taniwha placed a clawed hand on a place in the wall and grinned at the other two inmates. Pressing on it, the wall opened like a door leading to an escape tunnel.

"You've done this before," Keir noted.

"Not me personally, but I know a few people," Kapena said evasively.

"Do you dislike the Council?" Ilarys asked, moving down the tunnel. When the door shut behind them, Keir wished he could see in the dark as well as a taniwha could. But before them was nothing but a long expanse of stairs and darkness.

"My allegiance lies with my village," Kapena answered. "As long as they are safe, I have no opinion."

"And if they are not?" Keir asked. Ilarys smacked him in the dark.

"Then neither is the threat against them," Kapena answered.

"The Order can help protect people if there is an issue," Ilarys added.

"Like they protected the dragons three hundred years ago?" Kapena replied. There was a heavy silence to follow.

"They're trying to help with the rebuild and protection," Ilarys offered weakly.

"The dragons chose to help in that war," Keir replied boldly.

Ilarys winced.

"They knew the weight of their decision. The Order wouldn't have been able to stop them," he continued. There was a hiss in the dark before them and it took them a jolt of anxiety and another breath to realize it was a chuckle.

"You are correct," Kapena replied. "I like you speak your mind, but too much of a loose tongue can get you killed. And others."

"Which is why you won't tell the Order about your village," Keir surmised.

"To ask for help, others must know where you are," Kapena said. "Or that you exist. Without that knowledge, no help may come."

"But others knowing of the existence can bring unwanted peril," Ilarys realized. "So your village is safe, but to keep it that way, it needs to remain a secret."

"That is a secret I trust with no one," Kapena replied. "But my village is not as safe as I would have it."

"What about your crew?" Keir asked. "Do they know?"

"They are a part of the village," came the reply. "And they are why I agreed to help you."

"Oh?" Keir prompted when there was a lengthy pause.

"We are what's left of a dying village. Those mirror people you've spoken of," Kapena stated, the air seeming to chill around them the further down they went.

"What about them?" Keir asked.

"What do you know of them?" Kapena prompted.

"They take the form of the individual's reflection and move as they do. When the individual in question touches the mirror, the reflection moves at the last second and traps them. Sometimes they are lured, sometimes they strike without warning. Always with little to no witnesses."

"And when they strike," Kapena added, the voice danger-ously low.

The twins felt a sense of fear settle over them.

"Their eyes change, don't they?" she finished.

"Yes," Keir replied, barely above a whisper. He remem-bered the girl from the alleyway he'd seen taken as a child. It had haunted him ever since and he refused to step in a mirror ever again. "They change to solid red. There's no eye left. Just a red glow. Both-"

"Above and below the original set," Kapena finished for him.

A gentle glow seemed to fill the stairwell and they could make out Kapena's shape before them. The sound of the ocean reached their ears from beyond the wall. The taniwha had paused at a solid end before them, no door in sight. Reaching out and touching the stone, Kapena half turned and looked at them.

"You've seen them." It wasn't a question. Keir knew a fellow survivor when he saw one.

"They attacked my village," Kapena replied. "They stole seven. You are the first person I've come across that knows anything and has been actively trying to get to the source of the issue. I want you to speak to my crew and help us get them back."

"If I can, I will do everything in my power," he replied honestly.

Kapena pushed against the wall and opened the hidden door to reveal a shrouded dock and a large ship not too far offshore. The taniwha, stepping forward wordlessly, headed towards the ship.

The siblings followed.

The cry of the gulls taking roost on the mast and the crash of the waves against the side of the hull, causing the wood to creak, were the only sounds audible on the ship. Kapena had deliberated with her crew in private to see how much—if any

—information they wanted to disclose to the twins in exchange for the aid they were so wary of. They had concluded that they would not take them to the village, but they would let them see the sickness that plagued it through the Mourning Mirror. The very mirror that had taken five of their people.

Despite Kapena's reptilian appearance, her crew were of various creatures, all much smaller than her brutish form. They looked up at her glowingly, like a guardian of pure luck. It was quite a contrast to the mistrusting looks they shot the twins as they stepped onto the deck. Keir and Ilarys surmised they were not very welcoming to outsiders, but then again, that was common for people that wanted their cultures to be closed off to others. When at last they had made an agreement and moved to divulge the information, they gathered at the door that would bring them to the Mourning Mirror and spoke quietly.

"We will scry our village and show you the sickness," the first mate explained.

"Each time someone was taken, the village became more and more ill," Kapena added as two crew members entered the room and closed the door behind them, leaving them in the corridor.

They didn't have permission to see the process, but the twins were fine with that. They were more interested in getting to the source of the issue. "We take care of ourselves. And when we can't do that, our people take care of each other. And when there are some that our people cannot help, the village helps them. It heals and protects where we cannot. And if it cannot, it makes their passing easy and we return them to the earth to nourish it."

Keir nodded. "The living cities have similar ways. They often look after the homeless or change up their streets when someone that needs help escaping can't get away. The people respect the city and the city takes care of its people. If you do not take care of the city, the city does not take care of you."

Kapena gave a small smile. "The village is just as much a part of us as we are of it. So when it fell ill, we feared the worst. But we found the source of the foul energy coming from this mirror. We could not destroy it because we feel our people can still come home through it. But even removing it from the village did not aid in its recovery. It has stopped the disappearances, though."

"Until two weeks ago," the second mate frowned. "Another was taken."

"Salos." The captain nodded. "He wanted to find the others, but they took him with them. We waited to see if he would return, however..."

"He has not come back." Keir nodded grimly. "I've never heard of anyone coming back from the mirror world. Though there was a report of someone seeing a stranger on the inside of their mirror once, beating on it as if trying to get through. They didn't recognize them, but they said the image of them disappeared and they never saw them again. They dismissed it as overwork or insanity and swept it under the rug. Fortunately for them, I make a career out of collecting these stories."

"You believe they cannot return?" the second mate asked.

"I believe that if there is something preventing them from coming back, I'm going to search until I find a way past it," Keir replied, his gaze miles away as he lost himself in thought. He bit the end of his thumb in concentration.

"Trust me," Ilarys sighed. "Once he puts his mind to something, he doesn't stop until he makes it happen."

"Then we will depend on you to get them back," Kapena replied.

"If it's possible," Keir nodded. "I will." If they are alive, he added mentally, glancing at Ilarys. She had the same thought.

"You say you've dealt with these kinds of cases before," the second mate spoke up. "Have the others also seen the strange creatures?" The crew suddenly seemed unnerved, looking around the ship as if expecting whatever creature they mentioned to appear at any moment.

"Creatures?" Keir prompted, as he mentally tried to go through his other cases as they described it.

"Great metal beasts with eyes like fire," said one.

"Some with a roar like cannon fire," agreed another.

"Sometimes there are people inside them," another added. "You can see them through the glass-like skin of the beasts, screaming."

"But they aren't substantial," the second mate continued. "They are..." he hesitated.

"Ghosts," someone said, and several others agreed, nodding and repeating the word.

"Spirits?" Ilarys asked.

"No, not spirits." The second mate shook his head. "Spirits of the land and people and creatures we understand and make peace with." He paused, trying to find the words. "These are not of this world."

Keir thought back for a moment. "I remember in a few extreme cases of abductions over the years, there was mention of strange sightings in the areas. Most refused to describe them or take the sights seriously, so I could never get much information on them. It may very well be tied to it and now that I have a description, I can ask others if that's what they saw. If they know they aren't the only ones that saw it, they feel less crazy and are more forthcoming with information. I will find out more and let you know those findings."

There was an exchange of looks that was a mixture of relief and worry. If they weren't the only ones that saw the strange things, sure that made them less crazy, but it also meant they weren't just imagining things. And that was not the most comforting realization to come to when you weren't sure if said creatures could harm you.

The door opened to admit both the first mate and the navigator. They closed it behind them. The mirror was prepared and warded, but not before Keir got a glimpse of the room. There was a freestanding mirror bolted to the floor to keep it from moving as the ship did, and on it and surrounding it were flowers and seashells and other trinkets amongst candles and images of those lost. It was a memorial to the ones stolen away. The heavy weight of anticipation in the air was almost palpable. However, before the group could be escorted forward, Keir requested Kapena and Ilarys to move away from the door and have a quiet conversation.

"If you must say something, you can speak it before my crew. There are no secrets here," Kapena growled.

"I'm not keeping it from them, I'm keeping it from the mirror," Keir replied in a low voice.

This perked the captain's interest. She followed.

"When we go in there, I need as many crew members as we can to file in, to give Ilarys a chance to sneak past them unseen behind the mirror. I don't want them to know she is in the room. This way, she can cast a spell to see through my eyes and see what I see. Then, once I request everyone to leave, it will appear I am the only one left in the room."

"You would make yourself the bait for a trap," Kapena realized.

"Hopefully, one that will work." Keir nodded.

Ilarys nodded too, but seemed to have an argument she was holding back.

"I will tell them to come pay their respects to the city." The captain nodded. And with that, she turned and began giving out orders. The other crew members moved without hesitation to retrieve the rest of the crew. There was a heavy silence as Keir turned to Ilarys.

"Sister, if you think any louder, I won't need my abilities to know your thoughts," Keir prodded.

"What happens if you get taken as well?" Ilarys asked.

"Then I'll find out where they have taken the others," he answered.

"And if you can't get back or get them back?" she prompted.

"Then I will get the message to you one way or another," he replied. "Even if I have to haunt your dreams."

"You're going to die," Ilarys grumbled, exasperated with her brother.

"Then I guess I'll die," he shrugged. It was an attempt to make her loosen up. And though he appeared to make light of the situation, she knew he was contemplating his next move. Having her in the room with him rather than gallivanting off alone attested to that careful calculation. She just hoped it paid off this time. He at least had luck reversal on his side, and he'd had plenty of bad luck recently to build on up to this point. She bit her thumb - a habit they shared - as she considered their next move. If this went according to plan and they made contact, would they even be able to get information? Or would it prove fruitless and she'd lose her brother along with the missing villagers? What would

Aui'ani do? She glanced at her dual rings - one on each of her middle fingers. Should she consult her first?

"She would call us idiots and tell us not to do it," Keir replied.

"You said you couldn't read my thoughts," Ilarys glared.

"I said if you thought any louder, I wouldn't need to. I can read your face plain as day," Keir replied.

"She would say it's a stupid thing, but agree that it's a necessary step if we want to further our investigation," she sighed.

"She'd also tell us not to do it," he nodded.

"We've been searching for ages for an opportunity like this and now we've stumbled onto it," Ilarys said. Her tone was uncertain and frustrated, but she was itching to see where this went.

"That's how most cases work. Stick your nose in the dirt and dig until you find a root that leads you to a tree. Because where there are trees," Keir began.

"There is water," Ilarys finished. She knew the saying and hoped it was right. If they found even the smallest sign, it could be a breakthrough in their case. As she considered this, the captain returned, the crew members following in her wake, all privy to the plan. They opened the door to admit the captain, followed by the first and second mate, Keir, and several crew members. People lined the room, surrounding the mirror, as Ilarys slipped past and stood behind the mirror in the shadows. Keir faced away from the mirror and towards the captain. When Kapena met his gaze, his eyes glowed for a brief second before going back to normal. She'd set the spell.

He turned back to the mirror and watched as each of the crew members paid respect to their village and the captain gave a speech. The small ceremony sent energy to the village, hoping to make it well again. In the mirror, past their faint reflections, Keir could see the village. The edges were decaying at an alarming rate, blackened and cracked. There were places within - small growing patches - that looked bruised and diseased. There were people that gathered around the sick spots and tried to help them, but it appeared to make a minor difference. The colors of the walls and trees and earth seemed leached of vibrance, dulled and paling. The crops were weak, the air stale, the trees themselves withering. This living village would die if they didn't get it help soon.

As the ceremony ended, each of the crew members filed out one by one, their looks crestfallen. When all that remained were the twins, the captain, and the first mate waiting by the door, Kapena put a hand on Keir's shoulder.

"I'm going to stay longer," he said softly.

"We cannot leave the scrying spell up if you stay alone," Kapena warned.

"That is fine," Keir nodded. "I may do some scrying on my own, if that's okay?"

Kapena hesitated, then gave a nod. "Your fate is in your own hands. Know that I cannot lose more people to save you should the mirror take you."

"I understand," Keir nodded. "I do not expect you to sacrifice your crew for a stranger."

Kapena nodded, reaching into the pouch on her hip and slipping a crystal onto her palm, the strap across the back of her hand. She waved it before the mirror and the image rippled and disappeared, leaving just their reflections. Removing the crystal, she handed it to Keir. She gave him a nod and turned to leave. He watched her in the mirror's reflection for a moment before she turned the corner. He looked at the first mate, who hesitated in the doorway and gave a small smile.

"It's okay to close the door behind me," Keir said.

Only the crewmember had a strange look on his face as he stared not at Keir, but behind him at the mirror. Keir looked back at their reflections, not seeing anything out of the ordinary at first, but noting he hadn't seen the side of his face turn when he looked back. Realization dawned on him, but he kept a straight face until he looked back at the first mate. Giving a wink, he signaled he understood and not to worry. The first mate gave him an even stranger look and quickly shut the door. The only light in the room now came from the candles surrounding him and the tiny porthole in the wall that barely let in any light.

Moving over to the mirror, Keir studied his reflection. The eyes didn't look any different from his own. The movements were the same. But the energy was wrong. Not... quite right. There was a thick permeance of fragrance in the air from the surrounding candles, but just beneath it all, he could just make out the scent of decaying leaves. A crispness in the air that made his hair stand on end. Placing the crystal Kapena had given him in his hand, he hesitantly reached up to the mirror.

"Delmar," he spoke quietly. He called out the ley coordinates, and the section of the city he wanted to open a mirror link to, and waved the crystal in an arc before his reflection. The images sprung to life behind his image as if he were standing in the city. All he had to do was touch the mirror, and it would instantly transport him to the other side.

He swallowed. So many years he'd avoided mirror travel. And now he was deliberately trying to bait something into abducting him through one. His mouth was dry as he glanced away from his reflection to take the crystal off his hand and found it shaking. The memory of the nymph child's screams echoed in his mind as a red flash caught his attention in his peripheral vision. A cold feeling settled in his stomach and spread through his limbs like ice in his veins. This was it. He was going to get the confirmation he was searching for after all these years.

But at what cost was it going to come?

He looked back at the reflection, nothing showing on his face, as he reached forward to touch it. A hair's breadth away from making the connection, he saw the change in the reflection's eye and the ripple in the image. He jerked back, and the reflection went back to normal so quickly it was almost as if he had imagined it. Shaking his head as if he believed just that, he reached up again, touching the cool surface. He knew that wasn't Delmar. The colors were off. Almost muted. But he also knew he needed answers.

And this was how he would get them.

When his hand went through the mirror and he felt something grab his hand, he pulled back with a yelp and stumbled away. This time, the reflection snarled at him and beat against the glass. Two more sets of red eyes appeared above and below his own set. Neither sibling paid attention to any of this, however, for Keir had pulled back and stumbled, sprawling on the floor, his eyes flashing bright as images flickered before his vision.

A one-armed girl, dark-skinned, wide-eyed, standing before a mirror. Everything seemed to happen through her vision. She glanced away from her reflection, back down to a bag on the counter she was packing things into with a sense of urgency. The grim line of worry set in her forehead made her eyes seem too old for her youthful face. There was a sound from the other room, and she turned, poking her head around the corner to see another girl enter. This girl was in a chair with wheels. Much like a reverse chariot.

A type of wrap hid her hair, covering her ears, neck, and part of her shoulders as well. Her eyes were red rimmed and glassy, her breath coming in rapid spurts as she tried to calm herself, but failed.

"What happened?" the one-armed girl asked. It was a moment before the other girl could form words.

"He's- He's d-dead," she was sobbing. "He-He didn't call be- because he was dead." Rushing to her friend's side, the one-armed girl calmed and comforted her as best she could.

"I've got you," she murmured between comforts. "Just breathe. I got you." Her own vision blurred as tears formed in her eyes.

The blurry vision turned dark, and the dark boards of the cabin ceiling replaced it. The sounds of a snarl reached Keir's ears, and he sat up abruptly, gasping for air, taking a moment to get his bearings. His heart hammered in his chest and ears, and an icy breeze stung his eyes, blurring his vision again. He reached up and wiped it away, realizing there were tears staining his cheeks. He furrowed his brow, lost for a moment, until the voices pierced through his confusion and brought him back to the present.

Not possible! His reflection hissed, the voice echoing as if one and many were speaking at the same time. The voice faded in and out and as if it were reverberating in a large chamber, yet was close at the same time. *How? How!* the reflection demanded, its lips unmoving but set in a snarl.

"H-How what?" Keir asked, scrambling to his feet again. "Who are you? What do you want?"

How did you escape the Veil? the voice accused. It was angry and violent, and a growl seemed to emanate from its chest.

"Es-Escape?" Keir asked again.

How? the reflection demanded again, beating the glass with its fist. How it had not shattered was beyond Keir. The frame shook and he could feel the pulse in the air. Still dazed from the vision and the flood of emotions, he wasn't entirely sure what he was doing or asking. He stared at his reflection, his mind slowly piecing itself back together from that strange place.

"I don't know," Keir answered honestly. Then he remembered who he was dealing with. "Why do you keep taking people?" Had they given him the vision? Who were those girls?

Give us passage! Show us how! the voice demanded.

"If you tell me what's going on, maybe I will help you," Keir tried to reason. *Maybe.* If they were just trying to cause harm, then he wouldn't help anyone. The reflection seemed to simmer down and narrow its eyes at him. All six of them. Keir willed the second shiver threatening to shimmy down his spine to dissipate as the reflection seemed to weigh this option. Keir pressed on. "Why are you taking people?"

Free us, it replied, ignoring him.

"We'll get to that," Keir said. "You want out, I understand. Why does that mean abducting people?"

A long pause.

To pass through the Veil as others may, we must become the same, the reflection replied at last.

"You're trying to become like them?" Keir asked, confused. "How?"

One with the Fae, one with the spirit, the reflection said. It echoed a few times. *Partake of the essence, become the same. Once the same, the Veil gives way.*

"Partake...?" Keir said slowly. So, they called themselves the Fae... But what did 'partake of their essence' mean? Steal their magic? Steal their souls? Surely not to eat them... "Where are the others taken through this mirror? Can I speak to them? Can you release them?"

None who enter may leave again. The Veil will not allow it. You escape the Veil's iron grasp, the reflection said, eyeing him angrily. Almost... hungrily. *Tell us how you do this.*

"I don't know," Keir said again. "But I'm willing to find out." He thought for a moment, considering what it would mean to let these creatures into their world. Would they continue to harm and take people, or were they trying to do something else? "If you can get out of that world and into this one, what do you want to do then? What are your plans? Where do you go from there?"

Has your world been cursed by iron? the reflection asked. *It burns and bites our bones.*

"No, it interferes with most forms of magic. It's only used in protection and defense," Keir replied.

A haven is what we seek. We are dying in this world alone; the reflection replied. *There is no magic and no respite. The ancient ways are gone. Tell us how you escaped the grasp of the Veil that shuns our own,* it demanded again, the echoes of pain and long suffering weighted in its voice. It made Keir feel... sorry for them.

"If I search to find you a way into this world - you and those you have taken - will you stop abducting people? Starting now and once you are across?" he asked.

What promise do you offer we can trust? What can you give us you cannot bear to part with? Something you will fight to see returned once the deal has been complete? the reflection prompted.

"I... don't have any trinkets with me," Keir said. The reflection seemed to sniff the air for a moment, turning its head from side to side as if trying to place the scent.

Your essence is different, it said.

"Different? How?" Keir asked.

You stink of the magic of Eitû. It was a distasteful comment from the tone, but Keir didn't know enough to take offense.

"Eitû?" Keir asked, confused.

The murderer went by many names. Rynon Eitû-

"Rynon?" Keir repeated, recognizing the name as the name of his order. A growl emanated from the mirror, the images behind his reflection darkening.

He trapped us in this place. We will never forget his sins. The voice grew thicker, angrier with each word.

"He's not very well spoken of here either, from what I remember," he noted, despite the fact his very organization was based on dealings with Rynon; not everyone liked the old story. Keir wasn't overly familiar with it, but they had provided him with funding to do research on the strange sightings and the rest he hadn't much cared to find out. He was more interested in saving the nymph child and those like her than he was finding out more about the Veil. The fact the two overlapped was just a lucky happenstance. "I didn't think that story was true, though," he added. He made a mental note to research that later.

You are a Seer. It wasn't a question.

"Somewhat," Keir agreed. "How did you know?"

We have watched you since that day. We hunted you as you hunted us, came the reply.

Relief rushed through Keir. So it had been true. They had been after him. He hadn't been crazy to avoid mirror travel all those years ago until now.

The reflection added, *No trinket. We will make this bargain for a price.*

"What price?" he asked suspiciously.

A vision, it replied.

"I can't control them." Keir shook his head. "I've never been able to."

A vision! it demanded.

He held up his hands in a calming gesture. "I can try. But I make no guarantee that it will work. You may not get the answer you seek. Will you still agree if this is the case?" he asked.

The reflection made a noise that was caught between a growl and a gurgle as it considered this. *We will take no more from your world,* it agreed at last. *Touch the glass,* it instructed, placing its hand on the other side of the pane.

Keir took a deep breath, holding his hand parallel to his reflection. After a moment's hesitation, he pressed his palm against the glass, moving through it again. He felt the flesh of the reflection and an involuntary shiver ran over him. It was clammy and cold. Like mud and wet, decaying logs coated in a slimy mold and the scent of dying earth. It was putrid and overwhelming, but only for a second as a bright yellow light blinded his vision, drowning out all of his senses. He dropped to his knees, his hand still pressed against his reflection's, and gasped.

There were more people than before. A dark-haired boy with thin, hooded eyes and dual devices encompassing his ears; the girl in the chair with wheels from before; the one-armed girl; and another boy - a half-elf by the looks of him - with heavy-lidded eyes, a broad flat nose, and red, rust-colored hair that fell about chin length. All of them looked panicked. They were in some kind of small space that looked abandoned and derelict.

"Only Dai-Nē can pass through the Veil," the half-elf was saying.

A roar sounded through the cabin and the world shook as if rending itself in two. Keir fell back across the floor, dazed and confused. Another, more terrifying roar blasted through the cabin and the wood seemed to threaten to splinter beneath the mirror. When his eyes focused again, his reflection had thrown back its head, arms twisting as if in agony. A hole stretched across its chest and opened to reveal a gaping maw with rows of jagged teeth and a lolling tongue large enough to constrict its prey and drag it back into the throat of the beast. The purple hued ridges seemed to lead down into something much larger and more terrifying than the Keir sized form his reflection had taken. The Seer's scream joined Ilarys' screams as the image in the mirror started to pulse and flicker.

The voice, once hissing and distorted by echoes, grew deep and throaty, as if a spear had impaled an angered boar. Keir's former reflection rent in two, starting at the head and tearing itself down the center, winking out of existence. The pulse of energy exiting the mirror sent a crack sprawling across its length and blew out the remaining candles, plunging the room in darkness save for the palest light of the setting sun peeking through the small porthole, splashing across the ceiling.

Keir's chest heaved with panic as he stared wide-eyed at the mirror. It was deathly silent. When he could think again, he stood and approached Ilarys, who stood pressed against the back wall, wide-eyed with a heaving chest.

"Are you harmed?" he asked.

She shook her head, unable to speak.

"Come," he breathed. "Let's get out of this room."

Nodding fervently, she accepted his hand to help her to her feet. Before crossing in front of the mirror again, Keir took the sheet that he had set aside earlier and covered it. If he never looked at another mirror again, it would be too soon. Ilarys took a moment to dispel the eye enchantment while he did and was grateful to be in her own headspace again.

When the door opened, the hall was barren save for a lone shadow waiting at the steps to their right that was already retreating to alert the others. An alarm sounded and suddenly more shadows and shapes crowded the tops of the stairs, but only one descended.

Kapena.

As she came to a stop at the foot of the stairs and looked them over.

"We know why they are disappearing and we have an idea who is taking them," Keir responded. "We have made a deal that they will take no more people from this world as we try to bring them back."

"We can't get to them yet," Ilarys added. "But we know where to start looking."

Kapena let this sink in for a long moment. She then gave them a nod and ordered her men to give them food and drink.

"And what did you offer in return?" Kapena asked, her tone suspicious. She knew such a deal could only come at a price.

"A vision," Keir responded. "I don't know if they saw what they wanted or if it was utter gibberish. But they made the deal."

Kapena narrowed her eyes for a moment. "What was all that screaming?"

"After they saw the vision, there was this... thing... in the mirror. It turned my reflection into a terrifying sight. I was still dazed from the vision and wasn't expecting it," Keir answered honestly, rubbing the area on his chest he'd seen open to reveal a mouth in the mirror.

"The chest was a mouth," Ilarys added, motioning. "I'm going to have nightmares for weeks. I'm used to strange-looking creatures, but to see my brother turned into some-thing like that-" She shuttered.

Kapena watched them for a long moment, her stern features seeming less harsh and more satisfied.

"We will drop you off at the closest port after you eat and rest. You look like hell," she added.

"That's better than we feel," Keir replied, following the crew members to the stairs. Every muscle in his body ached as if he'd been the one to wrench himself in two instead of his reflection. "Thank you, Captain."

"Don't thank me," Kapena said over her shoulder. "If you had lied just now, you would have suffered severe burns."

Ilarys looked down to see a section of the hall doused with a truth spell... mixed with a fire spell.

"If you want to thank me, you get those people home safe," Kapena continued. "And yourselves."

"Wouldn't that have burned down your own ship?" Ilarys called, indignant.

"You think I haven't warded my ship against friendly fire, girl?" Kapena quipped with a grin. "To think I would be so foolish."

"No, it just feels rude," Ilarys bristled.

"Easy dear sister," Keir replied, patting her back as they made their way up the stairs. "We are unwanted guests on this ship. We did as we said we would, and they took precautions to make sure we would hold up our end. I cannot blame them for defending themselves."

"This is too much energy," Ilarys complained, not feeling up to arguing her point. "Just let me sleep."

"In due time," Keir agreed. "In due time.

CHAPTER 3
ALCHEMY

Amara's father had yet to call since she had started at Blemwick. And when one month turned into four, Rodney was worried for her. When Amara discovered her cell phone had been disconnected, she wondered if he was trying to cut her out of his life completely. Rodney suggested using the office phone, but she discovered her father's phone had also disconnected. She tried Liz's and found the same issue. No matter how the other two would try to cheer her up, it didn't seem to work. Winter break came and went, and nothing changed. She stayed at the school with Rodney and Tursanay over the break since she couldn't contact her father. Mr. Asher's face fell when she brought it up to him, but he planned for her to stay, taking the hassle out of it for her.

Rodney glanced back at the table where Amara sat, trying to finish her homework for her next class. Tursanay was standing in line with him to grab their food. "She's not been sleeping too well. And when she does, she wakes up screaming from nightmares," she said, following his gaze.

"Nightmares?" Rodney winced. "Yeesh. She can't catch a break."

"The last few have all been about the same thing, but different things happen. Same red-haired, green-eyed guy. Same urgency to the dream, like he's trying to figure out how to tell her something," Tursanay replied with a sigh. "She won't tell me what has her so afraid and I'm wearing out. We've had a few complaints filed from our neighbors, but no one's doing anything but lecturing us about being rowdy and telling us we have a curfew for a reason."

"We definitely have to talk to someone. I just feel like if something doesn't change soon, it'll get worse," Rodney murmured, pointing to the dishes he wanted and thanking the lunch lady.

Tursanay toyed with her necklace for a moment, lost in thought. "I have an idea, but if it doesn't help, I'll go to Mr. Asher or someone and demand they drag her dad down here so I can kick his ass," she grumbled. "Or at least get her to the counselor."

"Counselor first, ass kicking later," Rodney replied. "It doesn't really make sense to me, though. I mean, from what I've heard of him from you, he seemed like a nice guy. They seemed really close. Why would he just up and dump her here without a second glance and drop all contact?"

"They were close. Very close. Maybe he was just an asshole all along and was fantastic at hiding it," she shrugged.

Rodney watched the muscle in her jaw work and knew she was much more disgusted with Amara's dad than she was letting on. But he also knew she wasn't saying anything, for Amara's sake. Taking their trays, they walked over to the table to join Amara, and Rodney set a plate of food down on top of her textbook.

"Eat," he instructed her. "It'll make you feel better."

Amara sighed, sitting back. She covered her notebook and under her homework, Rodney caught sight of a doodle of a person with chin length hair and intense eyes.

"I'm not that hungry," she replied.

"You skipped breakfast, lady," Tursanay scolded. "You don't get to skip lunch."

Picking up the fork, Amara picked at her food a bit, lost in thought.

"So, what'd you dream about last night?" Rodney prompted, and Tursanay kicked him from under the table.

Amara glanced up at him, then over at Tursanay, who was trying to look innocent.

"You get like this when you have bad dreams," he added.

Amara looked back down at her plate, considering. "The creatures came back," she said at last, and Tursanay looked up, surprised. She glanced at Rodney.

"Creatures?" Rodney prompted.

Amara took an unsteady breath. "It's like..." she hesitated, chewing her lip. "It's like they know when the dream starts and they hone in and I have minutes before they find me. And it's always happening in this clearing in the woods, and it gets... smaller and smaller each time. And when they find us..."

"Us?" Tursanay asked.

"The boy," Amara replied, glancing at her homework, a small corner of her sketch poking out. "It's like he remembers the previous dreams, but something always goes wrong. He's... speaking in a language I don't recognize. It sounded similar to French at first? But it's not quite the same." She fell silent a moment, staring at her plate, but not really seeing it. "He keeps trying to communicate with me, but it's hard... It's like we're trapped in that clearing. Any time we try to leave, everything just goes haywire. The world turns into a blurry swirl of color and I get sick and..." Her voice caught, her hand shaking slightly.

"What happens?" Rodney asked softly.

This was obviously difficult for her to talk about, but he felt like if she could voice it, maybe she could figure out how to not be so afraid. He wasn't sure how... but maybe he could make her smile about it? Amara took a moment to try to eat, but her hand was shaking so badly she could barely manage to take more than a few bites.

Finally, she spoke again. "There are these creatures that keep showing up. They have bright yellow and black eyes and..." She shuddered and spoke again, describing the creatures with leathery-looking skin that seemed to be stretched over bones. "They have a dog-like face sometimes. Other times they-" she paused, taking a breath and folding her arms around her midsection. "They look like this thing that has a huge, gaping mouth with... needle-like teeth."

She looked up and blinked as if trying to will herself not to cry, and Rodney felt his heart sink into his stomach. He wasn't good at dealing with people when they cried.

"And the noise they make when they're getting closer, when they're hunting me-" She stopped when her voice broke.

"Hey," Tursanay said softly. She wrapped her arm around Amara and hugged her. "It's okay. They're not here. You're okay."

Amara suppressed a sob and struggled to recompose herself.

"I've got something for you, okay?" Tursanay said, rubbing her back. "It's a necklace my dad gave me when I was little. It would help me when I was having bad dreams. Maybe it'll help you too."

Rodney wanted to comfort her, but honestly did not know what he could do or say. Before he could deliberate for too long, Amara took a few deep breaths to calm herself, and furiously wiped her eyes with a napkin.

"I'm sorry," she muttered. "It's just I can still hear it when I wake up sometimes."

"Don't be sorry," Rodney replied. "I just feel bad you have to deal with that..."

"I just kind of wish he would stop showing up in my dreams and bringing those things with him," she muttered.

"You should tell him that," Tursanay replied, trying to joke with her.

"I tried," Amara grumbled. "I don't think he understood me."

"Have you tried looking up French phrases to say to him?" Rodney asked.

"I don't remember them usually," Amara replied, picking at her food again and taking a bite.

Rodney gave a small smile. At least she was trying - both to do something and to eat. It meant she was fighting, and that was better than doing nothing.

Even if it wore her out.

"Maybe this will help," Tursanay said, taking off the necklace from around her neck. The small black cord she held out had an amethyst pendant hanging from it - just a small, jagged cylinder no bigger than her pinky finger. "It's worth a shot anyhow," she smiled.

Amara took it, running her thumb across the stone.

"I'm willing to try anything at this point," she sighed, thanking Tursanay.

There were two weeks of school left to go before they were out for the summer. To end the school year, the school brought in a guest speaker to give the students some advice on their futures. Rodney, Amara, and Tursanay were late getting there, and were stuck in the second row behind the faculty members. Everyone else tried to sit as far away from the faculty as possible to get away with talking during the event, filling up every other place there was. Tursanay and Amara had been up late the previous night studying together because the finals were just around the corner, and Rodney sat between the girls, keeping them awake through the speech. After the fifth or sixth time being prodded awake by Rodney, Amara and Tursanay forced themselves to sit up straight and at least try to pay attention.

Rodney kept glancing between the two of them as he listened to the speaker to make sure they were staying awake. They seemed to do better, but a sudden motion from Amara made him do a double take. She was staring wide eyed and intently up at the stage near the side door. He glanced in that direction to look at what she was staring at, but saw nothing. Glancing back at her, confused, he noticed she looked terrified as she tracked something across the stage with her eyes. Abruptly, she tensed with a sharp intake of breath.

"LOOK OUT!" she yelled. Suddenly, everything blurred for a moment in Rodney's vision, and his stomach flipped, threatening to revolt. A piercing pain shot through his temples, and he doubled over. He covered his mouth, praying he wasn't about to vomit, when a loud crash from on stage made him shout in surprise. He looked back up with a wince, blinking to clear his vision. On stage, a heavy light fixture had landed on the podium the speaker had been using. The speaker himself had ducked to one side, barely escaping the crash.

The room was in an uproar.

It was a good ten minutes before the faculty got the students settled and sent out of the room to enjoy the rest of their free hour while they made sure everything was secure on the stage. The trio made their way down the hall and back towards the cafeteria, where some students were gathering for an early lunch. Endless chatter about what had just happened was everywhere.

"What was that?" Rodney asked as they sat down. None of them had gone to get food just yet, and Rodney was glad. His stomach still hadn't quite recovered, though the piercing pain in his temples was finally ebbing.

"That's what I wanna know," Tursanay agreed. "Why'd that just fall out of nowhere?"

"No, I mean," Rodney corrected. "How'd you know to tell him to look out? You weren't even looking at the light fixture. You were watching something on st..." His voice trailed off as Amara turned white as a sheet.

"Amara?" Tursanay asked, looking at her.

Amara swallowed hard.

"I-I thought I drifted back to sleep," she whispered.

"No, you were wide awake," Rodney replied. "Why? What were you looking at?"

Amara was silent for a moment. "I saw him again. And the creatures were chasing him. They went for the speaker like they could see him, too." She got that faraway look in her eye. "I thought I fell back asleep..."

Rodney and Tursanay exchanged glances.

"I got..." Rodney hesitated. "This terrible headache right after you yelled for him to look out..."

Amara looked up at him.

"And everything got really blurry, and I felt like I was going to puke."

"Hey yeah," Tursanay said, giving him a surprised look. "Me too..." They looked in between each other. "I thought it was because of the light fixture falling and the panic?"

"You don't have to say that to make me feel better," Amara said, her hands shaking.

"I'm not," Tursanay shook her head. "My stomach is still messed up."

"Mine too," Rodney agreed. "That's why I didn't want anything to eat."

"Me too," Amara whispered softly. "It's like that... when I have those dreams and he runs out of the clearing or I do... or when those creatures break into it." She looked between the two of them. "It's why when I was having them so much, I couldn't eat a lot."

"Why didn't you say anything?" Tursanay asked. "We could have tried to do something about it sooner..."

"I just thought it was me being afraid of something stupid," she replied softly, looking down at her lap.

"It's not stupid if it upsets you," Tursanay replied.

Rodney played with the ring on his right hand absent-mindedly. "What if you're not actually having dreams?" he said, slowly.

"What do you mean?" Amara asked.

"What if someone's actually trying to get in touch with you?" Rodney asked.

"I think she should tell the counselor about it, to be honest," Tursanay said, the skepticism showing on her face.

"For sure," Rodney shrugged. "But still, what if?"

"What would we even do with that information?" Tursanay asked. "There's literally nothing we can do for him."

"He's been consistently trying to tell her something since he first showed up since the beginning of the year," Rodney argued. "I mean... maybe we can try to hear him out?"

"I've tried, I don't understand him," Amara replied. "Well, back when I was having the weird dreams. It's been a few months... but if they're coming back..." She paled at the thought.

"Maybe I could give it a crack," Rodney offered.

"How are you going to do that?" Tursanay rolled her eyes. "Wait for her to take a nap between classes so you can yell in her ear for him to visit you next when she dreams and hope it works? Wait - why are we even talking like he's a real person?"

"She could tell him to come see me or she can try to write down some words he's saying and see if we can't translate them?" Rodney countered.

Amara leaned her cheek on her hand, exhaustedly, and gestured at Rodney with the other.

"Or you can take them and have them yourself and I won't have to deal with them anymore," she offered dryly and sighed.

Rodney grinned, grabbing her hand as if to shake it - a spur-of-the-moment idea, something to make her laugh.

"Deal," he agreed, but the shock that ran through their hands had them both pulling back with a yelp.

"Ow! What the hell!" Amara complained.

"I was trying to make a joke," Rodney grimaced, laying his face on the table as he gripped his injured hand, trying to make it stop stinging by applying pressure to it. "Man, that really hurt!"

"Yeesh, that shock was so bad it glinted off your ring," Tursanay commented. "Did you wear fuzzy socks or something?"

"No," Rodney replied with a grunt of pain. "Sorry about that. My joke sort of backfired."

"I thought it was shocking," Tursanay replied, seeing an opportunity.

"You come to my table and use my pain and my own joke against me," Rodney complained, pretending to be offended. Okay, he felt a slight offense that he had missed that punchline.

Tursanay laughed.

Because no one really wanted to return to class after such a long free period, the atmosphere around the end of the lunch hour was fairly lax. When the bell rang, the students shuffled off reluctantly, and the trio parted ways, heading to their next period. Amara and Tursanay to English, and Rodney to history.

Making it into his seat just as the bell rang, Rodney breathed a sigh of relief. He caught his breath as the teacher called roll, having sprinted the last little way to class. Settling in, Rodney flipped open the history book and leaned against his hand, preparing for a long, boring history lesson on... the molecular structure of glucose? He gave his book an odd look and realized he'd grabbed the wrong one. He mentally kicked himself and hoped the teacher wouldn't notice.

I'll just have to take good notes, Rodney sighed. Not like he was going to retain it very well anyhow.

Twenty minutes into the lecture, the door to the classroom opened, and Rodney glanced up. The person coming in now, Rodney thought, may have been a new student checking in to get things ready for starting school after summer break. He certainly didn't adhere to the school dress code. The boy in the doorway had on a green shirt that came to mid-thigh with some brown baggy pants. His shoes looked different from anything Rodney had ever seen and Rodney wondered where on earth he had gotten them.

Weird, Rodney thought to himself. In fact, the kid's entire getup was weird. He glanced up at the boy's face and noted the bewildered look in his eyes. He noted his rust-colored hair that hung past his ears and stuck out at odd angles at the ends, like it needed a trim. Definitely a new student. His hair cut was against school rules. He looked lost... *The office is on the other side of the school, my dude.*

Rodney understood his plight, though. It had taken him forever to memorize the halls around Blemwick. The boy's eyes roamed the room as Rodney watched him, wondering how long it'd take before Mr. Heinrick noticed him. The boy's eyes fell on Rodney, who gave him a welcoming grin and a nod. His expression turned from uncertainty to utter shock.

He demanded something in a language that was extremely foreign sounding to Rodney's ears, as if the red-haired boy were expecting someone else. The boy had stumbled backward, dramatically. Rodney blinked, surprised at his sudden outburst. He glanced at the teacher, who still droned on at the chalkboard about the history lesson, completely ignoring the commotion. Actually... No one was reacting to the commotion, he noticed, glancing around the classroom. Still half turned in his seat, Rodney's eyes flickered back to the boy. He pointed to himself silently and raised his eyebrows as if to ask, *What me?*

The boy fixed his bright green eyes on Rodney, flaring them with suspicion. He spat a rapid-fire sentence so accusingly, Rodney stared at him for a good five seconds before he could react. His face dropped into a look of stupidity that could have, in Rodney's mind, rivaled that of Trenton's.

"Wha-?" he managed.

The boy accused again; the language sounding like a mix of French, like Amara had mentioned, and Russian. A sudden panic came over him and he flickered like a ghost. He looked back at the door as if he expected someone to follow him - someone he wasn't looking forward to running into, and Rodney's mind flickered back to the creatures Amara had mentioned. His attention turned back to Rodney and spoke urgently.

"D-... Ele-... -nt," his voice was breaking up like someone with poor reception on their cell phone. He stood over Rodney, trying to make him understand, but the sound grew worse and worse. His whole figure started wavering like static on an old TV. Rodney stared up at him as if he really were seeing a ghost, wondering if he'd just officially lost his mind as he watched this flickering boy yell something inaudible at him. Suddenly something overlapped his image before it winked out of existence, followed by a whomp that Rodney felt more than he heard rush past him, causing his stomach to flip. He suddenly felt very dizzy, much like he had that morning.

"...oberts, answer me - are you paying attention? Obviously not, if I have to repeat myself. I said, What could be on the ceiling that could be more interesting than this review for your final?" Rodney looked up at the teacher like he hadn't realized he was there. He was vaguely aware of a few snickers behind him. He blinked a few times to come to his senses, and a fresh wave of nausea hit him.

"Um, actually, sir," he groaned. "I'm not feelin' so great. Can I go to the infirmary?"

"You do look a little pale," admitted the teacher reluctantly. "Alright - just try not to puke before you get there," he added, pointing to the pad of hall passes hanging by the door. "Would you like someone to go with you?" he asked.

Yeah, but neither of them are in your class, thought Rodney. "Er, no, sir," he replied out loud, and left shakily. However, halfway to the infirmary, he immediately started feeling better, as if a switch had flipped and turned off the nausea. It hadn't been nearly as bad as this morning. He debated ongoing back to class or not. Checking his watch, he noted that class was almost over, and the three of them had study hall together next. He'd have to tell the girls about the crazy incident in history class when he caught up with them. Deciding to skip the rest of the molecular intricacies of glucose, as told by a history teacher, Rodney gathered his things from his locker and headed for the library.

It was ten minutes until the end of class and that was the longest ten minutes of Rodney's life. The 'dream' had given him a really weird feeling. The more he thought about the weird incident, the more questions he kept drawing. Was the guy from this incident the same one Amara had talked about from the other incident this morning? He looked a lot like her description, but how was that possible? Maybe he'd fallen asleep in class and just had a dream about it. Maybe his imagination had just painted the picture for him.

Then again, maybe he was over thinking things. Had he really dozed off in class and had a dream? No... the teacher had gotten on to him for staring up at the ceiling rather than listening to the lesson. That meant his eyes had been open, for sure. Otherwise, he would have gotten into trouble for sleeping in class. Rodney thought about the look that had come across Amara's face when she said she had had the dream. Her eyes had been open. But that was just a coincidence...

Right?

If he hadn't been asleep, why had no one else noticed the guy? If he was certain it wasn't a dream, then what was it? A hallucination? Was stress getting to him too?

He thought about the boy's appearance again. Grabbing a piece of paper, he jotted down everything he could remember and wracked his brains for any of the words he could pick out. Something about 'e-day' or 'die knee' or 'key toe tea' were words he kept repeating, but none of that really made any sense. At least to him.

Maybe if she saw these things, she'd say the guy looked nothing like that. Maybe he was just making this up. There was really no way he was actually having those dreams, was there?

The stress from these upcoming exams is getting to me, Rodney thought to himself, leg bouncing with anticipation as he chewed on his pen.

If it was a dream or a hallucination or whatever and he was just getting himself worked up over nothing, then everything would be fine and he could go back to normal and laugh about it with the others. But if the sinking feeling in his gut had something more to it, he wasn't sure what he'd do. Ugh, why couldn't he make sense of this? Sighing, he finally made himself sit down, only to stand back up almost immediately when the girls entered the library laughing and talking. Rodney waved them over frantically, shifting from foot to foot, waiting for them to reach their table.

"What's up?" asked Amara, concerned. "Something happen?"

"Did it ever," said Rodney, immediately launching into the story as he handed Amara the piece of paper with all that he'd written.

The bell rang as he finished his tale, and all the noise in the school library died down. You could hear a pin drop. The girls stared at him, Tursanay's face transforming into surprise and disbelief, Amara's uncomprehending at first, then complete fear.

"You... actually saw him?" she said, voice barely above a whisper.

She looked like she was going to pass out. He motioned for them to gather at the table. They put all their things down and got settled and leaned in toward the center of the table as he spoke in a low voice so that no one would overhear. He told them what had happened, then of his speculations about not being asleep, and wondered aloud if he was going crazy or if it was just his imagination.

"When he came into the room and looked at me like 'Who are you?!' I was thinking 'Dude, same,'" joked Rodney, trying to lighten his nerves. It wasn't helping.

"Of course he'd look at you like that," Tursanay said sarcastically. "If he really is the same guy from Amara's dreams, he'd have no idea who you were."

"Well, that's true," muttered Rodney. He hadn't thought

about that. The idea made his stomach hurt. "No wonder he looked upset at seeing me," muttered Rodney aloud. "I wasn't who he was expecting at all... You realize that means it is someone trying to get in touch with her, right?" he hissed. His brow furrowed as he thought about what he'd just said. "You know, I didn't actually expect my theory to be true, but it's gaining a lot of support at the moment."

"Maybe he is more than just a figment of your imagination," Tursanay teased, elbowing Amara.

"Okay but one, that deal we made with the dreams was just a joke," Amara balked, shaking her head like she didn't want to accept any of this. She must have felt like she was going out of her mind, Rodney realized.

He was right there with her.

"Two, what if we're having a group hallucination and we need serious help?"

"Can't be," argued Tursanay. "I haven't seen him at all."

"You watch," warned Rodney, pointing at her. "You're gonna be next and something big's gonna happen since you said that."

"I'm sorry but it's going to take me seeing him to believe this guy is something other than a nightmare Amara's having that influenced you to have one too, because of the stress you're both under," Tursanay admitted finally.

Rodney made a face, but it cleared almost instantly, replaced with an evil grin.

"All right," he said. "You wanna have a dream too? I'll make a deal with you." He stuck out his hand, and she eyed it suspiciously. "If you dream about him, you have to interrogate him. Find out who he is, what he wants, and why he keeps popping up. You get to be the one to look crazy talking to an invisible person who speaks in another language in the middle of class."

"Psht," scoffed Tursanay, rolling her eyes. "Yeah okay." The sarcasm dripped from her very body language as she grabbed his hand. "Deal." Immediately, they felt the shock run through their hands. They yelped and let go, ignoring the scowls from the people in the surrounding library area, who shushed them.

"Pain," Rodney grunted, putting his face against the table. "I'm in pain."

"Rodney, I swear if you did that just to shock the hell out of my hand-" Tursanay threatened as she tried to make her hand stop throbbing.

"Why would I shock myself, too?" Rodney hissed back, suppressing a grunt. "I'm never wearing socks again."

CHAPTER 4
LIGHT

"Did I tell you my roommate got adopted?" Rodney was saying as they sat down at the table for lunch.

"What? Awesome!" Amara smiled.

"Yeah, he is going to live with them this summer and that means I get a room aaaalll to myself!" Rodney grinned. "Well, unless a last-minute enrollment comes through, but a room by myself for a short while is better than nothing."

"Right?" Amara chuckled, tucking into her food.

She seemed to actually have an appetite despite the nightmares she'd been having, Tursanay noticed. She frowned despite the pleasant change. Something was bothering her.

"I hope it's a good fit for him," Rodney nodded.

"Same," Amara agreed, turning to get something out of her bag. She said something else, but Rodney glanced up at her, brow furrowed.

"Sorry, say that again?" he asked. "I couldn't see your face."

"Sorry," Amara replied, turning to face him. "I said I need

to write the dream I had last night down in my dream journal the counselor gave me before I forget."

"How are they? Any better?" Rodney asked.

"Still lots of nightmares," Amara sighed. "The guy has stopped showing up since the deal went down, but it's made room for... other things."

"That sucks," Rodney frowned.

Tursanay glanced between the two of them quietly.

"You'd think now that you're free of him, you'd have a pleasant night's sleep. Can't catch a break," Rodney added.

He shook his head and Amara muttered in agreement as she turned to a fresh page in her notebook and began scratching notes between bites of food.

"Are you two trying to pull some kind of prank on me?" Tursanay asked abruptly. Rodney looked up blankly, spoon still in his mouth from taking a bite. He said something, then seemed to realize he still had food in his mouth, then swallowed.

"Not that I'm aware of..." he replied, looking at Amara. "Did I miss something and forget?"

"Why? Something happen?" Amara asked Tursanay. "To make you think we pranked you?"

"Just wondering about those dreams..." muttered Tursanay.

Amara frowned, her thoughts seeming to flash back to some unwanted image.

"You seemed to still be having them a few nights ago, but I guess not..." Tursanay continued.

Rodney looked up from his plate and in between Tursanay and Amara.

"Oh," Amara said softly, looking down as if she'd been hoping to forget about that. "No," she said at last. "They had nothing to do with that guy. That was... something else..."

"Anything we should be worried about?" Rodney asked. "I mean, I don't want to be right about anything else trying to contact you. If the guy is real, does that mean other things you dream about are? Are those monsters real?"

"Rodney," Tursanay warned. "Now's not the time."

"It's a legit concern of mine," Rodney disagreed. "I mean, if anything she dreams about could come and affect us, and she's having nightmares..." he trailed off to make his point.

"I don't think it's anything we have to worry about," Amara shook her head. "It was just a bunch of really gory dreams... One of them had your dad in it, Tursanay," she added.

"Did he say anything to you?" she asked, Rodney's words sinking in a little too closely at the mention of her father.

Amara shook her head. "It wasn't like the dreams with the red-haired guy. This was different. I wasn't there. It was just like... third person or something. But also weird, like a memory? There was this creepy enormous dinosaur lizard thing involved, so definitely just a really messed up dream."

Rodney's eyes grew wide. "If Godzilla shows up and starts destroying the city, I'm reminding you of this conversation."

Tursanay covered her face with her hand and groaned. As ridiculous as that sounded, if Rodney was right again, this could get terrifying really quickly. Except, she was also having issues, even believing that contact through dreams was possible. Yeah, it was a cool concept, but it was hard for her logic to accept.

"Yeah, okay, when I can reach out and touch one of my dreams in person then I'll be worried, but it wasn't even

Godzilla," Amara chuckled despite herself. "It was more like a raptor or a Komodo dragon mix, but, like, big enough to ride."

"That's still terrifying," Rodney complained, putting his head in his hands. "I don't want to meet those either! You saw how the movie ended - not good!" He gestured in frustration.

"Anyway," Amara interjected. "That's not going to happen. I'm allowed to have normal bad dreams, even if they are weird."

"For our sake, I hope so," Rodney shuddered.

"So, question," Amara said, turning to Tursanay. "what made you think you were being pranked exactly?"

Tursanay sunk into her chair. "I was kind of hoping to get a dream as quickly as Rodney did, but nothing's happened all week."

"I had a break between dreams for a while, remember?" Amara replied. "Maybe it's just break time again."

"Dude needs to hurry," Tursanay replied. "I want to get to the bottom of this. The longer he waits, the more stressed I get."

Rodney agreed heartily.

"Oh, speaking of dreams, thanks for letting me borrow this," Amara said, handing Tursanay her necklace back. "It helped a lot after the first few nights of bad dreams."

"I'm glad," Tursanay smiled, taking it back and putting it on. "Let me know if you ever need to borrow it again."

"Gladly," Amara agreed.

As the weeks counted down to finals and summer vacation, the trio found themselves short on time to hang out. They caught glimpses of each other throughout the day, but with all the reviews they were receiving in class, Amara and Rodney had minimal opportunities to engage with Tursanay, who felt extremely bored and practically pleaded for a weird dream just to have something to do. She was exempt from all her exams because of her GPA, but still technically had to attend class and take notes for participation and attendance.

The fourth day, with all the tests, Rodney and Amara were so preoccupied they'd forgotten all about the dreams since none had been appearing recently. Tursanay helped the two of them study until they couldn't absorb any more information, then waited all day for the testing to finish up by passing the time reading or staring out the window mindlessly.

The third and last day of testing was the last day of school before summer break began. Amara had planned to wait at the school until she could contact her father. She didn't have other family members to contact, but Mr. Asher was very forthcoming with attempts to find her father and getting a social worker involved in case the worst happened and he didn't come back for her. While this had devastated her to hear, Mr. Asher assured her they would do everything in their power to find out what was happening.

Tursanay, however, was just plain angry at the man for disappearing, and let Amara know exactly how she felt a few times, but after seeing her reaction, kept her opinions to herself. She spent the last day of testing in her room, lying on her bed, letting her mind wander. Watching the clock until it got close to the end of their last testing period, she jumped into the shower to get ready.

Putting on her jeans and t-shirt, she walked back to her bed while fixing her hair, and looked for her shoes. Unable to find her left one, she bent over to look under the bed and heard a loud ripping sound behind her. Thinking she had ripped her jeans, she shot back up, turning to check when something caught her eye.

Floating midair in the space behind her was a light that closely resembled a huge sideways pool of water that glowed with a bright blue light. Tursanay's jaw fell open in stunned, silent shock. Slowly, the strange pool of light shrank in size and at the last possible minute, something dove out of it and rolled across the floor toward her. She screamed and leapt across the bed, flattening herself against the wall on the other side, wielding her comb like a sword.

She stared wide-eyed at the thing that was now racing back toward the strange blue pool, trying to get a good look at exactly what it was.

Or rather, who it was.

The boy who had tumbled onto the floor then raced back toward the sideways floating puddle, drew a large, white knife out of his belt, and smashed the hilt against the blue light, causing it to vanish completely. The knife looked to be made entirely out of bone, and had a leather cord tied around its guard, a single jewel in the pommel.

The blade itself, however, was what Tursanay was concerned about. The only thing she had was a comb with a pointy end that would hurt really badly if she stabbed him with it. But to get close enough to do that meant getting close enough for him to use that nasty-looking blade. The odds didn't really sound good. She watched him for any hostile movements, but at the moment he only stood there, panting, staring at the place where the strange light had been. As if snapping to his senses, he began searching the room frantically, his chin length hair whipping about his face. He turned and locked his bright green eyes with Tursanay's startled brown ones. She flinched and squeaked, but her reaction was nothing to his.

Surprised being an understatement, the boy screamed as he began backpedaling away from her, until he tripped over his own feet, falling flat on his back. Tursanay screamed back, startled by his reaction, which caused him to scream again as he scrambled further away in a flurry of arms and legs until his back pressed against the far wall. He held his knife out before him defensively. They stared at each other warily for a time before a light seemed to flare in the boy's eyes, making him straighten. He pointed exasperatedly and said something accusingly, as if wondering how many more times he'd have to ask.

"Seriously?!" shot Tursanay, getting the gist of 'Who are you?' despite the language barrier. "You burst into my room out of some floating... *sideways toilet thing*," she burst out, struggling with words for a moment before they started flowing as fast as she could speak. "and have the audacity to ask me who I am?! Try again mister!" Tursanay aimed the pointy end of her comb at him like it would protect her, and the boy, to Tursanay's satisfaction, eyed it cautiously.

He held up his hand to show he meant no harm and slowly set his knife down. Still moving slowly after checking her reaction, he reached into his shirt pocket, keeping eye contact with her. Tursanay held the comb higher, and he ducked slightly, mumbling something as if to reassure her everything was okay. Pulling out a handful of something - beads? No... - he dumped it out in his other hand.

He held up a round, marble-like green thing as if to give it to her. She eyed it, then eyed the others piled in his left hand. It looked like candy. Was this a peace offering? He gestured for her to take it, and slowly she lowered the comb, tucking it into her pants pocket, but hesitated. Should she really take candy from a stranger? Especially one that appeared out of nowhere? When he offered it to her again, she slowly came forward, and reached out letting him drop it into her hand, then relief colored his face instantly. Taking another one in his hand, he held it up and popped it into his mouth, chewing it slowly.

He gestured for her to do the same, then gestured between the two of them, and motioned speaking. He repeated the motions again, and Tursanay furrowed her brow. Was he saying this was a way of communicating, or was this saying it would help them communicate? She sniffed it experimentally, the scent of cinnamon and cumin causing her to make a face. The pieces all looked identical, and nothing had happened to him.

This is how you get roofied, Tursanay thought to herself. *I don't want to be that stupid person in every horror movie, but my gut's telling me to try it.* She sniffed it again, trying to will herself to lick it, but pulled back, chickening out with a whine.

"Yeah, but what if I'm allergic?" she complained, pacing back and forth and gesturing to him irritably. "You don't know what allergies I have! I don't know what's in this! You cute, but you ain't that cute!"

He seemed to look frustrated. He gestured for her to eat it again, saying it in his weird hybrid language, like Amara had said.

"Wait, I took two years of French," Tursanay realized. "Part of that sounded French. Um, um parlez vous?" she tried. His eyes lit up, and he asked a question that didn't entirely make sense. Her face fell a bit as she tried to concentrate. Maybe simpler words. Holding up the candy, she gestured to it. "Pourquoi?"

The boy seemed to understand. "Parler," he said, gesturing to the candy, then to his mouth. He then gestured from his mouth to her and back and forth to him.

"This will help us speak?" she said slowly to herself. As if he understood, he nodded. She blinked. "Wait, can you understand me right now?" He nodded. "Because you ate that?"

Another nod.

She paused, trying to forget if she said he was cute before or after he'd eaten the candy, and wasn't sure if she wanted the candy to be poisoned or not now. She started pacing again, swearing under her breath. Every so often, she'd look back at him and pause, only to pace and start swearing again. She was trying to talk herself into eating it, but she was also trying to talk herself into not eating it. She wasn't entirely sure what she thought was a good idea.

"Okay," she breathed. "Okay, I'm going to do this. I made a deal. You show up and I ask questions. Okay." She bounced on the balls of her feet and swung her arm, trying to psych herself up. "I got this." She held the candy up to her face. "If you drug me, I'm so kicking your ass." With one last hesitation, she popped the candy in her mouth and bit down. It dissolved almost instantly, leaving a rather contradicting taste on her tongue. She wasn't even sure she'd swallowed it. "That is so weird..."

"Can you understand me?" the boy asked.

Tursanay let out a swear that the neighbors probably heard as she hopped backwards and on top of her bed, pressing herself into the wall. "*Could you speak normally the whole time?*" she exclaimed.

"It was a language spell," he explained. "Do you not have those here?"

"A what?" Tursanay demanded.

"It enables us to speak without a language barrier," he replied nervously. "I-I've had so much trouble with the language barrier. I thought this would be simpler?"

"Why are you even here?" she wanted to know.

"I-I am attempting to locate the lost Dai-Nē," he said, hesitating as if he expected her to argue with him. "I-" he continued uncertainly when she said nothing, only stared. "I have crossed the Veil in search of them." He hesitated again, confusion crossing his face as he ordered his thoughts. "I had found one, I thought, but now I am uncertain... There was another girl, like yourself. I thought she was the one I was looking for, but then there was that boy?" he added in a tone that was utterly confused. His voice had trailed off, and Tursanay stared at him as if he'd grown a second head.

"A..." she had to swallow, her mouth had gone dry. She tried again. "A... girl like me...?" she said at length. "And... a boy?" Her brain wasn't working. It wasn't processing what he was saying. She was reeling in shock that he was even standing there and talking, let alone that what Rodney had hypothesized was true.

Oh no, Tursanay realized. *If what Rodney said was true, then what if there really are other things that can come out of Amara's dreams?* What if, because they had traded dreams, anything Tursanay dreamed now could come to life? A list of celebrities she wanted to watch movies for ran through her mind. If she could watch enough to make herself dream about them, this could get very interesting. Especially if they really could come to life.

"You know of them?" the red-haired boy asked, disturbing her train of thought. She flushed, clearing her throat awkwardly, hoping that mind reading spells weren't also a thing too.

"Know of them?" she asked, trying to remember the last thing he said. Oh right, the boy and the gir- "HA!" she shouted abruptly, making the boy jump. She pointed at him. "The deal!" The poor boy pressed himself against the wall. She tried to think of something to ask - anything - but first she needed to calm down. She took a breath to gather her thoughts, and slowly she moved toward the boy.

"Are you Dai-Nē?" asked the boy before Tursanay could speak. Every question she had thought of or was forming suddenly dissipated and left her blinking at the boy blank-faced. She gave him an odd look and asked him what on earth a die-knee was.

The incredulous look that the boy gave her made her feel stupid. "You don't know of the Dai-Nē?" he asked, stunned. "I thought everyone knew about Dai-Nē just like they knew the fundamentals of common magic. Even to those who can't practice it... It's as common as children's stories, or -"

"Yeah okay," blustered Tursanay. "It's common knowledge to you. Just one problem with that theory, Einstein: I haven't got the slightest clue what you're talking about."

The boy gave her a curious look. "What is an Einstein?" he asked.

"Common knowledge," she responded with heavy sarcasm.

The boy considered this for a moment.

"Somehow," he began. "I did not expect our worlds to be this vastly different."

Tursanay faltered. "Y-your what?" World? She was getting a headache. I *have finally gone insane, lost my mind, or slipped on the bath soap and am having a hallucination... I finally dream about the guy they've been telling me about, and my brain makes him an alien from another planet. Brilliant Tursanay! Absolutely brilliant...*

The boy interrupted Tursanay's mental rant again. "The Mortal World has been sealed away from the normal world for a long time... Possibly millennia or more..."

Don't you have that kind of backward? thought Tursanay. She could only manage a strange look.

"You realize," she said out loud. "That nothing you've said, thus far, has made even the slightest bit of sense? I mean... Mortal World? Something about knees...? Magic? There's no such thing as magic unless you count those fake magicians that pull rabbits out of their hats. I mean, sure, I enjoy reading about that stuff, but I don't think it's real." She paused. "Said the girl who just watched a guy fall out of a sideways floating puddle and into her room to give her magic candy that eliminates speech barriers." She put her hand on her head, her eyebrows threatening to disappear into her hairline. "I'm literally losing my mind."

"You can lose those here?" the boy asked, worried.

She glanced at him out of the corner of her eye.

This was going to be a long day.

Making her way to the cafeteria, Tursanay kept checking over her shoulder nervously. How would they even sneak him around? How would she explain this? Entering the cafeteria, she caught sight of the other two and waved them down. When Tursanay reached the table, everyone started speaking at once. Rodney and Amara asking her if she was okay, Tursanay trying to get them to come with her. They tried again, but with the same result. Tursanay held up her hand for silence and continued urgently.

"I can't explain right now, but I need you two to come with me," she said, waiting for them to move. When neither reacted other than to give her an odd look, she added, "Now." She raised her eyebrows to imply she didn't want to talk about whatever was bothering her in the middle of the lunchroom.

"Can I finish my pudding?" asked Rodney tentatively.

"No!" snapped Tursanay indignantly.

"Can I take it with me?" he tried again.

"Rodney!" she growled, grabbing his arm and hauling him to his feet. Amara pushed back from the table and manually wheeled after her to catch up before they got too far, calling after Tursanay to slow down. As they went down the hall, the two noticed Tursanay was heading toward the side door that led to the dorms in the school's main building.

"Is it in our dorm?" Amara asked, but two men in suits speaking to a staff member in the lobby drew their attention away. One of them flashed a badge, gesturing to his partner. Tursanay seemed to pale slightly as her pace quickened. Amara exchanged a look with Rodney, who seemed to fall silent, a serious look on his face.

"T, what's going on?" he asked quietly. She shook her head wordlessly, casting a wary glance back toward the office where the police officers had disappeared.

They veered to a side exit and crossed out onto a covered walkway, but Tursanay veered off toward the back of the school. The sky outside was turning dark and thick with clouds, promising a long stormy night ahead. They made their way across the basketball court, over the grounds behind the school, and, before long, they reached the rear fence of the enclosure where some trees grew behind some hedges.

"What are you doing?" Rodney asked. "Do you want to get detention? We're not supposed to be this far out unless we have permission."

"Look," she said, a little more harshly than she intended. "If I understand things correctly, we've got a lot bigger problems than detention right now. You're just going to trust me on this one."

"Trust you on what?" asked Amara softly, worried. "Did those police have anything to do with this?"

"Oh, dude, I can't go to jail," Rodney balked. "I won't survive in jail."

"Rodney, calm down. They can't be here for us, can they?" Amara interrupted, looking at the other girl. "Can they?" she asked again when no answer came.

Tursanay looked back at the school, her hesitation not making the other two feel any better, then shook her head. "I don't think so, but right now, I think anything's possible." Rodney and Amara stared at her for a minute, silent, then exchanged looks. Rodney eyed Tursanay again, then sighed.

"I swear if I go to jail for you," he said. "You better bail me out."

"Just help push Amara through the grass," Tursanay replied, turning and going into the wooded area.

"So why did you pick the back of the enclosure where I'd have to muck through grass?" Amara asked, as Rodney helped steer.

The scent of rain was getting stronger, mixing with the scent of pine and oak. It wasn't long before Tursanay could hear Rodney trying to control his labored breathing to keep from seeming over dramatic or make Amara feel bad. He seemed grateful when they stopped.

"Because I didn't want the staff to see or anyone to rat us out," Tursanay replied. They reached a small clearing, and she paused. She turned to face them and took a breath. "Just... Don't... freak out, okay?"

"No promises," Rodney nodded, as if agreeing.

"Oh!" she said, reaching into her pocket. "Eat this first." She handed them each a green marble-sized candy like she'd received. "You'll thank me later."

"What is it?" Amara asked suspiciously.

Rodney sniffed it and jerked away.

"Ew!" he said, popping it into his mouth. "Whoa, it disappeared." He smacked his lips, trying to place the flavor. "That's like..." He made a face, then shivered, but then lifted his eyebrow and waved his hand as if to show so-so.

"I know, right?" Tursanay said, knowing just what he meant. It was weird, and gross, but also not bad? "Try it - I won't make you eat anymore."

"I... don't want to," Amara said slowly.

"Think about it. Eat it once, never have to try it again. Never eat it at all, never know if you like it," Tursanay tried.

"There are a lot of things I don't have to know I won't like it," Amara said, not listing the most obvious.

"Will you at least try this for me?" Tursanay begged. "I'll explain why in just a minute."

"Why did you bring us out here to make us eat strange candy and risk detention?" Amara asked, point blank.

"If you eat the candy," Tursanay replied. "I'll tell you."

"That's borderline extortion," Amara replied.

"No, it's bargaining," Tursanay replied. "If I threatened to get us all caught lest you eat the candy, that would be extortion."

"Fair enough, but I still don't want to eat it," Amara replied.

Tursanay sighed, then perked up.

"Actually," Tursanay said. "Don't eat it yet. I want to see if it actually works."

"Wait what?" Rodney said, wondering what exactly he'd just eaten.

"Hold on - don't lose that," she instructed Amara. She took a few steps towards the far side of the small clearing and gestured for something to come out. "Come on!"

"What are you..." Rodney began, then froze as the boy with rust-colored hair he'd seen in history class walked out from behind the bushes.

"This," Tursanay introduced to their wide-eyed faces. "Is Soren. He's here looking for these people called... the Dai-Nē?" she said hesitantly, looking at him to confirm.

He nodded.

"And he thinks one of us might be the Dai-Nē of Element? Still not quite clear on what that means. But anyway, the reason he keeps popping up was because he was trying to scry where you were? However, because you were across the Veil, he couldn't figure out how to communicate with you at first? But he kept doing it to pinpoint where you were so that he could bring a translation spell to you so that you could talk and actually understand each other."

As Tursanay spoke, Amara had slowly made her way forward, staring at Soren intently. When she got within a comfortable distance, she stopped, and Soren stared back wordlessly.

"Anyway, something seemed to go wrong," Tursanay added, hesitantly, giving Amara an odd look. What was she doing? "When he tried to contact you again, but ended up finding... Rodney..." her voice trailed off as she watched Amara lift her hand, finger extended and shaking.

Reaching out, she carefully, and subtly, poked Soren in the chest. Her breathing seemed to become unsteady as her eyes widened. Soren reached out and poked her in the shoulder as if returning the gesture, and Amara's breath caught.

There was a long moment of silence when something seemed to break. Shaking her head and backing her chair up, Amara turned around abruptly and pushed herself out of the clearing.

"No. No, no. No, no-no! Nope. No!" she yelled, as she drew further and further away.

"Ah crap," Tursanay panicked, remembering something she'd forgotten in all of her excitement.

The dreams had been a state of fear for Amara, not something weird and interesting like it was for Tursanay. She ran after her, trying to stop her, but had to get in front of her for it to be effective.

"Wait Amara, please! I'm sorry - I should have shown you this differently. Wait- Stop! Please!"

Amara didn't seem to hear her, however, as she stopped and covered both sides of her head with her hands.

"Please, don't let it start," she begged. "Please don't let those creatures come here. I can't deal with them anymore!" A sob caught in her throat.

"No-no-no," Tursanay said, hunkering down and pulling one of her hands away. "It's okay. It's okay - they're not coming. You're safe here. We're not in the dream clearing. We're at Blemwick, okay? You're here with me and Rodney. We're at school. The only thing you'll hear are irritable teachers and school bells, okay?" She squeezed Amara's hand and made eye contact with her. "Hey," she said again, softly. "I've got you. I made sure nothing was going to happen before I brought you to see him. It's just him. Just him and me, and you and Rodney."

Amara nodded, hanging onto her words, trying to reground herself.

"Just us," she repeated. "Just us."

"I'm sorry," Tursanay said softly. "Since I finally got some answers, and I got so wrapped up in my excitement that I just wanted to show him to you. I didn't think about how it would bring back the bad memories, too."

Amara pulled her collar away from her neck and wiped her face on the inside of her shirt.

"I'm sorry too," she breathed. "I just felt like I couldn't breathe and like I was right back in those dreams and it was like I could hear them coming after me all over again."

After a little coaxing, Tursanay convinced Amara to come back to the clearing, but as they came back, Rodney was pacing like a caged animal. The girls stopped, glancing between the boys.

"I don't like this," Rodney said. "You didn't mention the part about possibly having to deal with governments and political stuff! I'm not good at political stuff!"

Tursanay gave Soren a look, putting her hand on her hip. "What did I tell you about letting me break the news to them slowly?"

"He asked me a question. I merely answered," Soren

replied innocently enough. He didn't seem to understand her confusion.

"Yeah, well next time, just wait till I'm back," she replied.

"Wait," Amara said. "What's he saying?" She looked up at Tursanay. "You understand him?"

"You can't?" Tursanay grinned.

Amara shook her head.

"Huh? But... I can?" Rodney said slowly.

"But he's speaking in that weird language," Amara replied.

"Oh no," Rodney groaned. "Oh no, this really is a dream and I haven't taken my exam yet and now I'm going to show up naked to class agai-"

"Rodney!" Tursanay interrupted him. "The candy! You're not in a dream. The candy was a spell that helps bridge the language gap. Oh, man, this is too cool - it actually works!"

"Are you telling me," Rodney began slowly. "That the piece of candy you gave us early is why I can understand him and she can't?"

"Yes!" Tursanay beamed.

Rodney looked at Soren, offended. "Where were you when I was taking Spanish two?" Soren made a slight eyebrow lift in confusion, but didn't reply.

Amara rubbed her face, trying to process everything. "Okay - what's this about politics?"

"Right," Tursanay remembered.

Soren said something rapidly and quickly, but Amara waved her hand and stopped him.

"Hold on," she muttered, digging into her pocket and retrieving the green candy. She popped it into her mouth and blinked in surprise when it disappeared. "What is that like... mint cotton candy mixed with like..."

"Seaweed!" Rodney declared at last, placing the taste.

"Oh, that's so it!" Tursanay agreed. "Like what they put on sushi sometimes!"

"Ew," Amara replied with a shiver.

"Can you understand him now?" Tursanay asked.

Amara looked up at Soren.

"May I continue?" Soren asked.

"Whoa," Amara stared wide-eyed, not entirely believing it had worked.

"I knoooow," Tursanay grinned. "So cool, right?"

"It's... it's something alright," Amara understated.

"Okay, but seriously," Rodney interjected. "Tell them what you told me? Because I have questions."

"Hang on," Tursanay interjected. "Okay, we left off with how he found us, right? Let's start there. Start with why you were looking for the... the Die-thingies-"

"Dai-Nē," Sorren corrected her.

"Yes Dai-Nē," she amended. "Start with that."

"There are seven Dai-Nē," Soren replied. "At least we think there are still seven. Something is wrong with the power of Sight."

"Wrong how?" Tursanay asked.

"It's diminished," Soren continued. "When the last seer was killed, it was suspected that someone was hunting the rest of the Dai-Nē. Therefore, the new generation went into hiding for their own safety."

"Whoa, hold up," Tursanay stammered. "You left that part out before!"

"Your numerous questions prevented me," Soren replied pointedly.

"That's-" Tursanay balked, then amended. "That's probably true..."

"So, what happened? Where did the Dai-Nē end up? What happened to the other Seer-dude? Did they find out who killed him?" Rodney asked.

"It is still a mystery," Soren replied. "I am attempting to locate all the Dai-Nē, starting with the Dai-Nē of Element. Which is where I currently stand with you three. When I find out which of you is the Dai-Nē of Element, I can continue my search for the others."

"Wait, one of us are Dai-Nē?" Amara asked.

"I scryed for the Dai-Nē of Element," Soren replied. "And I discovered you first. Then... him. Then her." His tone wasn't approving, and the furrow of his brow gave away his persistent confusion. "Which is not possible, for there can only be one Dai-Nē of each," he added.

"Okay, so how is this related to the politics thing?" Amara asked.

"There are rumors the Order of Rynon is searching for the Dai-Nē as well," Soren replied. "My suspicion is they may have had something to do with the old seer's death, but we have no proof."

Amara looked confused.

"So, what are the Dai-Nē exactly, and why are they so important?" she asked.

"The Dai-Nē are the protectors set in place by Rynon long ago to keep peace," Soren answered. "They were supposed to be ambassadors between our worlds, but that became spoken of as a myth over time. I thought it was a myth until I found myself here."

"Why does there need to be an ambassador between the worlds?" Amara asked. "Do we have something like that here and it's kept as, like, this big government conspiracy style secret where they meet the second Thursday of every month?"

Rodney gasped abruptly, grabbing both the girls' shoulders, making them jump. Even Soren flinched. "Do you realize what this means?" he asked, shaking them. "The men in black are real and those two guys in suits who came here earlier know he's here and are tracking us down! They're going to take us to a government facility, and we're going to vanish without a trace!"

"Whoa-whoa, back up," Tursanay said, grabbing his shoulder in turn. She really hoped this theory wasn't true because holy crap Rodney had been on a roll lately. "There's nothing to support that evidence - we don't know they're here for us."

"But we don't know they're not," Rodney replied.

"Well," Tursanay said, "he also said that our world's considered a myth over there kind of how magic is over here," Tursanay said. "So theoretically unless both sides have secret government agencies that secretly communicate with each other and keep the public in the dark about everything, then those guys just showed up at the same time as Soren and this is all just a huuuuge-" she hesitated. "Holy Mary, mother of God, those men are government agents of magic and they're here for us-"

"A-g-ga-ah-guys," Amara stammered, trying to shake fear settling into her stomach. "Guys. Back up, okay?" She looked at Soren. "Why are they looking for the Dai-Nē? What do they want with them?"

"I am unaware if they are," Soren replied. "I can only assume if they are, then they want the power of the Dai-Nē," he surmised. "The Dai-Nē controls the power of Rynon."

Thunder rolled overhead as a brief silence fell over the trio.

"Who's Rynon exactly?" Rodney asked.

"That's a story for another day," interrupted Tursanay. "He tried to explain it and I got lost in the details. The important thing I got from it is that we, or at least one of us, is part Rynon."

"What does that mean for the men inside?" Amara asked.

Tursanay turned back to Soren. "If I'm understanding this correctly, it takes all the Dai-Nē to have the powers of Rynon, yes?"

"Indeed," replied Soren.

"But when I was interrogating you earlier, you said something about a Council of Dai-Nē," Tursanay reminded him. "They teach the Dai-Nē how to use their powers, right?"

"Correct," Soren agreed. "They unlock the power bestowed on the individual by Rynon for each Dai-Nē."

"Would they be able to protect us if these guys turn out to be some people trying to hunt down the Dai-Nē?" Tursanay asked, forming an idea. "The Council people I mean."

"No," Soren said slowly.

"No?" Tursanay repeated, her backup plan instantly falling apart. "Why not?"

"They," Soren began, but hesitated. "Do not... know I am here."

There was another heavy pause.

"Wait, then who sent you?" Amara asked.

"I wasn't," Soren began, a small flush on his face. He looked to one side, not meeting their eyes. "No one sent me... I... sent myself?"

"You... came across the Veil all on your own?" Tursanay said. "Why are you looking for the Dai-Nē?"

Soren hesitated. "I am also a Dai-Nē... I wanted to find people like me."

"Wait, you keep saying Veil," Rodney said. "What's that?"

"The way he explained it," Tursanay replied. "I think it's basically what separates the magic world from our world. What keeps us from being able to see them or cross over by accident?"

"Worlds..." Rodney repeated.

Tursanay patted him on the shoulder. "Just breathe; it helps." She was speaking from personal experience.

"Wait, crossover you mean, like, as in die? You mean there are things around us right now and we just can't see them? Does that make him..." Rodney paused and whispered behind his hand to Tursanay. "Does that make him a zombie? Or a necromancer?"

"I am half-elf," Soren bristled, offended he had to be asked.

The trio stared at him long and hard for a moment before Rodney found his voice again.

"We talkin' Santa, video game, Lord of the Rings, or Keebler?"

"He's not a Smurf, he doesn't smell like cookies, and while he is wearing green, he's not on a quest for Zelda, he's looking for Dai-Nē," Tursanay retorted. "One thing at a time. Besides, no," she continued before they got distracted. "The Veil's not like that—the way he described it, it's like our worlds are completely different and completely unaware of each other. Uh... Except for maybe the government thing..."

"Wait, so if magic is separate from this world," Amara began. "And one of us is supposedly this Dai-Nē thing; how'd we end up over here?" Amara asked. "If no one knew about all this..."

"I do not know," Soren answered honestly.

A bell rang in the distance.

"Oh, no, that's the last call for supper," Tursanay groaned. "Where are we going to hide him?"

"Hide him?" Rodney repeated.

Tursanay gave him an exasperated look as she gestured to Soren. Then he realized.

"Oh... Oh! Oh no."

"You see my problem," Tursanay agreed.

"Rodney, when does your roommate leave to live with his new family?" Amara asked, remembering him saying something about that.

"He's already gone. He went to eat supper with them," Rodney replied. "They shipped out his stuff this morning."

"Perfect!" Tursanay grinned.

"Whoa-no, not perfect!" Rodney balked. "What if we have a room inspection?"

"Then explain you have a guest?" Tursanay offered. "Say he's your brother." When Rodney gave her a condescending look, wordlessly reminding her to compare the two of them in appearance. She amended with, "Okay, at least say he's your cousin."

"I don't have a family. That's why I'm here, remember?" Rodney reminded her.

"Yeah, but the staff won't know that off-hand. They have so many students, they won't remember every single one," Tursanay replied.

"They'll still ask for the permission slip," Rodney replied.

"Then we'll go to the office and grab one and say we want to have it filled out in case our friend visits later. We'll forge the signature and bam, instant permission," Tursanay replied simply.

"Do you even hear yourself?" Rodney asked. "That's going to get us in so many levels of trouble I can't even count the ways."

"Well, hopefully by then we'll figure out what to do with him so that we can avoid all that," Tursanay replied.

"That's a big if, though," Rodney argued.

"Good thing I didn't say 'if'," Tursanay retorted.

"There is still the issue of finding out which of you are Dai-Nē and which of you are not," Soren interjected.

The trio looked at him.

"Actually," Tursanay began slowly. "I may have a theory on that." She looked at Amara. "Remember when you and Rodney made the fake deal to switch the dreams, and it worked?"

"Yeah?" Amara said.

"Well, when he first got here, he said he saw a girl first, then a boy. In other words, you then, Rodney. Then after you made the switch with me, Rodney," she said, looking up at him. "He came out of the floating sideways puddle thing-"

"Portal," Soren corrected her.

"The floating what now?" Rodney blinked.

"Long story," Tursanay dismissed. "We'll get to that. Actually, there's a lot more we need to get to, but," she said, holding up her finger and turning to Soren, but still partially facing Rodney so he could read her lips if necessary. "based on what you are telling me, they weren't dreams at all, but your attempts to contact her that just seemed like a random series of dreams on our end."

"I do not understand," Soren replied, confused.

"What I'm saying is, I think when we made a deal, we weren't switching dreams. We were switching the Dai-Nē power thing and didn't know," Tursanay surmised.

"That's not possible," Soren replied. "To remove the power from a Dai-Nē would result in their death."

"What if that's just another myth on your end?" Tursanay challenged. "Because we switched dreams twice, and because of that, you saw all three of us. Yet we're still alive."

"What you are describing does not seem possible," Soren disagreed.

"We can try again," Tursanay said. "See, I think you, Amara, are the Dai-Nē of Element. So, giving you the dreams back will give you the power back."

"Whoa-ho nope!" Amara said, holding up her hands. "I'm not taking those back. You can have them. Besides, I'm not interested in getting involved with someone else's politics either."

"No no listen," Tursanay said. "Since he's not trying to contact you anymore because he's physically here with us - that's the best part - you won't have the dreams anymore!"

"I can't go back to having those dreams," Amara shuddered.

"Okay," Tursanay reasoned, looking at Soren. "If you don't scry her any more, will she go back to that place you were meeting up at to talk to her?"

"No," Soren replied. "That was my established correlation in order to-"

"Seeeee?" Tursanay said brightly, turning back to Amara. "No scrying, no dreams, no creatures!"

"Are you sure?" Amara asked, looking at Soren.

"Those creatures cannot reach us here," Soren confirmed.

Amara was quiet a long time, the sound of thunder getting closer.

"Ready to take your power back?" Tursanay asked, holding out her hand.

Amara looked at it long and hard, but reached out and took it.

"Deal," Amara said hesitantly.

Both winced, waiting for the shock, but it never came. Tursanay peeked through one eye, then two.

"It... didn't work?" she said slowly.

"Maybe because he's here now?" Amara suggested, hopefully.

"No, I don't think so," Tursanay replied. "Him being here has nothing to do with who had the dreams. Just why the dreams were happening."

"You are correct," Soren agreed. "When I used the scrying glass, I looked for the Dai-Nē of Element. The current wielder of any individual power of the seven divisions of Dai-Nē can only be one person at a time. When that person passes on, the power is reborn into the next generation. For me to have scryed all of you in succession, you would all have to be the Dai-Nē of Element. However, such a feat is not possible."

"So that means my theory is right," Tursanay replied. "I just don't understand why it didn't work this time."

"It's one theory, doesn't mean it's the only one," Rodney argued.

"Fight me," Tursanay argued back, not seriously.

"We'll figure that out later," Rodney dismissed. "We need to get back before the curfew bell rings."

"Chicken, you just don't wanna square up," Tursanay joked. Then added, "But yeah, we haven't eaten. We should get back."

"What about the men in black?" Amara said softly.

The others hesitated. They'd forgotten that bit.

"It's probably just a coincidence," Tursanay reassured her,

though she didn't sound too convinced herself judging by the half octave rise in her voice.

"Probably," agreed Rodney, not convinced either.

Amara groaned, worried, as Rodney helped steer her back towards the school. Tursanay motioned for Soren to follow.

CHAPTER 5
DARKNESS

Ilarys sighed as they dropped their packs into their room in the inn. They had just taken a jitney dirigible back to the other side of the city, only to be deposited over half a league away from their inn at the nearest stop. Out of money for a ground level ride back to their room, they walked the two and a third miles back, completely exhausted by the time they arrived, well after dark. The inn was no longer serving meals at that hour. They'd have to wait until breakfast to get anything to eat.

"You'd think I'd be used to this by now," she said as she dropped onto the bed at a ridiculous angle. Kicking her shoes off, she used her toes to pull off her stockings and fell limp, arms half hanging off one side of her bed, feet off the other. "Used to you dragging me on ridiculous quests, running out of money, and having to walk back... but this is probably your worst yet."

"I think that time we encountered the crazy General in Alhalanadria that was convinced she was the next Dai-Nē of

Alchemy despite never having gone to the Council to confirm it might have given this time a run for its money, had we not just seen my reflection-"

"Don't-... remind me," Ilarys cut him off. "I want to sleep tonight, not wake up screaming and get us kicked out of another inn."

"I think we need to take a holiday," Keir muttered. "Especially after that encounter."

"I take back everything I said about your fear of mirrors," Ilarys mumbled. "To think they'd been hunting you all this time... waiting for you to take my dare and step through..."

"I have to say I would definitely feel validated by saying I told you so," he replied. "But just for your sake, I'll refrain."

Ilarys wanted to punch him, but to do so would require more energy than she had at the moment.

"On second thought, it would have caused me much less stress in life if I had pushed you in like Elise wanted me to," Ilarys grumbled, burying her face in a pillow and trying to ignore him.

Suddenly, the conversation was much too exhausting to keep up, and she just wanted an hour and a half of silence to unwind and not think. She could spend the day bantering with him, speaking to others about their current quest, interrogating who needed interrogating, but when it was time for food and sleep, she just needed peace and quiet. Time to process. Unfortunately, it was several hours past her normal processing time.

"Elise always was fond of planting both feet to face your fears and jumping in headfirst. Consequences be damned," Keir remarked. "Do you still talk to her?"

In response, Ilarys laid motionless on the bed, holding her breath for as long as she could so she could stay in that comfortable position for longer. When at last she could hold it in no longer, she let out a long, exhausted groan until her lungs emptied and her voice petered out. She waited a few seconds till her lungs demanded air, then turned her face to breathe lest she suffocate.

"A simple no would have sufficed," Keir shrugged, moving into the bathing area and out of her sight.

"I miss Aui'ani," she muttered, eyes catching sight of her dual rings again. "She puts up with you better than I do."

"I still don't understand how having a simple conversation wears you out so much," Keir grumbled from the bathroom as the sound of water running reached her ears. She opened her mouth to reply it wasn't the conversation, so much as his entire embodiment of seemingly endless energy, when Keir shouted in alarm, knocking several things from the counter into the floor.

"Please tell me you're decent," Ilarys called, sitting up on the bed and already forming the sigil in the air with her finger to start the eye spell. She would not get up if he was just being reckless, but that scream had a distinct note of fear in it that had her worried.

She blinked and suddenly she could see Keir's reflection in the portrait mirror in the bathroom. Fully clothed, brow furrowed, and a glare coming from six red eyes. It was probably quite the contrast to his wide-eyed startled look she felt her own features forming.

Another has breached the Veil, the reflection hissed.

"A-Another?" Keir repeated, trying to regain his composure.

What are Dai-Nē? it demanded. *What race is this?*

"They... they aren't a race," Keir stammered. "They are wielders of a power that is reincarnated. It can be born into any race." He hesitated a moment before gesturing to his eyes. "Can you make that a little less... not me? It's unnerving enough to speak to my reflection, but I keep feeling like those are on my face and I don't like it."

There was a moment as the reflection stared at him blankly before the face changed back into his own. Ilarys too breathed a sigh of relief.

Where does this power come from? the reflection asked.

"I-I don't know," Keir replied, shaking his head. "I can see if I can find out. Why is this important?"

The Dai-Nē are the key to our escape, the reflection replied. *Their essence is the same as the Veil. The same stench of Eitû.* It seemed to think for a moment.

"Does everything over here smell like him? Why do you hate him?" Keir wondered.

The village did not stink of his magic, it said slowly. *The Veil about the village was weakening. We could feel their magic more strongly. Take their people more easily. But they destroyed every link but one, and your The Veil is weak there, but we can no longer reach it to escape.*

"The Veil is weaker..." Keir murmured, thoughts swimming.

From her place in the bedroom, Ilarys whispered, "Is the village dying because of the weakened spot in the Veil?" Keir heard her and repeated the question.

Yes, came the reply. *The weaker the Veil, the more power it leaches from the tears. The more power it consumes, the more that falls ill.*

"Yet you were still trying to tear a hole in the Veil?" Keir balked. Ilarys shared his sentiment. If they were only going to abduct people and steal their essence, and create holes in a

Veil that would kill even more people, she wasn't sure she wanted to help them.

There is a spell to remake it, the reflection hissed. *It exists solely in our world. Once we crossed the Veil, we would have offered this to repair the damage. There is too much iron. Too much evil. We wish to separate ourselves from this place.*

Keir sighed, rubbing his face, and for a moment Ilarys could see nothing. She heard him mumble something about the Order not going to like that and agreed. One of the core beliefs of the senior members of the Order of Rynon was that there was a Veil between the worlds, and that the Dai-Nē were the bridge between them. Ambassadors that would make peace again eventually and reunite the two worlds. From the sound of it, the two worlds would do best to stay separated.

This breach is not the first. The reflection continued, making Keir look up. He blinked to adjust his vision and focused on the words.

"Wasn't I the first?" he asked slowly.

You have not breached the Veil, merely escaped it. The response was not comforting, and the implications were alarming.

"You're saying..." Keir hesitated, then tried again, not sure how to phrase his question. "You mean to say that 'another' has breached the Veil, means that someone has crossed over and... come into this world? Are people from your world entering ours? Why can't you join them?"

Ilarys considered the implications of this. If that world was of iron and evil, what would that mean if they breached the Veil and invaded this world?

Not into your world, the reflection replied. *They have crossed from your side to this world of no magic.*

"Wait, that means there is a Dai-Nē in the other world?" Keir thought out loud. Ilarys thought back to his vision of the four people in the small space. Was that a prediction? Keir didn't have predictions that didn't happen within the next few minutes. He mainly dealt in hindsight, amongst a few other things. Her brow furrowed.

There are several, the reply came. *They escaped through the portal hidden within the Council many years ago.* There was a long silence that made Keir look at his sister, then away quickly lest the Fae get suspicious and disappear again.

"How many?" Keir asked quietly.

At least two, possibly three now, the reflection replied. *They are gathered together. Exchanging powers using the Ring of Rynon as if it were a toy.*

"Ring of Rynon?" Keir repeated. They usually called him Eitû, Ilarys noted. She wondered why this time was different.

The Ring that brought Eitû his stolen power, the reflection replied.

"Rynon stole his power?" Keir asked, shock coloring his voice.

From the many eyed Seraphim, the reflection replied. The voice was growing angry, and the mirror growing dark. Its eyes, in the reflection, were changing. The pupils went cat-slit, and the red lines opened above and below, threatening to awaken again. *We will not forgive him for his sins.*

"Whoa," Keir said, trying to calm them down lest they bring unwanted attention from the innkeeper. "At least he isn't around anymore, right?"

His power lingers, the reflection growled.

"If he stole his power, then isn't the power that lingers that of the Seraphim, not Rynon?" Ilarys suggested. She couldn't bear to see the chest split open again. She was quite certain she wouldn't sleep tonight as it was.

Keir repeated it quickly, trying to calm the situation.

The power is tainted with his essence, the reflection began, as the mirror's darkness ebbed away and he could see the room behind him again. *But at least we can remember the power of the Seraphim.*

Keir and Ilarys both let out a relieved sigh.

"Is it possible to return the power to the Seraphim?" he asked after being prompted by Ilarys.

They perished with the spell that stole their power. They are the Veil. The power of Eitû. And thus, they are the Dai-Nē, the reflection replied. *They are not gone as long as we remember and honor them. But they must purge Eitû from their magic to truly be at peace.*

"How can we do that?" Keir asked.

Recast the spell, the reflection replied. *Set us free and recast the spell.*

"Can I view the spell?" he asked.

Come to us, the reflection replied. *And we will show you the spell.*

"I will postpone that offer to take up on another time," Keir replied. "But I need to learn more about this ring you spoke of—how does it work?"

It is needed for the spell, the reflection began, but cut off, half turning away from Keir as if hearing something behind it. Ilarys shivered at the thought of something behind the Fae that was threatening enough to distract it.

"What's going on?" Keir asked, noticing too.

The shapeshifter has returned, it replied.

"Aren't you a shapeshifter?" Keir asked, but seemed to go unheard.

She is hunting them, the reflection growled. *She is going to take our last means of escape-* The reflection shimmered, disappearing like smoke off of Keir's features.

"Wait!" Keir called, but it was too late. Ilarys released the spell and blinked.

"What do they mean 'she's hunting them'?" Ilarys asked. "Do you think they mean the Dai-Nē?"

"I don't know..." Keir replied, coming into the doorway. "But it makes sense if what I saw about Dai-Nē being the only ones that can cross the Veil is true, then that means the shapeshifter Dai-Nē is over there now as well. That means nearly all the Dai-Nē are on the other side of the Veil right now."

"Are you going to join them?" Ilarys asked. "Take the Fae up on their offer to see the spell?"

"I'm going to talk to the OOR first. We need them to set up an immediate meeting with the Head of the Order," he said.

"Forget going through the proper channels," Ilarys replied. "I have a contact that can get us inside by tomorrow afternoon." She grabbed her hand-held mirror, opening it up and running her finger along the circular edges of its surface. The mirror flickered to life with a blue light. A shadowed figure came into view, and a voice that was slightly distorted answered. "I need a meeting with the Head of the Council."

"Go through the proper channels like everyone else," the voice quipped.

"It involves the location of at least four Dai-Nē, possibly five," she added. There was silence for a moment, followed by a scratching sound.

"On the morrow by the eve," was the quick response. "This information source had better be reliable."

"Worst case, we only have one Dai-Nē, best case all of them," Ilarys replied. "That source is me."

The figure gave a nod and severed the link. Ilarys closed the hand-held mirror and put it away. Lying back down on the bed, she sighed.

"That was quick," Keir noted, trying to hide how impressed he was. "We should-"

"I'm not doing anything else until I have slept, bathed, and eaten," she cut him off. She had exhausted all her energy and was done with today.

Keir only grumbled something in reply.

CHAPTER 6
ETHER

They took Soren to Rodney's room, where they got him a change of clothes, so he wouldn't stick out like a sore thumb if anyone saw him. He and Rodney were relatively the same size, so they agreed to let him wear his uniform. Rodney, however, was a tad bit bigger, so Soren's clothes were awkwardly baggy in various places. Since Tursanay hadn't had time to eat yet, they dealt with it and headed back to the cafeteria. The smell of food that hit them as they entered the room caused Soren's stomach to growl loud enough for the others to hear.

Rodney laughed. "I speak that language! Come on, we'll get you a tray," he said, taking Soren to the almost nonexistent lunch line. The cafeteria was open late on Fridays and weekends, so they could still get a bit of food, despite the time. Amara waved the others into the lunch line, saying that she'd secure the table while they got their food. She grabbed an empty chair from nearby and set it at their usual table for Soren.

As they stood in line, Rodney explained what the different foods were and Soren stuck mostly to the things that didn't sound mildly worrying. Asking questions here and there as they occurred to him.

Rodney was in the middle of describing just exactly what meatloaf was as they got back to the table, none of them noticing Mr. Asher standing there talking to a pale faced Amara until they had all set their trays down. There was an awkward silence as everyone stared at each other, tensely. Amara was looking at the group with a mix of fear and uncertainty on her face, and Rodney and Tursanay looked to be praying Mr. Asher didn't start asking troubling questions about Soren that would be very difficult to answer. Mr. Asher, unfortunately, was staring fixedly at Soren, and Soren staring back, both with odd looks on their faces. Soren's surprised, and Mr. Asher slightly shaken. Soren could see a bead of sweat run down his face.

"If you're here," said Mr. Asher, swearing under his breath and not taking his eyes off Soren. "Then things just got very complicated."

The shock on the trio's face was indescribable. Mr. Asher seemed to shake himself out of a reverie and snapped his attention to Amara.

"There are two detectives in the office that need to talk to you, Amara," he said, his tone taking an authoritative note. "After what you've just experienced, I know you're a little wary of everything, but I promise you can trust them. Do you understand?" He grasped her shoulder for emphasis and locked eyes with her.

She blinked in confusion, and tried to respond, but couldn't seem to form the words.

"Just go ahead to the office for now. I need to talk to these three for a moment. They can catch you up later." When she hesitated, he instructed her to go with a tone that told her not to argue. Still casting a glance over her shoulder now and then, she rolled off to the office to see what the detectives wanted to talk to her about.

Mr. Asher looked at the remaining trio at the table and took in the bewildered stare of his two students. He sighed. He looked around the cafeteria to make sure there wasn't anyone nearby that would overhear them talking. Once satisfied that most of the students were far enough away or had already trickled out, he nodded at them to sit down and followed suit. He let out a very long sigh and rubbed his face as if he were trying to process everything at once. For the first time since meeting him, Soren saw just how tired he looked.

"Eat while we talk. It'll look like I'm welcoming a new student that you two know," he instructed, leaning back in his chair. They followed suit, and, after a moment's hesitation, Tursanay and Soren started eating. Soren, more hesitant than the others, cast a leery glance at her plate then his own. Mr. Asher allowed himself a grin. "It's okay, Soren. It's just mashed potatoes and gravy. I wouldn't recommend eating the meatloaf, though."

Tursanay choked and cupped her hand over her mouth before swallowing. Soren looked suspiciously at the dark gray lump. Tursanay had just put a piece in her mouth.

"I just mean, it's a little salty compared to the meat you are used to," Asher explained. "And the texture throws me off. Never could get used to it."

"How do you know his name?" asked Tursanay once she could breathe again.

"I think I should start at the beginning," replied Mr. Asher. "How much have you told them, Soren?"

"Not much," Soren replied. "They get easily distracted."

"Heeey," Rodney complained.

Asher laughed, but there wasn't much humor to it. "That is a common trait in this world."

Soren considered this. "They know about the Council of Dai-Nē, the Veil that separates our world from the Mortal World, and about the old Seer's death... And the basics of the Dai-Nē: why they exist, how many there are, and the reincarnation cycle... It amazes me how little common knowledge they know..."

"You've covered a lot... Eat, I'll talk." After hesitating, they obeyed. Mr. Asher took a deep breath and sighed again. "I can't tell you everything right off the bat, for obvious reasons," he said, casting another look around the lunchroom. "But you deserve a few answers." He paused, considering. "First, do not under any circumstances use that portal knife again, young man. There was a reason I told you to wait the first time." The stern look he gave Soren made the half-elf's voice disappear. He nodded quietly, color draining from his face. "Second, I bet you are wondering what my part in all this is."

Tursanay and Rodney glanced at each other, then back at Asher, both nodding.

"About twenty years ago, I lived on that side of the Veil. When this generation of Dai-Nē were born and the old Seer died, we sent them into hiding just in case their lives were in danger as well."

"As well?" Tursanay asked. "Wait, died? Didn't Soren say that someone killed him?"

"Well, there has been speculation that when the old Seer had found six out of seven Dai-Nē, the one responsible for his death may have seen the list. The only one he didn't find was the next Seer - his replacement for when he passed on," Asher answered.

"If the powers are reincarnated, how would he be able to find his own replacement?" Tursanay asked.

"The Dai-Nē of Sight can predict when and where they will be born, as well as their names," Asher answered. "You'll learn more about that later," he added, cutting off any more questions and returning to the story.

"Do you think there will be another Seer?" Soren interrupted, anyway. "They say the power is diminished, and that it is dying out."

"Diminished?" Tursanay asked. "He mentioned something about that before. What does that mean?"

"That one is a little harder to explain," Asher replied. "But it's important... so I'll touch on it." He cleared his throat and sat up a little more. "The Council of Dai-Nē has a pedestal. Now this pedestal is a device that holds the power of Dai-Nē until the next vessel is born and can retrieve their powers from it. Usually, they receive training first, and then unlock their full potential by gaining the powers.

"But... if it's reincarnated, how does that even work?" Tursanay asked, confused.

"That's just how it's always been," Soren began with a shrug, but Asher shook his head.

"No, it's not," he replied.

Soren looked up, surprised.

"The history behind that isn't something I can go into right now, but you're right, Tursanay. It was supposed to be reincarnated naturally without the powers going through the pedestal, but something happened long ago that made it necessary for the pedestal to be created. Now when a Dai-Nē passes away or killed, their power returns to the pedestal until the next generation can retrieve it. The Council protects the pedestal and trains the Dai-Nē; and are supposed to be the voice of the people to ask for help from the Dai-Nē when issues arise."

"That... makes little sense though," Soren continued, mulling over what he'd said about the pedestal. "If they are supposed to be reincarnated naturally, then how are they tied to the pedestal?" Everything he'd ever been told about the Dai-Nē started with them receiving the powers from the pedestal. If that was a lie, and the truth of the non-magic world was a lie, what else was? Things he'd grown up learning were unraveling bit by bit and he didn't like it.

"I can't get into that right now," Asher shook his head, then checked his watch before glancing back towards where Amara had left the cafeteria. "For now, I'm sticking with a few key points." He turned back to them. "The powers form into orbs on the pedestal. I'm assuming the power of Sight has diminished to the size of the powers of Light and Dark magic?" Soren's eyes widened, and Asher took that as confirmation. "I can sense the question you have. And the answer is yes. There is more behind that as well, and I will tell you more about that as soon as I can."

"But not now," Tursanay sighed, not liking the partial bits of information.

"You're catching on," noted Asher with an apologetic smile. "Just know that it will be addressed and fixed as soon as possible. But for now, I believe there is still a Dai-Nē of Sight out there."

"So, it doesn't mean they are growing weaker when they diminish?" Soren prodded. "People have speculated the powers were dying out for a while now... Some even feared it meant magic itself was dying."

"No, there is no fear of magic dying, but the secret behind the diminished powers is only known to those that were there when the pedestal was built," Asher concluded.

"But wouldn't everyone have passed since then?" Soren asked. "No one has been that long lived since... the days of Rynon himself."

"You are partially right," Asher nodded. "The ones who built the pedestal are the ones we were afraid killed the old Seer. That's why we sought to hide them where we believed no one could find them: here in the Mortal World."

"So, the people who built the pedestal are bad?" Tursanay asked.

Soren wanted to know, too.

"You'll find it's hard to define an entire people as wholly good or wholly evil. Same as an individual. There are a few. But even if the pedestal has outlived its usefulness, it had a good intention at one point. Even if it ultimately served a different purpose. Remember that as you gather more information about that world and be careful not to listen to prejudices. That world is as diverse and as vibrant - if not more so - than here in the Mortal World," said Asher.

"Mortal World?" Rodney repeated back. "Wait, so I'm confused. He just said no one lives that long, but you called this place the Mortal World? So, is everyone there immortal or no? Or is it like this is the human/mortal world and that's the afterlife?"

"No," Asher replied. "There is only one immortal left, but... they prefer to remain unknown. There are no other immortals... Not anymore, anyway." He seemed to add that last bit under his breath a bit darkly, but did not direct it at anyone in particular. "The term 'Mortal' has become more of a slang term used to describe non-magic—or rather—non-paranormal individuals, persons and or beings. It fell into myth over time that such people even existed, much like the existence of magic and paranormal people and things did over here."

"Oh, so like..." Rodney first pointed to those at their table, but hesitated and pointed to a random table across the room. "Normal people?" He took a slow sip of his drink.

"Normal to you, yes," Asher replied.

"Oh man, are humans the cryptids of the magic world?" Tursanay grinned.

Rodney snorted into his cup and choked a bit.

"Wait," she paused, a thought crossing her mind. "But if one of us is Dai-Nē, and no one knows about this world... then how did the Dai-Nē get over here?"

"There have always been myths and legends over time of how to get here. We tested a theory, and it worked," Asher answered.

She chewed her lip thoughtfully. "So, if we're the Mortal World, what is that place called?"

"For lack of a better term, I suppose you could call it the Magic World, but you'll get strange looks if you refer to it as that over there," Asher replied. "Same as you would if you called this world the Mortal World here."

"That's fair," Rodney noted, nodding.

"What happened after the Seer died and you started rounding up Dai-Nē?" Tursanay asked.

"We found four that would go across the Veil," Asher continued. "One we never found, the seventh was never located by the Seer, and the last one's family refused to go across the Veil point blank. When the day came to move them, the fourth never showed up, so only three made it across the Veil."

"Where are they now?" Rodney asked.

Asher gave him a sideways glance. "Aside from Ms. Ephraim, who is not at our table, all of you. The original four that were supposed to escape to the Mortal World," he answered. Tursanay's eyes lit up and Rodney's face paled. Soren sat up - he had done it? Had he found not one but three other Dai-Nē? His pulse raced in his ears.

"I have superpowers?" Tursanay beamed, hands pressed to the sides of her face before she remembered to lower her voice. "We all have super powers?" she repeated, more quietly, unable to wipe the grin off her face.

"Uh... I can't even do a single push up or walk down the hall without tripping on air," Rodney interjected. "If I have a superpower, I'm going to be the same, but instead of eating tiles, I'm going to take the entire building with me."

Tursanay disagreed with him, stating that would only happen if he had super strength, which Rodney argued back with several names and descriptions Soren didn't recognize. He wondered how people in this world could have such abilities and it not be magic.

"Did you ever find out if the rumors were true? Were the people that created the pedestal hunting the Dai-Nē?" Soren asked, trying to ignore their stray off topic. Again. He was more concerned about whether they were being hunted. The others looked over curiously.

Asher considered the answer for a moment, his expression grim. "While I'm not sure of the details, I know this... When we first came across the Veil, someone scattered us. They knew we were going to use the portal and when. Then, reptilian creatures that can follow a scent across countries hunted us. Creatures that could even hunt across waters." He looked at Soren for a long moment. "That's why I asked you to wait before you used that portal knife I gave you. I wasn't sure if it would cause the creatures to come again. I hope they haven't tracked you since they attacked immediately last time, but nothing has happened this time.

"Something happened," Soren blurted, looking abashed, but determined. "When I tried to contact the Dai-Nē of Element again-

"Also, like I asked you to not do," Asher interrupted, but Soren pushed on.

"When I scried her again, it was someone different," Soren finished.

There was a long pause and Rodney and Tursanay exchanged glances as if being told on for breaking the rules.

"What?" Asher asked pointedly.

"It was him," Soren added, nodding to Rodney. "Then her, once I tried again." A nod at Tursanay.

Asher was obviously unsettled to hear this news. "That's..." he began, his voice trailing off.

"Not possible," Soren agreed readily.

But Asher shook his head. "No, it's possible, but only under two circumstances," Asher said, doing a double take at something across the room but quickly looking away. He looked at the other two. "Don't do it again until we can talk more. It could cost you your life."

Rodney paled considerably and swore he would not. Tursanay hesitated.

"What two circumstances?" she pressed.

"Another time," Asher replied, a warning in his tone.

"I'm sorry but if it could cost us our li-" Tursanay argued, but he held up a hand abruptly.

"Ms. Valtteri," he said in a commanding voice. "I'm afraid

if you persist, you will skip a demerit and go straight for detention."

Confusion crossed Tursanay's face, but she fell silent for a moment, and Soren wondered just what a demerit and detention were to cause the argumentative one to fall silent. He noticed Asher glance at something behind her, just before Tursanay rolled her eyes and looked away. Soren followed her gaze. Nearby was a man mopping up the floor, giving her a side eye of disapproval. She gave the man a weird face, then looked back at her food. Soren watched the exchange quietly and sipped his water, wondering who that was and why they gave him a slight sense of fear in his gut.

"Do you understand?" Asher reiterated.

"Yeah, yeah, yeah," Tursanay dismissed. "No more talking back to the teachers, even when they are wrong."

Asher shook his head. "Remember: we welcome civil debate. To accuse one of being 'a hack' is not debating, just antagonizing."

Rodney, who appeared to be more lost than Soren, stared at the two of them. The utter confusion was apparent on his face, reminiscent of someone trying to solve complicated math problems and failing to see the connection.

"Mr. Roberts," Asher got his attention before he could say something to ruin their facade. "See that your... cousin gets a haircut before next semester starts." Tursanay rounded on Rodney with a smile that exuberated pure sarcasm. Rodney, seemingly instantly distracted by the subject change, glowered at her in return.

"Not a word," Rodney instructed Tursanay, who shrugged her shoulders and raised her eyebrows innocently. "Yes, sir, Mr. Asher, sir. I will make sure my *cousin* fits the dress-code standards by then. Hopefully, his uniforms will be in by then and he won't have to borrow mine. Like he is today." Rodney glared at Tursanay for good measure.

"I'll take care of that," Asher replied, rubbing his temple and trying to hide his amusement. He monitored the man with the mop as he moved away from the group and out of earshot. When he'd left the cafeteria, Asher sighed.

"Deets," Tursanay said immediately. "What are the conditions?"

Asher sighed again. "You are persistent."

"I mean hellooo? World of magic? I'd be crazy not to be interested," Tursanay scoffed.

"Call me crazy," Rodney interjected. "But I'm still a little hung up on the idea someone might be out to off us."

"I'm just being cautious at the moment," Asher reassured him. "I just don't want a repeat of history."

"Question," Rodney piped up. "Those men in the office..."

"No," Tursanay tried to shush him.

"The men in the office?" Asher asked, raising an eyebrow.

"It's a legitimate question," Rodney whispered to Tursanay, trying to gesture for him not to ask. Turning to Asher and just ignoring Tursanay, he blurted. "Are they secret government agents that interact with the other side of the Veil regularly and now that Soren is here, we are going to become the ambassadors between our worlds?"

Asher stared at him for a moment. Tursanay looked like she wanted to crawl into a hole, but also wanted to know the answer. Soren wasn't sure what he thought. When Asher's face fell a bit, Tursanay and Rodney exchanged nervous glances.

"No," he said softly. "I'm afraid they are from a local police department. The Mortal World and Magic World governments do not communicate."

"Why does the fact they are from a local PD make you have that kind of reaction—what happened?" Tursanay demanded. "Why did they want to talk to Amara-" she said, already getting to her feet, but Asher stopped her.

"They need to speak with her alone right now," he said, standing and barring her way. Then added softly, "But she may need your support when she comes out. For now, get him settled in your room, Mr. Roberts. I'll take care of the paperwork."

"But she doesn't need to be in there alone if something happened," Tursanay argued.

"Right now," Asher said, lowering his voice and putting his hand on Tursanay's shoulder. "There are things you need to focus on. You may be on the move in the next few days or you may be here for months. I'm not sure. What I need you to do is go to your dorms, pack some essentials should something go awry, and wait for Ms. Ephraim to come to you. Can you do that?"

When she didn't answer, he called her by her first name to get her attention. Tursanay looked up at him, a good deal of fear and uncertainty in her eyes. She backed down and nodded, but pushed past him without another word to head towards the dorm. Asher pursed his lips, watching her go.

"I'm sorry you have to deal with this all at once," he said, looking back at the boys. "I was going to wait until you had finished school and didn't have so much on your plates to deal with. School is hard enough without throwing this into the mix. You're just children and you're already getting in way over your heads."

"I mean... I guess it was bound to happen, eventually?" Rodney attempted to console him, but did not know what to say.

Asher nodded absently and rubbed his face again. He almost looked to have aged a few years after their conversation.

"I need to go take care of a few things," Asher said. "Finish eating. Get some sleep. I'm not sure what tomorrow is going to bring."

And with that, he left, leaving the boys to eat in an awkward silence.

CHAPTER 7
CONSEQUENCES

When Amara made it back to their dorm room, she could barely get the key in the lock. Partly because she was shaking so bad, partly because tears blinded her. When she pushed open the door, barely suppressing another sob, Tursanay's head poked out of the bathroom.

"What happened?" she asked. It was a moment before Amara could form words. Hearing it out loud again was so much worse than she'd imagined.

"He's- He's dead," she choked out. "He-He didn't c-call because he was dead!" Tursanay's face paled as she dropped what she was holding and crossed the room in three strides, instantly enveloped Amara in a hug.

"I've got you," Tursanay murmured between comforting words. "Just breathe. I got you." Her voice broke a bit as tears blurred her vision. They cried together until Amara calmed down enough to take a shower and crawl into bed.

The next morning, Tursanay went to meet up with

Rodney and Soren without waking Amara. There were some things they needed to figure out, but she felt Amara needed the rest right now. Whatever happened in the office had clearly been a huge emotional stress on her, and she needed all the rest she could get. When she got to the boy's dorm, Rodney and Soren were already awake. She shared the news with them, and the looks on their faces sobered from irritation at each other to shock quickly.

"And here I was thinking the most pressing matter was the fact that none of my clothes fit him," Rodney said, gesturing to Soren, who looked like he was wearing a poncho. Irritated with it, he tore it off and looked around for his old shirt.

"You know you're going to need to go to the store together and get him at least one outfit that fits besides your extra Friday uniform..." Tursanay muttered watching poor Soren finally give up fighting with the most recent shirt and throwing it to the floor. She had to clear her throat and look away to hide her blush. He had a decent build. Not exactly gym built, but I-do-manual-labor-for-a-living built. He had callused hands and a few old scars that were nearly faded by time. Wherever he came from, he worked hard there.

"Where are we going to go?" Rodney asked, picking up the shirt Soren had discarded on the floor. He went around picking up clothes as he went. "The Bargain Bin? I don't exactly have a lot of cash on me."

"There's a Goodwill around the corner... You can get him quite a few outfits for just a few dollars," suggested Tursanay.

"I don't really know if we can have him stay here long enough to wear that many outfits. I mean, what happens if he's here till school starts back? What do we do then? Hide him under the bed during classes and feed him honey buns as a snack? What about room checks?" Rodney pointed out.

Tursanay sighed. He had a point. "We can't hide him under the bed and feed him honey buns; we have to make a plan." She turned toward Soren. "What did you plan on doing once you got here?"

"I do not know anymore. I came to this world with the primary reason of locating the Dai-Ne of Element and requesting their aid in finding the other Dai-Ne that had been transported to the Mortal World. Upon Asher contacting us and informing me the three of you are indeed the Dai-Ne I am looking for, I am uncertain whether we should await his instruction or continue with what we originally planned."

"Which was...?" prompted Tursanay.

"Transport the Mortal World Dai-Ne to the Council of Dai-Ne safely so that they may unlock our powers, and thus begin our training," replied Soren.

"How long, exactly, do you think we would be gone? If we decided to go, that is," Tursanay asked.

Soren considered this for a moment. "I... did not consider you would be returning here... It never crossed my mind. My only concern was finding the Dai-Ne and getting them to the Council safely. After that, others would decide for us."

"Oh, first off, no one but me is deciding for me," quipped Tursanay. "Second, what do they want us for once we get there?"

"That is for the Council to tell you. I only know some, and expected to get more information once I got there," replied Soren.

"So basically, you created a mission you did not know would succeed or not with little or no information to go on and just hoped for the best?" scolded Tursanay.

Soren looked sheepish.

"I only wished to help," he replied. He seemed to be afraid of her.

Tursanay sighed. Why did no one ever think to ask questions? "Well, for now, let's just regroup with Amara and figure out what we need to do from here. We can get Soren new clothes later. Right now, we still need to fill Amara in on everything."

"Right," Rodney sighed. "This is going to be hard..."

Once Amara was up and awake enough to function, the four of them exchanged stories of what happened while the other was away. As they talked, Tursanay's nervous energy got the better of her and she went around the room packing things into her backpack that might come in handy should they need to go somewhere with Soren, after all.

But what did one pack when going on an adventure to another world? Tursanay grabbed the first aid kit her dad had always taught her to keep around, as well as what little cash she had. Though, she realized, that would probably be useless where they were going. She grabbed their toothbrushes and toothpaste, adding an unopened package of both for just-in-case purposes. Packed extra clothes, various toiletries, some pens and her favorite notebook, along with any other odds and ends she could think to pack. She wasn't sure what to expect on the other side.

That something exciting could be waiting around the corner was making her pace the room. She laid down on the bed, trying to calm her nerves as the other three chatted over the details Amara missed, but it wasn't long before she was up and walking around again. She would deviate between the bed and pacing and double checking her bag several times until she had memorized the location of every item in it. Returning to the bed, she tried to focus on something else. What would they see over there? Would there be magic? Magic schools? Would they get to go to one and meet all sorts of magical beings? If Soren was really an elf, was there more like him? What made an elf different from a human? And what about magic items? Like flying carpets or protective talismans - would they get to use those?

What kind of hierarchy was there between magical beings? Was one greater than another or did they find some form of equality? Were there species that she'd never even heard of? How would she be able to tell simple minded creatures apart from intelligent magical beasts? It would probably be insulting to walk up to an intelligent animal, thinking it was going to be like talking to a pet. What kind of etiquette would be proper? Would she be able to learn that, too?

The fact she was wondering about the proper etiquette for interacting with a magical beast made her pause a moment. She was going stir crazy just lying or walking around the room and looking for stuff to pack. She needed to get some fresh air and clear her head before it exploded with all the possibilities. Making an excuse to go get a snack, she headed down the hall for a bit of fresh air.

Were they really about to go on an adventure like in all the books she'd ever read? she wondered to herself as she walked right past the dorms and back into the school without paying attention. Her mind was in a million and one places. It wasn't until she noticed the squeak of her shoes that she realized she'd gone too far. The brick walls with rows of brown metal lockers separated only by classroom doors made the halls echo eerily.

Slowing her step, she looked around. Why did everything seem so dark suddenly? The air seemed displaced, like she was off balance. As if there was something else, something palpable in the atmosphere.

Watching her.

Following her.

Coming closer yet sticking to the shadows.

It made her pulse quicken, her breathing becoming unsteady. When did the hallways get so tiny? Something was different here. Wrong. The walls felt like they were closing in on her, slowly entrapping her in a cage.

Picking up her pace, she began looking for an exit. Every footstep she took sounded like two as she bounded her way almost blindly toward the back exit. Like something was chasing her. It sent panic rising in her chest like a snake wrapping around her rib cage, and she broke into a jog. She needed to go out into the yard and stand in the open. Needed to see the sky. She needed to feel the wind on her face. She couldn't breathe in here anymore.

She turned down another corridor and slowed down. It had taken a moment in the heightened creep factor to notice that something else was off... The air was different here. Colder. Crisp. Like a day fit for the middle of winter, not the first day of summer vacation. Air so cold it almost hurt to breathe it in.

Another shiver ran up her spine, causing goosebumps to run down her arms. She wasn't sure if it was the cold, or the continued feeling like she was being followed. Watched from some unseen place. She looked around, but the halls were empty save for her, and a leaky water fountain that had a steady drip... drip.... drip... echoing along with her footsteps that had all but stopped now. She turned back around and stopped. Why did the end of the hallway look so dark? Had a light blown?

Tursanay didn't like the dark. Ever since she was young, she had always had a nearly crippling fear of it. She had to have a light in the room with her before she could fall asleep, or even function enough to move. She didn't even like watching movies in the dark. And she was not about to step down there if a light had blown. She would find a different route if necessary.

Her breath formed a mist in front of her. Tursanay crossed her arm over her torso, rubbing her side for warmth, but the cold seemed to soak into every part of her, even as deep as her bones, causing her to shiver violently. From a distance an ear-splitting scream sounded, high pitched, wrenched with fear and the sound reverberated off the walls surrounding her. The sound had nearly sent her climbing the walls, shattering the silence with a force of a lightning strike to the chest, but she let out a sigh to calm her nerves. Someone was playing a sick joke, wasn't they? They got away with it more when there were so few people that stayed here over the summer. Fewer students meant more lax faculty watches. What moron was trying to scare her now? She took a step forward, wanting to confront them, but stopped dead, her lips parted to call them out, the words stuck in her throat.

Something in the shadows moved.

No... not something in the shadows...

The shadows themselves...

Was it.... Was it getting darker at the end of the hall? How did they do that? She squinted suspiciously at the blackness. Was it just in her head? Some kind of trick? She took a step backward, uncertain now. Thoughts of everything she'd seen over the last two days flickered back to her. Had something followed Soren through the portal that they weren't aware of?

The shadows spread toward her, gaining speed as they raced down the hall. And everything they consumed in their wake seemed to blot out of existence. First turning gray. Losing all color. Then disappearing into the depths of the shadowy mass.

Tursanay's heart stopped as she scrambled to run the other way. She remembered something Soren had said about people coming to get them. Could they do this kind of thing? Bring magic into the Mortal World? Wasn't that what the Veil was keeping separate? That would make it so much easier for someone who was trying to kill them.

Tursanay didn't have time to form any more coherent thoughts as her panic choked her. She slowed down enough to make the turn into the hallway that would take her to an alternative exit, but had to backtrack immediately. Swarming down that hall were the same shadows. Only this time, they seemed... thicker... darker... more potent. Her feet skid so hard to stop she slipped, having to push up off the floor to get traction again to run the other way.

She ran to the next hall and the next with the same results. Each time she looked down a hallway she passed, the shadows seemed to become thicker and thicker, taking on a more solid form as they converged behind her, chasing her. The more it thickened, the more it became almost a tar-like substance that seemed to grow and bubble and writhe, as if it were reaching out for her, but couldn't break through whatever was restraining it. She narrowly missed being hit by the strange tar-like mass as she passed the last branching hallway and caught a strange murmuring sound. The scent of decay coming from it in thick waves. It sounded alive, but it reeked of death. Like the decay of leaves in the winter, or a frozen carcass of an animal that died in the cold of winter. It was like the essence of fear, cold and dark, crawling up in her throat, making it hard to breathe as she ran as fast as her legs could carry her.

A fear of death swallowed her. She didn't want to die. Not now. Not like this. She didn't want to be devoured by this dark shadow, never to be seen or heard from again. It was burning her lungs as she gasped for breath, but she couldn't stop. Her fear wouldn't let her. She ran faster than she thought possible and broke into the lobby of the school at a dead run, heading straight for the front doors.

If she could get out into the open, maybe she could escape it. Something made her want to reach the sunlight at all costs. As if there were some way, it would protect her from the strange shadow monster gaining ground on her with every winded step she took. She needed to reach the fresh air and sunlight. She didn't want to be near the dark anymore. Artificial lights weren't bright enough. She needed natural light. The warmth of the sun to chase away this chill and make her feel like death wasn't at her heels. This shadow creature would not take her alive.

The entrance doors burst open with a blast of wind, and a wave of the same shadowy tar-like substance crashed through the doors like a flood, consuming her in a whirlpool of darkness. It threw her off her feet and slammed her into the floor of the lobby, and the last thing she heard was a crack of thunder and a dark laugh. Then everything went black.

Tursanay sat up with a gasp, her face pouring sweat. She was back in her room again - Amara on the bed, Rodney and Soren in the floor - all startled by her outburst.

"Are you okay?" she asked, concerned.

Tursanay's chest was tight, and she felt like she couldn't breathe. Her breaths came in short ragged bursts, as if she really had been running at full speed. It had just been a dream! Just a dream.... She let out a sigh of relief, trying to take calming breaths, and covered her face with her hand.

"Tursanay?" Rodney's concern grew. He rose from the bed and moved to check on Tursanay, but Tursanay waved him away. Where on earth had that come from? The nightmare had seemed so real she could still feel the cold shiver down her spine. She rubbed her arm against her leg for warmth, expecting it to be as ice cold as she still felt, and was surprised when it was pleasantly warm. It was an alien feeling, as if it didn't belong to her. It felt as if this wasn't her body and as if that shadow mass had really swallowed her up in the lobby.

"Just a really bad dream..." she managed, at last. "I'm going to go get some air, okay?" She felt as claustrophobic as she had in her dream. More so after the encounter. She needed to get some fresh air for real this time.

Tursanay stood and reassured Amara all was well, before heading down the hall again toward the school. Well, for the first time, she amended mentally. Taking the elevator this time, she paced inside the small compartment, the ride maddening, making her feel like a caged tiger. She was replaying the images of the dream in her mind. That cold chill she'd felt. The shadow-tar monster that had chased her. Those smells and sounds it made. The memories made her shudder. They were as vivid to her as if they had really happened. At last, she was free of the elevators and walking down the school corridors, praying for daylight to find her soon.

The nightmare still lurked in her mind as she went, the echoes eerily familiar as if she were reliving the whole thing. The sense of déjà vu was overwhelming and made her sick to her stomach. Speeding up her pace, Tursanay eyed the corridor coming up to her left. Seeing the sun would make her feel better. Getting out of this depressing, dark building that seemed hell bent on closing in on her and her thoughts would relieve the panic still wanting to claw its way into her chest. She turned into the last corridor that led to the back exit and froze.

The lights at the end of the hall were out.

The air in the hall about her suddenly took on a familiar chill that ran down her spine and seeped into her blood and bones. Her hair stood on end, and her heart picked up its pace. Suddenly, she didn't want to be here anymore. She wanted to be as far away from here as she could get. It didn't matter if it was just a coincidence. This was too real, too close to the details in the dream she experienced. She took a step backward as her breath formed into a mist.

From a distance an ear-splitting scream sounded, high pitched, wrenched with fear and the sound reverberated off the walls surrounding her, and the fear returned.

Before she had time to register if the shadows ever moved, she was running. Running back the way she'd come, never looking back to see if anything was chasing her. She ran down the corridor that connected the school with the dorms and ducked into the stairwell. It would be faster than waiting on the elevator, and she didn't want to find out if the thing from her dream could climb the shaft faster than the elevator could run. Three flights of stairs had never passed by so quickly for her, nor had the stitch in her side ached so badly. But she couldn't stop. Not now. Not yet. She had to reach the room first. Her fear compelled her to keep running, and her adrenaline pushed her forward. She had to make it.

Tursanay burst into their dorm room with enough force to send her rolling across the floor. Amara yelped in surprise at her entrance, nearly climbing the wall by her bed from the shock. Without taking time to explain things, Tursanay scrambled to her feet, slammed the door shut and locked it before throwing her bedside table in front of it, scattering its contents everywhere.

"What are you doing?" exclaimed Amara. "What happened?"

Tursanay could barely form a reply, but managed, "We have- to go- *now*-" between gasps for air. "Something's chasing me! We have to go out the window!"

"I can't get out the window," Amara replied, reaching for her chair.

"Soren, help Amara out the window," Tursanay instructed, quickly grabbing her bag. "Rodney, help me get her chair out the window. *Now! Let's move!*" she barked, sending them all scattering. Something in her voice wasn't playing.

Soren scooped Amara up in his arms as Rodney opened the window. Soren went out first, carrying Amara, and the other two finagled her chair.

"What are we even running from?" Rodney asked as they got the chair through the window.

Tursanay turned to say there wasn't time to explain, but her eyes caught something from behind Rodney and the explanation that had been ready to trip off her tongue evaporated into one word. "*That!*" she screamed, pointing at the door. Amara looked around to see a strange sight. Their door was bowing inward as if a great force were pushing against it, though he couldn't see any shadow underneath it. It creaked and groaned with the strain, and the hair on the back of her neck stood up, something about the sight sending fear clutching at her throat. Rodney shoved Tursanay the rest of the way out of the window, snatched up the other girl's bag, and dove out onto the grass outside.

Rodney, however, could see the same thing Tursanay could and turned on heel.

"Move it!" Rodney exclaimed, needing no more explanation. He grabbed Tursanay's arm and helped her up, half dragging her as he ran. Whatever that thing was didn't matter. After all, they'd seen and heard the last few days—after all the horror movies they'd seen in their lives—seeing an invisible force trying to break into the room only meant one thing: Flee.

Together, the four of them made their way across the grounds as quickly as they could, Amara back in her chair. From behind, they heard a crash as the door gave way to their pursuer, but the teens never stopped to look back. They fled for all they were worth to the front gates—the closest escape route from the school grounds.

Tursanay shoved the stitch in her side out of her mind at the sight of the mass trying to pry its way into the room. Adrenaline coursed through her body, pushing her faster. Rodney, not as winded, however, was just ahead of her bee lining for the gate guard hut that sat just beside the admit-one entrance.

"Mr. Ernie!" Tursanay screamed to get his attention as Rodney ran inside. "We need to get out of here now!" She watched Rodney disappeared into the doorway and Tursanay ran after him, only to run straight into his back as he skidded to a halt with a scream ripping its way from his throat.

Rodney was trying to backpedal as fast as he could, but Tursanay was in his way. There on the floor, his neck horribly twisted and broken, blood seeping from his mouth, was the old gate guard. The look on his face was of utter shock, staring directly at them.

And his eyes were solid black, the whites in them gone.

Tursanay wrenched her eyes away from the gore and shoved Rodney back outside, grabbed her student card out of her bag and slid it into the card reader, shoving her way through the gate.

"Come on!" screamed Tursanay.

"Should we just leave him?" exclaimed Amara.

"Do you want to end up like him?" Tursanay retorted.

Casting a panicked glance back at the school, Tursanay noticed for the first time the entire sky above it was a swirling mass of black clouds that seemed to have a column leading down to the building like a funnel cloud. Over by the dorms, the black shadow substance that chased them shattered through the window and exploded out and down the side of the building, seeming to recuperate for a moment before forming into a swarm again, moving toward them faster than before. Amara fumbled in her pocket for her card and slid it through, pushing through the gates as well. She didn't want to find out what the invisible force would do should it catch up. Rodney and Soren followed behind, Rodney swiping his card a second time to get Soren through.

They raced down the streets, pushing past people and watching behind them to see if whatever it was, was gaining on them or not. People glared at them as they pushed past, but other than a rude word or gesture, they did nothing else. And when the shadow passed through the crowd, not touching anyone as it followed them, the pedestrians didn't even give it a second glance.

"They can't see it," Tursanay realized. "Only we can see it!"

"I can't see anything!" Amara yelled over the noise of the city.

"How can you not see that?" exclaimed Tursanay.

"How should I know?" Amara said. Rodney grabbed Tursanay by the sleeve and dove down another street. Rodney wasn't sure where they were going, but he hoped it was far away from whatever was after them. He could see it whether Amara could and the tar-like substance that was chasing them was terrifying enough to make his heart stutter. Tursanay scrambled to keep from falling, and did her best to keep up as they turned and dove, twisted and scrambled to get away from the shadows that chased them. At last, they made a wrong turn and went down an alley that led to a dead end, and panic set in.

"What do we do?" Tursanay shrieked, on the verge of a nervous breakdown.

Both Rodney and Tursanay were grabbed by their collars and pulled into a side door, followed quickly by Soren being grabbed and Amara wheeled backwards by some unseen person. The door slammed shut behind them, casting everything into pitch black. Hands clamped over Rodney and Tursanay's mouths.

"Shh!" commanded a voice from behind them, just as they were wondering if the invisible forces had caught them.

Panic settled in, but the idea of someone helping them get away from whatever that was, ended up being stronger than her fear of whomever this was. Amara strained her ears to listen carefully, trying to slow her gasping breath. The ache in her arms was a full-on cramp now.

From a distance, a strange sound came to them. It was soft at first; hard to notice, but then it grew and grew to a sound that was like needles to the ears. It was like thousands upon thousands of tiny birds, all shrieking in angry protest, growing in volume and number, were flocking down the alleyway on the other side of the door. The teens held perfectly still, not even daring to breathe. At last, the sound faded, and they could exhale again. Tursanay felt a breath behind her as the hand came away from her mouth and realized their savior must have been holding their breath too. Tursanay turned and came face to face with Mr. Asher. There was a small glowing crystal in his hand, lighting up his face enough for them to see.

"What are you doing here?" Amara blurted out.

"Shh! They may still yet hear us," warned Mr. Asher. "Are you alright?"

"No, we're terrified! Mr. Ernie is dead, and that thing has been chasing us since Blemwick! What's going on? What was that thing? Why can't anyone see it but us?" Tursanay demanded.

"Because it's a shapeshifter," he replied. "Specifically bespelled so that those without magic can't see them."

"What?" Amara asked.

"Wait, Amara said she couldn't see it," Tursanay replied, realizing the danger that her being caught alone could pose.

Asher cursed under his breath. "I don't have time to explain much. It's hunting you. I wanted to do things differently, but they've caught up to us faster than I thought they would."

"But what should we do? What if that thing comes after us again?" asked Tursanay.

"I'm going to hold it off for as long as I can," replied Asher. "Right now, I need you to run and not look back. Get through the portal as fast as you can and keep running. When you get to the Council, keep an open mind, but don't be too trusting. You know nothing about that world yet, and people will try to take advantage of that if you aren't careful. Tell no one you're from the Mortal World. Trust no one. Make sure you know it's each other before you trust yourselves. And above all else, stay together. Now go!" He shoved them away toward another doorway that led out the back. "You can trust Soren, but no one else until you know more about that world. Understood?"

"But what about you?" Tursanay asked. "Aren't you coming with us?"

"I'll meet you there if I can," he replied. His tone didn't sound reassuring, but he shut the door on them before they could ask any more questions and turned back toward the other door that led to the alley and pulled out a crystal that dangled on the end of a chain. He whispered into it and it glowed with a ghostly light.

The door blew off its hinges into the alleyway and the kids scrambled away out the other side of the building Mr. Asher had directed them to as his scream tore out behind them, pushing them faster and faster. The sound of his gurgling breath haunting their steps.

The group had fled the sight of the Mr. Asher's end and made it all the way to the city park before they collapsed, unable to go any further at the moment. The stitches in their sides burned like knife wounds in their lungs, and their muscles ached from the exertion.

Amara picked up a rock and hurled it as far and as hard as she could with a scream of frustration and covered her face with her hands. Grabbing fistfuls of her hair, she fought back the urge to cry again. She was too angry to cry right now. Too confused. Too emotionally spent from the past few days alone. She couldn't take much more of this before she just snapped.

If she hadn't already.

Tursanay came over to her, sitting in the grass beside her, setting her pack down. The feel of the grass against her skin was almost surreal. How could normal things like this still exist in a world that was turned upside down? One minute you're worried about passing your exams in school, the next minute you're just hoping you can stay alive long enough to see your friends again.

"I half want whatever the hell this thing is to find us so I can kill it and be done," Amara tried to seethe, but her voice was cracking with emotion. She would not cry. She refused to cry.

"Personally, I'd rather know how to kill it first," replied Tursanay. "I just want to know what we're dealing with here."

"Well, I don't!" Amara said, trying to look anywhere but at Tursanay. If she met her eyes, she would lose it. She continued bitterly, saying, "They took my dad away from me, I've been sentenced to a boarding school, found out I was adopted, found out my biological parents are magical who's-a-what's-it's from some fantasy realm and *now* the one person who's supposedly our sole ally is sacrificing himself to an invisible force to save our lives from something that's trying to kill us, has probably killed the gate guard or whatever he was, and is probably in league with whom or whatever killed my dad!" She took a breath. She still refused to look at Tursanay, and buried her face again to hide the tears and sobs that threatened to escape. "Have I left anything out?" she demanded to no one in particular.

"Yeah," defended Tursanay, setting her jaw. "All the good parts. Like how you found me again - and Rodney! How you're still alive–and so are we. Yes, things are screwed up right now, but at least we have each other to lean on! We need each other right now, Amara," she said, leaning over to the other girl. "Don't fall apart yet. I need you. When we get away from all this, then we can fall apart together. Okay?" She was fighting and failing to keep from crying, too. Tursanay had never been so scared in all her life. She reached out and touched Amara's shoulder, more for her own support than anything.

Amara locked eyes with her best friend and saw the look in Tursanay's eye. Her anger fizzled out, leaving only the raw fear and tears that she had fought so desperately to hold back. There was nothing keeping them now, and they flowed freely, wrenching sobs from her chest.

"We've gotta keep it together, okay?" Tursanay continued, voice cracking. "We can't fall apart in front of Rodney, he'll panic and then things really will fall apart and I just don't think I can handle—"

Amara pulled Tursanay into a hug. Tursanay suppressed a sob, trying to fight back the tears and failing too. Amara could feel her trembling.

"Why do you guys get to be the only ones who get a hug?" Rodney cried, already falling apart, listening to them.

He went over and joined in on the hug as Amara struggled to recollect herself.

She couldn't fall apart on Tursanay. Tursanay was barely holding it together herself—if at all. She had to hold on. She couldn't fall apart now. Like Tursanay had said—they could fall apart together when they were safe and sound.

Slowly, though the unshed tears and fear formed into a ball of pain in her chest, she gained control of her nerves and sobs. She quieted, squeezing Tursanay in reassurance. Everything would be okay. They would make it through this together. She wouldn't make Tursanay worry. She wouldn't make Rodney worry.

"We'll get through this," Amara whispered. "I promise. I don't know how yet, but it'll be okay."

Tursanay couldn't speak anymore, only nod. They hugged until they could recompose themselves, then wiped their eyes. Tursanay smiled at Amara.

"We look ridiculous," Tursanay muttered with a sniff and a laugh.

"What are sisters for, right?" Amara smiled back. "They don't care if you're a mess. They stand beside you and beat up anyone who dares to upset you."

Tursanay nodded, then sighed. "We've got a big list, and we don't even know all the names."

"I'm bad with names anyway," Rodney sniffed, wiping his face.

"We need to relocate to a deserted area immediately, create a portal, and do so in secret. It generates an enormous amount of power that other magic kinds can detect, so we will not have much time to get through it," Soren informed them.

"Wait, so your arrival here brought them, after all?" Amara shot.

"I did not know, I swear to you! I knew nothing until Asher said something." Soren gulped sheepishly, afraid she'd get angry again. "If I had, I would not have acted so rashly."

"Amara," Rodney said, stepping between the two of them, trying to diffuse the situation. "Let's just calm down and work this out, okay?"

Amara cut Rodney a look. "Move."

Rodney held up his hands and stepped aside and asked her to just please not kill either of them. Amara turned her glare on Soren, who took a step away from her in fear.

"Don't you dare move a muscle."

Soren froze, afraid to disobey. Amara moved up to him until she was barely a foot from him.

"You. You brought this here. People are dead because of all this," she spat, causing him to blanch again.

"Amara!" called Tursanay. She was being too hard on him. He couldn't control all that had happened.

"But the one person who may have died protecting us from whatever this thing is..." she continued, ignoring Tursanay. "told me I could trust you. You and one other person in this whole mess. Part of me wants to just say forget all of this and tell you where to go and what you can do when you get there..." She stared into his eyes, making sure he understood every word. "But right now, you're the only option that keeps them safe." She pointed back at Rodney and Tursanay without taking her eyes off Soren.

His eyes flickered to them momentarily before fixing themselves back on Amara's.

"And if you betray that trust..." She put her finger in his

face and he flinched slightly. "If anything happens to them... So help me, I will kill you. Do. You. Under. Stand. Me?" She poked him for emphasis with each syllable that she separated.

Soren studied her carefully for a moment and nodded.

"Come with me," he said. "I give you my word that your trust is not ill-placed."

Momentarily satisfied, Amara backed away with a nod.

"Where to?" she asked, turning to the others. Together, they took the bus to a downtown area.

Tursanay knew of an old office building with a parking garage that was going to be demolished in the next year to make room for a new bookstore and recreational play area for the part of town it was in. It would be free of prying eyes and far enough away from the school that they would have some time before they were found again. If at all.

They entered the parking garage, and traveled a few levels down until anyone just passing by couldn't see them, and Soren took out the bone-carved knife. He glanced around carefully as he did so, half expecting something to lunge out and attack them or the shadows to come alive. Even in the middle of the afternoon, this far down in the garage was rather dark. And after their recent troubles, they jumped at almost anything, it seemed.

"When I create the portal, it will not remain open for long," said Soren. "It will also immediately attract unwanted attention from enemies. We have neither the means nor the ability to counteract at this time. Go through the moment I tell you to. Don't hesitate. We cannot tarry for long." He pointed to Amara. "You first." Amara came forward as he tore a portal through the air. The blue light flooded the area, dancing on the walls like the reflection from a body of water.

"I get the sideways puddle comment now," Rodney mentioned to Tursanay.

"Will this hurt?" Amara asked as she watched it expand slowly.

"No," replied Soren. "Because we are the ambassadors of both worlds." He turned and looked at her. "It's ready. Go!"

Amara pushed forward, her look of uncertainty slowly forming into a mask of determination. She reached out her hand and only hesitated for a moment before pushing through the portal. A violent shock traveled up her arm so forcefully that it pushed her back. Amara yelped in pain and grabbed her arm, which she could no longer feel.

"You are not Dai-Ne?" Soren demanded, confused. "But Asher said…"

"What?" Amara yelped. After all that? She wasn't a Dai-Nē?

"Only Dai-Nē can pass through the Veil!" Soren replied. "The deal!" he exclaimed, suddenly remembering. He muttered a curse.

"The deal?" Amara demanded between grunts of pain. The feeling was coming back to her arm, but now it was throbbing with pain. "What deal?"

"Crap, I forgot to mention that part," Tursanay cursed. "Me and you have to switch the dreams back," she told Amara. "That's why you couldn't see the shadows. You gave the dreams to me and now you don't have the power that makes you see them." It wasn't the best recap, but it got the point across. The wind rustled some old debris in the level above them and made them all turn and look nervously. Soren's brow furrowed as he turned back to look at the trio standing before him.

"Is there a way inside that building over there?" he asked,

gesturing to the building that the parking garage was attached to.

"I think I saw an open door one level up," replied Tursanay. "Why?"

"We must evacuate this area as soon as possible," replied Soren.

"Do you think whatever was after us will be far enough away to not have sensed that?" Tursanay asked.

"With our luck?" Amara muttered. "No."

"Let's move faster," Rodney whispered, afraid to talk too loudly and attract more unwanted attention.

They made their way back up a level and slipped into the door that led to the hallway. They went in cautiously. Inside was an abandoned office building. There were a few old broken desks still lying around in various rooms, pieces of scattered paperwork, fold up chairs, various broken office equipment lying around. Otherwise, it was utterly barren, save for the graffiti on the walls and the support columns scattered evenly throughout each main room.

Tursanay shifted her bag nervously on her shoulders as she looked around. This place made her anxious. Soren turned and looked at the group again and gestured to Tursanay and Amara.

"Perform this action once more," he instructed.

"What?" asked Amara, but Tursanay stepped forward, seeing where this was going.

"We need to switch back to get through," she concluded. Soren nodded. "But we tried once already and nothing happened."

"Are you sure?" Soren asked. "Perhaps there was a mistake."

"Yeah, there was a huge shock last time. It really hurt," replied Tursanay.

"No, you wanna know pain? I had to go through that crap twice!" complained Rodney.

"Twice?" asked Soren.

"Yeah, once when I got it from her, then again when I gave it to her," Rodney said, gesturing appropriately to each girl. "Until she tried to go through the portal thingy," he continued, pointing to Amara. "I was the only one that got shocked twice. Which I think is unfair to you," he added sarcastically to Tursanay. "Because that was a perfectly good opportunity you missed just now." She stuck her tongue out at him.

"You two," Soren said, pointing to Tursanay and Rodney. "Make this transaction again."

"What!" Rodney demanded indignantly. "I don't want to do that again!"

"We have names, you know..." muttered Tursanay, giving Soren a look.

Somewhere in the stairwell, they heard a shuffling noise, and all fell silent. Exchanging scared looks, Soren ushered them into one of the conference rooms that lead into three different hallways. He signaled them to close off all the doors as quietly as they could. After sealing off all exits, they gathered in the center, attempting to watch all routes simultaneously.

"Make the transaction," urged Soren in a hushed whisper. "If we are to escape, this 'deal' is pertinent to getting through the portal together!"

"What if it doesn't work?" Rodney asked, returning the hushed whisper. "Then I'll just get shocked again for nothing!"

"Would you rather get shocked again and it not work, or not try to get killed?" Tursanay whispered fiercely.

He glanced nervously at the doors. When he didn't respond, she hissed his name.

"I'm thinking!" he hissed back, and she hit him, giving him a look. "Alright, fine! Give me the stupid dreams back!" he whispered irritably.

"Wait!" Amara tried to warn, but it was too late.

"Take them!" Tursanay said, grabbing his hand and shaking it. The effect was immediate, and the shock ran through their arms violently, causing them to yelp involuntarily. Soren and Amara glanced around; their hearts in their throats, praying nothing had overheard them. The sound of something metal being scooted across the floor, came from outside of one door and the group scrambled as silently as they could to the exit farthest away from it, and ran down the hallway into a second stairwell, before they found an unlocked door, and crammed inside of it.

They grabbed whatever they could to barricade it before relocating to another closed off room, this one much smaller, but still with a back exit. This looked like it was a private office space rather than a room big enough for companywide meetings like the last one. They gathered in the center of the room and watched the exits and windows carefully for any signs or sounds of movement.

"Make the deal again," Soren said, breaking the silence after he made sure nothing had followed them.

"I'm not doing that again!" Rodney balked. "You said I had to make the deal so we could escape, and I did. You didn't say I had to go through that a fourth time!"

"It's the only way to get the dreams back to Amara,

Rodney," Tursanay piped up. "Apparently, it has to pass through you."

"Do you think it has something to do with his ring glowing?" asked Amara. "It did it again back there... but it wasn't on the hand you shook with. I just thought it was from the shock before, but maybe..."

"Did Asher not mention something about the ring?" asked Soren, looking at Rodney. "Show me," he instructed.

"It's... just a ring I got from my uncle..." he muttered, not really wanting to part with it.

"Rodney, just for a second," pleaded Tursanay. "I just want this to be over with, too." Rodney hesitated, but took the ring off his right first finger and handed it to Soren. The other boy inspected it, and his eyes widened.

"It says 'Ring of Rynon' on it..." he whispered in awe. He looked up at Rodney, surprised. "Who was your uncle?"

"It says what?" Rodney asked, taking the ring back and examining it. He'd never noticed anything but a few designs etched around the jewel in what he originally thought was a weird decoration. He put it back on his finger, thoughts swirling.

"That might explain why you can exchange the powers of the Dai-Ne," Soren said excitedly.

"What do you mean?" asked Tursanay.

"I scryed for the Dai-Ne of Element, however, I came in contact with each of you in corresponding order that you traded the dreams, did I not?" Soren asked.

"Yes," confirmed Tursanay. "You mentioned that."

"As I have said before the only way this should be possible is if all three of you are Dai-Ne of Element which is physically and magically impossible according to the laws set down by Rynon when he created the Dai-Ne to represent the different branches of his power. The only other explanation is that you traded the power with one another through this ring," he declared, pointing at Rodney's hand.

"So, this ring can switch our powers around? That's why we get a shock when we make the deal? And why Amara can't go through the portal or see those creatures?" Tursanay concluded.

"I believe so," confirmed Soren. "And if the two of you make the exchange one last time, then all will be right again."

"Wait a minute," Rodney balked. "You mean to tell me they could have put on the ring and switched it with each other and I wouldn't have had to do this a fourth time?"

"Oops," said Tursanay, wincing apologetically. "It should be the absolute last time, no exceptions, if it's any consolation."

Maybe they would get out of this alive and intact after all. Rodney looked at Amara, a rather grumpy looking frown on his face. He really didn't want to have to do this a fourth time. Especially not when it could have been avoided in the first place.

"It's my third time, Rodney. Trust me, I know how you feel," said Amara. "Though I never want to experience anything like that portal shock again," she added.

"We'll have to be ready to get out of here for it once you make the trade again. It will attract attention," noted Soren.

Rodney looked at Amara and held out his hand. "Want 'em back?" he grumbled.

Amara took a deep breath and nodded. If this worked, it would change everything...

What were they getting themselves into?

"Yeah..." she said with a nod, bracing herself. "Yeah, I do." They shook, and once again the effect was instantaneous, the shock running up the length of their arms, causing them to yelp in pain and jerk away from one another.

"That's a very interesting ring you have there, Rodney Roberts," came a voice from behind them. The group jumped and turned in unison to see, sitting in the windowsill, was the last thing they expected to see. With its tan fur and yellow eyes, the coyote watched them from beneath hooded brows. "I know some people who would be very interested in getting their hands on it."

Rodney, staring wide eyed at the creature in the window, desperately started patting Tursanay on the shoulder to get her attention, and the more he patted, the more frantic he became until he was basically slapping her shoulder for her attention.

"That coyote knows my *name*," Rodney whispered in a strained, panicked voice as he continued to slap at Tursanay's shoulder, trying to force himself to wake up or come back to reality.

"That coyote is *talking*, Rodney!" exclaimed Tursanay, smacking him back, equally panicked. "I think that's a little more disconcerting right now!"

The coyote scoffed, then threw its head back and howled.

"*Run!*" exclaimed Soren, taking off for the door farthest from the howling beast. The others needed no more convincing as they crammed through the door, trying to get through. A snarl ripped through the air from behind them, and Rodney, the last to get through the exit, turned to see the coyote lunging for him as he tried to slam the door closed. The beast wedged enough of itself between the frame and the door to grab hold of his arm in its teeth and yank his arm back through.

Rodney screamed in both sheer panic and pain as all his

weight pushed against the door, while teeth dug in on the other side. The others scrambled back to his rescue, fighting with the door and the coyote to get his arm free. At last, the beast seemed to slip on its grip, and they pulled Rodney free. Soren slammed the door shut, barricaded it with a nearby discarded board, then barked at the others to get moving. Rodney cradled his arm against his chest with his good hand and ran with them.

When they reached the end of the hallway, it split in two different directions. After a moment's hesitation, the group turned left, away from the wall of windows and deeper into the building. If the talking coyote had somehow gained access to the fourth or fifth story from the window, there was no telling what else might come through.

They dove into an office, this time with no second escape, and locked the door, hooking a stray two by four up under the handle. This was it. They found themselves trapped. If they couldn't get through the portal this time, they wouldn't make it through this alive. The group exchanged looks for a moment, but didn't waste time waiting to see if the coyote followed them this time. They gave Soren some space, and he cut open the portal.

"One of you assist me in holding the door. They'll be on us in moments," instructed Soren, as the portal stabilized.

Rodney started toward the door, but Tursanay beat him to it, glancing at his injured arm, then up at him, shaking her head.

"When I give you the word, go," Soren said to Amara. She nodded back, then faced the portal as Soren and Tursanay barred the door with their weight.

"Amara," came Tursanay's voice. Amara turned and looked over her shoulder at her friend. "...Be careful."

"If you don't follow me immediately, I'm coming back for you, do you understand?" Amara replied pointedly. "I don't care if I have to drag you by the hair kicking and screaming. You're coming with me! We're in this together, okay?"

Tursanay nodded, her throat going dry as she tried to swallow. "Okay."

"Go!" Soren called. Amara turned back to the portal and rolled forward. This was it. It was now or never. She would either go through this portal or die trying. Whatever waited for her on the other side could be far better or far worse. She did not know what she was getting into, but at this point, it was her only choice. Die now or take a chance and live? She had limited options. Taking a deep breath, she pushed herself towards the portal.

And disappeared inside.

CHAPTER 8
COUNCIL

The click of her boot heels across the stone floors echoed in the quiet halls as Ilarys made her way to the grand hall meeting. Tall columns and green and blue marbled halls were much colder to her eyes with the weight of this news on her shoulders. The enormous arched doorways she walked through as the wooden doors to the hall grew closer, only made this enormous space more off-putting and intimidating. Could she do this with as little rest as she had gotten? She and Keir had just arrived back and though they were exhausted, but they needed to report immediately.

"'Laris!" the familiar voice interrupted her brooding thoughts and washed through her like warm relief. A dark-haired, black-eyed beauty with a shapely face came into view.

"Aui'ani!" Ilarys exclaimed, looking up as the other woman ran to her. Aui'ani tackled her in a hug and Ilarys spun her around before burying her face in the other woman's shoulder. Her scent perforated Ilarys's senses, grounding her and easing her nerves and welcoming her home at last. Taking Aui'ani's hands in her own and kissing them, she breathed, "I missed you so much. I was hoping I'd get to see you before I went in there."

"You'll do fantastic," Aui'ani reassured her, cupping Ilarys's face in her hands. "I'll be right there with you, watching from the crowd."

"I'm so glad you could get us in. This information could change everything," Ilarys replied. "Thank you again."

"It's what I do," she winked. She nodded over her shoulder. "Now go. They've assembled and I'm due as well." Ilarys gave a nod and watched her go, taking a breath and squaring her shoulders. She could do this. She had to. Standing before the doors, she swallowed, putting on a mask of determination and urgency. They needed to listen to her if any of this was going to go well at all. She swung open the doors and stepped inside, marching down the center of the room to where the Head of the Order and the other members sat, muttering amongst themselves and trying to figure out what was going on. When she entered, the chatter quieted down, and all eyes fell on her.

There was a brief silence as she came to a stop before her podium.

"What information do you bring to the Order that requires an emergency meeting?" the Head of the Order asked.

Ilarys lifted her chin. "I think it would be best to show you what I've seen."

A murmur ran through their ranks.

"You consent to have your memories displayed for all to see?" the Head of the Order asked.

She clenched her fist to keep her hands from shaking, not wanting to relive this. She would rather do anything but relive the moment she saw her brother's chest wrenched open again.

"Yes," Ilarys answered as bravely as she could. Her voice was soft. Small. Almost a whisper. She felt a bead of sweat drip down her back.

"Then proceed," the Head of the Order replied, gesturing for the mind reader to present her memories to the court. A figure moved forward from the side of the room to join her by the podium. He placed his hand on her forehead and stretched the other to a blank wall. The scenes that played out before them were of their investigation from the aziza child all the way to the incident at the inn with the mirror. When Keir's chest had ripped open on the ship, a horrified murmur went through the crowd as they watched, enraptured. When the face returned in the inn's mirror and Keir's fears proven to be more than just the ramblings of a madman, there were more whispers and gasps.

When the Dai-Nē information presented itself, there was silence.

When it was finally over, Ilarys pulled away, shuttering at having to relive each moment in just as much detail as she had to in the first place. She had a fantastic memory, and it was both a gift and a curse. Right now, she wished she could vomit it away and never relive that again. She would probably have nightmares for weeks, judging by the unsettled feeling churning in her stomach.

"You were right," the Head of the Order said heavily, breaking the silence that followed. "The news that the other world is so wrought with iron and unwelcoming to our kind is not good news for us." He sighed. "But we have proof that it exists, and I think we should do everything in our power to find out everything we can about these creatures before we let them into this world. It could vastly change our ecosystems if they are as violent as they appear to be."

"I feel like there is a small group that lashes out whereas the whole is more interested in escape," Ilarys said. "But I agree we need to do more investigation before they may enter this world. We'd need to find a way to bring them across in the first place."

"The Dai-Nē you mentioned... Do you propose they are those four from the visions?" an Order member asked.

"At least one, possibly three," Ilarys agreed.

"Three Dai-Nē," another Order member said. Her tone was hushed with excitement threatening to spill over. "They may be the missing three that disappeared over a decade ago."

"And your brother," another spoke up. "Since he escaped these... Fae? That means he is a Dai-Nē as well? I don't understand that part."

"We believe the Fae can use mirror travel to change the location to somewhere between this world and the Mortal World," Ilarys began. "As if inside the Veil itself, but they can't seem to breach it. Neither can someone escape once they cross into it if our research has proven true. My brother once saw a nymph child stuck in a mirror by her hand, her reflection pulling her in, but she couldn't pull herself back out. We think that since only Dai-Nē can pass freely through the Veil, should you pass partially through with mirror travel, you are stuck in the in between and cannot cross back out without the help of a Dai-Nē cast spell; or unable to pass through at all if you have created a portal as we saw those four children do."

"Where is your brother now?" the Head of the Order asked.

"Attempting to contact the Fae once more to glean more

information. We agreed I would present the information to all of you and he would continue the investigation, since the Fae will cooperate with him freely," Ilarys answered.

"We will need time to process this information," the Head of the Order replied. He turned to Ilarys. "Good work. Your investigations have paid off."

"Thank you," Ilarys breathed.

"We will reconvene in a few days once we have had time to process and discuss our next move. Meanwhile, if you have any more contact with these Fae, you are to report it immediately."

"Yes, sir," she nodded.

"Meeting adjourned," he dismissed. Everyone got up, slowly dissipating and buzzing with this new information.

Aui'ani made her way over to Ilarys again, putting a hand on her arm gingerly.

"You've been through so much," she said softly. "I'm sorry I couldn't be there."

Ilarys held up her dual rings, one on each hand. "You're always there with me," she smiled.

Aui'ani smiled, touching her matching rings to Ilarys's.

"You always were a romantic," Aui'ani teased. "Come, tell me of your adventures that you didn't tell the Order about and I will draw you a bath, love."

"You're amazing," Ilarys almost cried. She wanted a bath almost as much as she wanted another hug. If not, perhaps a bit more and then another hug afterwards. Aui'ani's hugs could always heal her tired soul.

"I know," Aui'ani smiled, leading Ilarys by the hand down the hall. She let slip a small giggle.

"Hello?" Keir said, tapping the mirror in front of him. "Anyone... there?"

He'd been trying to contact the Fae for over an hour, with little to no success. Ilarys was still in the meeting, but he was getting nowhere fast. At this rate, he was going to come up with nothing to add to their investigation. He really needed to get in contact with them rather than have random encounters. He sighed, setting down the stick he'd used to tap on the glass, and jumped when he glanced back up to see the red eyes flicker to life on his reflection's face. The noise he made was rather undignified.

"Stop doing that!" he breathed, trying to calm his heart rate.

Why do you call us? the Fae asked in the mirror.

"I, ah," Keir began trying to regain his wits, "needed to ask you some more questions. To help me find out what I need to help you."

Ask. A command.

"Something you said before threw me off," Keir said as he paced before the mirror. "You knew about the Council but you didn't know about the Dai-Nē. What do you know about the Council?"

We have had dealings with the Council for centuries, came the reply. *They have made deals with us many times. They owe us even now.*

"Owe you?" Keir asked.

We granted them a favor. Something they could not do on their own, the reflection replied without moving Keir's lips.

"What did you do for them? What do they owe you?" Keir asked.

That is between us and the Council, the Fae replied.

"What has the Council been doing across the Veil?" Keir prompted.

No response.

"Look, you need to tell me something. If the Council has a way to move freely across the Veil, then they should have a way to help you cross as well."

They do not, came the reply.

"How do you know?" Keir countered.

Because they have tried and failed, it replied. *Even now, with the Ring of Rynon, they say they cannot help us.*

"The Ring of Rynon?" Keir repeated. "You realize that is something that could potentially be the key to your freedom? If it does what we believe, it does."

Explain, the Fae demanded.

"Well, if what you said was true, and those kids were exchanging their powers, why couldn't they exchange it with you long enough to get you across the Veil one person at a time?" Keir said simply. The anger that flashed across his reflection's face gave him heart palpitations. "It's just a thought. I don't know if it's plausible," he added quickly. "Maybe if the Dai-Nē's magic works on both sides of the Veil, covering you with a Dai-Nē protection spell could do the same?"

We must get the ring from the Council, the Fae growled. *They have lied to us.*

"If the Council has a way across the Veil, there may be more than one way to get you across if we can find these other Dai-Nē and ask for help." Keir was nodding. "The first place to look would be the Council. They hold several celebrations a year to cover up the fact they are secretly searching for people to test themselves against the pedestal in order to find the next generation of Dai-Nē. While they are distracted, we could attend the next celebration and see if we can find the ring and unlock my powers. If I really am a Dai-Nē like you seem to think I am."

How long?

"The next celebration is in a week. It'll take everything we've got to get there on time unless you allow us safe passage," Keir replied.

This we can agree to, the Fae replied.

"Then I will talk to my sister and begin preparations. We'll see how far we can get," he concluded.

"Absolutely not," Ilarys bristled. "Do you have any idea what you're asking? There's no way we can pull something like this off, let alone get there with enough energy left to lift a finger! We'd have to leave by dawn to get there in time! I can't Keir - nay, I won't!"

"We've been granted safe passage by mirror, sister. We don't have to leave until an hour before the ceremony to pass through customs."

"Regardless, the ring will be heavily guarded! Your hind-sight is no good to us in a fight and I am not getting thrown in jail again, thanks to your antics!" Ilarys balked.

"It has become a habit, Keir," Aui'ani agreed as she set some food down before Ilarys, who gave her a lovingly thankful look. "The Order has gone to great lengths to get most of your records destroyed or sealed. You really should be more careful."

"Listen," Keir defended himself. "If the Council of Dai-Nē really has ties in the other world, then there may be something more nefarious going on here. They could try to gain more power, take over both worlds—it could be anything! Or worse, they could try to find and corrupt Dai-Nē to help them take over places across the Veil."

"He has a point," Aui'ani said.

"Whose side are you on?" Ilarys complained.

"My own," she answered, as if it were obvious.

"That still doesn't help us figure out how to get the ring or what it even looks like," Ilarys argued. There were too many variables to deal with when she was so tired.

"Well," Aui'ani mused, sitting down beside Ilarys and across from Keir at the table. "If I'm not mistaken, since there will be so many people from all over the world coming to celebrate and join in the Council's underground mission to find the Dai-Nē, I would imagine customs would have their guard spread rather thin."

Keir brightened. "She's right. And we could get in as part of the Dai-Nē seeking crowd, claiming to want to try our hands at it and sneak off during the ceremony and rejoin once we have it, so no one suspects us."

"It could work," Aui'ani agreed. "If you had a shapeshifter that could change her appearance to an animal and confuse them to chase the wrong individual and lead them the wrong way."

"This is a bad idea," Ilarys sighed.

"But you know it could work," Keir countered. "And you get a week to rest up before we have to do anything."

Ilarys took a deep breath and let it out slowly as she picked at her plate. "You promise you won't drag me into anything for a week and that we can mirror travel safely?"

"You have my word," Keir replied, making a promise gesture with his left hand. "Me, of all people agreeing to mirror travel, should cement that fact."

Ilarys raised and lowered her eyebrows in agreement. "Fine, but you're leaving me be for this entire week until the night before so we can corroborate our story."

"Works for me," he grinned. "Meanwhile, I'm going to go take care of a few things I've been meaning to since we got back."

Ilarys waved him away and looked at Aui'ani when he closed the door behind him. "So, you're coming with us this time?"

"Can't let you have all the fun," Aui'ani grinned.

"Yes. Fun. That's what it is," Ilarys said, rolling her eyes, making Aui'ani laugh.

"At least I can monitor you two and keep you out of jail this time," she said.

"There is that," Ilarys agreed, digging into her food. She needed to build up strength now if she was going to be of any use on this mission.

CHAPTER 9
FAMILY

Tursanay let loose a rather unladylike curse under her breath after following Amara through the portal, then looked around in awe. Rodney came through next and Tursanay looked at him. The surrounding woods were dead or dying, filled with a thick, cold fog. The darkness hanging over them like a blanket made it hard to see very far past the trees a few yards off.

There were very few sounds other than chirping insects, a few nocturnal creatures, and the wind rustling the dead branches, making them click and snap. The sky was clouded over, and now and then a half-moon would peer through at them, huge, close, and much larger than normal. The grassy earth was damp, and the smell of marsh and rotting wood was almost overpowering.

"It worked. This is all real," she breathed. "It's actually real," she kept repeating, as if she couldn't wrap her mind around what she was seeing.

"Don't say that," Rodney whispered, his voice cracking, his eyes wide. Shaking his head as he backed away from the glowing portal, he prayed there wasn't anything in these woods that would eat them. "Don't say that. Middle Earth can't exist - I don't want to fight a dark lord! This was supposed to be a really weird, really bad dream! I was supposed to wake up by now!"

"It's not a dream," Tursanay murmured, turning to Rodney and grabbing him for support. Her knees were threatening to buckle, and she wasn't entirely sure how she was still standing. "It's not a dream," she repeated over and over, her panic rising.

They were both panicking, but Rodney gripped her arm in return, trying to get a hold of the situation.

"What are we going to do?" he asked. She always had the answer, but now she was looking to him for it. Only, he didn't know either. In his mind, the only thing he could compare it to was sci-fi movies. And in sci-fi movies there was always some gigantic creature and someone or something looking to eat you. Or kill you. So far, the only thing they hadn't encountered was a gigantic creature. Rodney tried to wipe that thought from his mind.

Just ahead of them, Amara was looking around, her breath forming a mist in the cold air. Something in her vision seemed to flitter past... like a shadow. She turned and looked back at the portal. Something was wrong... Had it just flickered? She pushed past Rodney and Tursanay, staring at it intently.

"What?" asked Tursanay. "What's wrong?"

The portal flickered again, and Tursanay's fear sparked.

"It's flickering! It's going to close!" Amara panicked.

"What?! It can't go out yet! Soren's not here!" Tursanay squeaked.

"Wait, we don't know it's going to close. It might just be what it does!" Rodney argued, not wanting to go near the thing again.

"Since when is flickering ever good with these kinds of things?" Tursanay countered.

"I don't know!" Rodney shouted in full on terror. "When have we ever seen something like this before? Cause unless you've had an encounter of the third kind, this isn't exactly your day-to-day source of normal!"

"Third kind or not, if we get stuck on this side of the portal without our elf, we're screwed!" Tursanay argued.

"I just got my arm chewed on by a talking coyote that knew me by name—I'm not prepared to go through that again!" Rodney countered.

"Wait, Amara—what are you doing?" Tursanay called, watching the other girl move toward the portal.

"I've gotta go back," Amara decided, ignoring their arguments.

They couldn't last in this world by themselves. They needed Soren. He promised he would get them through this safely, and she wouldn't let him go back on that. She wouldn't let anyone abandon her a second time.

"What? No! Wait," Tursanay scrambled over and grabbed Amara's arm.

"We need him here!" argued Amara, her anger rising. "The three of us can't do this without him! We're blind. We don't know what we're doing. He promised to get us out of this mess!" She jerked her arm free and pushed herself toward the shrinking portal. "I'm not letting him off the hook that easily," she growled under her breath.

Besides, it was his fault they were in this mess. If he had just left well enough alone, maybe things wouldn't have turned out like this. She needed someone to blame to keep a handle on things, and right now, Soren was her current target of irritation. Scrambling to stop her, the other two called for her to stop, but Amara ignored them, reaching out for the portal just as Soren came sailing through, taking all three of them out like dominoes.

The portal winked out of existence and left them lying on the ground, groaning in pain. Soren had head-butted Amara when he'd dove through and knocked himself senseless. Groggily, he rolled over, clutching his head, and grunted in pain.

"Ooovw," muttered Rodney as he rubbed the back of his head and tried to sit up. He looked over at Tursanay sitting up next to him, then at Amara lying across them still. "Everyone okay?"

"My butt's a little sore, but otherwise I'm okay," replied Tursanay. "You gonna live, Soren?" Soren replied with a grunt as tried to stand with a stagger. "Amara? You okay?" When Amara neither responded nor moved, Tursanay shook her shoulder. When there was still no response, her heart skipped a beat. "You knocked her out!" she yelled at Soren, smacking his arm. "What do we do now? She might have a concussion!"

"Our destination contains a healer," replied Soren as he moved away from them, the knife in his hand again. He staggered slightly, his head swimming.

"We can't move her like this!" argued Tursanay.

She looked over at Soren when she heard a familiar rip and saw him opening up a portal. Soren walked away from the portal, picking up his pace, and tore another one through the air. Tursanay looked over at Rodney, confused, and he returned the look. What was he doing?

"Uh, Soren?" she ventured as she watched him open four more in various places around them before coming over to stand beside them, digging the knife into the ground and dragging it to open yet another portal. "What are you doing?"

"Didn't you say that opening one of those would attract a lot of attention?" asked Rodney. "Why are you opening like fifty?"

"Disguising our trail. The portal is traceable. But the individual one we transfer through is not," replied Soren. He watched the last one stabilize and looked at the others.

"Wait, why are we going back across the Veil? Didn't we just come from there?" Tursanay demanded.

"There is more than one use for this blade," was all he would offer as an explanation. "Hurry. We must move from here. This opens close to a place of refuge where we may find some assistance... And medical aid," he added, gesturing toward Amara's unconscious form and Rodney's bleeding arm.

Rodney glanced at his arm, the sharp pain still throbbing, but temporarily forgotten in their panic. His eyes grew wide as he looked up at the others.

"Guys! I have a problem!" he blurted.

"What?" Tursanay asked, her voice almost hoarse with fear as it was.

"What if I turn into a werewolf because that talking dog thing bit me?" he asked, his words slurring together in his panic. He lifted his upper lip, angling his head so Tursanay could get a good look at his gums. "Are my teeth getting any longer?"

"Rodney focus! We don't have the time to panic!" Tursanay squeaked, already doing just that. I can't think about that right now. Tursanay repeated to herself several times. Rodney's not a werewolf! He's *not a werewolf.* She had to reassure herself, otherwise, she would panic. Are werewolves even real in this world—I can't think about that right now. I can't.

"*Grab her!*" commanded Soren, gesturing at Amara. "We must depart!" Responding to the authority in his tone, the other two scrambled, picking up their unconscious friend between them and balancing her in her wheelchair. "Go!" he instructed, pointing toward the portal on the ground. Rodney and Tursanay hobbled over after exchanging uncertain glances and stepped inside. Soren jumped in after, and slowly all the portals disappeared.

The first thing they registered was water everywhere. Tursanay was the first to surface, followed by Soren, then Amara and Rodney. Sputtering and now awake, Amara glanced around, trying to get her bearings. The woods surrounding them were nowhere near as dark and foreboding as the previous woods had been. There wasn't an air of death about them, but of life. There was no swamp, only a wide creek just deep enough for them to be submerged past their heads.

"Where are we?" Amara coughed. She'd inhaled some water in her shock.

"Guys! I can't swim very well!" Rodney called. "Can someone help me get to the bank?" He was struggling just to keep his head above the water, let alone move. It seemed no matter how much he kicked or moved his arms, he never could get anywhere but exhausted. Amara grabbed his shirt and moved him to the bank. Laying out on the bank, Tursanay looked around curiously, trying to figure out if there would be something here to come after them as well. It was getting dark, and soon they wouldn't be able to see anything.

"Where are we?" Amara asked again, half of her still in the water.

"In a creek to throw off our scent," Soren panted, crawling onto the bank and rolling onto his back. "We must keep moving."

"Thank you, Captain Obvious," Tursanay muttered.

"I am not a captain," replied Soren as he struggled to his feet. Tursanay rolled her eyes exasperatedly, letting the comment go as she got to her own feet.

"Ugh, I have a pounding headache," Amara muttered, holding her head.

"You head-butted Soren," Tursanay replied. "I'm surprised you still have a head."

"Where's my chair?" Amara noted.

"Uh oh," Tursanay said, looking back at the water.

"Maybe I can dive in and get it," Amara said. "I've always been good at swimming."

"Just be careful," Tursanay said as Amara dove. A large fin popped up behind her as she disappeared beneath the murk and Tursanay screamed. Amara popped back up almost instantly.

"What?" she asked.

"There's a giant fish thing in there with you!" Tursanay shrieked, moving towards the bank as fast as she could to

help Amara out, but when she pulled herself up on the bank, Tursanay shrieked again. *"It's trying to eat you!"*

This time it was Amara's turn to scream as she vaulted herself onto the bank and started trying to wriggle her way out of the scaled beast's jaws. Only the more she wriggled, the more it splashed, making it hard to see. She tried to climb further onto the bank where Rodney was already grabbing a stick to beat the thing off of his friend, but when the stick contacted the scales, Amara yelped in pain.

"Ow! *Ow! Stop! Stop!*" she yelled, out of breath. She turned over and sat up and examined the creature thought to be halfway devouring her and realized she now had a fin. "Get it off! Get it off! Why do I have a fin! What is this?!" She thrashed about and her fin thrashed too. The yellow and orange glittering scales reflecting the light beautifully with a rainbow sheen.

"Amara! *Amara!*" Tursanay called, trying to keep her from hyperventilating. She wasn't too far from it herself. "Okay, okay—you're okay. Let's just take a second to lie down and breathe—okay, good," she nodded, as Amara did just that. She couldn't look at the thing that had just replaced her legs and still function. She covered her face with her hands.

"This can't be happening right now. No, no, no, I can't take one more thing going wrong or weird! I can't handle having a tail instead of legs! I'm still trying to process if any of this is real. Why do I have a fin?"

She started sobbing. She started and couldn't stop, and Tursanay had to just rub her arm as she regained control of herself. This was too much for any of them.

"Uh... Tursanay?" Rodney said slowly. A bit loudly. "That's not the only thing that changed..." She looked up at him and he slowly pointed to her, just behind her. She looked over her shoulder to see a pair of soaked, iridescent wings. She scrambled to her feet.

"Oh god," she blurted out. "Oh god, what is that? Get it off of me!" The more she wriggled her shoulder, the more they flapped and buzzed and she nearly sent herself airborne, trying to run from them.

"I think that is you!" Rodney called as she ran past.

She screeched to a halt and ran back to him.

"Hold up," she said, trying to catch her breath. "You're telling me that this isn't some kind of huge bug on me and I've got wings now?" She tried to process that. "So what, Amara's a mermaid, I'm a pixie, and Soren's an elf? What are you? Do you have a tail?"

"What?" Rodney asked, trying to keep up with what she was saying. "I think my hearing aids got short-circuited. Why does Amara look like a mermaid?!" Tursanay signed nearly everything she just said, and Rodney's panicked look grew more and more frantic with each word.

"*Hold it right there!*" came a gruff voice, surprising all of them.

"I don't have a tail! I swear! Please, I don't want to be a werewolf!" he pleaded, shaking.

"*Stop!*" Soren called, standing between the others and the woods from where the voice had sounded. He held out his arms to make himself a bigger target. "*They are my friends!*"

"You don't have any friends!" the voice called back, making Amara and Tursanay exchange glances.

Did they know each other?

"Gregory, that's enough. Soren!" called a different voice that made the boy straighten. "Where have you been? You disappeared with just a note. Nanako is worried sick, and now you pop up with three strangers out of some kind of strange blue light and call them friend? What's in your head, boy?"

As he spoke, a man, followed by two younger males, made their way out of the woods. The man was tall and round, a scruffy black beard covering his face, his hair blending into it. The boy to his right was taller and leaner than him, with dusty red hair and a disapproving glare directed at the group. To the man's left was another boy, probably ten or eleven, much shorter than the other two, and a crop of black hair poking out at odd angles, a grin plastered across his face.

"Th-they're..." Soren stammered, hesitating. His voice shrinking as low as his confidence. "They're Dai-Nē."

There was a silence that followed that seemed to make Soren shrink back even more. The air was thick, uncomfortable, and the others felt as if they'd walked right into a personal conversation to which they weren't welcome.

"Didn't you say we needed to get away from here?" Tursanay murmured behind him, as if to give him a little help.

Soren seemed to breathe again.

"We need to get back to the house," he called to the strangers. "Away from this area."

"Those people are not welcome here," growled the older man. "If what you say is true, then you are endangering my family."

"It's my family, too," Soren argued back.

"Not if you continue to put the rest of us in danger!" the older boy growled back.

"Hamnet!" came a distant female voice. The three strangers straightened, and the older man cursed.

"Nanako, stay back! It's not safe!" he called.

"*Nanako!*" called Soren, a hope in his voice. "*I found them!*"

"Soren!" the bearded man snarled under his breath, knowing it was too late to silence the boy.

"Soren?" the woman called back, surprise and relief coloring her voice.

The man cursed. When she topped the hill behind the trio that barred their way, a small Asian looking woman pushed past them, ignoring their protests, and seized Soren in a hug. She had long black hair pulled into a partial twist; her eyes an inviting warm brown. She had a tiny frame and was the same height as Soren. "You're soaking wet," she fretted, murmuring softly as she smoothed his hair down. "But you're okay," she sighed, then glanced at the others behind him.

"My friends... they are Dai-Nē. I found them, just like I said I would." Soren breathed in utter relief, the exhaustion he'd been hiding weighing his frame down. With this woman here, it seemed he could relax.

"Let's get them inside and dry them off," she murmured, putting her arm around Soren. "It looks like your friend there needs to have his arm looked at, too. And who made this mermaid cry? My dear, I haven't much in the way of comfort for you, but you are welcome all the same."

"Nanako!" protested the older man in a hushed whisper, muttering something they couldn't hear as he gestured to the trio.

"Hamnet!" Nanako barked. "I will not have you speak in such a manner to our guests. Soren trusts them, and that is enough for me."

"They fed, clothed, and housed me. They are good people," Soren agreed.

Tursanay and Amara glanced at each other, then back at

Rodney, who had finally joined them, holding back a bit of an uncertain look on his face.

"Then they shall have the same here," Nanako reassured him. "Anyone who takes care of my son as such is welcome here."

"Thank you," Tursanay murmured gratefully, a shiver running through her as a breeze blew past.

Amara pulled herself together enough to fetch her chair from the bottom of the creek they'd landed in, and Rodney and Tursanay helped her get back in it.

"Let's get you into some dry clothes," Nanako replied with a kind, but determined, smile. She turned her gaze to her husband and an unspoken word passed between them. Both scowled, but it was Hamnet that looked away, jaw set, before ordering the group to follow him to the house. Once inside, they received clothes and food before being given a place to crash for the night, as their adrenaline rush had faded and left them exhausted.

* * *

The sound of a creaking door opening roused the girls from their sleep as Nanako peeked inside. The smell of food wafted in from the other room, and the group stirred, hungry. They had accommodated Amara with a tub of water, her new form needing the moisture, and Tursanay had slept on Soren's bed, and the boys given padding to sleep on in the floor.

"There is enough food for all in the kitchen if you are hungry," she smiled kindly. She invited them to take as much time as they needed, and they thanked her as she closed the door, heading back to the main part of the house.

Groaning, Tursanay sat up, stretching and rubbing her face as Amara covered her head with a pillow, uttering a curse when she didn't wake up to find this had all been a really bizarre dream. Tursanay glanced over to find Rodney still asleep as Soren sat up - the boy's hair a tousled mess as he tried to regain his bearings.

Finally stirring Rodney awake with the promise of food, Tursanay skipped pleasantries and got right to business, demanding Soren tell them what was going on and what was with yesterday's exchange. Soren, however, was less than forthcoming, replying they should wait to talk about such things when there was no one else around.

Unsatisfied with his answer, Tursanay could only scowl as he ducked out the door before she could argue. Following him and planning to get some straight answers, the girls led the way and Rodney fell a step behind, unable to really understand anyone as they whispered fervently.

The food smelled and tasted amazing, and though they still wanted answers, the food seemed much more interesting as they filled their bellies with a warm, freshly cooked meal that made the cafeteria food they were used to pale in comparison.

"This totally makes up for the nightmare I had last night," Rodney said, speaking with a tad higher volume than the others as he spooned more food into his mouth. He paused mid-bite, a worried look crossing his face. "There ah... isn't such a thing as a magic spell that can turn someone into a pink ostrich is there?" Rodney asked nervously, looking at Soren.

The other boy looked up from his plate, confused by the question. "As I am uncertain what this ostrich is, I cannot confirm nor deny this inquiry," came the reply.

"Speaking of things that we don't know about," Tursanay

spoke up. "We need to know what's going on and who's after us."

"Yeah, are we even safe here?" Amara agreed, also looking at Soren, who paused in taking a sip of his drink as he caught their stares.

"Those things that chased us won't follow us here, will they?" Rodney wondered out loud, still worried about talking coyotes. Soren set his cup down, glancing around the room and lowering his tone.

"Not here," he warned them. "Not now."

"No," argued Tursanay. "We need to know what we're up against and why they want to kill us."

"Yeah, what'd we do to tick these people off?" Amara asked, agreeing they should get some information.

"You gotta tell us something," Tursanay continued. "We've followed you on blind faith so far; we deserve some answers."

"There's no one else in here right now," Amara began, but Soren cut her off.

"I'll not endanger my family by speaking where it is not safe-" he bristled before a creaking door that had them all sitting up straight interrupted his words. Three pairs of eyes fell on Nanako, who calmly walked over to the table of guilty looking teenagers, and Rodney, who was still pondering over the pink ostrich to himself.

"Soren," she began softly as she moved. Gracefully, she sat down at the table with them. "I couldn't help but overhear, and I know you feel obligated to protect this family after the information you've found out, but remember, it is our responsibility to safeguard you." Soren opened his mouth to argue, but Nanako held up her hand to silence him. "There is a reason your parents entrusted us to look after you, my love. Entrusted me." Soren looked up at her, confusion coloring his face, but she directed his attention to the others. "As they have helped you, so must you help them. Since they share the same fate, they are warranted to have the same information you have."

"Whoa, back up," Amara interjected. "What fate? I didn't agree to join any kind of magical quest to reclaim a kingdom here, I just want to find out what happened to my dad and why people we don't know are trying to kill us. I want to know how I can make things go back to normal..." Though, as the words left Amara's mouth, it seemed to dawn on her that things would never quite go back to normal.

"Do you really want to drop all this and just go back to Blemwick for summer vacation?" Tursanay asked. Things were just getting exciting - she didn't want to leave just yet. Not with all that had happened already. Yeah, things were terrifying and frankly, she wasn't sure what tomorrow might bring, but wasn't that the best part? The thrill of adventure she'd read about in books and stories? She'd been a military brat most of her life, traveling a lot, and having sat still for the past few years had been driving her nuts. The prospect of an adventure with actual magic wasn't something she wanted to pass up. This kind of thing didn't just happen to people every day. Not in real life, anyhow.

"If it means I won't get turned into a pink ostrich and eaten by undead coyotes, yes," Rodney replied. "Give me boring classes over being eaten any day."

"Rodney, no one's going to turn you into an oversized pink chicken. It was just a bad dream," Tursanay reassured him.

"You don't know that," Rodney argued. "You got a

premonition about shadows coming to life." He took a breath to calm himself.

"Guys, we're getting off topic here," Amara interjected.

"Right... Sorry," Tursanay apologized, realizing she probably sounded crazy arguing living shadows and pink ostriches.

"It's a legit fear! I don't want to be a pink ostrich!" argued Rodney.

Taking a breath and letting it out, Amara looked at Nanako. "We know how we got to the other side of the Veil, but we don't know what a Dai-Nē is or anything about this world. A couple of days ago, we didn't even think it existed... Help?" Putting it as simply as she could think to, Amara cut to the chase, and Nanako looked a little relieved to have the subject back on something she understood.

"So, it's true there is a Mortal World where no magic exists?" she asked.

"Until yesterday, the closest thing I'd ever seen to magic was a guy pulling a rabbit out of his hat for my sixth birthday," confirmed Amara. "Then the secret compartment failed, and the rabbit ran away."

Nanako considered this for a moment.

"Then perhaps I should begin at the very beginning," Nanako sighed. "Soren needs to know some of this, as well. They chose us for a reason to look after him once they were told he was a Dai-Nē. I am a keeper of history. Of the truth of the old days. And it was important he knew the truth one day of how things began, and not the altered history people talk of nowadays." She reflected for a moment, standing to retrieve some yarn work from a shelf by her chair, and returned to sit at the table with the others, setting to work with her fingers as she spoke. "In the beginning, there was only one world."

"That must have been chaos," Rodney said, watching Tursanay sign the words to him as they all looked at her in awe. Tursanay shushed him and they all turned their attention back to Nanako, Rodney aside, who was watching Tursanay sign most of the story she could.

"Magical beings and non-magical beings coexisted alongside each other harmoniously, actually," she chuckled. "Until," she said, the smile fading, "there was an uprising. It began with the stirrings of unrest between the two kinds. Battles broke out, each side feared the other; thinking the other inferior.

"A man and woman of great power, Rynon Eitû and Moidra Faekind, gathered leaders to themselves from all over the world. It was called the Council of Nations. Two from each—one to represent the magic kind, the other to represent the non-magic kind. The two of them oversaw the event, for Rynon had been born of the non-magic kind, and Moidra was born into magic and was the queen of the Fae. They were great friends and wanted peace between their people."

"So, what happened?" Amara asked.

"Many nations wanted peace, but they couldn't meet the demands. Then Rynon stated he knew of a way to end all the arguments, but that he would have to go up into the mountains alone to find the solution. He was a wise man, and the Council of Nations trusted him to come back with an answer. But Moidra did not, and followed him in secret."

There was a pause as she frowned again.

"No one knows what happened between them when they were in the mountains, but when Rynon came back, he smelled of magic that did not belong to him. And he was a new, forceful power to be reckoned with. Because of this, the two kinds began to war with each other, the magic kind calling for Rynon to give up his obviously stolen power, and the non-magic kind wanting to use it to their advantage. A slaughter ensued where magic kind were driven back by the new found forces of Rynon, even though Rynon claimed he wanted only peace. Things devolved into madness."

"So, how did they fix it?" Tursanay asked. "Or did they?"

"When they feared their extinction," Nanako said. "The magic kind demanded Rynon fix what he had started. So, he came up with a plan. He would separate the magic kind from the non-magic kind with a Veil between the worlds. Those who wanted to come were welcome, those who wanted to stay, could."

"But who would have stayed when you're literally being hunted?" Rodney asked, horrified.

"When he created the Veil," Nanako continued. "Rynon's power split into five parts. It passed down this power through reincarnation. These people were called the Dai-Nē."

"But I thought there were seven Dai-Nē?" Soren said.

"There were originally five, but something happened in the past that changed this. I do not know what, but that is something you'll have to discover on your own," Nanako replied.

There was a moment of silence as this information sunk in. The entire world, as they knew it, seemed shifted slightly. Like growing up and being told Santa wasn't real, only to have the world turn on its ear when he flew you around in his sleigh.

"So, Dai-Nē are like superheroes," Rodney concluded, breaking the silence. When Tursanay gave him a look, he defended himself. "What? They go around saving the world with special powers and go up against people that want them dead!"

"So Rynon created this world to save magic people and passed his power down to us," Amara continued talking over the other two as they delved into fandom arguments, and looked at Nanako. "Somebody killed someone else, and they thought they'd try to kill us too, so they sent us across the Veil so that we'd be safe. Only now that someone's found us and really wants to kill us." She took a breath and let it out in a huff, running her hand across her face. "Here's my question: There are a lot of 'theys' in there. Who's doing what and why?"

"No one knows for certain who murdered the old Seer," Nanako replied, quickly getting the impression Amara would be the only one to stay on a topic she could understand.

"Right. Soren mentioned something about that." Amara nodded.

Nanako replied, "As I have said, we have limited knowledge about the Seer's death, only rumors."

"Some have also speculated," Soren added. "that the reincarnation of the Dai-Nē of Sight was impeded when the old Seer died in a meditation state. But Asher stated that wasn't true. I am uncertain what to believe now."

"Why would dying in the meditation state prevent the power from being passed on?" Tursanay asked.

"It was the way he died. People believe his death was magical because there was no mark on his body, and no evidence of poisoning," Nanako replied. "They could not detect the spell used on him, so it remains unknown."

"And additionally, his power returned to the pedestal," Soren agreed, as if trying to prove his point.

"But the orb was half the size of the others and severely

diminished. If there is a chance the line survives, it will be greatly weakened," his mother argued back.

"I thought you said we knew little about his death," Amara commented, watching their exchange.

"We know very little about the details of his murder," Soren corrected with a tone that conveyed his belief that there was more information to be gathered.

"Wait, back up," Tursanay interjected. "You lost me at pedestals and orbs."

Nanako looked at her. "When a Dai-Nē passes on, their powers are stored in a pedestal for safekeeping until the Dai-Nē can be found and gathered, and brought to the Council to have their powers returned and unlocked."

"I thought you said it would pass on by itself through reincarnation," Amara interjected.

"It was supposed to," replied Nanako. "But there was an incident in the past that made it safer for the Council to look after it and distribute it to the Dai-Nē safely." Nanako took a breath, trying to word her sentence carefully. "You need to work with the Council because they have Dai-Nē power and the ability to train you to be the best you can be. But you need to understand that not everything the Council will tell you is true. And that while there are still good people within, there is corruption as well."

"But if the Council is corrupt, don't we need to avoid it?" Rodney asked.

"It's political, Rodney. Everything's corrupt," Tursanay replied flatly.

"Whoa, hold it right there," interjected Amara. "That's signing us up for a quest we haven't all agreed to yet."

"Well, you can be a party-pooper and stay here and wait for something to kill you," Tursanay replied, patting her hand against the table impatiently. "Or you can come along and find a way to kick its butt before it kicks yours."

"We still don't even know what we're up against!" Amara argued, bristling. "How can we fight something when we don't even know what it is?"

"By learning what's out there so we can prepare for it," Tursanay quipped.

"I dunno. I'm kind of torn here," Rodney piped in. "On the one hand, I'm with Amara on this. Things like quests and missions seem cool to read about and watch, but when the danger and death is real and you're getting your arm chewed off by a talking coyote... All you want to do is go home, hide under your bed with something to fend off things that go bump in the night."

"See?" Amara defended. "Thank you!"

Rodney glanced down at the table and took a breath, looking back up at Amara. "But like Tursanay said... we had shadows come to life and chase us... How do you—how do you fight shadows? How do you fight things that aren't supposed to exist? Do you just hide in a corner and pray it doesn't notice you when it clearly has already, or do you find a way to survive?"

A small silence filled the room as Amara and Tursanay both let that sink in. The gate guard was dead. Mr. Asher was probably dead. Someone or something wanted them dead. And now they were in a completely different world where they could face all sorts of unknown dangers.

The only sound was the fire crackling in the next room. Tursanay spoke up.

"I'm curious though," she began, looking at Nanako. "Why does the Council hold the Dai-Nē power still? Why not destroy the pedestal and have things return to the way they were before?"

"And why did you speak of five Dai-Nē? Are there not seven?" Soren pestered again.

"If the legends are true, then there were only five Dai-Nē in the beginning," Nanako replied. "Though I am uncertain what happened to the power. All I know is that there were originally five. No information I can find on the pedestal speaks of what happened. The information seems to have been purposefully forgotten. As for dethroning the Council of its authority over the device, I do not know if it is possible. Nor do I know what happened so long ago that caused the Dai-Nē to relinquish their power to them in the first place."

"Okay, so who would want to hunt us down?" Tursanay asked, her thoughts straying back to survival. "And why? Do they want our power? Do they just want us dead? Is it because of something our parents did that they're punishing us for? I mean, is there anything that would give us an idea of who's doing this and what they're after?"

"It is impossible to target the parents of a Dai-Nē before they are born. There is no indicator that would allude to anyone being capable of producing a Dai-Nē child," Nanako replied.

"So that leaves someone wanting our power or just us dead," Tursanay concluded. "but since we haven't known about any of this long enough to tick people off, it seems like the obvious choice would be-"

"Someone wants our powers," murmured Soren, nodding. "It is plausible."

"But not probable," Nanako argued. "Only the Dai-Nē can extract the power from the pedestal, and the power immediately returns once the Dai-Nē pass. There is no way to transfer the power to someone else. You would have to control the person directly. This plan would be folly."

Rodney glanced down at his hand and noticeably paled as he met Tursanay's eyes, then exchanged glances with Soren. Nanako didn't miss it, her brow furrowing.

Tursanay glanced at her, a worried expression on her face. "Well, they do now," she said softly, wondering how bad this situation really was.

"What do you mean?" Nanako asked, urgently.

"My ring," Rodney breathed. "The coyote got my ring."

CHAPTER 10
WANTED

"What?" Nanako asked, confused.

They explained what had happened before they got there.

"We believe it to be the Ring of Rynon, capable of switching the powers of the Dai-Nē between individuals without loss of life," Soren explained.

Nanako paled. "If that is the case, then you must find and retrieve that ring as soon as possible. In the wrong hands, it could very well mean an imbalance of power the likes of which our kind has never seen before."

"No pressure," Rodney squeaked when Tursanay finished signing what Nanako had said.

"I need some air," Amara sighed, excusing herself from the table. She wheeled herself backwards, then paused. "Thank you for the meal," she murmured sincerely to Nanako before going out the front door.

"Is your friend well?" Nanako asked the others.

"We've... been through a lot the last few days," Tursanay

let out a breath. "Amara a little more so with this investigation into her dad's potential murder. This alone would be a lot to take in, but she's dealing with some personal stuff too, and she just needs some time," Tursanay murmured.

"That's part of the reason I've been trying to get her mind off it by trying to make her laugh or get irritated at us so she could focus on something different," Rodney admitted. "She's the kind that can pull herself together if she's got something else that needs focusing on. Like all this Dai-Nē and magic stuff."

"You know you're not as clueless as you try to make yourself out to be," Tursanay smiled softly.

Rodney shrugged, embarrassed at the compliment.

"I just don't like seeing my friends upset," he murmured, looking at anything but the surrounding people at the table.

"Amara..." Tursanay explained to Nanako. "just needs some time to adjust."

"I understand," Nanako nodded solemnly. "If there is anything I can do to help relieve her stress, just let me know."

"Is there a way to help her in her mer-form?" Tursanay asked. "We just found out today that we are magical creatures and we're not exactly adjusting very well." She wriggled her shoulders and her wings buzzed experimentally making her flinch slightly at the movement and sound.

"I know of a spell that can help her move around freely, but you would have to travel to town to get it. I do not have the power to make it," Nanako replied. "You will need a moisture spell and flying spell. This will allow her to swim through the air as easily as she would move through the water."

"That would be so rad!" Tursanay beamed, then hesitated.

"Oh... but we don't have any money..." she deflated. "Those things probably cost money."

"They are not expensive," Nanako smiled. "We can spare the money for all that you have done for our son, Soren."

"Oh, you don't have to do that," Tursanay began, not liking the idea of taking their money. She wasn't sure how well off or poor they were and had no basis to judge from.

"It is the least we can do to help you on this journey you are to begin. You have a long way to go before you can reach the Council of Dai-Nē, and we are too far out in the country to mirror travel. I'm afraid you'll have to make part of the journey on horseback to reach the nearest town, then mirror travel from there." Nanako stood and moved to a box on the counter where she took out a few coins and placed them in a pouch. "I have a nephew that works at a blacksmith shop there. You can take the horse to him and he will bring it back to us from there."

"How can we travel on horseback with Amara?" Tursanay asked, pointing out the obvious. A mermaid on a horse was not an image she had expected to think about. "We still need to bring her chair with us."

"You can take the wagon," Nanako decided. "That will also help you carry the supplies we'll send with you. Just enough to get you to the Council where they will take care of you after that if you truly are the Dai-Nē they are searching for."

"Well, we made it past the Veil, so here's to hoping," Tursanay replied. "And thank you," she added softly. "For everything you are doing. I know this must be so much to deal with, but we appreciate it. Very much."

"You are welcome," Nanako smiled warmly. "I am sorry we could not do more, but I am glad we could do this much."

"It's more than enough," Tursanay smiled.

"Come, let us prepare your bags," Nanako prompted.

Soren watched as Rodney and Tursanay moved to help Nanako gather some needed items and pack them away, and sidled out the front door to where Amara was sitting on the porch trying to get her breathing steady.

"Please don't try to pep talk me, Tursanay, I just need to have one freaking minute where the world isn't about to come crashing down around my-" she paused, turning to see Soren standing there instead of Tursanay and she felt heat creep into her face as she clamped her mouth shut. Looking away, she cleared her throat. "Sorry, I thought you were..." but her voice trailed off.

"I'm sorry," Soren said awkwardly.

She looked up at him.

"I think I may have made you angry at some point, but I wasn't sure... If I have upset you, please understand it was not my intention-"

"It's not you," Amara sighed. "I'm sorry I took my irritation out on you. I didn't have anywhere to direct it, and this whole mess started when you showed up in my dreams." She looked up at him again. "I shouldn't have blamed you and taken things out on you. I should be the one to apologize. You've just been trying to help, and I've just been a mess." She looked back out at the scenery. "I just didn't ask for this. Didn't ask for any of this. I don't know what I'm supposed to do."

"I don't think anyone asks for life to unfold the way it does... And anyone that thinks they know everything, truly knows nothing," Soren replied. "Nanako told me that once."

"Nanako is wise and very kind," Amara smiled softly. She

took a deep breath and let it out slowly. "I'm sorry I stormed out. It's just every time I process one thing, I have something else to process and sometimes it just piles on until I don't have any thinking room left and I get..."

"Frustrated?" Soren asked, and Amara gave a rueful nod. "That I understand. Every time I think I've got an understanding of how people react to things around me, I'm told it's more complicated than that and I get frustrated. Why do things have to be complicated all the time? Why can't people just say what they mean and mean what they say?"

"I notice you have a hard time picking up on sarcasm," Amara said with a small smile. "Sometimes I think life would be easier if people just spoke simply. Sometimes it makes things harder. I get in trouble for speaking my mind a lot, so I've learned to keep most of it to myself."

There was a small silence between them.

"If you wish, you can speak your mind to me," Soren replied, breaking said silence.

Amara nodded. "I might take you up on that, eventually."

Soren smiled, then hesitated. "Was that sarcasm?" he asked. Amara shook her head, and the smile returned. "Then I will listen when you feel you can speak it again."

"Thank you, Soren. That means a lot," she replied.

They spent the next few hours preparing themselves for their journey. Once they had everything ready, and Amara loaded into the wagon with the help of the others in Soren's family, Tursanay hooked her own bag over her shoulder and made her way over to the front of the wagon, where Soren sat at the reins.

"You know where we're headed, right?" she asked for the umpteenth time.

"Indeed," Soren replied yet again. "Do not doubt me. I have traveled this path many times."

"It's the only one he knows, honestly," Hamnet spoke up. "Any other place and I'd be sending one of my boys with you. That child can get lost in a tunnel that goes one way."

"All tunnels have two directions," Soren corrected. "It was an easy misunderstanding."

Hamnet took a breath, then thought better of what he was going to say, and looked at Tursanay. "After you get to the inn, don't give him the lead. Look for someone who can point you in the right direction from there."

"I'm fantastic with directions. I just need to have them," Tursanay shrugged. "If someone can point us and name some landmarks, I can get us there. If not, we can wing it." With a buzz of her wings, she climbed into the seat beside Soren, Rodney already in the back with Amara.

"Good luck," was all Hamnet would reply as he patted the horse's backside. Soren clicked his tongue, and they set off.

The ride was much smoother than they expected; the wheels enchanted to absorb the bumps and holes so that it felt like they were gliding on air. It was almost like riding a magic carpet, but with a more solid base, you could move around on freely.

When an hour had passed as they continued on, they started talking amicably, asking about the city and what was different about it and the place where Soren lived.

Soren described the cities and how they were alive. That each of their citizens were responsible for helping take care of it. If you didn't take care of the city or were destructive, the city didn't take care of you if you needed help. It was a mutual bond and benefit, and could even help the sick and dying heal as much as possible. There were streets that would change up and lanes that would stretch out depending on what the city wanted to do that day or if someone needed help to escape someone chasing them, it would help block off their pursuer's paths. Soren had seen that happen once, when a man had been falsely accused of some crimes.

He spoke of the way graffiti moved across buildings to chase birds or how he once saw one make a rude gesture to someone cleaning it off the side of the wall. Told them of the witch's breweries that could give you a shot of luck in your morning drink or a pastry for courage or charisma if you had, say, a job interview. He spoke of the ways the city would change throughout the day for whomever walked its streets at the time.

Those of dawn and day would live in the sunlight and enjoy the shade of the buildings in the heat of the day, whereas those of dusk and night would have just enough glow from the streets bouncing off the reflective surfaces of the buildings to help them see at night without being a nuisance. There were vendors that sold food for different creatures.

There were touristy things like talismans that had an enchantment on them or fun toys for toddlers to play with that made noises or would light up and write their names for them. Street performers with magic poi that created sigils and alchemic circles to produce flashes of light or butterfly shaped light spells to awe the crowds. That had been one of his favorite shows growing up to watch while his family brought their crops to town to sell. He would watch the street performers and enjoy being somewhere he could get away from his worries and fretting about his family for just a little while.

When another hour of stories passed, they finally came upon one of the living cities Soren spoke of so highly. The center of the town was a giant tree, its roots creating a wall around it with smaller trees and the like. Inside the barrier were large buildings with a layer of mirrored windows all along the first levels. During the day, you could see through them and see inside the shop's windows where they displayed food, trinkets, clothing, and such.

"Man, I wish we could buy some clothes," Tursanay breathed, looking at some of the more flowy robes. "Those are gorgeous and our school uniforms make us stick out like sore thumbs."

"True," Soren commented. "You are dressed strangely, but this is Sendew and they are used to strange people passing through." They paused by an inn with a stable where they were planning to house the horses for the night and pointed across the street to a blacksmith's shop. "My cousin works over there," he added.

"Oh?" Tursanay brightened. "Your cousin's a blacksmith?"

"Indeed," Soren replied. Once they had stalled the horses and got Amara out of the wagon, they made their way to the blacksmith shop to speak to Soren's cousin. Once inside, they found the shop to be empty except for a black cat who watched them curiously from the counter. There was a fire glowing in the hearth and the smell of hot metal filled the air. Strangely, though, the place wasn't overly hot. In fact, it was a rather comfortable temperature near the counter. Almost like there wasn't a fire nearby at all.

"Tohru?" Soren called.

"He has stepped out. How may I help you?" the cat asked.

"Please tell me that wasn't the cat that just said something," Rodney tried and failed to whisper to Tursanay, who could only stare openmouthed.

"Don't be rude," the cat hissed, its ears laid back and tail swishing. "My husband isn't in. What do you want?"

"Akram?" Soren asked, coming around the other side of the group where the cat could see him.

"Soren!" Instantly, the ears were up and so was the tail. "It's good to see you, child! How is your family?"

"They are well, and yours?" Soren asked politely. It was a custom.

"Tohru and Kadin are the same as ever," the cat chuckled. "What brings you here? Are these rude children with you?"

"Sorry," Tursanay stammered, finally getting back to herself. "It's just... A talking animal attacked us without reason the last time we came across one.

The ears went back again, and the eyes narrowed. "I'm a shapeshifter, not a talking animal, child. Learn some manners."

"That's actually one reason we are here," Soren interjected. He lowered his voice. "They are the same as me."

The cat blinked for a moment, as if processing, then understanding seemed to dawn on it. "Oh, you mean they are the missing...?" The ears went forward again, tail swishing, eyes wide.

Soren nodded. "We need to get to the Council. We stored the horses in the stable at the inn across the street, but now we need to get a spell set for her," he said, gesturing to Amara. "And mirror travel to the Council."

"What sort of spell set?" the cat asked curiously.

"Flying and moisture," Soren replied.

"I know a witch," Akram said. "I can only use alchemy, but Kadin can create those spells."

"We can pay," Soren said.

"Nonsense," Akram declared. "You are family and these are your friends. My kindness will extend to them and so will my forgiveness if they at least try to behave."

"S-Sorry again," Tursanay replied. "We just found out about this world a few days ago, so we're still adjusting."

"World?" Akram repeated, squinting, and Soren winced.

"Let's discuss that later," Soren said quickly. "I'm worried about... others overhearing."

"I think that's a wise decision," Akram agreed. "Come. I will ask Kadin to watch the shop until Tohru returns. Meanwhile, you may enter my house and we can speak freely."

"Thank you," Soren said, relieved.

Their guide led back into the house that sat behind the blacksmith shop, and taken into a room that was lined with glittering trinkets, vials of various liquids, dozens upon dozens of crystals, and various herbs and concoctions that were unrecognizable to them. There were shelves upon shelves of books, various circles and scorch marks on the floor, and on the table in the middle of the room was scattered papers with diagrams and many scribbled notes, some of which seemed to be lists of ingredients. There at the table, pouring over a book, was a tall, broad-shouldered man with long brown hair to said shoulders, and an angular face with a long straight nose. He was quite handsome.

"Kadin, my love," the cat spoke, walking into the room and leaping onto the table. "I need you to watch the shop. We have some guests."

Kadin blinked and looked up. "Oh! My apologies. I didn't

hear you all come in... Nor do I recognize any of you but one..."

"It's alright my love, they are Soren's friends," the cat answered.

"Ah," Kadin realized. "That makes much more sense. Alright dearest, I can tell when you're impatient to do whatever it is you're looking to do, so I'll go to the shop and leave you to it."

"Thank you, my love, you understand me so well," the cat seemed to grin cheekily. If that were possible for a cat. Once Kadin was out of the room, the questioning began. Soren explained everything, down to the Ring of Rynon and how they exchanged powers before the shapeshifter stole it from them, and how they escaped across the Veil. The cat listened silently as he told the story, only interjecting occasionally for questions and clarifications. "Well," it said as he finished. "You certainly have gone through quite a lot. And that explains your lack of manners. How can you be polite if you do not know what is considered rude?" The cat looked at Tursanay. "And you. Why do you keep making those gestures?"

"I'm translating," she answered. "As best I can. Rodney is partially deaf, and I'm giving him the gist of the conversation."

"So, you need a hearing spell as well?" the cat asked. "I'm sure we have the ingredients for that. But he'll have to wear a crystal on his ear. Will he be comfortable with that?"

"He's used to wearing hearing aids, but they quit working when we went across the Veil," Tursanay answered. She signed this to Rodney, who perked up. He nodded fervently. Being left out of half of the conversation was isolating, but he'd wear a dress if it meant not having to put Tursanay through signing everything for him. He knew she didn't mind, but with one arm, it had to be tiring for her. Especially having to finger spell words that just didn't get used normally.

"That's settled then," the cat said. "Three spells and some lunch."

"Whoa!" Amara exclaimed as the spell lifted into the air. "This feels weird... How do I direct where I'm going?" She wheeled her arms, trying to steady herself.

"Just as you would your chair: with intention. Lean in the direction you want to go," Kadin explained.

"Holy-" Rodney swore as his finger gently ran over the crystals hanging from his earlobes. "These things make everything so clear!"

Amara yelped in the background as she crashed into a shelf. Kadin called for her to use her tail as a guide, wincing as she swung it the wrong way and took out a row of books.

"Guess that makes things crystal clear for you now, Rodney," Tursanay grinned, elbowing him.

"You had a chance to make the first thing I heard you say with perfect clarity something profound, and you go with a pun," Rodney accused.

"I saw an opportunity, and I took it," Tursanay grinned.

"Go to your room," Rodney replied in mock irritation, making Tursanay laugh.

"Guys!" Amara called. "A little help?" They turned to see her upside down and floating past the light fixture hanging from the ceiling. She was desperately holding her shirt down in embarrassment. It took some time, but after a half hour of practice, Amara could somewhat maneuver without too much issue, and was getting a grasp on how far up or down she was from the ground. There was a limit to how high the spell would go, but there was also a good distance she could fly up.

"The spell will last for a year," Kadin was explaining as Rodney and Tursanay helped Amara make a complicated maneuver in the air.

"What about these?" Rodney said, gesturing to his ears.

"Every three or four months, charge the crystals in sunlight or full moonlight, and the spell should last as long as the crystal does. Should the crystal break, you'll need a new one, but otherwise it will last forever if you keep charging it," Kadin answered.

"Best. Hearing aids. Ever," Rodney said.

"Ah, I see you are coming along well with your new spells," Akram said, entering the room. This time she was in human form - long dark braids for hair, a shapely frame, and light brown skin. She was beautiful as she was terrifying, with piercing eyes despite her soft face.

"I take it Tohru is back," Kadin said, greeting her warmly. "Tell him not to stay up late working tonight and to close shop early. I have a feeling you're going to escort these children and I want to spend time all together before you leave."

"You have an uncanny way of reading my mind, love," beamed Akram.

"I just know you that well," Kadin grinned.

Akram went and fetched her husband from the forge and when he entered, the kids stared in awe at the massive, muscled person who walked through the door. He was at least six and a half feet tall, possibly taller, and filled up every inch of the massive doorways they had in order to let him pass through with ease. He was head and shoulders over Akram and a full head over Kadin.

Soren was the only one not intimidated.

"My love," Akram greeted him. "These are Soren's friends." She gave their names and his in turn. Rodney waved and gave a weak hello and Tohru gave a small nod in his direction. "Don't worry, he's just shy," Akram added. They wouldn't have believed her if a small blush hadn't sprouted across his cheeks.

Tursanay perked up. "Are you the blacksmith?" she asked.

Another nod.

"That's so awesome!" she beamed. "I've always wanted to meet a blacksmith! You're so strong!"

Akram grinned and elbowed her husband. "He appears to have a fan already," she teased, glancing at Kadin. "Now that you have the hang of your spells, it's time for some food and a quick trip to the Council to see you off."

After they had filled their stomachs with food and drink and gathered their supplies, they made their way into the parlor, where a large mirror stood against the wall. It was large enough that had it been a doorway, Tohru would have no trouble entering it. Akram stepped in front of the mirror.

"Delmar," she said, giving the coordinates. The image in the mirror shimmered to life, showing the city behind her as if she were already standing there. "Alright," she declared. "Who wants to go first?"

When no one stepped forward, Tursanay took a breath. "I'll go," she said bravely. "What do I need to do?"

"All you have to do is touch the mirror and go through and you'll be transported there," Akram instructed.

"Will it hurt? Will I feel anything?" Tursanay asked.

"You'll feel a cold sensation as you pass through the mirror, but otherwise, nothing," Akram replied.

Tursanay took a deep breath and reached out to the mirror, hesitating for a moment before touching the cold, smooth surface. Something seemed to ripple in the mirror, the colors changing slightly. She pushed her fingertips through and felt the cold sensation pass through her hand before something grabbed it. Yanking her forward, she yelped and instinctively pulled back, bracing herself with a foot against the wall.

"Something's got me!" she yelled.

Without thinking, Rodney rushed forward, wrapping his arms around her waist and pulling her backwards. Yanking her free with the added weight, they tumbled to the floor, landing in a heap. There was a thump against the glass as Tursanay's reflection grew two more sets of eyes above and below her own, all turning red, and hissed at them - a deep throated feral sound that shook them to their bones - before disappearing.

Everyone backed away from the mirror quickly.

"Please tell me that wasn't normal!" Tursanay "I can't do that again and lose another arm."

"That was most definitely not normal," Akram confirmed. "But legends have spoken of it. The mirror people were supposed to be a myth. I've never heard of a legitimate sighting before."

"Mirror people?" Tursanay accused. "Seriously? I almost got abducted by a mythological creature in a world of mythological creatures?"

"You okay, T?" Rodney asked as they got up.

"I will be," Tursanay lied, brushing herself off and realizing she was letting her anger get the better of her. "As long as there is another way of traveling to the Council because I'm not doing that again."

"You would be foolish if you tried," Akram agreed. "Well," she sighed. "It appears we'll have to take your horses, Soren. I hope your family doesn't mind you using them for longer. We'll write to them and explain that it'll take me longer than expected to bring them back, but that I'll return them as soon as possible."

"I'm sure they will not mind," Soren replied. "They are not due for a trip to town for some time."

"Excellent," Akram beamed. "Meanwhile, we'd better hurry and begin our actual journey if we're going to make it before the celebration."

"Something just nearly took my arm off and we're just ignoring it?" Tursanay asked.

"Far from it. I know a person who was researching such a thing a while back but was nearly laughed out of the town. Perhaps there was more to what they were researching than I first believed," Akram muttered. "I will get in contact with them and discuss it further, but in the meantime, it's a few days' travel by horse to get to Delmar and we need to hurry."

The group took some time to get going, but once they set out, a speed spell from Kadin sped the journey along to give them a bit of headway. The first day's journey ended in another city where they found an inn and got some rest for the night. As they were leaving the next morning, Soren looked groggy and as if he had not slept in the least.

"You okay?" Amara asked.

"I am unwell," he replied, sounding like he felt like throwing up.

"What's wrong?" she asked.

"I had a strange dream," he began. "The city... it... it spoke to me. It said it could feel some of its sister cities getting ill and asked me for help. Only, I didn't understand how I could. It told me I would understand soon, but that I needed to hurry if I wanted to save the other cities. Then it touched a vine to my forehead, and a light surrounded me. I felt the energy drain from me and I collapsed into a pool of water and woke up with a start. That is when Akram called for us to rise, and I started feeling unwell."

"I know the feeling," Amara said softly. "When I would wake up from our shared visions, I would feel the same."

"I am sorry I put you through that," Soren said.

Amara shook her head. "I don't blame you anymore. I'm sorry you have to experience it, too."

"We can see about getting something to settle your stomach if you aren't feeling well, Soren," Akram said from across the room.

"I should be fine soon," he said, though he looked rather green. "Thank you."

"You're as stubborn as ever, child," Akram said, raising an eyebrow at him. "Come, I will get you something before we leave and you won't have to deal with travel sickness either."

"You get travel sick too?" Amara said. "You should definitely take something. I insist."

"Alright," Soren sighed. "I will."

"What's this? Soren agreeing to something so easily? I like your new friends. They can talk some sense into you better than we ever could," Akram grinned. "Let's keep it that way."

"Just this once," Soren frowned. Akram winked at him. "What?" he asked. "I don't understand..."

"Let's just chalk it up to her being glad you have friends that are interested in your good health," Amara explained, though she didn't want to address another potential meaning behind that wink. At least she hoped Akram didn't mean flirting. Amara was no good at it and was in too much turmoil to think about that sort of thing at the moment.

They finally set out for the morning, Soren feeling much better with a bit of nausea healing spell in his stomach and a nap in the back of the wagon. The group stopped for lunch in Alhalanadria and found it to be a military-like city of alchemists. The city itself was bright and colorful, families walking the streets, going in and out of shops and not paying much attention to the alchemists in uniform marching around the streets - some headed to destinations with arms full of papers, some making sure that there were no issues in the shops they passed. Others still seemed to discuss things in groups, as if taking a break from their duties and sharing the occasional joke. It was a pleasant atmosphere and far from what they expected when they saw so many uniformed soldier-looking figures walking around.

"The food here is the best thing I've ever tasted," Rodney said around a mouth full of sandwich. "It doesn't matter where we go. It always tastes homemade from scratch and fresh."

"Do you not make your food fresh in your breweries?" Akram asked.

"Long story." Tursanay waved the question away. "Rodney is just a glutton for good food." It was a harmless tease.

"Can you blame me?" he asked, unphased. He pinched off

a bit of his sandwich and put it on her plate. "Try it! It's amazing!" Tursanay did and agreed it was good, sharing some of her own. When they finished eating, Rodney, both stuffed and sorry he didn't have room for more, they sat to rest for a few minutes, talking amicably until a shadow fell across their table as three men in alchemist uniforms stood over them.

"Yes?" Akram asked. "Can we help you?"

"These four need to come with us," the first one stated flatly.

"Why?" Tursanay asked, furrowing her brow. She wasn't just about to walk off with some strangers. The alchemist held up three wanted posters with their faces on them and a second alchemist held up a fourth with Soren's.

"You are wanted criminals," he stated firmly.

"Whoa, wait, what?" Rodney blurted out. "All we've done since we got here is travel, eat, and sleep—is that illegal and no one told me?"

"Come quietly without making a scene and you can speak to General Hartmut to plead your case," the first alchemist said. "Make a scene and it's straight to the Council, who have very little mercy for those accused of treason."

"We're traveling to see the C- oof-" Rodney got cut off with a kick under the table.

"They'll come willingly," Akram said. "But only if I get to speak on their behalf."

"Fair enough," the first alchemist agreed. "Get up and let's go."

Slowly, to show they would not try to make a run for it, the group got to their feet (Amara just floating off the floor) and made their way to the door, one alchemist leading the way, the other two taking up the rear. They marched them across to the main building and brought them through a series of doors until they finally halted before a chamber door. A female voice inside told the first alchemist to enter. After entering, he made them wait outside, and then after a few moments, he brought them inside as well.

"General Hartmut will see you now," he stated.

The office before them was organized chaos. There were books everywhere, lots of dark wood cabinets, and a large desk filled with papers sitting in the middle of two windows on either side of the room that brought in most of the light.

"State your case," the General said. She was blonde, her hair pulled back in a tight bun, with golden brown eyes and pale skin. She was young, too. Much too young to be a general.

"First," Akram spoke up. "What are the charges?"

"Treason," the General said. "According to your posters."

"What treason? We have violated no laws," Akram replied.

"You'll have to take that up with the Council," the General replied. "If you can't make a case for yourself here, then there is nothing I can do but turn you over to the proper authorities and let them deal with you."

"Wait, but all we wanted to do was go to the Council and get to the Dai-Nē thing," Rodney spoke up.

There was a pause.

"You believe yourselves to be Dai-Nē?" the General asked.

"I mean, after being hunted like we've been, I certainly hope we are," Rodney grumbled.

"Rodney," Tursanay whispered to shush him.

"Hunted?" the General hummed to herself. "Perhaps a trip to the Council would benefit us both, then. I'm the Dai-Nē of Alchemy after all."

Soren perked up. "If you are Dai-Nē as well, that means we have nearly found them all!"

"Then it's settled. We'll take you to the Council. If you are who you say you are, the Council will pardon your crimes. If you are not, then you will be subject to their form of punishment. May they have mercy on your souls should it come to that. Though I doubt there will be any."

The group exchanged nervous looks.

"So, you're just going to let us go like that?" Rodney asked.

"Of course not," the General said. "I'm going to escort you."

"Can we not do the mirror travel thing?" Rodney requested.

"Rodney," whined Tursanay, who mentally half begged him to stop talking and saying things that could brand them as not of this world. She didn't think telling everyone that judging by Soren's family's reaction was such a good idea. Akram was the only exception to that. She went out of her way to help them, but Tursanay got the feeling that she wouldn't be in the majority.

"What? I'm going to have nightmares if we try that again," Rodney whispered back defensively.

"A man unafraid to admit when he is scared," the General commented with a smirk. "I like that. But there is no need to request such. It is protocol to escort via caravan, not mirror travel. There's too many of you and having you travel through the mirror between guards would require too much security for this simple matter. I will not have you overpowering guards on either side and escaping."

"No worries there. The only place I'd get would be lost," Rodney replied, half to himself.

The General let out a laugh.

"You are most entertaining. I certainly hope you are who you say you are," she grinned.

"I'm just Rodney, that's all I claim to be," he replied. Where he got this sudden burst of confidence to talk was beyond him, but he was going with it. It was easier when you could make someone laugh anyhow.

"General Tryn Hartmut," she replied. "You can call me Tryn."

"Tryn," Akram began.

"I said he could call me Tryn," she snapped coldly. "You can call me General or General Hartmut."

Rodney's eyebrows shot up into his hairline and suddenly he wished he'd listened to Tursanay and shut up. He exchanged a sideways glance with her as an awkward pause filled the air.

"General," Akram continued coldly. "We are hoping to reach the Council before the celebration in a few days. Can we arrange this?"

"As that is when I hope to arrive, I should say so. We'll leave immediately. I'll gather my things and assign a guard to you."

And with that, she gave a nod to the alchemist standing to the side, and sent him after more guards. Ten minutes later, they herded them into a caravan, with Rodney and Soren riding in one cart and Tursanay and Amara in another. These carts were much nicer than the farm cart Soren's family had lent them. The carts had seats covered in a plush material and windows for them to look out from.

Tryn herself rode with the boys for extra security and because she wanted to question them further. Akram rode with her to be a mediator, much to the General's dismay. By the time they reached the Council two days later, Tryn had questioned Rodney to his wits' end, and regardless of what he seemed to say or do, the General was infatuated with his answers and twisted their meanings to her own liking. In her eyes, he could do no wrong and anyone that said differently was obviously mistaken.

By the time they reached Delmar, they were all exhausted.

CHAPTER 11
INFILTRATION

Keir, Ilaris, and Aui'ani arrived in the city of Delmar. Keir shivered and pulled away from the mirror as if he had experienced an electric shock. He checked to make sure he was still all there and looked up at the other two, smirking at him bemusedly.

"What? It's my first time since I was five. You can't expect me to get over it that easily," Keir pouted.

They walked through the mirror station and into the open city, bustling with activity. The centaurs were working on trash duty, carrying carts behind them and throwing the weekly waste into them. The mail couriers - riding great winged elk and carrying their satchels of holding - flew up and down the street, quickly delivering letters and scrolls at a brisk pace. There was new graffiti painted on the side of one of the mirrored buildings with a political statement about the Council etched into the glass. It moved and waved to get people to see its message. Some stopped and read it, others continued on with their heads down against the wind. There was a storm moving in soon.

Once they reached the palace in the center of the city, they made their way inside, wading through customs like everyone else. There were so many people here just itching for a chance to see if they were a Dai-Nē, others here for the Prince's birthday celebration, and some for both, that it was all they could do to keep their patience as they were granted entry into the main hall.

"Now," sighed Ilarys. "Where do we begin?"

"You two act like tourists," Aui'ani said. "I'm going to turn into a mouse and find out just where we need to go to find something interesting."

Slipping behind a column and transforming, Aui'ani skittered out along the walls and made her way down the corridor. The mouse went unnoticed by the patrons and waitstaff, as it hopped behind decor and stayed to the shadows. Several corridors down where the people became sparse, and the guards became more frequent, the mouse slowed its pace until it came upon a door guarded by two burly looking guards. Swiftly changing into a beetle, she crawled past them and under the edge of the door, careful not to set off the sensor in front of her. Peeking around the room, she saw several artifacts placed on pedestals throughout, one guarded by a third guard.

That would probably be it. Something that powerful would need all the guards they could spare. And with the Prince's birthday party and the Dai-Nē event coinciding, their resources were stretched extremely thin. Making its way back past the guards, the beetle crawled until it was around the corner, then shifted into a mouse. The mouse made its way back towards the party before ducking behind a column once more before turning back into Aui'ani. She bounced out from behind the column and practically skipped over to the twins.

"Simple job. Three guards, two outside, one in. Basic magic sensor on the doors so I can't pass through. Disarm and defeat the two outside guards quietly, disarm the barrier, take out the guard inside, grab the ring, make a run for it," she replied simply.

"She makes it sound so easy," Keir grumbled. "Take out the guards quietly. How do you expect us to do that without alerting more guards?"

"I have an idea, but you'll need a spell," Ilarys said.

"Oh great, I hate when you have ideas," Keir cursed to himself.

"We need to go to the nearest brewery and get a sleep spell, and to a blacksmith and get a light spell," Ilarys said.

"You're going to give them some sleepy tea, then give them a nightlight in case they get scared of the dark?" Keir asked sarcastically.

"Then we'll need some lock integration tools," she continued, ignoring him. "This job might actually be fun."

"Fun? Oh, I definitely hate where this is going," Keir replied.

They made their way to the marketplace and gathered the spells they needed for the job, then went back to the party. There were more people than before and it was difficult to maneuver through the crowd, but once they were down a few corridors and away from the main body of people, they could breathe more easily and talk without shouting or being overheard.

"I've been here enough times on diplomatic missions that I can get us to the corridor we need without running into too many guards, but we're going to have to take a roundabout way to get there," Aui'ani said as she led them down another hall, peeking around a corner to see if there were any other guards coming. So far, they'd done decently enough. If their luck could hold out, they could pull this off without a hitch. They rounded another corner and crossed two halls before they had to stop. There were voices up ahead and a slightly ajar door they needed to sneak past.

"You let them escape?" demanded a voice from within.

Keir told the others to hold as they listened closely. "We are this close to losing our hold on the Fae and you let those children get away? If we don't find at least one other Dai-Nē soon and make good on our promise, we won't have access to the Mortal World at all. The Fae will see to that. We can't lose our hold over there. We need the other Dai-Nē to make this work."

"The Fae interfered, and the phoenix was there," a female voice replied. "What was I supposed to do? Fight all of them?"

"You're fully fledged, why not?" the male voice spat back. "You should have been able to get at least one of them here!"

"I nearly had one of them, but he slipped through my teeth," the female said. "But I got the ring. That has to count for something!"

"It does," conceded the other voice. "It makes our plan that much easier. If we can convince them to combine their powers into one, we can transfer all of them at once to the new wielder."

"Then what's the problem? There was a half-elf with them. They'll turn up eventually," the female said. "They know we exist now."

"You better hope they show up sooner rather than later,"

the male voice spat. "Otherwise, we'll lose everything we've been working towards."

The three standing outside heard footsteps and quickly scrambled to hide behind the corner and hope the footsteps didn't follow them. After a few moments, the sounds of footsteps receded and they could breathe a sigh of relief. They eased past the door quickly and inside they could see a dark-haired female with her back to the door slam her hand on a desk in irritation. She was short with tan skin and seemed to have quite the temper. Once they turned the next corner, however, they ran into a boy with reddish brown hair and bright green eyes and a shocked look on his face.

"Lost," he muttered under his breath.

Keir pointed behind himself.

"Party's that way," he said in a whisper as well. He stared at the boy as if he'd seen a ghost, but said nothing. They quickly parted ways with nods of thanks, praying the footsteps didn't come back, nor that the black-haired girl over would hear them. They rushed as quietly as possible to the next corridor and only then did they slow their pace.

"I think I knew that kid from somewhere," Keir muttered under his breath. "But my mind won't place him."

"We'll have to figure it out later," Aui'ani whispered. "We're here."

"Here's the plan," Ilarys said quietly. She whispered it to both of them and they exchanged looks, horrified, but with no other ideas, they went along with it.

Stumbling down the hallway with his arm around Aui'ani's shoulders, Keir laughed raucously. Aui'ani giggled maddeningly as they made their way closer to the guards. They swayed back and forth, going in a zigzag pattern, clearly drunk, and seemingly oblivious to the two guards standing before the door at the end of the hallway.

"And then I told him if he wants another errand done, he gets to be the one eaten by the dragon," Keir said loudly, finishing a joke. Aui'ani burst into more giggles and laughter and they came to a slow stop as they seemed to notice their surroundings. "This isn't the hallway to our rooms. I swore it was a left," he said, slurring his words.

"Oh! Maybe those shiny people know," she said, pointing to the guards in their armor.

"Let's ask them," he said, then raised his voice, stumbling towards the guards. "Hey shiny people! Man, it's dark in here... where's my light spell?" he muttered to himself, digging in his back pocket.

He let the small orb out of his hand and let it float behind his head far back enough so that his shadow extended a good way before him. The guards tensed for a moment until they realized it was a harmless spell, then relaxed but only a little.

"This is an off-limits area. Please return to the main area, sir," the guard to the left stated.

"I think we're lost," Keir said, coming closer. His shadow linked with theirs on the floor as he spoke. "See, we're trying to find our rooms," he continued, but he was trying to keep them from noticing what was going on behind them.

As the orb behind him grew brighter, the shadows darkened. And emerging from the shadows was Ilarys, with a sleep spell in hand. When he turned his attention to the other guard, going on about a wild account that required great gesturing, Ilarys covered the first guard's nose and mouth with the sleep spell and whispered the activation word in his ear. The second guard turned in surprise and Keir smashed the second sleep spell into his face, grabbing the back of his head to hold him still. The guard's eyes went wide and Keir growled for him to sleep, and slowly, after a moment of struggle, he slumped into Keir's arms, unconscious.

Ilarys pulled herself free of the shadows and helped Keir and Aui'ani pull the guards out of the way of the door and out of sight of the main hallway. Aui'ani got down on one knee and examined the lock, pulling something out of her hair that was holding it up into a loose bun, and pointed it at the barrier just under the door. She held out her hand for the lock integration tool, and carefully set to work disarming the barrier spell that would set off alarms. It took several painstaking moments, but when she felt the shimmer of the spell turning off, she gave Keir a nod.

Stepping forward, he knocked twice on the door.

"Shift change," he said.

There was a groan of a stretch and a shuffling of feet from inside the room and as soon as it opened, Keir head-butted the third guard, sending him crashing to the floor. Ilarys was on him in an instant with another sleep spell. They darted into the room and looked around. All kinds of trinkets littered the hall. One in particular that caught Keir's eye was a serrated bone knife with a cord wrapped around its jeweled pommel. He briefly wondered what it was for when Ilarys found the object they were looking for sitting on a pedestal in the center of the room in a glass box and called his attention back to their task. Carefully lifting the spell surrounding the box, Ilarys motioned for Aui'ani to grab the ring before she lowered the spell again to keep it from going off. Once they had their target, they quickly left the room, shutting the door behind them and made their way back into the main party area.

Their hearts pounded in their ears as they tried to stay

calm, but when someone went running past, they tensed. It was a boy with black hair and a panicked look on his face, followed by what they could only guess to be a bounty hunter, judging by the snarl on her face. They breathed a sigh of relief.

"We're not out of the woods yet. They'll be looking for someone trying to leave the premises immediately," Aui'ani said. "Stick with the crowds and wait for your scrolls."

"You're lucky I studied how to reflect spells back on themselves to avoid detection," Ilarys mentioned to Aui'ani.

The other woman gave a snort as they turned another corner.

"And you're lucky I learned to decrypt spells with a lock pick set," Aui'ani quipped back.

"Keir, stop sweating nervously. You'll give us away," Ilarys scolded.

"Stop saying things like you'll give us away or you'll give us away, idiot," he replied sarcastically.

The two of them whispered back and forth viciously until a waitstaff interrupted them, bringing them their scrolls. They thanked them and cleared their throats awkwardly. Reading the directions on the scrolls, they moved into the designated area, going through the guards' checkpoint and trying to pretend they hadn't just taken out a few guards just moments earlier.

"What if we're not Dai-Nē, you think?" Keir asked under his breath to his sister as the guards checked their scrolls and eyed them suspiciously.

"Then we'll probably get chewed out, but here's to hoping," she replied.

Once the guards were satisfied, they let them pass, and they joined the others milling together in the room below.

CHAPTER 12
POWERS

When at last the General and company arrived in Delmar at the location of the Council's headquarters, the Council's staff escorted them to a holding area. When they explained their situation, they had talismans strapped to their wrists to prevent them from leaving the building, and that would alert the guards to their locations at all times.

They couldn't take them off until they were unlocked, but this allowed them to move about the place freely until they could process their wanted posters. Since there was a major celebration in the works, their guards were stretched thin and it would take time to work their case. In the meantime, they could enjoy the celebration so long as they stayed within the confines of the building.

"Well, that was certainly more generous than I was expecting to be treated," Tursanay murmured.

"This is unacceptable," the General growled. "I can understand the treatment for Rodney because he is the least likely of all of you to truly be guilty, but the rest of you should at least be in a dungeon cell for treason."

"So, we're basically under house arrest and are free to enjoy the party before we get sentenced," Amara confirmed with the man at the desk.

"Since you are here for the Dai-Nē ceremony, yes. Otherwise, you would be in a cell awaiting your trial," the man replied.

"Oh... why does that make a difference?" she asked.

"Because Dai-Nē will receive a pardon for any prior crimes accused of them upon receiving their powers. It's why so many people come this year. It's a clean slate and a chance to be taken care of for the rest of your life. Everyone respects the Dai-Nē title," the man replied.

"Oh," Amara replied.

"Where did you say you were from again?" the man asked, squinting.

"We didn't," Amara replied, turning to break up another argument between Tursanay and Tryn. "Guys!" she clapped her hands to get their attention. "Let's get out of this office and give the man some space. Tursanay, Rodney, Soren - a word?" They filed out, much to the man's relief, and made their way down the hallway. Amara repeated what she'd learned and added, "I have a feeling where some people respect the title, there's gonna be someone that resents it. Just be careful about who we tell what for now."

"Especially if there are people vying for the position and their lives hanging on it," Tursanay said. "The Council sure is on a path to making a lot of enemies that way."

Tryn snorted. "The Council already has lots of enemies, child. You don't become a world power with the most powerful people in the world working for you without making enemies."

"Most powerful people in the world?" Rodney repeated.

"The Dai-Nē, my little meat pastry," Tryn smiled. "We are the most powerful people of magic."

"Hoo boy," Rodney sighed. "I'm not sure how to unpack everything she'd said in those two short sentences."

"I'm sorry, whomst is your what?" Tursanay bristled, wanting not to unpack that little tidbit, but to throw the whole thing away.

"Okay, focus!" Amara called. "Where do we go to find out about this Dai-Nē event? If we can just go ahead and get this over with, then that'll be one less thing to worry about for now. Actually, like, ten less things to worry about."

Soren started counting something on his fingers and Amara told him it was just an over exaggeration and the confusion on his face cleared as he stopped counting.

"It will not be happening until sometime tonight so there will be sometime between now and then where we can rest, bathe, eat, and prepare ourselves for the event," Tryn replied, and the trio brightened instantly.

"A bath," Rodney sighed dreamily. "I'm so ready for a bath. It's not even funny. I'm really tired of that corn chip smell."

"I'd give just about anything for a bath right now," Amara agreed. It had been a long time since they had received amazing treatment at Soren's house.

"Then let's get you settled into a room and work on those tasks," Akram said. She led them down the hall and to a worker who was passing by and, after a few moments of conversation, had arranged for them to have four rooms given to them, two people a piece. She would stay with the

General, Rodney and Soren would stay in one room, Amara and Tursanay in another, and the two alchemists that stayed behind to help Tryn in the fourth.

Once the talismans were in place, they sent the other alchemists back through mirror travel to the Alhalanandria, so they didn't have to worry about them anymore. Escorted to their individual rooms, the groups bathed, dressed with new clothes provided to them from the Council, and got fed, and then gathered in the General and Akram's room, relaxed and clean for the first time in what felt like weeks.

"What's the plan?" Amara asked, settling on a cushion on the floor beside Tursanay and Soren. Her fin wrapped around Tursanay's seat as there was no way to tuck it underneath herself comfortably. Rodney sat on Tursanay's other side and Akram and the General stood before them, hands on hips as if caught mid disagreement.

"We were just trying to decide that," Akram replied. "Tryn feels we should confine you to your rooms for the time being, and I think it would do you some good to get out and experience the atmosphere."

"I think we should play it safe and keep them from getting into any more mischief than they already have with treason on their heads. I'll not risk them escaping and-"

"Escaping how?" Akram reminded her for what seemed not to be the first time. "They have the talismans on them. Are being tracked at every step. They are safe and well kept up with unless you think there is something else we should worry about that you're not sharing."

Tryn hesitated just a moment. "No. Nothing like that. But if you are Dai-Nē, I'm worried you'll be able to overpower the talismans and escape."

"They don't have their powers unlocked yet, they can't overpower the talismans," Akram argued.

"True," Tryn seemed to concede. "I still do not think it's a good idea to let them roam about. If they stumble onto something that could get them into more trouble, it'll be even harder to dismiss the case over your heads already."

"What if we promise to be careful and to stay out of trouble?" Rodney prompted. Honestly, being stuck in a room with Tryn sounded a lot scarier than roaming around a palace-like place that contained all manner of mythological creatures.

"Of course you would be careful, my Rodney," Tryn cooed. "It's your friends I'm worried about."

Rodney got an idea. "What if I keep them in line and out of trouble?" he asked, playing on her weakness for him. "I can make sure they stay safe and away from things that they shouldn't be around."

Tursanay cut him a look.

"Well..." Tryn hesitated.

Rodney looked up at her with big, hopeful eyes.

Tryn sighed. "Agreed then," she caved at last.

"Awesome!" Rodney beamed.

He turned and grinned at Tursanay, who rolled her eyes at him.

When they made their way to the chief center of the celebration, there were dozens upon dozens of species running around. Some with animal-human hybrid, some fully animal, and some that looked like regular humans - then others still that looked like random objects or unidentifiable things that moved about in inhuman ways. There were centaurs and afrits and azizas, cynocephali, djinn, nymphs, and so many more that they could both recognize and not recognize. Creatures that seemed like stuff of dreams, others like the things of nightmares - all mingling and talking amongst themselves and to each other and eating snacks that floated through the room on trays like invisible waitstaff.

There were rock beings that ate gems, large bats that chewed on fruit as they hung from a horizontal pole just above a table of food on one end of the room. The talking animals were one of the more fascinating things to Amara, who liked animals more than she liked people. To talk to one like a person was like a dream come true. There were people and creatures with wings of all sorts, making Tursanay feel less like a sore thumb and more normal. Amara saw others with gills and fins of sorts and also felt more normal in this strange new world.

"This is amazing," Tursanay breathed.

"I'm literally speechless right now," Rodney agreed.

Amara just nodded, unable to really vocalize her awe.

"You act like you've never seen a crowd of people before," Tryn commented. All three of them shut their open mouths with a snap, remembering they needed to blend in and not let people know they were from another world.

"Well, being out in the country tends to have smaller groups of people," Rodney hedged, trying to cover their tracks.

"Oh, that's right, you're not from around here, are you?" Tryn recalled. "Where did you say you were from again?"

"Fayd Morn," Soren interjected. "It's where I grew up."

"Sounds like such a quaint place," Tryn mused.

She ruffled Rodney's hair, being nearly five inches taller than him and loving their height difference. "I joined the military when I was fifteen, and have been all over the place since. It's been a good four years."

"They let you join that young?" Tursanay asked, concerned.

"I was a prodigy," Tryn explained. "They trained me how to hone my power before I could rise in ranks. They quickly saw how well I adapted to situations and I made general in no time. I'm the youngest general there ever was." She added the last part proudly.

"So, you're only a year or two older than us and you're already a general? That's astounding," Rodney commented. It was unheard of, was what it was. How could they let someone so young have so much power? None of them were ready for that kind of power. Perhaps they had seriously underestimated Tryn.

"Thank you, my Rodney," she beamed.

"So, let's go check out that thing over there," Tursanay said, grabbing Rodney's arm and jerking her head at Amara to come with them.

She had to get Rodney away from Tryn before they did some more bonding. The General was bound to take it the wrong way. Rodney meant well and all, but he did not know when he was being mistaken for flirting or doting on others. Tryn took every sign as something more and it was getting on Tursanay's nerves. 'My Rodney'. Where'd she even get off calling him that? It was almost as creepy as 'my little meat pastry' but less so thankfully. She hoped it was just a mistranslation in the speaking spell they'd taken rather than her actually calling him a meat pastry.

The trio made their way into the crowd and almost instantly got separated, looking at various things. Amara got swept up in, watching a performance in the center of the room involving people that could control various elements, and Rodney found a table full of snacks and drinks whilst

Tursanay moved to get some air on the balcony in order to clear her head.

She didn't want to take her anger out on anyone and figured the quickest way to calm herself down was to get out doors without overstepping the talisman's boundaries. Leaning on the railing overlooking the city with a sigh, she tried to take it in, but all she could think about was the general calling Rodney 'my Rodney' repeatedly. She ran her hand over her face and sighed. So much for clearing her head.

"Hello there," came a voice. She turned to find a boy very near her age with pointed ears like Soren's, making his way over to her in a friendly manner. He had dark brown hair and eyes, and medium brown skin. His slender frame was just slightly taller than her own and he had a kind face.

"Hello," she responded politely, though she wasn't entirely in the mood to talk to people.

"A little too crowded in there for you?" he smiled.

Tursanay returned the smile. "You could say that."

"It's always this ridiculous every year," he said apologetically. "Not much I can help. My father thinks it's necessary to have all kinds of entertainment for my birthday, so it just gets more and more extravagant."

"Oh, well, happy birthday," she said, not realizing this was a birthday party as well. "I honestly didn't know," she apologized in turn.

"Ah, you must be here for the... other event then," he said.

"I am," she nodded. "My friends and I have come a long way."

"Then I hope you are not disappointed." he smiled.

"Honestly, even if it doesn't work out, being here made the trip worth it. This place is amazing," she said.

"I'm glad you're enjoying yourself then," he replied with a grin.

"Very much so," Tursanay smiled. She introduced herself.

"I'm Prince Kyoden," he greeted back.

"Nice to meet you, Prince Kyoden," she said, trying not to panic that she was having a conversation with an actual Prince.

"Call me Kyo," he winked. Tursanay couldn't suppress the smile very well that threatened to spread across her face just then.

"Kyo it is. How old are you turning, Kyo?" Tursanay asked.

"Nineteen," he said. "Where are you from?" he asked.

"Uh," she hesitated, trying to remember the name of the place Soren gave. "Fayd Morn," she added quickly.

"That is a way," Kyoden agreed. "I've never met someone from so far out in the country.

"I've never met so many different types of crea- ah- people before either," she replied, correcting herself from calling them creatures, as that could come across as offensive.

"It's like a different world, isn't it?" Kyoden grinned.

"You have no idea," Tursanay laughed.

"Prince Kyoden," came another voice. They turned to see a satyr emerge from the party carrying two scrolls on a platter.

"Udo," greeted the Prince.

"My Prince, there is a message for you," he said, then looked at Tursanay. "And if this is Lady Tursanay, then I have one for her as well."

"I am," she nodded. He handed each of them the scroll and gave a quick bow. Tursanay struggled with the scroll for a moment before getting it open and read the contents.

"I have to go," Prince Kyoden said. He bid her farewell, and she opened her own scroll with some difficulty.

"I ah…" she began looking back up at the satyr. "I can't read this."

"It is a summons to the Dai-Nē ceremony, my lady," he replied, trying to hide the surprise in his voice.

With that, she gave a nod, and he added, "There's a map that'll lead you there. Just follow the yellow lines."

"Thanks," Tursanay replied. She pushed through the crowd to find the others running into Akram.

"There you are," Akram snapped. Something was off about her eyes, Tursanay noted, but she couldn't place exactly what. "Good, you intercepted the scroll. Find the others and round them up before they catch on. "

Before she could ask to catch onto what, Akram disappeared and left Tursanay feeling more confused than ever. She heard a voice behind her that sounded suspiciously like her own, followed by a curse. When she turned around, her eyes went wide.

She was staring at herself, speaking to Akram. They spotted her again, and she ran into the crowd.

Rodney ran for all he was worth through the crowd and into a series of halls. He did not know where he was going, but wherever it was, it was better than getting strangled by Tursanay with her arm on the wrong side. He ran down a few sections of halls before he came to an intersection where he saw Tursanay run out, this time with her arm on the correct side. But how could he be sure it was his Tursanay and not another duplicate? He had to think of a quick way to confirm it was her and not some random shapeshifter pretending to be her quickly and concisely without giving himself away in the process.

"Jackie Chan!" he shouted, pointing at her. She glanced behind her, bewildered for a second, and his heart dropped. Then something lit up in her face as she seemed to understand.

"Chadwick Boseman!" she shouted back. So, apparently they'd found her too. Relief flooded through Rodney.

"Oh, thank goodness," he sighed. "I just got strangled by your twin, but they had your arm on the wrong side."

"Yeah, that's who I'm running from. Her and Akram. Quick, we gotta hide," Tursanay said, grabbing Rodney and ducking into a room. She quietly shut the door behind them and waited until they heard someone run past the door, talking amongst themselves. There was silence for a few moments and Tursanay let out a breath she'd been holding. "When I met up with Akram, there was something off about her eyes. She told me to intercept the others before they realized what was happening, but before I could ask her what she meant, she disappeared into the crowd. Then when I heard a curse behind me, I turned around and there was my double you mentioned. I ran as quickly as I could."

"Yeah, I would have given myself away instantly when she told you to intercept the others," Rodney shook his head. "I would have had the dumbest look on my face."

"It's a good thing your friend seems very astute," came a voice from behind them.

"Aww man, not again," Rodney said, turning.

There, sitting in a chair and drawing, was a lovely girl with long dark locks and soft brown eyes. She bore a remarkable resemblance to the prince Tursanay had met earlier, and she had a very regal air about her.

"You're one of the royals, aren't you?" Tursanay guessed.

The girl smiled.

"You really are very astute. I am Princess Mira," she said calmly, as if she hadn't just had two strangers duck into her drawing room to hide.

"Royals?" Rodney repeated, paling.

"Sorry, ma'am," Tursanay gave a quick, polite duck of the head as a bow. "We didn't mean to intrude."

"Who were you running from?" she asked as she set her sketching tools down.

"Honestly, we don't know. We just know they're hostile," Tursanay replied.

"Probably bounty hunters then," Mira replied. "What are you wanted for?"

"We're... still unsure about that too," Tursanay replied.

"Apparently we're wanted for treason? But all we've done is travel and eat food and travel some more, so I don't understand what we did wrong?" Rodney piped in, making Tursanay wince. It wasn't good to tell a future ruler that you had a wanted poster for treason over your head, but here they were. This statement earned a small laugh from the Princess.

"Are you here for the Dai-Nē trials?" Mira asked, mirth shining in her eyes.

"We are," Tursanay nodded, confused. "And we're trying to find our friends."

"Any chance you could help us out?" Rodney asked.

Amara looked at the map in the scroll and turned it a different way, then completely upside down.

"Yeah," she sighed. "I'm lost."

She looked up in time to see Akram run past and call out to her.

"Carla! Go to the western tunnel! We'll corral them into the major intersection and surround them!" And with that, she turned, without a second glance, leaving Amara floating there in a daze.

"Wh...?" she began, then sighed and shook her head. "Yeah, okay, whatever you say, lady." She threw her hands up and picked a hall at random.

She made it about halfway down the hall before she heard something behind her. She turned to see a girl with dark locks emerge from a room and motion for her to come, before taking another glance around the hall. Amara looked over her shoulder, then back at the girl, and followed her into the room.

"Are you Amara?" she asked.

"Yes," Amara replied with uncertainty.

"You must come with me. Your friends are waiting for you. The Council is about to assemble. You must go quickly," she said. As she spoke, she ushered Amara over to the fireplace and crawled into it. She pushed against the back wall and it gave way, sliding easily aside. "Here is a passage that will lead you safely to your friends. They are waiting for you. I have given them further directions on where to go from there. Lady Akram and the general will wait in the gathering place. Now, go before they come in here."

"Wait, but who are you?" Amara began as the girl pushed her into the passage and began closing it behind her, leaving her in total darkness.

"Your friends will explain," came the muffled voice on the other side. "Follow the tunnel!"

Amara tried letting her eyes adjust to the dark, but even after a few minutes, she still couldn't see a thing. She felt for a wall to her right, shaking with the effort to move. Amara hated the dark. Night was okay when you had the stars, but pitch black was awful. She stood trembling and felt along the wall. She had traveled for some time, feeling carefully with her hands, when she noticed her tail scrape across what must have been a set of steps in the dark. Had she been walking or in her chair, she would have gone tumbling forward and onto the ground.

She ran into something and sent what sounded like a person tumbling down said stairs. The person yelped in surprise, scaring her into yelping in return as she pressed against the wall, and didn't dare make another peep as she heard them groan when they reached the bottom of the short set of steps.

"Who is there?" the person demanded, trying to sound confident, but was clearly just as surprised as Amara.

"S-Soren?" said Amara, relieved.

"No, I am Soren," he replied defensively.

"No, I know it's you, I'm just relieved it wasn't someone else," Amara replied.

"Amara, is that you?" he asked.

"Yes," she replied. "Sorry for knocking you over. I can't see anything."

A brief silence.

"Do you know which direction you came from?" Soren asked.

"Yeah, why?" asked Amara. So far, it had only been a one-way tunnel. She hoped it didn't have more directions.

"I... am..." he hesitated. "Lost."

"Yeah, it's pretty dark in here," Amara agreed. "You haven't come across other tunnels, have you?"

"No, I just got turned around and subsequently—" he stammered.

"Yeah, no, all good," she said, recognizing his defensive tone again. "I just wanted to make sure we didn't have to worry about other pathways." Amara nodded, then realized he couldn't see her. "Here, grab my hand if we can find each other."

After several seconds, and Soren stepping on her tail fin a few times, they linked hands and continued down the tunnel together. It was much less scary to travel in darkness with someone by your side than it was completely alone. It was several moments of comfortable, if not slightly confused, silence as they made their way further down the tunnel and realized they could start making out shapes.

"Hey, I think there's a light up ahead," Amara said, breaking the silence after what seemed like an eternity. They emerged into a small, lit room where Rodney and Tursanay were standing there talking to each other next to a small bench. "Hey!" Amara greeted, relieved.

There was a moment of hesitation where fear crossed both her friend's faces.

"Bruce Lee!" Rodney exclaimed, pointing at her.

"Angela Bassett!" Tursanay said, backing him up.

"Uh... Hugh Jackman?" Amara replied uncertainly. "Why are we naming famous actors?"

"Amara!" they exclaimed, relieved, moving over to hug her.

"Wait-wait-wait-wait-wait how do we know that's Soren?" Rodney said, backing up.

Tursanay looked at him confidently. "In what way did we all greet you when we first met you? Show don't tell."

Soren hesitated a moment, then reached out and poked her on the arm. Amara let out a small laugh.

"Was that wrong?" Soren asked, flushed.

"No, no, that was what we did," Tursanay grinned. "And it tells us exactly what we needed to know."

Amara looked around the room, but saw no other way out than the way they came. "Sorry to derail this conversation, but which way do we go from here?" she asked. "I don't see any other doors."

"We go up," said Tursanay.

"Up?" Amara repeated, looking up along with Soren.

"Yeah, there's a loose tile in the floor above us. We'll come out behind some tapestry apparently," Tursanay replied. "At least that's what Princess Mira said."

"Princess? Was that who that girl was?" Amara asked. "Why was she helping us?"

"Apparently this sort of thing happens a lot? Where people come to see if they're Dai-Nē to get pardoned? But they try to get here before the bounty hunters get them - which is apparently who is after us - and sometimes they make it and sometimes they don't. So far, they haven't found the Dai-Nē, so most of them get caught, regardless."

"Oh, fun and she just helps these people?" Amara asked.

"She only helps the ones who are honest about why they are here," Tursanay answered. "Thanks to Rodney's blabbermouth, we actually got her to help us. Apparently, her power is being able to tell when someone is lying and when they are telling the truth."

"Sweet," Amara replied. "I wish I had that kind of power."

"One of us might just get it if we can get to this Dai-Nē thing," Rodney added.

"Right," Tursanay remembered. "We were just discussing how we could get up there. Who's the tallest?" she asked.

"I can literally fly up there and you and Soren can help boost Rodney up and we can pull you and Soren up once we get up there," Amara replied.

"Oh dude, that's perfect," Rodney agreed. They set to work on their plan and, after a bit of a struggle, they were up and out and peeking around the tapestry to see if anyone else was looking for them. There at the end of the hall was a guarded door. They walked up to the guards, who then stopped them.

"Go play somewhere else, children," the first guard said. "This is no place for the likes of you."

"Then it's a good thing we're not here to play," Tursanay replied, holding up her scroll. He took the scroll, examined its contents, took out a knife and slashed it, then, once satisfied, he handed it back to her. The other guard opened the door, and she started in. The others followed, but they were blocked.

"Scrolls," said the guards. The others produced their scrolls one by one, and the guard did the same procedure to each of them before letting them through. They walked down the dimly lit hallway until they came to a set of stairs that opened up into a large room, lit by enormous chandeliers that glowed as if they were lit by a fire, but there was no flame inside. They looked down the stairs to see a gathering of nearly a hundred or more people. Some entered from three other wall length stairways that led down to the main area. In the center of the room was a white stone pedestal. Its broad base held an equally broad oval with several grey stones with seven smaller stones framing each. Above the pedestal, floating in the air, were several orbs of different colors. Upon closer inspection, they were gems, glowing with an inner fire. An opal looking one, an amber colored one, a purple one, a white and black stone, a sky blue, and a green stone. Tursanay named them all off, wondering just what they were and why they were floating there.

Everyone in the room gave the pedestal a wide berth and gathered in groups to talk in undertones. The four looked at each other as if expecting the other to know what to do next.

"Should we go down?" asked Rodney, stating the obvious of what everyone was thinking.

"We need to look for Akram and Tryn," Amara said.

"Oh yeah," Rodney remembered. They looked amongst the crowd below as if they would materialize out of nowhere.

"Um, maybe we should go down there," suggested Tursanay.

"Or we could... wait for them to find us?" Rodney suggested. "Looking for someone didn't turn out so well for me last time."

He rubbed his throat, and Amara gave him a questioning look, but he just shook his head.

"Alright, let's just start down and stay together," Tursanay decided with a sigh. "We can't stay up here forever. People will stare."

She started marching, and the others followed like little chicks, not wanting to be left behind by their mother. They looked through the crowds for nearly ten minutes when Akram and the General found them and revealed their scrolls. The group told them what had happened since their parting and how they got there and of the guards at the door.

"Bounty hunters?" Akram looked at the General accusingly. "So that's what you were worried about."

"I told you parting was a bad idea and that they should have stayed in the rooms," Tryn replied indignantly.

"That's probably the first place they looked. I guarantee that when we get back, someone will have ransacked our rooms. They probably found the wanted posters in your bag, confirming their presence here," Akram replied. She turned back to the others when the general refused to take responsibility for putting the group in extra danger. "It was very brave of Princess Mira to help you. We should thank her when next we meet. As for the guards, they were checking to see if the scrolls were shapeshifters in disguise. The only way to do that is to cut it. The shapeshifter will bleed when cut, whereas the scrolls would not. It's why we had you meet in our room. The General and I checked our room for anyone listening in," she added.

The man standing beside the stone pedestal captured everyone's attention, causing the murmuring of the crowd to fall silent. He spoke slowly and precisely so that everyone could hear him.

"Alchemy, Ether, Element, Shapeshift, Light magic, Dark magic, and Sight," the last of the man's words hung heavy in the thick silence. "Never before has there been a summoning quite like this one." He placed his hand on the pedestal. "We have come together from the four corners of our world and beyond, seeking the knowledge that was lost to us nearly one score ago. The Seer had been murdered and the Dai-Nē children were scattered abroad and thrown into hiding." His eyes scanned the crowd. "There are fifty members of the Council present that represent each power under the seven divisions."

Behind the speaker, a group formed. The fifty members of

the Council descended the stairs directly behind him and stood in a square formation. They wore ceremonial robes and the lights from the room flickered across their faces in an almost menacing light. The room was deathly silent.

"They are the masters of their arts," the speaker continued. "And are prepared to teach the Dai-Nē if found, all that they know. Therefore, we have gathered here today. Somewhere amongst you could be standing some of the lost Dai-Nē."

The crowd had become tense. Some glanced at one another, their long history of rivalries showing between their glares. Each one daring the other to make a move.

Four children shifted uncomfortably.

"Some may not have been found yet," he said in a reasoning tone. "But with strength we move on, with courage we continue our search, and with faith we continue to work towards a better future," he shifted and straightened then, gesturing towards the pedestal. "What you see before you is a stone pedestal which harbors the powers of the Dai-Nē once they have passed from this world, and relinquished the title of Dai-Nē. In the past, when the old Seer told us the name and location of the next generation of Dai-Nē, we brought them here once they became of age and awakened their powers. From there, we trained them for years in order to gain the skills to protect our world. That is not how it shall be this time, however. Since the Seer was killed before he could find his successors, we scattered the located Dai-Nē for protection. Today, this pedestal will tell us which of you are Dai-Nē and which of you are not." He walked a few paces away from the pedestal. "For the past three generations of Dai-Nē, I have begun the ceremony. But now that I am moving on in years, I fear I will not see another generation of Dai-Nē. So, this year, I will step down and pass to my successor the honor of leading this ceremony. Please acknowledge my son, Prince Kyoden, who has, as of today, become of age. May his reign be long and prosperous!"

A respectful cheer rose to greet the Prince as he came and stood aside his father and addressed the crowd.

"That must be Lord Xeshin," Akram murmured to the four of them. "He is the leader of the Council and of all of Delmar."

All eyes fell on the Prince.

All but two.

Rodney looked around curiously at all the faces in the crowd until he saw a pair of eyes staring at him. Recognizing the fake Akram instantly, panic rose in his throat as he tapped Tursanay on the shoulder and pointed them out. The bounty hunters started making their way towards them.

"So, without further ado," the Prince's words rang out over the crowd, catching their attention. "Please separate into the two groups I have asked: candidates and caravans."

The crowd moved, and a look of annoyance flashed across the face of the lead bounty hunter. They lost sight of their prey again and had to join the caravan group, which was heading in the opposite direction their prey had gone. Once the crowds had settled, Prince Kyoden addressed the candidate's side, which had decreased by more than half the original size of the crowd.

"Would the first seven candidates please step forward?"

There was a slight hesitation, then a few near the front stepped forward. Two seemed eager to best one another in most every move they made, shouldering one another as they reached the pedestal. They stood on opposite sides to face one another as other candidates filled in the gaps between them. They stared one another down smugly.

"I will not lose to you, Saaken," the first one said.

"Nor I to you, Ablos," replied Saaken, meeting Ablos's gaze.

"It comes down to this," Ablos said.

"May the best man win," agreed Saaken.

"You're not the only ones with much at stake over this," said a man beside them. He looked haggard, scarred, and as if this were his last hope on earth. There was a glint in his eye that said he would survive this or die trying. The other two frowned at him, then squared their shoulders and looked at one another again.

"Candidates!" called the Prince. "Please place your hand on the stone plates before you."

Slowly, one by one, each placed their hand on the smooth gray stone plate, framed with small stones of the same dull gray. When all hands were touching the pedestal, it came to life.

From the flat top of the pedestal, the seven colorful orbs rose and circled above it in a hazy, dim light. The once gray stone plates glowed white beneath their palms. All eyes stared, transfixed by the floating orbs. A man standing at the forefront of the caravan crowd smirked as the orbs circled before the candidates.

The stone plates grew dull and lifeless once more and the orbs began freely floating, no longer circling. The smirk fell from the man's face.

"Thank you, my friends, but please step away from the pedestal. You are not Dai-Nē," announced Prince Kyoden.

"What!" came a sharp voice from the crowd. The man from the caravan crowd stepped forward and marched with cane in hand in front of the Prince. "What is the meaning of this?" he demanded.

"It means, good sir," replied the Prince steadily. "That amongst these fine candidates, however strong or powerful they may be, there is not one Dai-Nē. If you have a problem with this outcome-"

"Yes, I have a problem with this outcome! It's not the correct one! Try it again! I have not labored for years to train that boy to be anything less than a Dai-Nē!" the man exclaimed.

"Then I am afraid your labors have been in vain, for he is not Dai-Nē. The pedestal has proven that."

"Then it's wrong," the man with the cane growled.

"No no no," the shouts from the pedestal caught their attention as two bounty hunters set in on their prey. The scarred and desperate looking man backed away in panic as they lashed out at him with chains. "NO! It was a misunderstanding! Let me try again, please! I have to be a Dai-Nē! I have to!"

The bounty hunters tied him in chains and gag him before saluting to the Prince and marching their way back out of the steps. They had what they came for and didn't need to stick around for any more. That was just poor sport for the other hunters. A thick silence hung in the air as the man's muffled screams disappeared into the distance.

"As you can see, my good sir. It is not the abilities that make one a Dai-Nē, but what you are born with," the Prince stated firmly. "That is not something that can change. You do not command this court. You have no authority in this place and should not act as if you do. What the Council decides here is what happens." The Prince's voice was very stern and cold, commanding attention. "We will lay laws that will ensure we live in peace. We swiftly deal with those who disturb the peace. If you continue causing this ruckus, we will consider you a disturber of the peace and take action. Do I make myself clear, sir?"

The man looked at Lord Xeshin, his jaw muscles flexing. When the Lord gave him no response, he glared harder.

"Transparently," he managed at last. "Saaken! He called, still glaring. "We are leaving." And with that, he turned and strode up the stairs, calling once more for his protégé to follow.

Saaken turned and glanced at Ablos with a grin. "This isn't over, brother," he called.

"I would be disappointed if it were," Ablos replied. Saaken turned and followed his master out of the room.

"Will the remaining former candidates please step away from the pedestal so more may come forth?" stated Prince Kyoden. His calmer voice returned once everything had settled. Those remaining at the pedestal joined their groups in the caravan crowd. Seven more candidates came forward, and they repeated the process. When they placed their hands on the stone plates, the glow returned and the glowing orbs in the center swirled about as if seeking their new host. Yet, once again, there were no Dai-Nē amongst the seven. A third group came and went with the same results, and one candidate ran up the stairs and out of the room sobbing, followed by their caravan calling after them. The remaining candidates in the crowd grew anxious, and fewer and fewer volunteered to go forward.

Rodney, Amara, Tursanay, Soren, and Tryn all stood together amidst the diminishing crowd, watching as another group of people got sent away or carried away by bounty hunters - all with the same results: no Dai-Nē. They glanced over the caravan crowd and quickly found Akram. She gave them a confident look and a nod of reassurance.

"Next seven candidates, please step forward!" called the Prince. This time there were no volunteers at all, and the guards began picking people one by one to go up to the pedestal. One girl shoved her way through the crowd, as if late to the proceedings, and marched her way up before the guards could pick a seventh member. She placed her hand on the pedestal and waited for the others to do the same, as if impatient to get this over with.

When the others joined her, the orbs spun around again and one dove down into the pedestal and disappeared. The girl lurched back and held up her hand. There, on her palm, was the bright blue stone surrounded by the mark of the Dai-Nē: the symbol of the many eyed seraphim.

"Congratulations! We have our first Dai-Nē!" The crowd erupted in a mix of cheers and outrage. Now the stakes were getting higher. "If you would please step up here and join us on the stand, we will try to find more!" But even as he said it, it still took several minutes to calm the crowd down.

Beside the four, two folks, who looked to be related, eyed the pedestal wearily and one let out a small curse.

"Looks like we'll have to go up," the female one said.

"Looks like it," agreed the male.

"You see this going well at all?" the female asked.

"Everything goes black once I touch the pedestal," he replied.

Another curse.

"Guess it's our turn," Rodney sighed. He, Amara, Tursanay, Soren, and the two siblings looking duo from before stepped forward slowly, parting the sparse crowd and standing around the pedestal. Tryn squared her shoulders and marched up with the group. She marched up as smartly as the first Dai-Nē had and placed her hand on the pedestal, waiting for the others to join her.

When the prince raised his hand to gesture for them to put their hands on the pedestal, a cry from the caravan crowd grabbed their attention.

"*Stop!*" a woman called. Three people emerged, two women and a man.

"What are your reasons for stopping this?" Prince Kyoden asked.

"Four of them have a bounty on their heads," declared the head woman, standing between the other two.

"So have many others that have come forward. What makes this time any different?" the Prince inquired.

"They have a bounty even the Council cannot ignore. One of treason of the highest degree," came the reply. "We intend to collect on it."

"You cannot and will not do so here. This is the Council of Dai-Nē and as such we have the authority to remove said bounty if necessary in order for the Dai-Nē, should they be such, to receive proper training," Lord Xeshin interjected, irritated with the outburst.

"We want that bounty, Lord Xeshin," the woman snarled.

"Then," Prince Kyoden replied. "If they are not Dai-Nē, you shall have it. If they are Dai-Nē, you shall not."

"It's a hefty bounty, and we won't give up so easily," the woman warned. "Someone will pay for their heads."

"What are the odds all four are Dai-Nē after the results we have had today?" someone from the crowd complained. "Just get on with it!" A round of agreement rose and the bounty hunters booed back into submission.

The four treasonous children with bounties on their heads

glanced at one another nervously. A few of them had turned considerably pale. A lot more now weighed on whether they were Dai-Nē than just getting away from some unknown shadow creatures.

"Please place your hands on the pedestal!" Kyoden called once more.

The entire room held its breath as slowly, one by one, they put their hands on the stone plates. A bounty of treason would be one hell of a payoff and would be an interesting showdown. But if one of them were Dai-Nē, what would happen? The plates glowed brightly, and the orbs circled. The air itself felt electrified, if not from the stakes, then from the powers that pulsed before them.

They could each feel the crackle as they reached for the plates on the pedestal. Could feel it tingle up their hands and down their spines. The pulse of their hearts pounded in their ears and deafened the room. Whatever Lord Xeshin and Prince Kyoden were saying seemed completely drowned out now. It was them and the pedestal now.

As their hands touched the plates on the pedestals, the orbs sped up, then all six of the remaining ones shot back down as the first one did, and up the various arms of those standing around it. An electrical light shot out of six of the plates and up the arms of those whose hands rested there. All of them pulled away with a shout of alarm, and three of them fell on the ground, having lost their balance.

There was a long moment of silence as the crowd registered what happened. Even Prince Kyoden stood transfixed for a moment before shaking himself out of his reverie.

"Congratulations! We have found all the Dai-Nē!"

A roar rose from the crowd. Some of it cheer, some of it out rage, all of it chaos. The authorities quickly barred the crowds away from the Dai-Nē to prevent them from storming the group.

"Wait! Which of us are Dai-Nē?" the raven-haired woman asked.

"There will be a mark that bears the stone of Dai-Nē. This not only marks you as Dai-Nē but tells you which one you are," Prince Kyoden replied over the roar of the crowd.

"Where is the mark, exactly?" Tursanay asked with an edge of nervousness in her voice.

"It varies from person to person. Some have it on their hands, some on their chest or shoulder. Some on their legs or other places."

"Other places," muttered Tursanay, looking around for her mark.

"It's a black stone on the back of your shoulder, T," Amara said as Tursanay pulled back her sleeve with her teeth and could just barely make it out. "Do you see one on me?" she asked. Tursanay helped her get her back facing the room and checked under her shirt but found nothing. When Amara turned back around and opened her mouth to say something, Tursanay noticed it at last.

"It's the opal colored one on your tongue," she replied. "Easy to conceal if you need to," she added in a whisper.

"Great," Amara said sarcastically.

"You have the white one on your back between your shoulders, dear sister," said the man from earlier that joined the group. He muttered it low so the others wouldn't hear, but Amara and Tursanay overheard.

"Mine is on the back of my hand," Soren replied. "The green one."

"Mine's on my foot," the man muttered to himself. "The purple one. Only, it looks like half of it's missing?"

"I don't see mine anywhere," Rodney said. He was bent over, looking at the bottom of his feet.

"Nor I," Tryn said, all but stripping down.

"Uh Rodney," Amara said, pointing at him. "You have one."

"What?" he and Tryn asked simultaneously.

Rodney straightened. Then he narrowed his eyes. "Where?" he asked suspiciously.

"Right above your butt on your lower back," Tursanay answered.

"Excuse me?" Rodney asked indignantly. "You're saying I have a tramp stamp?"

"But that means," Tryn said hesitantly. "That's all seven... there must be a mistake. I'm supposed to be a Dai-Nē! I built my career off of it! That one day, I would have the ultimate power through alchemy!" She looked around at the others. "Which one of you? Which one of you has my stone?"

"Uh... which stone is the one for alchemy?" Rodney asked, praying it wasn't his.

"The amber one!" Tryn said, staring down at the girls.

"Please tell me mine isn't brown," Rodney begged hoarsely.

"Yeah, it's amber," Tursanay said.

"I have a brown tramp stamp," Rodney repeated, closing his eyes with a sigh. "Because of course I do."

"You can always conceal it with makeup?" Tursanay suggested weakly.

Tryn's face seemed to reflect the broken emotions running through her. Denial had been first when she couldn't find her mark, followed by anger at the others for stealing it. Then she seemed to skip right past bargaining and straight to depression when Rodney said it was his, for how could one take the power of Dai-Ne from another? It was simply impossible. Now the look slowly coming across her face wasn't exactly acceptance as she closed her eyes, took a deep breath and let it out slowly.

"Well," she said, straightening up and clearing her throat. "Obviously if it couldn't go to me, it had to pick the next best candidate. I suppose we met Rodney because I was destined to help train you. As the best alchemist in the world, I think I can accept this honor graciously." She had circled back to denial.

"That was a quick recovery," Tursanay muttered to herself as she watched the scene unfold.

"Time to make our exit," Keir said under his breath as the others had become distracted, either controlling the crowds or figuring out which Dai-Nē they were. Quickly they shuffled into the crowd that was raging and suddenly the ground shook and the people shoved up the steps which had slackened into a slope, and out the doors on every side. The twins with them. The doors shut firmly, leaving only Akram, who'd made her way over to the five of them before the others were taken away, and the Council themselves.

"Thank you, Master Loki," said Prince Kyoden, giving a nod. "Now that we have our Dai-Nē, there is no need to deal with the crowds." He turned to the others. "Dai-Nē," called to get their attention. "Please step forward so we can-" he stopped. "Where are the other two?"

The others looked around curiously.

"Uh, they were just here," Rodney said.

"Guards," Lord Xeshin barked. "Locate them and bring them back here. We can't lose them again." A group of guards were admitted through the doors before they were shut behind them.

"You," Prince Kyoden barked, pointing to Akram. "You are not one of the final candidates. Who are you?"

"I am their caravan," Akram replied confidently. "But there is a reason I stayed behind. I have pertinent information the Council needs to hear."

"Go on," Prince Kyoden sighed.

She gestured to each of them and said, "A fortnight ago, my husband's cousin, Soren, brought these three children to me." "Soren single handedly, armed with only a small amount of information and a portal knife-" a murmur ran through the crowd of Council members and Akram had to raise her voice to be heard. "Went and retrieved these Dai-Nē and brought them to me for help," she said. "Under ordinary circumstances, I would have responded to some strangers knocking on my door and claiming to be Dai-Nē by slamming the door in their faces."

"And what was different this time?" Prince Kyoden asked, disinterested.

"When they told me their story, they told me who sent them," she continued. "Asher."

Another murmur ran through the crowd.

"You have spoken with Asher?" asked Ansari, one of the elder looking members with a bald head and a long goatee.

"What news do you bring of him? Speak!" demanded another.

"He is alive?" came another voice.

"He-he died," Amara spoke out, looking like she'd rather crawl under a rock right then than face these people. But she had to say it. The guilt weighed too much on her mind. The murmurs died down again, and she found her voice once more. "He died trying to protect us."

"So, he has finally met his end, then," said Master Ansari solemnly.

"He died protecting the Dai-Nē... Let us honor his soul and let his spirit give all of us new strength. Let it be a testament to each of us," called another member, and a round of agreement rose from the Council members.

"Asher was missing," Lord Xeshin spoke up. "Where did you find him?"

"He found us actually," Amara replied. "And brought us together."

"That brings me to my statement," Akram spoke up. "When Asher found them, he was undercover in a place we thought did not exist… The Mortal World."

Murmurs and gasps filled the room, rising to shouts and questions as the room broke into another fit of chaos. The guild members had broken ranks. Some were discussing things amongst themselves, others were rushing down the steps to surround the children and ask them questions, pulling at their sleeves, reaching out just to touch them and see if they were real or any different. Prince Kyoden and Lord Xeshin tried to call and yell for order, but the crowd drowned their voices out. Some of the guild members were trying to help control the crowd, but to little avail. Then the ground shook beneath them and lifting the Dai-Nē children and their guardian into the air on an earth pedestal with gates surrounding them to keep them safe from those below and Prince Kyoden yelled at the top of his lungs for order and finally things seemed to settle down.

"Thank you, Master Loki, again for your assistance," Prince Kyoden said, rubbing his throat. "Back to your ranks, all of you!" he scolded. "That is not how members of the

Council of Dai-Nē are to behave!" The Dai-Nē safely put back on the ground. "Now," Kyoden huffed. "Begin at the start."

And so, they told them everything. From Asher and Soren's first contact, to the strange dreams Amara had. How they switched the dreams around and came to meet Soren and the strange happenings between then and now with the mirrors and the shapeshifters. They were there for a solid hour, telling their story before every detail was gleaned from them. Once they finished, they asked about the switching of the dreams and subsequently the powers, from Soren's theory, and told them about Rodney's ring.

"You lost the ring to this shapeshifter?" a Council member exclaimed.

"No, I almost lost my hand to the giant dog with gnarly teeth," Rodney replied defensively. "She just so happened to grab the ring."

"Alright," Lord Xeshin declared before an argument could break out. "What is done is done. We will need to find that ring as soon as possible to keep it under protection. Something of that power can be dangerous in the wrong hands."

"Meanwhile," Prince Kyoden agreed. "You are to go to the training grounds to become fully fledged Dai-Nē."

"Wait, we have to what now?" Rodney repeated.

"We will train you in our special training grounds set aside for this moment," stated Kyoden. "We will train you to be fully fledge Dai-Nē by the end of a fortnight. There has been an attack on the Council and we fear they may be after the power of Dai-Nē. Mixed with what you have told us, we now believe them to can take it."

"That's impossible," Akram said, shaking her head. "There's no way to train them in that amount of time. We have to mount a defense-"

"Actually, they can be, and efficiently so, within three days," Lord Xeshin said.

Akram gave him a sharp look. "What are you suggesting? The amount of power something like that would take just for one day is immense, but three?"

"And now thanks to Attalira here," he said, gesturing to the girl that was declared a Dai-Nē first. "We have that kind of power. We have collected three heart stones."

"*Three?*" Akram shouted. "How long have you been preparing for this day?" she demanded. "You said you had only just received word!" she accused.

"I have been preparing since the day the last Seer was murdered and the other Dai-Nē were scattered into oblivion," Xeshin replied.

"You've spent nearly a score hunting down dragon kind and stealing their soul stones?" she balked.

"It was that or sacrifice the last remaining phoenix, but apparently Asher is already dead!" Xeshin snapped. "This was to save the lives of millions. Three lives are but a small price to pay for the safety of many."

"For protecting the world, Xeshin? Or for protecting you precious Council?" Akram countered. "That's what you truly fear: the Dai-Nē can function without a Council to guide them, but the Council are nothing without the Dai-Nē to look over. You fear a shift in your power status!"

Lord Xeshin roared a reply, and Akram growled one in response. The Dai-Nē and Tryn stood looking back and forth between the two, suddenly feeling forgotten.

"Any idea where this is going?" Amara asked.

"I'm not even sure where it began," Rodney replied.

"It seems they have a long history," Tryn commented.

Even the Council was arguing amongst themselves. Prince

Kyoden, who had been looking helplessly between the two, soon dropped his look of concern and replaced it with one of defeat. He moved to sit on the steps with a sigh and just waited for things to calm down. The noise was becoming louder and louder, and soon everyone was shouting to be heard.

"The dragons are going extinct and the soul stones are sacred to their kind!" Akram was saying as Rodney got fed up at last.

"Alright, that's it," he muttered, looking over at Tryn. "Can you use your powers to make a really loud noise?" he asked.

"My alchemy? Well, of course, but why?"

He used both hands to gesture to the Council vaguely.

"Ah, to get their attention." She gave a nod and pulled out a couple of crystals that lit up in her hands and cast a transmutation circle on the ground.

A large column shot up from the floor with a wide top and a very weak-looking base. Tryn gently nudged it and sent the thing careening to the ground, and with it created a loud thud that caught everyone's attention.

"*Listen!*" Rodney barked.

Tursanay put her hand to her chest as she watched him, surprised.

"What's done is done. Let's just get over it and move on. No, it probably wasn't right and there are going to be... consequences," he said, faltering slightly. "But I have been dragged across two worlds, chased by people and things that want to kill me, and now I have to sit here and listen to all of you bicker like children. I don't know all the circumstances of what's all wrong, but if it keeps me and my friends alive, right now I'm just going to go with it. I want to get this stupid thing over with so I can go home and pretend this was all one really weird, really long dream. *Okay*?" he huffed. "So, can we please just move on?"

There was a silence as everyone stared at Rodney, and suddenly he wished he hadn't opened his mouth.

"The boy is right," said someone at last. "What's done is done. We need to stop arguing over the past and begin planning for the future."

"Well said master Zhi," agreed Lord Xeshin. "And well said..."

"Rodney," he filled in.

"Well said Master Rodney," he continued. "It is time to begin preparations for departure," he addressed the room. "In two days, four dwarven ships will arrive and we will travel up river, over the Sarasul mountain range, and dock where the east road crosses the river. From there, we will travel to the wooded marshlands south of the river. In which lies the Oheqia: your training grounds." He looked down at the Dai-Nē. "Your trainers from the Council corresponding to your power will pair you."

"You may abide by this, my friends," Akram interjected. "But I cannot. I will take my leave of you here and if you should come to your senses and see the evil that resides in this choice, you can join me again. But I will not stand by and watch this."

"Thank you for bringing us this far," Soren said. "I understand your desire to leave and not be affiliated with this. I am afraid we have no choice. But I trust your judgment and will listen and watch carefully."

"That is all I can ask of you," Akram replied, smoothing his hair back. "Be careful, little cousin. We do not wish to lose you."

"Nor I you," Soren replied. With that, Akram turned and left, making her way up the steps and out the doors. When silence settled over the group, Rodney held up his hand.

"Um, hi, yes," he stammered. "Me again. Uh, how do we know which Dai-Nē is which exactly?"

"By the stones in your markings," Xeshin replied. "Each stone represents a different power."

"Mine is the black," Tursanay piped up.

"Then you are the Dai-Nē of Light Magic," he said. "You will have dozens of teachers to teach you each aspect of your power. However, your primary teacher will be Master Ross."

A man with cold piercing blue eyes lifted his chin to look at her. He leaned against his cane and said nothing.

"Mine is an opal looking color," Amara said.

"You are the Dai-Nē of Element," he answered. "Your teachers will be Loki, master of the art of earth; Yasar, master of the wind, Nuri, master of fire; Anan, master of water, and Nyx, master of plants."

"Mine is green," Soren said.

"You are the Dai-Nē of Ether," Xeshin answered.

"And I already know I'm the Dai-Nē of Alchemy," Rodney added. "What about her?" he pointed to the first Dai-Nē girl. She was rather short with black hair to her shoulders pulled back into a ponytail, and dark eyes and tan skin.

"I am the blue stone," Attalira answered. "The Dai-Nē of Shapeshift."

CHAPTER 13
OHEQIA

It was two long days of preparation before the dwarven ships arrived to take them to the training grounds. They measured and gave the Dai-Nē clothing they could wear for all occasions, including several for training. They carried them over their shoulders in bags of holding as they yawned and rubbed their eyes sleepily. It was barely light out and they'd spent most of the night fretting over what was to come. Since the last two Dai-Nē hadn't been located and only a portion of the Council members were coming with them.

"Attention everyone!" Lord Xeshin's voice rang out over the small, bustling crowd. "The ships are docked and being supplied as we speak. You shall depart shortly. We are going to disperse you between the four ships. There are forty of you, so ten per ship. This is just as much for safety as it is for spacial purposes." He continued to give them instructions on what was to come and other things before announcing that neither he nor his son would join them in the Oheqia. They would stay behind to help search for the remaining two Dai-Nē that had escaped them.

"There are only thirty-nine of us," Soren noted, looking around. "Thirty-four Council members and five of us Dai-Nē."

"Was there a question in there?" Rodney asked.

"Who is the fortieth?" he asked.

"Uh... maybe they rounded up? Or miscounted?" Rodney suggested. He wasn't sure why it was so important.

"Rodney my love!" Tryn chirped from behind them.

"Oh no," Tursanay and Rodney both groaned. Tryn came up behind Rodney and swept him into a hug, spinning him around. It was quite comical to see, as she was nearly a hand span taller than Rodney. Well, it would have been, had she not been so irritating to them.

"Is this not exciting?" she said happily.

"I thought they said you weren't Dai-Nē," Tursanay balked. "Why are you here?"

"What does that have to do with anything?" Tryn asked.

"Why are you coming then?" Tursanay asked, noting the bag over her shoulder as well.

"She got special permission to join you," came the reply as Xeshin walked over to them. "I think she has shown some rather important skills that could come in handy for you down the road, Master Rodney."

"I mean, will she really have time to fit in a lesson?" Tursanay asked. "It's not like we'll have time to learn much in three days."

"But you will have more than just three days where you are going," replied Xeshin. "The Oheqia is a special gate that once you pass through it slows down time inside of a small area designated for different terrain training. You will have several years of training in that time and only three days will pass for us."

"*Years?*" blurted Rodney, before covering his mouth. "Dude, I still gotta take physics next year at school - I'll forget everything I've already studied for it! I'll fail!"

"Rodney, you realize there's a slim chance of us getting back to Blemwick, right?" Tursanay said softly. A hush fell over the group.

"All our friends and fa—the people we knew," Amara said. "They'll just think we vanished." She had almost said family, but now none of them had family left to go back to. At least, not a family the state would let them go back to in Rodney's case.

"I know it's hard," Xeshin began.

"No, you don't," Amara snapped. "You haven't had your whole life turned upside down and inside out. You live in a comfortable castle where people cater to your every whim. Yeah, you stress about political stuff, but you don't know what this is like and don't you dare pretend you do."

Tursanay placed her hand on Amara's shoulder. "Amara," she began softly, but Amara pulled away with a shake of her head, moving to load up on the ship with some of the others.

"Your friend has a temper," Xeshin commented.

"She just lost her dad," Tursanay replied. "She's not been doing so well with it."

"My condolences," Xeshin replied. "I can understand a bit of her outburst now."

Tursanay only nodded.

"What I came to tell you is that you will have one of the Dai-Nē of Sight's trainers going with you to help in any way he can. Master Zhi is one of our senior members and has a great deal of knowledge he can pass on."

"Cool," Rodney muttered. "Maybe he can help me remember what I've learned in school."

"Really?" Tursanay asked. She cocked her eyebrow skeptically.

"I'm not giving up on going back. I'm just having a really long summer break," Rodney replied with a shrug, following Amara. Tryn watched him go and looked at Tursanay for a long moment, a frown creasing her brow, before following him silently.

"I hate being the bad guy," Tursanay muttered, letting out a long breath.

Once the ships got loaded and were ready to go, the Dai-Nē gathered in the middle ship, and their voyage began. Staying above deck and watching the scenery pass, the trio of Mortal World Dai-Nē watched curiously as a crew of very short men running around on deck called back and forth to each other and made the ship work like a well-oiled machine. All had beards of some sort, whether it was just stubble and scraggly to long and bushy. Some wore clothes on their heads to help tie back the mass of hair, others were lucky to find a thread of hair on their shiny, bald heads. They all looked like sea weathered men despite their current river journey.

Rodney looked at the other two. "I don't know if I should make a Lord of the Rings joke or a Pirates of the Caribbean joke."

"How about neither, you dork," Tursanay grinned, glad he was in the mood to joke with her again. She didn't want to be stuck in the funk she'd put them in for very long. Thankfully, Rodney was good at breaking the ice and bringing them back to normal. They wandered over to the railing and looked out at the beautiful mountain scenery passing by.

"You really do love those old movies. Things have been so hectic, I've barely had time to be homesick," she admitted.

"Maybe after we train, they'll let us actually go home," Rodney said hopefully.

Amara sighed. "I doubt it," she said, agreeing with Tursanay's earlier surmise. "I think they are setting us up for something."

"Well, apparently this whole Dai-Nē thing is a big deal to them," Rodney said.

"More than you know," came a bemused voice. They turned to see a man older than them, but not by much. Perhaps in his early twenties, at best. He wore his dark hair to his chin.

"Hello," Amara said timidly.

He smiled and nodded once. "Hello. I am Council Member Yasar. I am the wind elemental."

"Really?" Amara stammered. "I ah... They said I was the Dai-Nē of Element."

Tursanay elbowed her with a grin, and she shook her head back, trying to hide her blush.

He raised an eyebrow. "So, you are my student."

Amara turned another shade of red.

"Are there other elemental teachers here?" Tursanay asked.

"Yes, all of them," he replied. "Master Loki, Mistresses Anan, Nyx, and Nuri."

"Oh nice," Tursanay commented. "You all traveled together."

"We prefer it to traveling with the other factions of the Council. Our views differ from theirs and it starts political debates over nonsensical things."

"Oh," Tursanay nodded. "That I understand."

"Hey, are there any of my teachers here?" asked Rodney.

"There are only ten passengers per ship for space," Yasar replied. Rodney counted on his fingers the number of passengers mentioned. When he reached ten, he gave a nod as if he understood now, and Yasar suppressed a smile.

"Having trouble with those numbers, Rodney?" Tursanay teased.

"Shush, it's been a long week," Rodney replied with a grin.

"Try a month and a half," Amara corrected.

Tursanay made a noise of agreement, and Rodney leaned against the railing.

"Hey, I just noticed something," he piped up. "I'm not looking for a place to hide. Where's that General lady?"

"General Hartmut?" asked Yasar. "Escorted to another ship."

"Oh, thank goodness," Rodney sighed, relieved.

"Why do you say that?" Yasar asked.

"One," Rodney said. "She's scary - and not in the don't-tick-her-off way, though she's also that kind of person. If it was just that, I wouldn't mind. She just genuinely creeps me out. Two, she keeps... calling me 'my Rodney'? And like it's cool to be appreciated and all, but can she not?"

"Not what?" Yasar asked.

"Fawn over him like a lovesick puppy," Tursanay muttered loud enough for everyone to hear.

"Yeah, that," Rodney nodded. "Like no offense meant, I just can't handle being coddled like that."

"Glad for a moment of peace?" Amara grinned.

"Ugh, not quite peaceful," Rodney said, looking a little green in the face. "I think I'm getting seasick."

"Perhaps you should go down below deck, Master Rodney," Yasar suggested. "That may help."

"Anything to make this feeling go away," Rodney agreed.

"I'll go with you," Tursanay said.

"I will come as well," Yasar said. "I believe there are some herbs on board that can help."

Amara looked around at Soren. They were the only ones left on deck besides the crew. She wasn't sure where the shapeshifter Dai-Nē was, but she hadn't seen her since they all came aboard. She opened her mouth to ask Soren if he wanted to go below deck as well, but he cut her off.

"I need to speak with you," he said in a low voice.

"Is everything okay?" she asked just as quietly.

"I am uncertain," he replied. "I overheard something at the Council and I fear it may be important for the others to know as well."

"What did you hear?" Amara asked in a quiet voice, checking to see if anyone nearby could overhear them. She wasn't sure how good a dwarf's hearing was, but she hoped it wasn't good enough to hear them from where they were.

"Some of it made little sense, but I think you are right in that the Council is setting us up for something much bigger than this. There was talk of combining our powers and a ring. I do not know if they meant the same one we lost, but something I heard makes me think it was and that the shapeshifter responsible for biting Rodney's hand and stealing the Ring of Rynon is working for the Council."

"What was it?" Amara asked.

"The way the woman said 'I almost had one, but he slipped through my teeth' makes me think..." Soren trailed off, not sure if he was just jumping to conclusions.

"That it's the same shapeshifter," said Amara, horrified.

She let out a small curse. "What else did you hear? Did you see what they looked like?"

"I did not. I only heard that they wish to combine our powers to exchange them with another wielder. And something about the Fae and their hold over them."

"The Fae?" Amara repeated.

"Yes. She said the Fae interfered, and the phoenix got in the way. Perhaps the same phoenix that the Council was speaking of?"

"Asher..." Amara murmured.

"Do you believe Asher was a phoenix?" Soren asked.

"I don't know," Amara said. "But it would make sense." Well, as much sense as any of this did in the long run, she thought to herself. "Do you think that invisible force that chased us was the Fae they were talking about?"

"Perhaps, but there is no way for us to confirm that," Soren said.

"Wait," Amara said. "We may be getting ahead of ourselves. You said only Dai-Nē can cross the Veil without issue, right?"

"Correct," Soren agreed. "As confirmed when we switched your powers back around."

"Then how can Fae get across the Veil to chase us?" Amara asked.

"The Fae are magical beings?" Soren asked.

"Yeah, there're all kinds of stories about them in our world," Amara replied. "Hm..."

"What?" Soren prompted.

"Our world isn't supposed to have magic, but we've seen evidence of it left and right still existing. The concealment spells, the speech spells, whatever was chasing us, I couldn't see."

"I believe the speech spell worked," Soren added, "because I made those myself."

"So, they were Dai-Nē made," Amara said. "So, you were right in that Dai-Nē and Dai-Nē spells can cross over the Veil?"

"That's what I've been told," Soren said.

"Tursanay is better at putting together ends like this," Amara sighed.

"What ends?" Soren asked, curiously.

"I was thinking of who could have been chasing us and who could have killed Asher. And I was wondering if they were the same people, or different."

"Perhaps we should see if the others know what we could be missing," Soren suggested.

"I think we're going to have to wait a while to bring it up to them. I don't think it's safe to talk around the Council members. To have them know what we know. We'll have to figure out a way to tell Tursanay and Rodney without being overheard," Amara said.

"How do you suggest we do that?" Soren asked.

"I hope they brought stuff to write with," Amara said. "Because I've got a long message to write."

"If you're so keen on keeping things from the Council," said a passing dwarf casually. "You need to learn which ones can hear you from a distance and which ones can't. There are elves on these ships, children. Be aware of that."

Amara flushed bright red at the passing dwarf. "H-how much did you overhear?" she asked.

"Enough to know you trust the Council about as much as we do," he said.

"So, you'll not tell them what we said?" Amara asked hopefully.

"If they didn't hear it themselves," the dwarf replied. "Then they should learn to listen better."

"Thank you," Amara said.

"I'm not doing it for you," the dwarf replied gruffly.

"I'm still grateful. For this and for the use of your ships," she added. "We wouldn't be this far without your help. So, thanks for that."

The dwarf eyed her for a moment.

"Hmph," he replied, walking off without another word.

The dwarves of the ship seemed hostile all day until that night, when the Council members were asleep. The five Dai-Nē were welcomed back above deck, where they found the crew singing around a fire in a large barrel. They passed around drinks that seemed to lighten their spirits, even though the captain supposedly did not allow alcohol on the ship.

They laughed and strummed away on their instruments, encouraging the children to join in the fun. Sometimes the dwarves would tell stories, others would suddenly burst into song, and the others would join him in the chorus.

"Sing with us!" one dwarf called to the children.

"Oh, we don't know the lyrics," Tursanay replied. "We're not from around here."

"Then sing us a song from where you're from!" suggested another. There was a round of agreement until the three of them exchanged looks, trying to think of a song they could sing.

Rodney started singing a random song that Tursanay recognized. The two of them joined in until they reached the chorus, and Amara finally recognized it too, and she joined in as well. When the song finally ended, a cheer went up and everyone drained their mugs.

"Now, that was some awful singing!" called the dwarf Amara and Soren had spoken to before on the deck. This time, he had a grin on his face to show he was kidding. "Where did you say you were from?"

"Oh, the ah, Mortal thingy - Mortal World," Rodney said before realizing he just blurted out something he wasn't supposed to. "Oops... I don't think the Council wanted us to tell people that..." A scowl crossed all the faces before them at the mention of the Council.

"Mostly," Amara interjected. "Because someone is trying to kill us, but we don't know who."

"Wouldn't surprise me if it was the Council themselves," one dwarf said and spat.

"Wouldn't surprise me either," Amara muttered.

"Do you trust the Council, lass?" one asked. It was the one she'd spoken to on deck before.

"I trust these three," she said, pointing to her companions. She turned to the Shapeshifter. "I don't know you yet, sorry."

"No offense taken. I don't trust you either," she said flatly.

"I'm Amara, by the way," she said, then introduced the others.

"Attalira," the shapeshifter replied with an inclination of the head.

"You're smart, lass," the dwarf continued. "Don't trust the government. They're only in it for themselves."

"Mm," Tursanay murmured in agreement, taking a drink of water.

"Oh my god," Rodney realized. "I missed a perfect opportunity to sing Far Over the Misty Mountains Cold from the Hobbit!" he added, smacking himself in the head.

Tursanay closed her eyes with a sigh. "Don't sing that. I will smack you."

"But," Rodney complained, gesturing and making noises. They're dwarves! This is a perfect chance! his motions conveyed wordlessly.

"I'm serious. I will smack you," Tursanay replied.

Rodney took a deep breath and let it out, trying to get rid of the urge to sing it anyhow.

"Man," Rodney mumbled. "And I really liked those old movies too."

The conversation shifted to tales and stories, and the group listened enraptured, until they were yawning and rubbing their eyes to stay awake. At last, the fun died down and the crew scattered to their positions and to bed for the night. The Dai-Nē went below deck to their assigned barracks and tucked in for the night.

"How did you get the dwarves to open up to you like that?" Yasar whispered, scaring the life out of Amara.

"What do you mean?" Amara asked, putting a hand on her chest.

"They never open up to strangers," Yasar said. "They're a tight-knit group."

Amara shrugged. "They just seem like good people to me? We just spoke to them normally."

"Strange," Yasar murmured before settling back into his covers. "Strange indeed."

The last thing they heard as they drifted off to sleep was the sound of the ship's creaking and the sound of quiet feet heading back up the stairs.

"Wake up Council! We're under attack!" yelled one dwarf from the stairs. The five Dai-Nē woke with a start to see all the Council members scrambling to get on deck.

"What's going on?" Tursanay asked.

Yasar, who was last and nearly up the stairs, jumped back down two and pointed at them. "All of you stay here. No matter what you hear, no matter what happens. Stay below deck and keep hidden," he cautioned. A thunder clap sounded overhead, and he turned back with a look of horror. "A sorcerer's storm..." he murmured. Turning back to the Dai-Nē, he gestured for them to stay silent. "Anything you say under the storm will give away your position and confirm you are here. Don't speak. Don't make a sound. Stay below deck - I'll try to divert the storm." And with that, he ran up the stairs with bare feet thudding against the wood like a racing heartbeat.

When he disappeared above deck, they could hear shouts and chaos ringing out above. Yasar's voice rose above the chaos, shouting orders. Suddenly, the boat lurched and groaned as it tilted dangerously to one side. The Dai-Nē went tumbling, involuntary noises of surprise escaping their lips. Above, as the ship righted itself, Yasar yelled more orders.

"Loki! Form an impenetrable barrier between them and us. Anon get those dwarves out of the water. Nyx! Turn the landscape against them. Nuri - destroy any more projectiles they launch at us. Dwarves!" His voice got louder for the crews. "I will give you a wind to push you forward and Anon will give you a swifter current. I need you to do what you do best and sail your ships out of here!"

A roar of acknowledgement came as everyone raced to do

their job. From below, where the Dai-Nē waited, the light that filtered through the cracks in the ceiling were suddenly shadowed by something that towered over the ships. High over. The sound of the wind whipping above them and filling the sails was almost as loud as the shouts of the dwarves as they organized their crews to sail the ships. Suddenly, the ship shot forward, and the Dai-Nē went sprawling again.

When Rodney could sit up and see Tursanay, he signed "What is going on?!" But before Tursanay could answer him, he turned a sickly color and ran to the nearest bucket, throwing up into it. All the motion was too much for him to handle. A voice seemed to answer from above as Yasar called to the captain.

"They will have lost us in a few minutes," he called. "The river splits in two ahead. We'll take the road to the east. They'll lose our trail there. They won't follow us until they finish fighting the land. Thank you, Mistress Nyx," he added. "And all of you - well done for putting up with me and my orders."

A few people laughed. The ship never slowed, and after a few moments, the Dai-Nē wondered if it was safe to emerge.

"He said no matter what we heard, but do you think it's safe now that it's all over?" Tursanay signed to Rodney.

He gave a shrug.

"I vote we stay put," Rodney signed back.

WHAM!

The ship shuddered to an abrupt stop, sending the Dai-Nē sprawling all over again like dice spilled from a cup. Rodney groaned an "Ow" as he hit the opposite wall of the ship, before he thought about keeping silent and thunder cracked overhead and lightning flashed. There was a hatch open above them and lightning struck down and formed into the shape of a white wolf before them, sitting down and lifting its head to howl. Thunder crashed again, masking the howl. It pulled its head back down and stared directly at Rodney, then in another flash, it was gone.

"Uh oh," Rodney said, realizing what he'd done. He smacked a hand over his mouth and felt the boat jostle so hard that he launched into the air and hit the planks below again with a thud and a scream. The other Dai-Nē weren't much better off being tossed about like a salad as well.

There were snarls above and laughter. Yasar yelled something incomprehensible as the sound of steel against steel rang out overhead, distorting his words. A roar of an angry lion sounded on deck and began running towards the hatch. One dwarf yelled for the hatch to be closed and suddenly the light from above became blotched out, save for the stairs that led on deck. There were shadows guarding the stairwell, and they flickered and danced as if there were firelight above as well.

When an explosion went off, Amara screamed, terrified, and curled into a ball to protect herself. Tursanay was doing her best to stand on her own two feet, but the turmoil of the ship that was now bobbing up and down like a lure in the water was making it impossible to get a purchase on the wood beneath her feet.

There was a struggle at the top of the stairs and suddenly three dwarves got shoved down below deck, bouncing down the stairs ungracefully and landing on the floor with groans; the air knocked out of one. As he struggled to breathe, another shadow descended the stairs and glanced around.

"Well, well, well," the figure said, grinning broadly and showing his fangs. "It looks like our precious cargo is alive. This will be interesting."

"Wh-what are you talking about?" Tursanay said, finally getting to her feet. Her nose was bleeding from slamming into the floor, and the stranger took one look at her and breathed in deeply.

"Oh," he sighed happily. "And such a rich scent you have. Perhaps I can have at least one of you as a snack."

Another roar sounded above as the fighting continued.

"Who are you? What do you want?" Tursanay demanded.

"Isn't it obvious?" laughed the stranger. "I'm obviously here to steal the precious cargo this ship holds. I'm a pirate, idiot," he explained as if to a small child. "Not a very bright snack, are you, my dear? Oh well, no need for my food to be intelligent. Sometimes it spoils the flavor."

"F-Food?" Amara squeaked.

The stranger looked down at her and flashed his fangs again.

"Oh, a mermaid," he said, curiously delighted. "We could collect your tears and sell them for a high price. I hope you don't like pain. It'll make it so much easier to extract your tears."

"You stay away from her!" Soren called, grabbing a nearby box and hurling it at the stranger.

Blocking it with little effort, the fanged stranger frowned at Soren.

"I don't like it when the treasure fights back. Be a dear and stop that nonsense," he said. "I don't want to break you to make you come along nicely, but I will."

"Are you a vampire?" Tursanay asked, putting two and two together.

"My, aren't we observant?" the stranger replied sarcastically. He blinked rapidly, as if trying to process why that wasn't obvious to begin with. Fangs, nighttime, the scent and sight of blood exciting him, and of course there was the fact he referred to her as food. "You children really aren't all that bright. Why were you considered precious cargo by the spell?"

"Wait," Rodney said, finally getting to his feet. "We're the precious cargo? I thought you were just going to rob us and be done—I don't want to be stolen food!"

"Such is life, I'm afraid," the vampire replied with a shrug. "Now line up like good little children and come to me." The last word he spoke became laced with some kind of spell that filled them with the urge to go towards him. They all picked themselves up or took steps in his direction as he hummed a tune that was both haunting and beautiful. It eased their fear and anxieties and brought them closer and closer to the vampire, who smiled and grabbed some nearby rope to tie them together as he continued to hum. The struggle of fear trying to fight its way out of their trance warred with the feeling of peace that eased them into a lull. Everything was fine—no, they were going to be kidnapped! —this would pan out fine—what if they were killed?— Nothing bad could happen. After all, they had a rope to secure them in place. That was a safe thing to have on a moving ship.

"Good, good," he said soothingly, tying knots around their wrists and waists. "Now follow me," he instructed. He went back to humming and led the children peacefully up the stairs and into the hellscape that was the deck. Like the Pied Piper singing his tune, he lead the children from the lower decks and into the fray above.

There were dwarves lying prone and fighting. There was a lion headed female attacking the crew. The council was fighting for all they were worth to free the ship from the iceberg that froze them in place, consuming half the ship. The plants, growing from the shore over to the ships, were fighting with the pirates and throwing a few overboard. Master Loki was the only one besides Nyx that could fight the pirates, while the other three were fighting the hold on the ship. Every time they'd make progress, more ice would grow and consume more of the ship.

Moving the children to the port side of the ship, the vampire waved for someone on shore to bring their ships closer. Yasar, panting as he stopped trying to drill a hole in the ice with his wind power, turned and noticed the Dai-Nē were being led away like little minions under a siren's spell. Yelling for the others to take notice, he stopped trying to fight the ice and started sending spirals of air to slice through the ropes holding them hostage. With a hiss and a glare, the vampire looked in his direction and grinned evilly.

Taking one of the Dai-Nē hostage—Amara, in fact, because she was the most valuable to him in that moment— he held a knife to her throat and glanced back at Yasar.

"Give me one and you can have the rest," he bartered, realizing he wasn't getting out of this with all of them. He checked for the ship coming closer and back to the wind user.

"No," Yasar yelled. "I will not give up my pupil!"

"That explains it: why the spell considered them your precious cargo. The sentimental value, of course!" His grin broadened. "I can trade in sentimentality."

"You will not be trading lives today," Yasar warned him.

The vampire glanced back over his shoulder; the rowboat getting closer.

"Perhaps," he hedged. "But you'll not endanger the lives of your precious pupil to stop me," he said.

"You're wrong," Nuri said behind him. He turned in

shock to see the fire wielder with a fireball in hand, throw the flames at him and catch him on fire. Hissing and screaming in pain, the vampire released Amara, who suddenly awakened from the trance she'd been in and yelped at the fiery being that was trying to put itself out behind her. Unable to douse the flames, the vampire fell overboard and turned to ash before he hit the water.

The dwarves ran the lion headed female off the ship and the other pirates, their plans having unraveled when the captain was murdered. When the pirates retreated, they could free the ship from the ice and set off again, the sun beginning to rise over the treetops.

"Who was that back there?" Tursanay asked. "Who attacked us?"

"They were some pirates that use that pass to ambush ships and travelers," Yasar replied.

"What was that weird hypnotizing thing they did to us? That was terrifying," Amara shivered.

"A vampire can control its victims like that sometimes. They can't make them do complicated tasks, but they can get them to follow them somewhere else," Yasar replied.

"It's creepy is what it was," Tursanay agreed with Amara. "Like I could feel myself wanting to go along and go with him. It was like it made everything make sense."

"It's most like that of a siren song," Yasar explained. "Rare is it, to find someone who can escape such a call. However, we escaped them and are nearly at our destination." It was an obvious change of subject, but they looked around at the change of scenery as the dwarves picked up their wounded and began the healing processes. The Dai-Nē got healed as well, given that they had gotten bashed a bit at the beginning of the fight when the ship was in tumult. When they weren't sore anymore, they stretched and moved around and helped around the ship until things calmed down.

"So, this place we are going to, what's it like?" Tursanay asked Yasar.

"You know as much as I," Yasar replied. "None of us have ever been there."

"Well, that was helpful," Rodney signed to Tursanay.

"Maybe that lady over there can give us some information," Tursanay signed back, pointing at a fiery-looking redhead with hair pulled back into a tight braid and icy blue eyes that pierced your soul. She dressed to the teeth in leather armor as if ready to fight at a moment's notice, but carried no weapons. She was an elf by the looks of it, and an intimidating one at that.

As if she'd understood what they were signing, the redhead turned her icy stare on them and they instantly knew she did not want to be disturbed. The scowl across her face even made Soren flinch.

"S-Sorry," Rodney muttered out of reflex. No reply came, just a turning of her head to look away. "She's scary," Rodney whispered to Tursanay.

"Glad she's not my teacher," Attalira muttered.

Amara questioned her life choices until this point, as she realized that was one of her teachers.

"Maybe they know," Tursanay said, pointing to a person with short, spikey white hair and a narrow frame, sitting on the railing with their legs crossed under them as if they weren't worried about losing their balance nor looked as if they'd just experienced a fight with pirates. They had the agility of a cat, and the friendly face that welcomed them over. Even their eyes were catlike, yellow and green with extremely narrow pupils.

The group of Dai-Nē made their way over to them and they gave a little wave.

"Hello!" they greeted. Their voice was light and lilting. "What brings you into my council?"

"Well," Rodney began nervously, casting a glance back at the red-haired elf. The gray-haired Council member caught the glance and chuckled.

"Do not fear, dear Nuri," they said. "She may not look inviting, but those who earn her friendship never lose its loyalty."

"Yeah, well, she's downright terrifying to a bunch of teenagers who do not know what they've gotten themselves into," Rodney replied. They all cast another glance in Nuri's direction in time to see her smirk.

"To those who have never met an elf that can bend fire to their will, Nuri can seem intimidating. Most elves have an affinity for ether styles of power. However, they all like to listen in secret to the fearful whispers of their victims to see if their private jest was of a desired effect," the white-haired Council member said, not looking at the Dai-Nē but calling to the elf.

Nuri frowned at her. "You have ruined my fun, Nyx," she said. "Things were going according to plan."

"But I have not gone according to plan," Nyx chuckled.

"Indeed, you never do," Nuri replied.

Nyx laughed again.

"All of you seem a lot nicer than I was expecting," Amara remarked. "I half expected the Council to be a bunch of grumpy old men who were more concerned with political status and power than anything else."

"Oh, there are those that are," Nuri added. "Especially in the magical divisions. But the younger members are more concerned with actually changing the world for the better than fitting into a corrupt system. The older generations don't like that and think we are ignorant because of it."

"Well, that's ridiculous. If you have the skills and the potential, you can be just as good as any of them. A lot of times even better," Amara replied.

"Ah man," Tursanay groaned.

"What?" Amara asked.

"I have to work with a bunch of grumpy old men who eat, sleep, and breathe politics," Tursanay complained. "I get so heated when I have to talk about political stuff."

"Then there's no one better to fight them and their crap than you," Amara grinned. "You won't put up with it."

"True," Tursanay conceded. "Oh, we came over here for a reason," she remembered.

"Do not waste your breath," Nuri interjected, but not unkindly. "No one on this ship has been to the Oheqia. What we know is rumors scare people away from it. They are not worth spreading."

"Have you considered that some of those rumors might be true?" Rodney asked. "And maybe we shouldn't be going there?"

"Oh, some of them are definitely true and meant as a warning," Nyx nodded. "But some of them are just wild tales."

"Wait, so if you've never been, how do you know that?" Tursanay asked, then she realized. "You said on this ship... So, there's someone on another ship that's been?"

"Perceptive," giggled Nyx. "That will come in handy. But to answer your question, Master Zhi has been before. He is ancient and wise. One of the few in the group of Sight that does not care for politics either."

"Wait, so if the Seer and that other Dai-Nē—who did they say it was? The Dai-Nē of Dark Magic?—if they ran off and disappeared, why is someone from the Sight group coming along?"

"Master Zhi is here to teach you of our world. Its history, its ways, and to impart knowledge that will strengthen your minds against others' influences. He is here to train your minds while the rest of us train your bodies and reflexes."

They arrived without further incidents at the port and unloaded all of their caravan and livestock. The dwarves bid the Dai-Nē farewell, and they set off towards their destination. They traveled for two more days, first past a small river-side town that dispersed into occasional houses, then into a flat, grassy plain dotted sparsely by trees. After the plains, they reached a wooded area that soon turned into a marshland. Insects swarmed them, and the livestock had to have a dry path made for them. They traveled well into the night until they reached a large cave and two massive doors. Before the doors, on either side, were two massive stone lionesses with wings sprouting out of their backs.

At the top of the door was a stone dragon with its mouth agape, staring into the distance. As the few travelers in front stepped into the stone area, the doors lit up with a deep blue sheen, and the lionesses came to life, their eyes aglow with the same deep blue. They stepped off their perches, walking in unison in an arc, until they met in the center near the edge of the platform where they sat side by side, facing the large group.

"What is your purpose for coming here?" they asked, their voices like whispering echoes.

Master Ansari stepped forward. "We come in the name of the Council of Dai-Nē," said the old man. "We bring the new generation to be trained, and ask permission to enter the Oheqia to do so."

"Why should we permit entrance for something done outside the room for hundreds of Dai-Nē generations?" they asked in unison.

"We have our motivations, which is known that you care nothing for. We do not ask to enter freely, but suggest a trade," Master Ansari replied.

"What is it you have brought us?" they asked, tails swishing silently.

"Three heart stones," Master Ansari replied.

"In exchange?" they asked.

"For three days inside the Oheqia," he replied.

The winged lionesses were quiet for a moment, gazing at the man before them.

"Do we have an agreement?"

Their eyes narrowed suspiciously. "If you have such power, then we will permit you three days inside the room once they are in our possession and the doors are closed. Should you try to fool us, the moment the doors close, you shall all perish and your life forces shall feed us for many years to come."

"Then the deal is done. Three heart stones for three days inside the Oheqia, with safe departure when our time is up," Master Ansari repeated carefully.

Three of the Dai-Nē exchanged nervous looks.

"Agreed," replied the winged lionesses in unison.

Master Ansari produced a box from his robes and opened it, revealing three fist sized blood red stones. They were uncut and unpolished, but resembled large blood droplets. He offered them to the stone guardians, who took a few steps back so that he might place them on the stone before them. He did so, then stepped back, waiting. The two guardians stooped and took one stone each in their mouths and swallowed it, leaving one in the box. From above, the stone dragon came to life, slithering down the side of the doors and up to the box. It took the last stone in its mouth and scrambled back up the other side and took its place atop the door once again.

"The deed is done," they said hauntingly. "The trade is complete. Follow now this path into our domain where time is skewed and knowledge gained."

They returned to their stone perches on either side of the doors, their wings forming an arc over their heads and mouths into a snarl. Stone returned to stone, and the doors opened behind them.

Everyone ushered forward, and the procession began. The further they went into the cave behind the doors, the darker things became around them until at last there was no light and they were all stumbling forward in darkness. The door shut behind them and the darkness enveloped all of them, cutting off all their senses. There were no smells to smell, no sounds to hear, and soon they couldn't feel anyone beside them or the ground beneath their feet. All melted away, and it was as if they were walking through air with no ground on which to purchase their feet. They became weightless and hollow as if floating amid the nothingness. They found themselves suspended in a void, with nothing to anchor them,

causing them to feel weightless and detached from everything, and all was lost to them.

The nothingness enveloped them and they were no more.

CHAPTER 14
ROSS

There was nothing. Only darkness. They walked for what seemed like seconds, or perhaps hours. No one could tell. Then, just as suddenly as all melted away, their senses came back one by one.

First was the sound of others shuffling alongside one another. Then the smells of livestock and of a fresh breeze blowing their way. Then the smell of grass and trees reached them, the sound of the wind ruffling their foliage. Before them, a light appeared. At first, it was a small glow that showed nothing in the surrounding darkness, not even the shape of the cave walls - if that's what this was. There was only an endless expanse of nothing. Then it became bigger and brighter, enveloping them in a warm light that had them shading their eyes from the intensity.

When the light died away, they were standing in a grassy field. Off in the distance was a crop of trees, and the sound of a creek nearby. There was sunlight above them and mountains in the distance, as well as a lake off to their left, but far enough away, it would take a good hour to reach from there on foot. There were cliffs to the northeast, and from where they were, they could just make out the ruins of a city in the far distance beyond the trees.

"We'll set up camp just over that hill, staying close to this area," Master Ansari said.

He called out orders for everyone to set up camp. The alchemists were to create living structures, as well as the elementals, to prepare a gardening area for crops to sow. Once they had a barn area up for the livestock, they herded them into their proper places and building started on their living quarters.

"Well," Tursanay said, helping unload some supplies from the carts. "I can honestly say this isn't what I was expecting.

"Yeah, no, right there with you," agreed Rodney.

"I don't know what I was expecting," said Amara. "But it wasn't this."

As the three of them chatted over what would be their new home for the next three years, a man with a thick, graying beard called them to the common area.

"The five of you will gather outside tomorrow morning two hours before dawn to face an evaluation. We need to see what level of training you've had to know where to begin," he said.

"Oh, I can save you time right here and now," Rodney said. "I can't even climb a rope in gym class. I'm pretty sure I'm a level zero. Tursanay can climb it one handed, so she's at least a level one, and Amara had an excuse not to go to gym on account she was in a wheelchair and couldn't use her legs, so she's probably level zero like me."

"Thanks Rodney," Amara said sarcastically.

"Hey look, no offense, I just don't want to get up two

hours before dawn when I can answer their question without even taking a test."

"You are still required to join us," the man said.

"Dude, the sun doesn't even get up that early! And I can't wake up that early without some kind of wake-up call to help me get up," Rodney replied.

"Oh, you'll get one," he said. "Do not worry about that."

And without waiting for further questions, he turned on heel and left, leaving them looking after him a bit worried and confused.

"Is it just me, or does anyone else not like the way he said that?" Rodney asked.

No one answered him.

Once the buildings were up and the Council members assigned to their quarters, the Dai-Nē got led to a larger building at the head of the campgrounds where they each had their own room and a common area to eat in. Made of wood and fabric, the doors slid open and closed. The table was low to the ground with cushions for them to sit on. There was a porch that ran the entire length of the front of the structure and comfy looking chairs to sit on lining the deck.

An enormous fireplace on the right side of the main entry, and past the common room was a long hallway that branched off into various bedrooms, each complete with a small assortment of furniture and a bathing and toiletry area. There was a set of drawers, a mat for a bed, a blanket, a pillow, and a small table that was low to the floor as well, much like the one in the common area. Each room had a fireplace, some rooms sharing one between the walls.

Taking out their bags of holding, the Dai-Nē unpacked their things into the rooms they had chosen and made things look a little more homely. The clothes given to them in

Delmar got packed away into the drawers, and some decorative trinkets they could buy in the city before they brought onto the boat ride to the north through the mountains and put in various places, making it look more lived in.

Amara set up a small shrine in her room to honor her father, placing the tattered picture Tursanay had grabbed and stuffed in her bag for Amara before they had left Blemwick. It was near where she prayed every night, so she'd have some company while she did so. She was less interested in trinkets, as she was preserving as much of her father's memory as she could. So, she got a picture frame that could take one memory and play it on repeat like a small movie. The memory she'd chosen was one of him smiling at her with the sun setting behind him, and his lips forming the words 'Hello my little dragonfly'. It was a nickname he'd given her when she was younger because she'd been obsessed with dragonflies, originally thinking they were actual dragons, just in a miniature form. It had been a memory that brought warmth every time she remembered it.

Tursanay had bought three small potted plants and named them after her friends. She placed each of them in the windowsill of her room and smiled as she scribbled their names on each. A peppermint one for Rodney because it was one of his favorite candies, a lavender one for Amara because she was always the calming spirit of the group, and the last, a basil, for Soren. Mostly because she wanted a basil but also because the shape of the leaves reminded her of his little top knot where he tied the top part of his hair back. She looked after them as if they were her friends, and should one of them look a little sickly, she would check on her friends to make sure they were okay, and see if there was anything going on that needed tending to.

Rodney had gotten what the Council members had referred to as childish toys, but he honestly hadn't cared. They were neat little artifacts to him, and his favorite was a glass ball with lightning inside of it that would strike the glass wherever you touched it and make your hair stand on end. He placed this toy on the top of his drawers next to his bed on a little pedestal that came with it to keep it from rolling away. Another trinket he particularly liked was a notebook that let you write notes to your friends in one tab, whilst taking notes from conversations around you for you in another. If your friends had a matching notebook, your notes would appear in their binder, much like a chatroom. He'd bought one for each of them and was planning on giving it to them on their birthdays or for a holiday. He hadn't decided yet. They were neat leather-bound books that had lined tea-stained pages. Made to be enchanted to only open with a password or familiar touch, Rodney had yet to set it up in fear they'd only open to his touch by mistake.

Soren had more things he'd packed from his room at home. A picture of his family, including his cousin and his cousin's family; as well as a quilt that Nanako had made him out of his old clothes that no longer fit him anymore and some of her own old clothes, as well as Hamnet's and their children. There was a piece of each of his family member's clothing sewn into each square and it was as if he carried them with him wherever he went. It smelled like home, which eased the homesickness he experienced the longer he was away. He hoped having this with him would ease the transition of being closed off from his family for so many years. One of the first things he wanted to do when this Dai-Nē mess settled down was visit Hamnet and Nanako again and hug them.

Attalira had been the only one of them that had bought no trinkets or brought any from home. Her room was bare save for her clothing items, and things the Council had provided her to make traveling and living in the training grounds for so long easier. Yet while her place did not seem homely nor well lived in as the others did, it seemed to comfort for her to have her own space and sense of privacy. She'd chosen the furthest room from the entrance, next to the side door at the end of the hall, and relished in the peace the evening brought.

Rodney rolled over in his sleep on the uncomfortable floor mat that was provided for them to pass as a bed. He groaned, rubbing some of the drool off his chin, and tried to get in a position that didn't hurt. Faintly awake, something caught his attention in the room. A sound of sorts and the sense of a looming presence. He cracked an eye open and closed it again before they shot open in horror.

There, filling his open doorway, was an enormous creature that looked like a dog's head on an ape's body. Now fully awake, Rodney stared wide eyed at the creature, fear striking him motionless until it snarled, pulling its lips farther back over its already frightening muzzle. Its jaws parted and let out a low growl, saliva dripping to the floor. The creature charged and suddenly Rodney's immobile limbs began scrambling as fast as they could to get out of the way. He crawled backwards towards the corner next to him and dodged out of the way just in time for the creature to smash into the small corner where he was just lying. He ran to the adjacent corner, and the creature tore after him, snarling.

Rodney screamed in terror as the creature tore through the

dresser drawer containing his trinkets and notebooks and destroyed them all with one wave of its arm.

Amara stirred in her sleep, coughing violently. She sat up, thinking she'd heard someone shout, and her body shuddered with a fresh wave of coughing. Her room was scorching hot and clouded in smoke. She looked around her with alarm to see fire springing up in the corners and up at the ceiling. And it was getting closer to her.

Amara pushed herself off the floor, floating away from the flames and moving as quickly as she could towards the sliding door, but hesitated, rushing back to get the picture of her father and going back to the entrance. Something cracked loudly above her. She looked up through the smoky haze and flew back, in time for a falling beam to block her only exit. A wave of fear rushed over her.

She had no way of getting out.

Soren woke to a loud crashing noise, then a sudden large rumble that seemed to shake the entire building. With a start, he sat up and tried to figure out what was going on. He heard a loud cracking noise and in the center of the floor, an enormous gaping hole ripped open, stretching to the opposite corner of the room than he was in. More were popping up in various places - one right behind him he nearly fell backwards into.

He let out a shout of surprise and scrambled to his feet, trying to run towards the door, but the ground shook violently again, causing him to lose his balance and fall to his knees. He rose again, taking a step towards the door, but a large fissure opened up at his feet with a great lurch, and he fell into the hole, screaming.

Attalira woke when a shudder passed through the building. The hair on the back of her neck stood up, her gut telling her something bad was coming. She was instantly on her feet, looking around and listening carefully for what had woken her up. Though she listened and watched, the room was empty, giving away nothing that could have set off her internal alarm.

The floorboards began to rise and fall quickly, as if something beneath them was trying to get through. She scrambled back in surprise just as the floorboards cracked and a large green vine shot out and straight for her. She didn't have time to react before the plants seized her. Another large vine with a giant purple and yellow flower on it reared up from the floor and seemed to look directly at her. Attalira stopped biting at the plant and her eyes widened in alarm as another tendril shot towards her.

Tursanay rolled over in her sleep and heard a soft thunk. Her brow furrowed slightly as she vaguely wondered what it was. After a moment of sleepy debate, she rolled back over to see a figure clad in black with a mask and veil only showing their eyes. Tursanay shot up in bed and backpedaled away from the person, demanding to know who they were. In response, the figure drew a knife from their sleeve, their eyes flashing maliciously. Tursanay's heart leapt into her throat. She crawled backwards, her breath coming in short ragged bursts, and tried to get to her feet.

The assassin took a step forward.

Rodney tore out of his room, skidding slightly in his socks, and looked to his right. There was a long expanse of hallway with a tiny door at the very end. The emergency exit! He remembered they were at each end of the hallway. Looking to his left to find a much shorter expanse of hallway with a much closer emergency exit, he ran as fast as his feet could carry him, straight for the door, with the creature not far behind him skidding out of the room in pursuit.

It slammed against the opposite wall and raced after Rodney, who got to the door and slammed against it, trying to open it, but it didn't budge. Slightly jarred, he looked for a handle and noticed a huge, heavy beam barred across the door. He nearly punched the door in his panic as he dropped to one knee, trying to pry the door open by lifting the beam, but to no avail. The harder he pushed, the closer the beast got and the more Rodney realized he would not make it. He turned, falling to the ground in time to see the creature lunge for him.

Rodney screamed.

Amara coughed and looked at the fireplace that connected her and Tursanay's rooms.

Tursanay! she thought.

She flew over to the wall and started banging against it and screaming for help, hoping she could wake Tursanay in time. The more she banged, the more tired she became, with no fresh air getting into her lungs. Her voice went hoarse from all the screaming, but she had to get someone - anyone's - attention, but no one seemed to hear her. She was sure of it. Someone would have heard her by now. No one was coming. No one could hear her.

She sank slowly to the floor, unable to fly up anymore, no matter how hard she tried. Something was wrong with her flying spell, she thought. *Please let them have gotten out in time!* Slowly, she lost consciousness, as that thought was the last thing to go through her mind.

Soren gripped the floor as hard as his fingers could. At first he'd been about chest level out of the hole when another great shudder hit and he'd slipped down to his fingers, just barely keeping him up. He hoped the shaking would either stop or not get any worse, because his fingers were quickly losing strength. Why was this happening? Were the stones they had given the creatures guarding the room not real after all? Was that why? They were being punished for trying to trick the creatures? Did everyone else fall to their deaths? He tried to readjust his grip while his feet dangled beneath him, scrabbling for something, anything, to gain purchase on. The ground gave another shudder, and Soren's grip slipped.

He fell into the black abyss below him, screaming.

Tursanay had thwarted the assassin in the first attempt on her life, but now she had to make it to the door before another could be made. Glancing over her shoulder, she ran for the door and saw another knife in their hand. Slipping on her blanket, Tursanay went tumbling to the floor, but quickly scrambled back up. She glanced at the assassin again, who had his arm outstretched towards her, then back at the door. She skidded to a stop and her blood ran cold.

There was a knife dead even with her neck embedded in the door. She looked back at the assassin and her heart leapt into her throat.

Attalira tore out of her room at a high speed, barely taking the time to open the main entrance door before sprinting over the low table and out the front and down the stairs. She sprawled onto the grass, panting, and looked around for anything else that was going to attack her. There was no one around but her. Did the others get attacked, too? Was she the only one that got away, or did they just leave her behind to get eaten by rabid flowers? The hair on the back of her neck stood up again, and she whirled around.

"About time one of you got out here," came the gruff voice of a man from the shadows. He stepped forward with a cane, though he looked fairly young, and stared down at her coldly with old eyes that had seen much. Attalira stared at him blankly for a moment, then scowled.

"You sent the killer plants after me?" she demanded.

"Shut up," he barked. "You were late. If you are ever late again, something worse will happen."

Attalira looked at him incredulously and barked, "What kind of demon are you?"

"Wait and watch, then I'll explain." He looked back up at the house and ignored her.

Sitting in the grass outside, waiting for the others to come out, Attalira eyed the strange man suspiciously. If he had sent those plants after her, who knew what he could do? She made a note of his face, committing it to memory. He had short scruffy brownish red hair with dark roots that were just beginning to gray at his temples. His scruffy beard and stubble hid his mouth and chin, the stubble covering his neck and jawbone. His mouth set in a perpetual frown, his eyes an icy blue and constantly vigilant. He stared at the house of Dai-Nē intently waiting for something to happen.

"Hm," his frown deepened. With a sigh, he raised and lowered his eyebrows and pursed his lips. He looked to the side and called to someone in the darkness that Attalira couldn't see. "Call it off their dead."

Attalira shot him a look. "Dead? Why would you kill them?"

The man looked down at her callously and barked. "I said watch and wait. Then I'll explain everything. So, shut. Up."

The creature had lunged at Rodney. He screamed and braced for impact. The creature had its teeth bared and claws outstretched. Ten inches from his face, the creature disappeared, and Rodney stared wide eyed at the space. He was still screaming despite the lack of creature before him, his mind expecting it to reappear at any second. When he ran out of breath and the creature was still nowhere to be seen, it left his mind reeling. What the heck happened?

Suddenly Soren's foot thunked against something hard, causing him to yelp in pain mid scream and roll over. As he gripped his foot, wincing, his eyes popped open, and he realized he was lying on something solid. He looked around, confused, and saw he was lying on the floor in his room screaming for what apparently seemed no reason. There were no holes in the floor, the ground was no longer shaking, and he was lying near his door, holding his foot he had kicked against the boards. He looked around the room cautiously, then straightened.

The Dai-Nē shuffled out of the house, muttering amongst themselves. Attalira looked back in surprise and stood to greet them.

"I thought you were dead," she commented when they reached her.

"Oh sure, now you care," the man muttered beside her.

"Who are you?" Tursanay asked, trying not to sound as shaken as she was. Her voice cracked, giving her away. She was already trying to keep tears from streaming down her face, and it wasn't working.

"I'll introduce myself when I feel like it," the man replied sharply.

The Dai-Nē gave him an odd look, glancing at each other over his response.

"I think he's the one who sent those things after us," announced Attalira.

"What'd she say?" Rodney asked. He'd taken his earrings that aided his hearing out so he could sleep for the night, and now he couldn't hear anything. Tursanay signed for him.

Now all the Dai-Nē focused on the strange man in a new light.

"You sent that assassin?" Tursanay asked.

"You sent that… that creature?" Rodney asked.

"The fissures? The quakes?" asked Soren in disbelief.

"I sent nothing," declared the man. "You were late, so we gave you a wake-up call."

"We almost died!" accused Tursanay, shaking with anger.

"No, you did die. Well, technically," the man added as if it were a minor detail. "If that were a real scenario, you'd all be dead."

"What about me? I got out," Attalira scoffed.

"Oh yes, little deserter. You got out, but at the cost of the lives of your comrades here. Did you even once think to stop and go back for them? Or were you just too busy saving your own skin?" retorted the man.

Attalira looked stunned, bristling defensively. "I was under attack!"

"Yeah," scoffed the man. "So was everyone else. But you didn't care. All you cared about was getting away."

"We all wanted to get away!" defended Tursanay. "We all thought we were going to die!"

"Good!" the man barked. "Then the exercise did its job!"

The Dai-Nē gave him incredulous looks.

"Look, I don't know what your problem is dude, but-" began Rodney.

"My problem is that I must deal with a bunch of snot-nosed brats who don't have an ounce of skill in their being yet have half the world depending on them to save their hides from any crisis that might pop up!"

The Dai-Nē continued to stare at him, not sure what to make of him. So far, it wasn't anything good.

"What's going on?" asked Tursanay after an uncomfortable silence.

"Oh, I'm so glad you asked. It's about time someone got to the point rather than standing here belly-aching," said the man, his tone dripping with more sarcasm. It was as if that's all he spoke. "I am here to give you a series of tests to define and discover what your level of skill is currently at, and to take the results from them to present the trainers to give them a basis to begin with. So far, you're doing miserably. Congratulations." He said, sounding as if he were reading a script.

He flashed them a smile that didn't reach his eyes and continued.

"The terrors you have just been through were the first test in the series I had planned to give you. This one was to force you to apply yourself to a sudden, unexpected situation and see how you fared." He paused and looked at them. "All but one of you died, and the one that survived left everyone else to die to save her own skin. If I were you," he said to the four Dai-Nē to his left. "I would watch out for the short one over there." He gestured to Attalira with his cane. "Not very trustworthy in a dire situation."

Attalira let loose a string of words that had the others' ears burning in embarrassment.

"Now," he said, ignoring her. "I have three more tests. I had planned to give you another physical one, but I can clearly see none of you are up to it, so I will resort to probing your tiny minds to see if any of you can pay attention."

The Dai-Nē watched him suspiciously as he paced slowly.

"First test will be a scenario. Stranded in the middle of the forest, laden with your traveling gear, you have gone two days without food. It is early spring, and the sun is rising." He turned to face them. "Question: What do you get for food?"

The Dai-Nē were quiet for a moment, staring at him as if he'd lost his mind.

"Come now. Don't be shy - this is an open question. Anyone can answer," he prodded.

The Dai-Nē exchanged glances for a moment, unsure what to say, then Rodney spoke uncertainly.

"Berries?" he suggested.

"Berries?" asked the man, looking at Rodney.

"Yes…" replied Rodney hesitantly.

"What berries?" asked the man as if he thought Rodney was stupid.

Rodney's brow furrowed. "Um… the red kind?"

"The red kind?" repeated the man.

"Yeah, cause green'll make ya vomit…" replied Rodney.

"Uh-huh," nodded the man with an exaggerated manner. "Well, there's just one problem with that theory…"

The Dai-Nē looked at him.

"It's early spring…. There are no berries yet," he barked harshly.

Anxiety flushed through Rodney's cheeks and he fell silent.

The man spoke again.

"Okay, let's skip ahead a bit, I can see this is a little too complicated for you…" reasoned the man. "Say you found some herbs in the forest that you can turn into a stew… Question: Where do you get the water?"

"From a river?" replied Rodney, hoping to redeem himself.

The man looked at him. "Did I say you were anywhere near a river?"

"No, but-" Rodney replied even more softly.

"Next! Anyone else got any brighter ideas?"

"Perhaps we can collect the dew from the plants," suggested Soren.

The man gave him a look. "What are you, a gnome that can go around collecting dew? Do you realize how long it would take you to collect enough dew to fill a pot? You'd be dead before you could get enough for a sip!"

"Well—then—!" Tursanay tried to smart back, but was having difficulty coming up with a retort. "We'll... We'll—dig a hole! And find some water!" she barked. "The trees gotta get it from somewhere!"

"They do!" the man smarted back. "The little gnomes your friend there was trying to steal the dew from brings in their little pixie friends to water the big stuff!" he made a face at Tursanay. "You have nothing to dig with, idiot. If you dug with your hands, by the time you got to water, you'd die of exhaustion! Especially in your conditions."

"Then where do you propose we get it? You've shot down every idea we've had!" argued Tursanay.

"Because they were all stupid! You aren't stopping to think!" he argued back.

"Sorry if we're a little off!" snapped Tursanay. "Guess we're not used to nearly being *murdered* this early in the morning!"

"We'll get used to it!" yelled the man.

Tursanay felt shocked.

"There are a lot of things and people out there just waiting to rip you to shreds every day. If you don't step up and learn how to deal with the unexpected, you won't last one day out there! The only reason you've survived this long is by dumb luck!"

"*Shut up!* Just - *Shut! Up!*" yelled Tursanay. "I'm sick of you and your abusive and insane remarks! What did we ever do to you? Sleep in late and miss your big test? Oh, *sorry* but we've kinda had a lot going on lately if you haven't noticed— we've been ripped away from our lives and thrown into this imaginary place where you expect us to just pick up the ball like it's all natural and *play along!*"

"*Yes*! That's *exactly* what I expect you to do if you want to *survive*. So, if you take *five minutes* to stop thinking about me, myself, and I, you'd see there's a way to *do* that!"

Tursanay glared at him with tears streaming down her face, still upset after being nearly killed by an assassin. She hated this guy. She just wanted to go back to bed, but she knew there was no chance she'd get to go back to sleep with this guy in charge, but was stuck with this creep.

"Now. If your complaining and screaming is done, I'll tell you the answer to the question." The man looked at them, his cocky, sardonic attitude back. "If you want to make a stew, you get the water from your canteen."

"Canteen?" Rodney asked. "You said we hadn't eaten in two days! How the heck do we still have water in the canteen?"

"I said you hadn't eaten. I didn't say you'd become dehydrated," came the reply.

"But you didn't tell us we had a canteen!" argued Tursanay.

"I said you had your traveling gear with you. That includes a canteen. *Think* children!" he retorted.

Tursanay opened her mouth with a full-on scowl, ready to argue the point of how that made little sense, but the man was already two steps ahead.

"Next scenario!" he declared, pacing again. "You are on a grassy plane. You have set up your tent for the night, you crawl inside and go to sleep. In the middle of the night, you wake up and look at the clear night sky. What is the first thing that you notice?"

"The stars?" came the reluctant reply.

"What about the stars? What can you discern from these stars?" asked the man.

"Well, a lot of things…" replied Rodney.

"Like what?" probed the man.

"Well… you said it was a clear night sky, so that means there are no clouds, which should mean it won't rain… that's good…" he reasoned.

Tursanay, still angry at the man, reluctantly added. "You can tell the time by the stars…" not that she knew how, but she wasn't about to admit that.

Rodney said, "Ooh, and you can tell like those zodiac things, or like um, see a lot of stars and galaxies…"

The man stared at them for a moment with an odd look on his face.

"Can anyone tell me why you can see the sky if you were inside the tent?" he asked slowly.

The Dai-Nē fell silent.

The Rodney said, "Cause… we put a… skylight in it?"

"Rodney, don't encourage him," sighed Tursanay.

Soren said, "The tent is missing… Perhaps a gust of wind blew it away."

"A gust of wind?" asked the man. "What did a tornado come by and take your tent away but somehow leave you untouched, gnome boy? It would have swept you away too genius, besides, did I say there was a wind blowing that night?"

"Y-you did not," began Soren, confused. "However,-"

"Then it wasn't a gust of wind. Your tent was stolen, you morons! If you had taken the time to look around you rather than get distracted by the pretty shiny things in the sky, then you may have noticed that your tent was nowhere to be seen!"

"How were we supposed to know that the tent got stolen? You didn't give us any details about what the surrounding place looked like. You just said that we suddenly saw a starry sky!" Tursanay argued angrily.

"I said you saw the clear night sky. I never said it was starry," replied the man. "Which brings me to the last scenario… I'll give you an easy one."

"You said that about the second part of the first one!" Tursanay reminded him. "You're just setting us up to fail!"

"Sorry, I didn't think you were this stupid. This one is reaally reaaally easy. Promise." He gave a mock look of assurance. "Question," he began. "What time is it?"

The Dai-Nē exchanged blank looks.

"No one? Well, why don't you try looking at the sky? As you said before, you can deduce the time by looking at the stars!" retorted the man.

"I don't know how to do that!" yelled Tursanay indignantly.

"Yeah!" agreed Rodney. "Plus, the constellations are probably different here - we wouldn't have a clue how to tell!"

"Oh yeah? Well, tell me this: What time was it preordained that you would rise this very morning?"

The Dai-Nē paused and fell silent.

Soren spoke. "Two hours before dawn?" he recalled.

"Yes. So, what time do you think it is now?" asked the man.

"T-two hours before dawn?" asked Rodney sheepishly.

"Wow! You finally got one!" the man said sarcastically. "Maybe if you had taken the time to actually *look* at the sky when I told you to, you'd notice there are little to no stars around here this close to dawn!"

The Dai-Nē looked at their feet self-consciously.

"Nearly dawn, almost dawn, close to dawn, nearly daybreak! I would have taken any of those! Yet you stand there arguing that you can't tell me what time it is because you can't read the stars even when there are none! You are worthless individuals! You can't fight, you can't adapt, you can't think for yourselves! All you do is cower and wait for someone to come save your frightened little hides or throw everything to the wind to save yourself and make sure you aren't to be blamed when you get something wrong! Own up to your mistakes, protect your team, and learn how to defend yourselves or just let yourselves get killed now and save your enemies the trouble!" He stamped or pointed his cane at them as he yelled.

Most of the Dai-Nē felt like crawling under a rock and never coming back out, but some were too angry at the accusations he had thrown at them previously to feel guilty.

"You have also not noticed a very crucial thing in all this time," the man continued. "Not all of you made it out of the scenario." Rodney and Tursanay exchanged looks, then looked around them at Soren and Attalira.

It clicked instantly.

"Amara!" Tursanay exclaimed, running back towards the house without a second thought. The building erupted in flames, pushing her back from the heat as the inferno enveloped the entire structure.

"NO!" Tursanay shrieked.

Rodney had to pull her back. Soren watched in horror as the flames lit up the faces of the other Council members surrounding them in the dark. They watched with blank faces, and none of them moved to help.

Was this it? Was this the real reason they'd brought them here? To round them up like cattle and steal their powers as they murdered the Dai-Nē one by one?

Without warning, Soren hauled off and punched Ross right in the jaw. If they were going down, he was going to fight it, apparently. A set of vines suddenly restrained him, and Attalira backed away cautiously.

Abruptly, the flames disappeared in a flash of light, and the structure had gone with them. Not burned to ash, but simply vanished. And in its place on unscorched earth in a patch of green grass was an unconscious Amara, unharmed and still breathing.

Rodney and Tursanay ran to her, Soren not far behind as soon as they released him, checking on her, and, after a few coughs, she was up and blinking at them curiously.

"You got out," she murmured, relieved. "I was so scared you got caught in the fire."

"It was a test. Since we didn't wake up on time, they sent us all horrors to force us to wake up," Tursanay sniffed bitterly, hugging her friend.

Why couldn't she stop crying?

"I think I failed that one," Amara muttered.

"Well, Master Ross, have your tests determined their level of skill?" asked a Council member emerging from the shadows to stand next to the rude man. It was the one that had warned them the day before.

Ross looked him in the eye. "When you have trained them enough to get them to a level, General Eizo, let me know. They don't even have a level zero of skill, they have negative skill! It's nonexistent! Never has been, never was, and at this rate, never will be. If this is the future of the world, then we're very much in trouble."

He hobbled away on his cane, leaving the Council member with the five Dai-Nē.

"Well… That went rather well, considering…" the Council member acknowledged, watching Master Ross go, then looked back at the Dai-Nē.

The Dai-Nē looked at the Council member, not sure if they wanted to know what he meant by that.

"Breakfast is ready for those of you that can still eat. Get yourselves prepared for your first day of training."

CHAPTER 15
LESSONS

The Dai-Nē separated and went to their respective teachers for the first part of the day, then around mid-day, the trio of Mortal World Dai-Nē gathered at Master Zhi's house to learn about history.

Amara's fly spell had worn off for some reason after coming into the Oheqia. Until the components for her flying spell could grow and get compiled, she got another chair constructed specifically for her fin's comfort so she could get around without issue. The really pleasant part was being able to get over difficult terrain much like that of the wagon wheels. Her chair was bespelled to not feel the bumps and dips. It was like riding a magic carpet, but less wobbly.

Since Kadin had been a potion's dealer, mixed with Akram's alchemy, they'd had everything they'd needed on hand to make her one. But here in the Oheqia, they didn't have everything right off the bat. So, for now, she was back in a chair and feeling a little more grounded than she had since she started flying. As for Rodney's earring hearing aids, their personal items had survived the artificial fire, and he put them back in shortly before breakfast.

"Before we begin," Master Zhi said, his gentle, quavering voice surprisingly full of energy. "I would like to give the three of you, and your two companions who are not with us, a special gift. It is a stone that will prevent your thoughts from being read by mind readers like myself. As Dai-Nē, you will learn very important information that can get used against you in a time of crisis should the information fall into the wrong hands. So, from now on, I would ask that you wear these around your necks to keep your thoughts safe."

"Wait, you can-?" began Rodney.

"Read your minds? Yes. Have I been listening to you fret over having to memorize dates and names of a completely different world on top of your own?" Master Zhi smiled. "Only by accident. Which is why I would like to quiet the room for myself so I can focus on our lessons and not your collective thoughts." He gave them a reassuring smile. "But no, you won't have to worry about that. This is to get you up to speed, not test your knowledge."

"Oh, thank goodness," Rodney sighed. The Dai-Nē reached out and took the stones, thanking him and placing it around their necks.

"How, uh, how far out could you hear our thoughts?" Amara asked.

"Don't worry," he comforted. "I only tune in to people knocking on my door to see who it is. I can tune out things that are outside the room I'm in. It just makes going to a market very difficult sometimes."

"Oh good," she said, relieved. There had been a few private thoughts she had wanted no one to hear out loud. It would just be too embarrassing. The only place left she felt safe was in her own mind. Take that away and she'd have nothing.

"Today will be your first lesson in how our world works," Master Zhi was stating as he paced back and forth before the three Dai-Nē. "We will start with the history of the world and how it formed." Rodney raised his hand and interrupted his train of thought. "Why are you doing that?" Master Zhi asked curiously.

"Oh, uh, it means I have a question," Rodney replied.

"Ah, well, feel free to interject with questions," he replied. "It's how you learn. You talk and debate the presented subject and stay interacting with it."

"Oh cool," Rodney said. "Well, we've already learned how Rynon sacrificed himself to create this world and the veil between the worlds and how they used to be all in one place, but-"

"Oh no, child, Rynon didn't sacrifice himself," argued Master Zhi. "He paid the price for his crimes. He got what he deserved."

"Wait, 'what he deserved'?" Tursanay asked curiously, furrowing her brow. This was an interesting start to their history lesson. "What do you mean?"

Master Zhi took a breath and thought for a moment. "Where do I begin?" He considered how to present the information for several seconds before he finally answered them.

They all waited silently.

"Rynon," he began. "Was a very wise man. And, at the height of the war between Mortal Kind and Magic Kind, he sought a power that would help turn the tides of the war. And he found it: a spell that would give him the power of the Many-Eyed Seraphim. Great and powerful creatures that could do all forms of magic, alchemy, shapeshift and more. They existed on a different level than most magical beings. They were nearly godlike in power, and many feared them. For though they could be a gentle race, they would smite those who incurred their wrath with no remorse. Their judgements were swift. Rynon found a spell that would give him this power and he wiped out the entire race, stealing their power for himself. They say he had a ring that gave him the ability to steal their powers, but the spell he used drained their life force to power it."

The girls looked over at Rodney, and he looked back at them. They had lost the murder ring and now some unknown shapeshifter had it.

"So, ah, back to my question," Rodney said, clearing his throat awkwardly. He didn't want to think about that right now. "How did the Dai-Nē come into existence? I know it has something to do with Rynon splitting his powers, but why did he create them exactly?"

"Possibly to prevent one person from having all that power, possibly to keep the legacy of the Many-Eyed Seraphim alive, possibly even to be ambassadors between the worlds, as many believe they are. Possibly all these things, we may never truly know," Master Zhi replied.

"So, when did the pedestal come into play, and why was it built?" Tursanay asked.

"Rynon created the pedestal when he split his powers to protect them from being stolen by anyone with the ring between reincarnations of the Dai-Nē," he explained.

The Dai-Nē exchanged looks, remembering what Nanako had said about the pedestal not always having existed. Something didn't add up. They'd have to make a note to find out just what, when they got out of here.

"So," Amara said, changing the subject. "Why do we get these marks when we got our powers?"

"It is the mark of the Many-Eyed Seraphim," Master Zhi explained. "It was their symbol, and is now the mark of the Dai-Nē."

"So, we basically have the power of the Many-Eyed Seraphim," Tursanay reiterated.

"Yes," Master Zhi replied. "It's why the Dai-Nē are so important to our world. They are a living legacy, and protectors of our kind."

They let that information sink in a moment.

"Why were some orbs smaller than others?" Tursanay asked. "Is it because they are weakening? Or because of something else?"

"Goodness, you three ask very good and complicated questions," Master Zhi chuckled. "There are some that fear the powers are dying out. I believe it has something to do with the generation of Dai-Nē that tried to destroy the pedestal so they could keep the powers for themselves and control who got said powers once they were to pass on."

"What brought that on?" Amara asked.

"There was a great struggle that nearly wiped out all the great dragons because of their greed, and I believe it destabilized the powers and made them weaker. Ever since the battle," he continued. "The Dai-Nē of Light and Dark Magic have had difficulty with their powers interfering with each other."

Tursanay looked around. "Do you have anything I can take notes on? I want to make sure I remember some of this stuff in case I have questions later."

"Of course," Master Zhi said delightedly. "Ah! And that reminds me. I have a reading spell for you all so that you can understand the books you'll go over in the course of your lessons here in the training grounds."

"A reading spell?" Tursanay's eyes lit up excitedly. Being able to read magical tomes in a magical world about magical things? Oh, this was right up her alley.

"How long ago did the generation do that?" Amara asked as he handed Tursanay a notebook and writing utensils. She quickly began scribbling notes.

"A good five thousand years or so, I would say," Master Zhi commented, scratching his white bearded chin.

For the next hour, and for a week or more, each class they asked about everything they could think of. Things like how the education system worked. Master Zhi explained witches were anyone with the ability to use magic that had minor schooling; sorceresses and sorcerers were those that were apprentices in magic with higher schooling; and wizards were masters at the art and could take on apprentices of their own.

He also told them of when he was in school how friends would make friendship talismans for each other. Or if they were at a secret party - hidden in plain sight by spells - that got broken up by the police, they would send out mass luck spells to keep from getting caught.

This opened up questions about the law enforcement in the magic world, and they learned about necromancers that would work with the dead to solve homicides and cold cases. Or living lie detectors that worked as regular cops and detectives, and werewolves that used their heightened senses to track down criminals.

They spoke of the murals some people would paint on the sides of buildings that moved and could even talk to people as they passed. Sometimes the living drawings would hide from law enforcement to keep from being erased if they got too rowdy or insulted one too many people.

They spoke of the money trading system and how one could barter in some places, or have a medium of exchange. Some people preferred monetary exchange, while others wanted something precious to the buyer because they could feed off the sentimental value.

This opened the subject of demons that fed on negative emotions as therapy, therapists that could read auras, psychics that would take jobs as teachers, or something as simple as hairdressers. Anything that would make money. Like how some alchemists dealt with experiments on the side to support their experiments. By the time their lecture was up each day, they had more and more questions to ask, and it absolutely delighted their teacher.

The first few months of training, on the other hand, were grueling. Given things to study, unable to escape homework even in the magic world, their days usually composed of lessons in history, then they traded off to their respective teachers to learn aspects of their powers and how to use them. Then came the physical training to get stronger and that had them so worn out by the end of the day, they barely had the energy to do their homework, let alone eat something before bed.

They rebuilt their cabin in its former glory the same day it had disappeared on the first rude awakening, and their personal items got restored. At night, they were so exhausted they would collapse into bed, but their anxiety of another rude awakening kept them waking up at odd hours of the night to check out of their windows to see if the stars were disappearing. Several times, they got up too early and were even more exhausted by the end of the day. It wasn't long, however, that they finally fell into a routine and things weren't quite as nerve-wracking as they had started.

"Keir, stop pacing. You're making me nervous," came the irritated command.

"Ilarys, I'm already nervous," Keir replied. "We just stole the actual Ring of Rynon, and now we're branded with the mark of Dai-Nē which makes us responsible for fixing the veil!"

He walked over to the wall and pointed at the research he had plastered against it in various forms: floating magical projections, news clippings, glowing crystal-pointed high-lights, etc.

"I've been studying all the living cities that have shown signs of being sick while you were making fun of my mirror people's research. There are rumors of a disease going around, but when I cross-referenced it with the cities we visited for missing people and mirror people sightings, it's exactly the same! Every last one! The veil is deteriorating. There are more and more ghost sightings of iron beings."

"Wait, all of them match up?" Ilarys said, standing and inspecting his research. "That's… impossible." But there it was, right before her eyes. "Can we bring this up on a map and see just how far it's spread?"

"Already compiled it," Keir said, pulling up the map. "It's bad. It's headed towards the seven cities next."

"With that many people"…" Ilarys breathed. "Thousands could die! Much like in Kapena's village… But didn't the Fae say they would stop if we helped them?"

"I think the Fae may have started it, but the tear is

growing on its own now. I don't think stopping the Fae will stop the deterioration of the veil. We're going to have to get the Fae across the veil and get the spell to fix it."

Tursanay woke up in a cold sweat. The veil? Deteriorating? Fae? What kind of dream was that? Yet even as she wondered, she knew it hadn't been a dream. It felt just as her vision had before when the shadows came to life. Real. Tangible. Alive.

She glanced out the window to check the time and saw a night full of stars and laid back down, though she wasn't sure she could fall back asleep. If what she dreamed was true? The Magic World and the Mortal World would clash together and all sorts of mayhem would ensue. Many people would die just from the initial panic, then a war could break out again.

With a sigh, she sat back up and grabbed her notebook, scribbling down every detail she could remember. If this were another vision, she'd need to warn everyone, including the Council.

The next morning, however, didn't go as planned. None of her teachers would listen, no matter how much she begged, and all of them treated her as if she were insane.

"I'm telling you I had a vision!" Tursanay balked.

"Nonsense," the fifth teacher of the day declared with a sniff. "only those with the power of Sight can have visions. You do not have that power."

"Will you at least listen to it?" she asked. "It's important!"

"I'm sure it felt that way, but as I said before, you do not have that power. So, stop wasting our lesson time and let's get back to your spell work."

Tursanay bit back a rude reply and sat back against the chair, defeated. She'd been through five teachers and none of them would listen to her. She hadn't even had a chance to tell Amara, Rodney, and Soren yet, and was ready to scream.

After class, they sent her to her first healing lesson with Master Ross. There had been a few days where he'd not been feeling well, and told her to use her class period as a study period by leaving a note with her previous teacher beforehand. This time, there was no note, so it looked like she'd finally get to meet the elusive Master Ross again for the first time since the rude awakening he'd given them. Hopefully, this would be much less harrowing. Grudgingly, she went over to his hut to knock on the door, but it was slightly ajar.

"Master Ross?" Tursanay asked, poking her head into the house where she was told she could find him.

"Sorry," came an irritated reply. The man with the cane came hobbling into view, grabbed the door handle, and moved to close it. His watery blue eyes fixated on her with a grumpy sneer. "We're closed. No more foot cream available. I'm afraid you'll just have to live with three toes for the rest of your miserable life. If you have any complaints, please file a letter with the head of the Council."

"No - wait! I'm supposed to learn to heal from you," she replied, trying to finish before he shut the door.

He paused, an inch from closing it.

Tursanay stared, uncertain if he was going to open the door or just close it and ignore her. It swung open enough for her to see his face.

"Oh! Well, that changes everything," he remarked sarcastically. "I'm afraid I must inform you he died. Abruptly. Three days ago. They had a quiet funeral. No students allowed. I'm not surprised you didn't hear about it. Guess you'll have to go elsewhere."

He shut the door abruptly, and Tursanay stood there blinking for a moment. Slightly annoyed after the day she had, she to get stubborn and just a tad bit annoying back.

Taking off her messenger bag and sitting on the doorstep, she pulled out her homework and set to work. There was a ton from the other classes, and if Master Ross was just going to refuse to teach her, then she might as well make use of the time. After a good five minutes, the door behind her jerked open.

"What are you doing?" the man from earlier demanded.

"Homework," she replied, not looking at him.

If he was going to be rude, two could play at that game. She was tired of being out of her depth on everything, and all of her teachers either hating her or thinking she was a moron for claiming she had visions. Or both. And she wasn't putting up with it anymore.

"You can't do that here. This is my doorstep," he griped.

"Correction," Tursanay replied, writing something down. "According to them," she said, noting with her pen to a group of Council members talking together across the street. "This is Master Ross's doorstep. And according to you, he's dead. Therefore, there is no one to contest whether I can sit here."

"Well, they're idiots," he scoffed. "And they don't know what they're talking about. So, move."

Tursanay laughed wryly. "No argument there. But that's an issue you'll have to take up with them, not me. It's not my fault Master Ross is no longer amongst the living and his body burned and ashes scattered into the wind."

She made a sarcastic hand gesture to further emphasize her words, no longer caring what people thought for the day.

"I never mentioned burning his body or scattering his ashes into the wind," the man argued.

"While I concede I have no proof that his ashes got scattered into the wind," Tursanay admitted, scratching down another answer on her page. "And that he was either buried in the dirt or sitting in an urn on some shelf collecting dust - I highly doubt he was buried."

"What makes you say that?" he asked.

"There are no grave markers or freshly dug plots around the campsite," she replied, wondering why she was having this conversation. "and he wasn't buried outside of the camp because it would have taken the better part of the day to take the body from point A to point B, dig the hole, have the ceremony, then bury him. And since no one has been missing for any more than the time it takes to go to the restroom, then wherever it is he resides, I doubt he is there whole… Therefore, burned is the other option… Unless he got fed to an animal, in which case, may he rest in pieces… Or… cooked in a stew and fed to everyone because waste not, want not… In which case, he was delicious."

Tursanay realized she was rambling irritably and stopped. Her bitter sarcasm that had mostly stayed in her head throughout the day was now flowing freely from her lips and directed at this man, but she had a hard time caring what anyone thought any more since no one apparently cared what she thought.

"Regardless, I still don't want you doing your homework on this doorstep," gripped the man.

Tursanay sighed, irritably. "I was told to go to Master Ross's house. Master Ross is dead. I was also told to do my homework, so here I am. If you have a complaint, I suggest you file a letter with the head of the Council," she snapped, throwing his previous words right back at him.

The man was silent a moment, and Tursanay felt a slight flicker of triumph.

"Do you always do what you're told?" the man sneered.

Tursanay tilted her head back to look up at him, towering over her. "Apparently not if you go by this conversation," she quipped.

He stared at her silently, glaring. But also, with something else... He was thinking. She could see it in his eyes. Calculating. Tursanay, too irritated to be phased, just met his gaze cooly.

"...Don't get ink on my porch," he replied, disappearing into the house and slamming the door behind him. Smiling to herself and feeling like she finally accomplished something today, Tursanay felt immensely better despite all that she'd been through. She scribbled happily and finished her work in the time it took for her healing hour to be up.

When the day finally drew to a close, and the Dai-Nē returned to their house, Tursanay asked them to hear her out before they went to bed. She told them about the vision she had and how she was worried about what it could mean.

"But only the Dai-Nē of Sight gets visions like that," Attalira argued.

"I've had visions before that saved our lives," Tursanay replied, tired of hearing that excuse. "I'm not counting it out. It felt the same as before." She turned to Amara and Rodney. "Like when we got chased by those shadows that I predicted?"

Rodney shivered. "I really don't want to think about that."

"You can't possibly believe this," Attalira scoffed. Though

her face looked like she was doing a terrible job of hiding surprise.

"It is true," Soren piped up. "I was also there. I thought it was a residual effect of switching powers, but apparently there is more to it. By all logic, you should not be having these visions, Tursanay. But I believe you when you say you are."

"Thank you," Tursanay said, relieved. "None of the Council will believe me or even listen to what I saw. They just dismiss me and think of me as an idiot."

"That'll bite them in the butt when they find out this is true," Rodney replied.

"Why do you believe her? She has no proof," Attalira asked Soren.

"Because when I was in Sendew," Soren answered. "The city contacted me. It asked for my help. I didn't understand why then, but I think I do now. If the veil weakening is leeching the life from the living cities, then we need to stop it."

"How can we stop it? We can barely get through our studies," Amara asked.

"We will train here for several years," Soren replied. "but only three days will pass in the outside world. That will give us the time we need to come up with a plan to help. We'll have the ability to do something then."

"True," Amara said. "Let's just hope a lot doesn't happen in three days. I can't handle another mess."

Over the next few months, they learned more about the Magic World than they believed possible. From its good side to its bad, its quirks and cultural shifts. Little things and big. They grew stronger from their constant workouts and even got a small handle on their powers. Though Tursanay seemed to struggle with hers more so than the others because of a hard disconnect between her and her teachers. She believed them to be idiots for not listening to her, and they believed her childish and delusional for insisting on the visions.

As for Rodney, Tryn proved to be a very hard teacher. Very hands on and almost violently corrective. If something he made had the wrong set of ingredients to his alchemical reactions, she let it blow up in his face. It was her way of teaching him to pay more attention. More than once, Rodney had to regrow his eyebrows.

Soren was having a trial, learning inner peace when no one could give him a proper definition of just what it meant to have it. He excelled at communicating with the spirits of the living things around him and learning to heal them, but other monk style training was proving difficult for him. He couldn't focus his ether into a physical manifestation, nor could he channel it into his limbs to enhance his fighting capabilities.

Amara was struggling with the different elements. Water she excelled in, but fire and lightning were terrifying to her, and earth and plants were just as stubborn as Tursanay when she set her mind to something. Air wasn't as hard, and she'd even combined it with water to create a cloudy mist. The learning was slow going, but her teachers were patient. When they finally gathered the spell ingredients to get her a flying spell back together, they had to reteach her to fly as well. They started by letting her swim in the water to build up muscle in her fin that she'd never used before in her life.

As for Attalira, she was a natural in all forms of

shapeshift. She seemed to take to each fluidly and rose to higher levels of training rather quickly. She seemed to understand how to change her shape and grasp her powers better than any of the other Dai-Nē in training combined. The other four watched on in silent jealousy that it was so easy for her, but also in awe. She was a sight to behold and all of her teachers were very pleased with her progress.

Some weeks passed as they settled into this routine, then they would change it up and put them on night classes so that the other Council members could come out and train with them, being people of the night. There were vampires, a werewolf, an aqrabuamelu, which was a scorpion man, and several, many more that preferred to work at night rather than in the daytime. Some preferred it because they couldn't exist in the sunlight. Others, more so because their own sleep schedules let them work better at night time.

On these days, the Dai-Nē got two days to adjust their sleep schedule before switching to nights, and two days to switch back once nights were through. Rodney had the most difficulty with this after getting used to one sleep method, changing it every so often really messed up his sleep schedule to the point he was falling asleep in class and being rudely awakened by having water dumped on his head at one point or another.

One night, after a grueling day of testing and training, the Dai-Nē awoke to the sound of a scream that contorted into a feral snarl. Shouts followed it, then an explosion. Everyone scrambled to their feet and out of their rooms to see what the commotion was, and when they pulled back the front door and made their way onto the front lawn, they saw campgrounds were on fire. Several people were running around in a mix of panic and urgency whilst the elementals worked to put out the inferno.

One Council member spotted the Dai-Nē and yelled at them to get back inside and stay there, before disappearing into the fray.

"I-Is this a test?" Rodney asked, uncertain.

"I don't think so," Attalira responded, eyeing the blaze and the passing faces lit up by the flames. "We need to get back inside."

"What's the hurry?" came a voice from behind them.

They turned to find Master Ross leaning against his cane and watching them intently. "You might miss something important."

The light from the fire gave his face an eerie glow.

"What do you mean?" Amara asked.

"I think we should go inside now," Attalira said as the same scream rang out again, followed by shouts of surprise.

It was the scream of a person losing their mind.

"What if they need our help?" Amara hesitated.

"You can barely make a cloud. What good will you do?" Attalira snapped.

"You can glean much from just watching," Ross said again.

There was something off in his tone. Something almost sinister. It made Amara's skin crawl, but Tursanay's brow furrowed into a determined line.

"Something's going on they don't want us to know about," she said out loud. "Something that would put the Council in a poor light."

She knew what Ross was doing. He would never give a straight answer unless you asked the right questions. She just had to figure out what the right questions were.

"Perhaps. Perhaps not," Ross shrugged. "The only way to find out is to observe."

Then again, sometimes he still wouldn't give a straight answer, Tursanay reminded herself.

The screaming became frantic and animal-like, closing in on their position.

"What is that?" Rodney asked, taking a step back.

The sound was like a human-animal hybrid being tortured, only it seemed like it was on the move and searching for something as well.

"Stay here and find out," Master Ross said. "It's making its way to the strongest power source."

"What?" Rodney squeaked, taking another step back.

"Get inside! Now!" Attalira demanded, stretching her arms to encompass them all and shove them backwards towards the cabin.

At first they hesitated, but when the screech wailed into the night, fear dripped down their spines and sent them scrambling for the doors. As they reached the porch and struggled to close the thin door behind them, they caught sight of a figure in the dark running straight for them, but they couldn't make out its features. The only thing they knew was that it was humanoid, and was making an ungodly noise as it ran towards them.

"Close it! Close it! Close it!" shouted Rodney.

A barrier rose around the cabin and the creature ran to it, beating against the red energy field. It looked like it had once been human, but the skin was melting away from its face as the flames licked at it. The thing was on fire and screaming - not in pain, but in frustration - as it beat against the only thing standing between it and its prey. There was a glint in its eyes was red from the fire, and its teeth shone through its cheek, making the menacing snarl that much more terrifying.

The Dai-Nē slammed the door shut and clambered back from the entrance.

"What was that thing?" Amara asked hoarsely.

"Someone please tell me that wasn't a zombie!" Rodney begged.

"Sure looked like one," muttered Tursanay. "Is it still out there? The barrier muted the sounds. I can't hear anything, but I'm too scared to look."

"Don't," Attalira said. "It could antagonize it enough to break through the barrier."

It was a grueling ten minutes before they peered cautiously out the windows to see the creature gone and the flames dying down to smoldering cinders at last. The barrier was gone now, and there were a few people walking back and forth outside. Getting up the courage to go back outside, the Dai-Nē poked their heads out one at a time.

"Is it safe?" Amara called to one of the nearby wanderers.

"It is safe now," he answered.

It was Master Ansari.

"What was that thing?" Rodney asked.

"I'm told it was a creature from the island in the lake. It escaped the barrier we placed around the island and made it to shore," he replied.

"There are more of those things?" Rodney exclaimed.

"Stay away from the island and you will be safe," Master Ansari replied. "I fear not everyone made it out safely tonight. We are doing a headcount now. Stay inside and get some rest. Tomorrow you will continue your training as usual."

"After an attack like that?" Tursanay asked, furrowing her brow again, perplexed this time.

"We have no time to waste," he answered. "Should there

be a next time, you'll need to be prepared to defend yourselves."

The Dai-Nē did not like the sound of that as they shuffled off to join the others, leaving them with that nightmarish thought for the night. None of them slept well for days.

"Lesson one," Master Ross began, walking over to a shelf of notebooks and selecting one without a title on the spine. He made his way over to Tursanay and handed her the book, but when she opened it, the pages were blank.

"There's nothing in here," Tursanay said.

"Yet," Master Ross replied. "You are to fill that book with all the information you can gather on the Council. Do not let them know you are collecting information. Do not let them see the information you collect. This is strictly for your eyes only."

"You want me to spy on the Council?" Tursanay asked, confused.

"No, I want you to gather all the information you can. And then get more. Understanding the people you work with and your enemies alike will save your hide in the future. Get their descriptions, get their family history, get their strengths and weaknesses, get their virtues and faults. Get everything that makes them tick and write it down in that book. When you think it's complete, bring it back to me and I'll tell you if you've got enough."

"But that'll take ages!" Tursanay said.

"Years, even," Master Ross agreed.

"I thought you were supposed to teach me healing," Tursanay said.

"I thought you wanted to learn something," Master Ross countered.

"I do, but so far most of my teachers think I'm an idiot and you keep giving me weird metaphors and odd assignments that have nothing to do with what I'm supposed to be learning," Tursanay complained. "Learning magic is supposed to be fun. I thought I could learn to… I dunno, construct a giant fist out of pure light, and punch through rocks or something."

"Then what's stopping you?" Master Ross asked.

"Wait, that's possible?" Tursanay stammered.

"Light Magic revolves around solar energy, light, spells that are strongest when the sun has risen. Warmth, drawing energy from positivity, drawing energy from the surrounding things to influence them. Clean energy that recharges you or the spell receiver. Light Magic users are often critical thinkers, extroverted, and creative."

"That… that explains why I'm not getting anywhere with my teachers," she said. "They give me a lot of negativity. Is there any way to draw energy from somewhere else?"

"Sometimes Light can draw energy from more calming places rather than bustling places, but their strength lies in drawing energy from their surroundings and socializing. The reason you can't get a grasp on your powers is because you are stopping yourself because you don't believe something is possible. If you don't believe in yourself and your abilities, then you'll accomplish nothing," Master Ross replied.

Tursanay was quiet a long moment, processing that.

"What does Dark Magic do?" she asked quietly.

"Dark Magic revolves around lunar energy, moonlight, and stars. Spells that are strongest at night, in shadows, calmness, stillness, and draw off inner strength and peace. They draw influence from the wielder's own emotions to influence their spells," Master Ross replied.

"So like opposite of Light Magic, naturally," Tursanay nodded. "So, if they are opposite, does that mean they're like introverts and shy compared to a Light Magic user who's extroverted?"

"Dark Magic users are emotionally driven, are good at de-constructing things, introverted yes, and self-reliant to a fault. This doesn't indicate a shy spell caster, but someone who works better with a clear head and heart. They can work well with others who resonate well with spell work," he added. "You can strengthen your magic by practicing it more, but sometimes there are physical limitations to what some can do by nature and predispositions of genetic influence. Since you are a Dai-Nē, you can push past those limitations and do great things. But only if you try."

Shock colored Tursanay's face as he gave her a straight answer rather than a sarcastic one. Perhaps she'd finally asked the right question.

"So, are there Light spells and Dark spells?" she asked.

"Spells are neutral," he replied. "It's how the wielder is capable of interacting with them that makes it Light, Dark or-" he paused, cleared his throat, then continued. "If you draw on outside forces, it's Light. If you draw on inner forces and base your actions on emotions, it's Dark."

"So Light and Dark doesn't stand for good and evil, it just stands for how the magic is used," she realized.

"It's not good versus evil, its unique personalities working in different ways and sometimes they bleed into each other. As for evil, it would depend on what you did with the magic that would make it good or bad. The magic itself is a neutral device. Just as a knife can be."

Tursanay was quiet again for a moment, thoughts racing. It was the first time someone gave her solid information about how magic worked that she could use and implement. This she understood. This she could work with. Shoving the book into her bag, she stood up abruptly and headed for the door.

"Where are you going?" he asked.

"I'm gonna punch a rock with an arm made of light," she replied and sprinted out the door.

CHAPTER 16
GROWTH

Soren had been chipping away at his emotions for months and still had trouble finding his true inner peace. What was it supposed to be like? Clear water rippling beneath a waterfall? The sounds and the movement of the water distracted him. How was that peaceful? Water was gushing down and splattering against the rocks below. That was a rush of sound and movement, not peace.

His teacher had tried different thought patterns, such as a quiet walk in the forest. But the forest wasn't quiet at all. There were creatures living in the trees, the wind that brought the smell of moss and soaked wood from the fresh rain. There were the sounds of his footsteps as he moved through the underbrush.

His teacher tried perhaps a small room indoors with shelves filled with books, and glittering lights from the night sky with the soft crackle of a fire in the corner, but Soren was too busy noticing the hum of magic that lit the fire, kept the bugs out of the windows, and powered the lights inside to really relax with that kind of setting.

Master Ryu sighed. "Magic doesn't have a hum."

"It does. I can hear it," Soren responded.

Another sigh from his teacher.

"Perhaps we can try something different," Master Ryu said. "Close your eyes and feel the auras around you. Find one that stands out and focus on it."

Soren closed his eyes and colors of auras from the land and the people living there filled his mind. He narrowed it down to just the land, mostly muted colors, but nothing stood out to him. He took a deep breath and let it out slowly as he focused on the auras of the people in the campgrounds. This was the part he excelled in. This he could do. One by one he dismissed the auras of those around him until he came to one that gave him a warmth like no other did. The spirit of the person in question was strong, but at the moment, they seemed unsure of themselves. He focused on it.

"Have you found it?" Master Ryu asked.

"I have," Soren said, not opening his eyes as he watched the colors change.

"Describe it to me," Master Ryu instructed.

"It is warm. Strong. Unsure of self, but determined," Soren replied.

"Let it fill your senses and let your focus fall on that," Master Ryu replied.

Allowing the warmth to fill his senses wasn't hard, as it was already spreading through his chest, but he hesitated, fighting to keep it at bay as it tried to spread further. It brought back memories that were hard to deal with. Though he had been just a small child, he remembered when his parents gave him to Hamnet and Nanako. He remembered them saying goodbye and watching them leave. He remembered losing that warmth - that connection - he'd had. His parents had promised they would be back soon. That they would see him again one day. But they had lied. He never saw them again, and for that he was angry. But more than that, he hurt. Giving in to this feeling that was creeping through his chest now meant allowing himself the chance to be hurt again. He couldn't let himself give into that warmth so easily. He couldn't risk losing that warmth again.

"Where do you feel the warmth trying to spread?" his teacher asked.

"My chest, but-" Soren began.

"Don't fight it," Master Ryu warned. "Grief blocks that gate. Do not allow the past to fill you with doubt or fear. Allow the warmth to spread and let it center you."

The hesitation was great. On the one hand, he wanted to learn what this inner peace meant, but on the other hand, he was afraid. Afraid of gaining something only to lose it again. The aura ignited a warmth in his stomach now, still threatening to spread, but could he let it? His stomach was doing somersaults at the feeling, and the warmth was enticing. It was gentle, calming, soothing. Not at all like the fear that felt like pins and needles in the back of his mind. He was afraid to embrace it, but he was afraid to lose this feeling too. It felt wonderful from what he had experienced so far, and to let such a feeling in would mean feeling it through all of his senses.

But at what cost? Could he trust it? Could he trust losing something he found comfort in? He decided he wanted to try.

Slowly, hesitantly, Soren let it slip past his defenses and fill his entire chest, running down his limbs and up into his head. Relief washed through him unexpectedly, and his shoulders relaxed on their own accord. He breathed in deeply and let out another slow breath. This. This was what inner peace felt like, he realized. What they had been babbling about finding through loud places and lively spirits of the forest. This was quiet. This was peace. But it was also more. It was a roaring flame, but not one that crackled and snapped, but one that warmed and glowed gently. It was something he'd always wanted to feel, but had never had the words to understand. He still didn't understand it, but he never wanted to let it go.

"Now," Master Ryu continued, interrupting his thoughts a bit, but not so much that he lost the feeling. "Let your spirit go to it."

"I can do that?" he breathed, his eyes still closed.

"Yes," Master Ryu said gently.

And so, he did, reaching out towards the warmth for the first time. His head fell to his chest as his body went slack where he sat. His spirit astral projected its way to the aura, but not before tethering itself to his body so he wouldn't lose his way. There, sitting atop a wall that looked to be in ruins, was Amara, practicing her fire powers. She seemed unsure of herself as she worked, but there was a determined line on her brow as she made her first few flame attempts. She was alone, and as soon as he saw her, he felt a peace settle over him even more solidly than before. He watched as she worked, unable to tear his eyes from her. Her movements were graceful despite her hesitations, her new fear from being caught in a fire on the first day of training having been holding her back from working with fire - but when she finally produced a flame and kept it alive, the look of triumph on her face made his heart skip a beat. He couldn't help but smile, too.

Love. Love was what he was feeling.

"Soren," he heard Master Ryu's voice from a distance. "It's time to come back."

He felt a tug pulling him away, but not before Amara looked up in his direction. She didn't seem to see him, but Soren felt as if they locked eyes for a moment. He quickly let the tug pull him back and when he returned to his body, the warmth had faded, but wasn't entirely gone.

"Did you find the source of your peace?" Master Ryu asked.

"I believe so," Soren replied, though his cheeks flushed at the thought.

Amara? His source of peace? Though it made sense, it still came as a shock. She always took the time to explain things to him he didn't understand. Could calm him when he was angry with just a few words. She was always so kind and patient when he got frustrated. He was glad to have made friends with her and now she was helping him even more by being his source of peace, and she didn't even know it. And now maybe something more? He only dared to hope.

Peace to him hadn't been some tranquil place filled with sounds and movement and creatures. It'd been being comfortable around someone he knew with no expectation of having to act a certain way or be a certain way. Like he was with Amara, he could show confusion or speak his mind and not get judged for it. She didn't give him backlash for not knowing something that was obvious to everyone else, but not so obvious to him. She just explained it. Simple as that. It wasn't sarcastic, or at least he didn't feel it to be sarcastic despite not really understanding sarcasm; it was just a natural thing she did. And it made him feel at ease.

"Then let's begin again," Master Ryu smiled.

Perhaps there really was something to this inner peace thing after all.

"So, how does alchemy work, exactly?" Tursanay asked, watching Rodney prepare his crystals. "And what does it have to do with those rocks?"

"They're crystals," Rodney corrected, though he knew she knew what they were. "with magnets inside of them to help the alignment of the transmutation circle match up with the astrological positioning and magnetic fields of the earth so you can transmute anywhere. See how the transmutation circle rotates when it's cast on the ground? That's the positioning needed to use alchemy. It's gone from stationary to mobile in the last century and really changed things up for alchemists." Rodney said excitedly because he actually knew what he was talking about.

"Before you'd have to either know by feeling," he continued. "study astronomy and science for years before you could make your first successful alchemical reaction, or go by the four directions north, south, east, and west to guestimate where to put the circle. Some people even carried pocket magnets to put in water to help pinpoint the magnetic fields if it was daytime and not night where you could actually see the planetary alignments. Others would have these special glasses that were bespelled to let them see the stars through the daytime sky and through clouds! It's really cool, actually."

"That does sound cool," Amara smiled, listening too.

Rodney added, "The crystals store the necessary information needed to project the kind of transmutation circle you need for whatever type of transmutation you are trying to make. Often, you have to have special ingredients on you in order to make the transmutation work, but other times you can use what's around you to make it work. Just like we learned in science, matter can neither be created nor destroyed. So, you have to have some form of equivalent exchange for things to work. You can't make a mountain out of a molehill."

"Okay, I understood about a third of that," Tursanay said slowly.

"Basically," Rodney began. "it's defined by the ability to use one's spiritual energy to manipulate surrounding matter from one object or substance, into another, following the laws of equivalent exchange. You can deconstruct, then reconstruct matter within the capabilities of your spiritual energy. The weaker the spiritual energy, the greater the difficulty to manipulate anything, and the more heavily you rely on transporting chemicals and compounds for transmutation use."

"So, kind of like magic, right?" Amara asked.

"Well… you can't like… curse people or levitate things like magic. Only alter an object's physical makeup. You can't, like, turn lead into gold or make counterfeit money—well, I mean you can—but it's illegal. And human transmutation outside of medical necessity is also illegal.

"That's a frightening thought. Can you, like, bring people back from the dead or something?" Tursanay asked.

"Nah, nothing like that," Rodney replied. "That's necromancy, and apparently you can only bring them back for a short period before their body starts decaying and makes it impossible for the spirit to stay connected to it. Which is why it's used to solve crimes rather than, say, create huge armies of undead."

"Thank goodness," Amara noted.

"Seriously," Rodney agreed. "But basically, any transmutations or experiments done on living creatures and beings must be for medical purposes only—so like open heart surgery, or fixing a broken bone, things like that. You can't just, I dunno, merge yourself with a horse because you wanna be a centaur."

"Oh yikes, but also like, wow, I kind of wish I could try alchemy now. It sounds pretty cool," Amara said.

"Okay, I have the right crystals and the right transmutation circles," Rodney said, taking a breath and letting it out as he examined his handiwork. "I just need to concentrate."

Standing up and wiping the sweat from his brow, Rodney took his stance and held out the crystal that projected the transmutation circle onto the ground. He took another breath and activated the circle. It glowed brightly before him and in moments the light faded with a blast, leaving a rather melted looking lump on the ground.

"I DID IT!" he exclaimed. "It didn't blow up in my face this time!"

"What is that supposed to be?" Amara asked, tilting her head.

"It's a flowerpot," Rodney replied.

"That is the poorest excuse for a flower pot I've ever seen, Rodney," Tursanay laughed.

"Granted, it's a little melted, but it's still a flowerpot," Rodney argued.

Amara was laughing now, too.

"A little melted!" she cried. "It looks like someone took a dump and stepped in it!"

"You laugh now!" Rodney pretended to bristle. "But come spring, when you need a flowerpot to put your potted plants and herbs in for whatever healing you learn, you'll be sorry! 'Oh no!'" he added in a falsetto voice. "'I don't have anything to plant this dumb turnip in! Maybe I'll ask Rodney for a flower pot since he's mastered them now!' And I'll be like, 'No, you had your chance to be supportive.'" he added in a lower voice before switching back to the falsetto. "And you'll be like 'Rodney I'm so sorry! I should have been more supportive of your endeavors!' and I'll be like 'That's right. Now suffer'."

The two girls all but shrieked with laughter at his voice, changes and gestures until they cried. This was top tier Rodney humor and the more he gestured to the flowerpot, the more it seemed to melt, which made them only laugh harder.

"Oh my god," Tursanay gasped, trying to catch her breath. "Rodney, I'll take your melted flower pot and make it into a beautiful work of art by planting stuff in it, and everyone will love it."

"No," Rodney said pompously, still pretending to be offended. "I'm going to take my first flower pot as a trophy. You can have the next one."

"Deal," Tursanay giggled.

"Maybe it won't be as melted this time," Amara whispered conspiratorially.

Tursanay snorted.

Amara struggled with the flame in her hand, her palms sweating, hands shaking with the effort not to burn herself. Her teacher was explaining how fire was alive and that it should be respected, but that just made the butterflies in

Amara's chest fly up into her throat as an unsteady, racing heartbeat replaced them. The flames danced with the sound of her pulse and Nuri barked at her one more time to steady herself or the flames would consume her.

Amara doused the flames again and took a shaky breath.

"I can't focus on being calm when you're yelling at me!" she complained.

"You're a Dai-Nē, you will have people screaming at you that their houses are on fire, that they're loved ones are dying, that their world is falling apart because of flames dancing before your face that you will be too afraid to tame because you can't focus! Learn to take the good with the bad. Fire can give you light and food and warmth, but it can take everything from you in an instant just the same. Steady your heart rate. Steady your nerves in the face of danger. Learn how to face adversaries with a calm mind and you will know what it is to understand fire." Nuri snapped.

"I get what you're trying to say, but can we please stop with the yelling?" Amara pleaded. "I'm still not sold on being a mermaid, let alone being able to control the elements. This is still scary to me!" She was on the verge of tears. Fire was terrifying. It ate everything in its path and while she understood the principal meaning behind the whole 'fire neither good nor evil, just a tool to be used', it didn't stop it from biting her hands and burning her scales when she dropped it.

She was still getting used to the fact she had to say scales.

Nuri took a breath and let it out roughly. "Start with your breathing," she said at last. "I'm going to yell at you. When you can breathe calmly through my yelling and your heart rate not speed up, then we'll take up the flames again."

"But—" Amara began, but Nuri didn't give her a chance to speak.

"I said work on your breathing Dai-Nē!" she yelled, making Amara jump and lean away from her. And so, it began. Nuri yelled, walking around her in a circle. She attacked her personally with her words. Called her weak. Called her names. Crossed lines. Amara begged for her to stop, but she wouldn't. Finally realizing that she wouldn't get through this without at least trying to work on her breathing, Amara closed her eyes and tried to block her teacher out.

It was hard. Inhale. The hardest thing in the world right then to block out the screaming and berating and the words that cut deeply and personally. Exhale. They cut through her peace like a knife. Inhale. Slicing into her with each syllable, each word carving a fresh wound. Exhale. Her heart rate sped up until it was the only thing she could hear as she tried to clamp her hands over her ears to block out the sounds. Inhale. When her ears rang with the sound, she focused on it, trying to ignore Nuri. Exhale. But it was then she realized she hadn't heard her in several minutes, the sound of her own pulse thudding in her ears the only thing she'd been able to hear. Inhale.

Something came back to her then as she realized her pulse was slowing as she breathed in and out carefully. Exhale.

"Light the fire Dai-Nē!" Nuri's voice instructed. Inhale. "Light it!" And though it was still the same cutting tone that she'd used all along, it didn't penetrate Amara's anxiety. Exhale. Didn't send her heart into palpitations and scrambling to crawl into her throat to hide. Inhale. It was just a voice. Exhale. Instructing her to light the fire, she realized she now felt like she could.

Taking a breath and letting it out again, Amara held out one hand, removing the other from the side of her face as well. She opened her eyes as the flame roared to life in her palm, steady, strong, and warm. She had done it.

Inhale.

The fire grew in her palm.

Exhale.

The fire shrank back to its original size.

The flickering matched her heart beat. A slow and steady flame.

"Good job," Nuri praised. "You not only have mastered yourself, even more impressive, you've mastered dealing with me."

Amara contemplated throwing the fire at her for the comment, but shook her head instead.

Tursanay breathed hard as she wiped the sweat from her brow. She'd been at work for hours and she still had made little progress. At least, not as much as she'd wanted. She'd been trying for weeks to solidify the arm of light, but she hadn't solidified it enough to pick up anything, let alone punch something.

It had been much harder than she had anticipated, but the fact she had made an arm of light in the first place had excited her to no end. She had learned to form the hand and could even flex the fingers. Seeing herself with two hands when she looked down was an unfamiliar experience, but it was one that sent her heart pounding with pure exhilaration every time she saw it. Not necessarily for having two arms. That part was just plain weird. Rather, it was the fact it had been possible at all. Positive energy had created this. Positivity and hard work. And all of it her own.

Soren sat atop the rock she was attempting to punch repeatedly, with little to no success, as the light scattered when it touched a surface. His eyes were closed and his legs folded beneath him as he concentrated on the surrounding auras.

Rodney was sitting a little way off, perfecting his transmutation crystals and Amara sat behind Soren, practicing her fire powers.

There was a little stream running past them and the sound of the water was a pleasant background noise as Amara dipped her tail into the smooth surface, gently splashing occasionally as she curled her tail in concentration.

Attalira was running in circles around their little sitting area, changing her form as she went from animal to animal to human to hybrid beasts. Her movements were getting even more fluid than before, though that hadn't seemed like a possible thing. Now she was moving with the grace of a master, far earlier than the others.

"You're not focusing your energy into your hand," Soren commented, not opening his eyes. "You begin to, then it scatters at the last moment. It is as if you are hesitating."

"I know, I know," Tursanay sighed irritably. "I've thrown a punch before, so I know what it feels like, but every time I go to hit something with the light arm my brain thinks 'This is going to hurt' even though I don't feel it, and it messes me up."

"Perhaps you should try punching something softer first," Amara suggested. "I can make you some sand to put in one of Rodney's flowerpots and you can punch at it until you get a feel for it. Sand is soft, but it adds a lot of resistance to build muscle."

"Maybe," Tursanay said. "Let's try it. I'm willing to do anything to make this work."

Rodney created a pot, much larger and steadier than any they'd seen him make before, and Amara filled it full of sand. Tursanay took a punch at it, but the light scattered at the surface again. Her shoulders dropped with a defeated sigh.

"Start by putting your hand on the surface of the sand and making it keep the shape," Attalira suggested. "By first touching the surface, you are creating a solidified form. Remember, you're not used to having this many limbs. I know how that feels from being a shapeshifter. It takes time to build up muscle memory. Trying to use your nondominant hand to do something you've only done with your dominant hand is hard. You have to train yourself to use your nondominant hand enough so that it solidifies first."

Tursanay's eyes lit up at the idea. After several more tries, she kept her hand formed on top of the sand.

"Ay! Get it T!" Rodney cheered.

Tursanay beamed from ear to ear.

"Try sticking your fingers in the sand next!"

As she made her attempts, Rodney cheering her on and Attalira offering pointers.

"Yes!" Tursanay exclaimed, picking up a handful of sand with her arm of light and holding it steady as she sifted the sand through her fingers back into the pot. With a look of triumph, she ran straight for the rock and tried to knock a solid punch into it, but once again the light scattered and she smacked right up against the rock, knocking herself to the ground.

Tursanay cursed under her breath. "I thought for sure that time would work!"

"You okay, T?" Rodney asked, moving over to help her

up. She checked to make sure her nose wasn't bleeding from how hard she'd hit, but gave a nod to Rodney. She turned and looked at the rock again and abruptly dove for it, forming the fist as she went, and knocked a solid punch into it, jarring Amara and Soren with the effort.

"*Yes! Yes! Yes!*" she cheered. "*Look I cracked it!*"

"Dude, that's so cool!" Rodney said, going over and examining her handy work.

"Hey, watch it!" Amara called. "We're still up here," she laughed.

"How'd you manage it?" Rodney asked.

"I figured if I didn't give myself enough time to think about it, I couldn't chicken out," Tursanay said with a grin.

"Interesting method," Attalira grinned, admiring Tursanay's handiwork.

"I'm gonna punch a tree next!" Tursanay cheered.

"Do not hurt the trees," Soren pleaded. "They'll ask me to heal them."

"It'll be good practice for both of us then!" Tursanay grinned.

Soren groaned, and Attalira laughed.

"We are going to teach you a special technique each of your elements is capable of tapping into if you are of a high level of skill. Only those with the precision to tap into this power can accomplish this technique," Yasar was saying as he watched Master Sharrod set up a barrier around them.

Another magic user stood off to one side, but Amara hadn't caught his name.

He was a large man with tan skin. His shoulders were

broad as was his torso, but his legs were much narrower in width than his upper half. He was bare chested, his curly black hair running down in ringlets and waves over his shoulders. His nose was broad and flat with wide nostrils, and his eyes were a warm brown color. He wasn't a hairy individual despite his mass of hair on his head, but he was a well-marked individual. All across his skin were shapes and markings. Waves, triangles, lines, circles. All making a map of a story that only those who knew its secrets could read. He stood stoically by watching the process of Master Sharrod putting up the barriers and said not a word.

"What are Tursanay's teachers here for?" Amara asked.

"To prevent you from doing one of two things," Nuri said, stepping forward with hands on her hips as she examined the handiwork of the other Council members. "Telling others of what you learned here... and dying."

"Dying?" Amara squeaked, terrified.

"This barrier will keep your form in a localized place so that we can... reassemble you if necessary," Yasar tried, but the look of horror that crossed Amara's face said he'd clearly made a mistake in saying those particular set of words to her.

"I don't know if I want to learn this technique," Amara said hesitantly.

"You must," Nyx laughed as if sharing a good joke and not talking about Amara's life hanging in the balance. "All Dai-Nē of Element must learn this method to be the best they can be."

"What exactly am I supposed to be learning?" Amara questioned, still concerned.

"How to turn yourself into the elements themselves," Yasar replied.

Amara blinked once, furrowed her brow, then blinked again.

"I'm sorry what?" she said.

"Observe," Yasar said. He backed away into the center of the dome Master Sharrod had prepared, the other Council members backing away to the edges of the barrier. She did the same, not sure what to expect as Yasar spun in place once, twice, then suddenly, with a great wind, swirled into a great tornado, his body disappearing entirely into the surrounding air.

"What's going on?!" Amara yelled over the wind. "Where did he go? Is he in the tornado?"

"He became the tornado," Anan shouted back, explaining.

The wind died down, and Yasar's form appeared bit by bit in the wind and dust swirling around, and when he fully formed, the wind petered out completely.

"You will learn to do this with all the elements," Yasar said. "Wind is the most dangerous because it can sweep you away without this barrier in place to keep you together. Hence why we have Master Sharrod here."

"Then what's he here for?" Amara asked, pointing to the tattooed man.

"Master Lakshmi is here to prevent you from telling others of this technique, as it is a highly guarded secret. Master Lakshmi is a secret keeper. Every tattoo on his skin is a secret locked away. Each one holding a story. Every mark, every symbol, is another secret kept," Yasar said.

"Wait, you're going to tattoo me?" Amara squeaked, sounding more terrified of that than she had been of being turned into wind. "Can I object to this?!"

"Do not worry, it does not hurt," Yasar began, but Amara balked.

"I don't want to expose myself in order to be tattooed in the first place!" she argued.

"Then perhaps somewhere else," Master Lakshmi said, stepping forward. "Somewhere not revealed to the world, but that exposes itself every day."

Amara hesitated, highly doubting there was such a place. And even then, would she agree to have it there? She didn't like this idea at all. But, much to her surprise, Master Lakshmi stuck his tongue out at her. She blinked, confused for a moment until she realized he was showing her his tongue. It also had black stripes marking it.

What kind of secret would hide there?

"You already have the mark of Dai-Nē on your tongue," Lakshmi said. "Perhaps adding another mark there will keep you from being exposed whilst keeping a promise to never speak of this to an outsider."

Amara considered this. "You're not going to stab my tongue with a needle, are you?"

"There is more than one way to get a tattoo. There is the traditional way, and there is the magical way," Lakshmi said. "The magical way involves an incantation only. No marring of the skin. Or tongue."

"Can't I just promise you I won't tell anyone and you believe my word?" she tried again.

"This will keep others from being able to discover your secret by other means. Truth rings, telepathic connections, torture, and much more. You will not be able to speak of it, nor will anyone be able to derive it from you by nefarious means," Lakshmi said. "I hold no secrets." He smiled. "And if you asked me to set a truth ring around me, I would say the same thing. I know no secrets."

Amara let that sink in and considered his words for a

moment. He could lie through his teeth about any of his secrets and no one could get the truth from him, no matter what they did. She briefly wondered if there was a way to unlock the secrets, but filed that away as a question to ask later, as something else was weighing more pertinently on her mind.

"You promise its incantation only?" she wanted to confirm.

"I promise," Yasar said, stepping forward.

"Okay," Amara consented at last. Truth be told, being able to turn herself into water and wind or maybe even lightning sounded amazing. She could take one step, turn into lightning, and travel across the plain in the blink of an eye. What if she could turn herself into a cloud? The ideas were bubbling up inside her the more she thought about it, making her excited to take the step, rather than nervous that something bad might happen. "Can I learn water first?" she asked hesitantly. Wind still scared her, but perhaps this wouldn't be so bad. They at least had a tub for her to sit in for this one.

"Of course," Anan smiled, stepping forward.

"Again!" Tryn called as Rodney blew up yet another attempt at alchemy, singeing off part of his eyebrows. This would be the third or fourth time Tursanay would have to heal his face. She was probably tiring of it, despite her saying it was good practice to heal him. Not that he minded her healing him, either. He could look at her unabashedly as they talked. Right now, however, he was more frustrated with his work than he was considering what it would be like to be healed by Tursanay.

Again.

"Oh my god, what am I doing wrong?" Rodney finally demanded, frustration coloring his voice. He all but threw his hands up in the air with the effort. "I've got the ingredients. I've got the crystal transmutation circle in place. Activated the circle like I was supposed to. I just don't understand what I'm doing wrong! And I'm tired of losing my eyebrows!"

"Think! My little meat pastry, think! You've got to consider the steps and break it down further," Tryn replied. "Start with the ingredients. What did you have?"

"I used the clay because I want to make a clay pot," Rodney said. "Simple enough. It's pre-made clay, so I know that's not the issue."

"Then if it was not the ingredients, consider the crystal," Tryn said, making him think rather than give him the answer. Why did all their teachers teach like that? Even the alchemists that worked with the Council taught like that. They didn't spoon feed you anything like the teachers back home did. They let things blow up in your face and told you to get up and try again. Imagine the horror of the science teachers out there who wanted to forewarn you. Something would blow up in your face? They'd have none of this nonsense. But they weren't here, were they? he reminded himself.

"I just used a fire crystal transmutation circle because the clay has to be heated in order to form!" Rodney replied.

"And there's your issue," Tryn said, folding her arms and looking at him as if it were obvious.

Well, it certainly wasn't obvious to him.

"What's my issue?" Rodney repeated.

"The fire transmutation crystal. That's not what you use to transfigure earth. You use the earth transmutation circle," she explained.

Rodney mumbled something about the clay needing heat to form again, and Tryn gave him a look.

"If you want to change earth into another earth substance, you use the earth transmutation crystal. If you wish to create a blast of fire, you use the fire transmutation circle, and if you don't want your eyebrows snatched off your face, then I suggest using it in a direction other than downwards. When using the fire algorithm, you must direct the fire somewhere otherwise, it will just explode in your face. When using the earth algorithm, you must focus the earth into a shape. Same with water. If you want it to become ice, you must think of a shape. If you wish it to flow differently, then you must give it direction. You cannot form earth with a fire transfiguration circle."

Perhaps she was spoon feeding him the information after all.

Rodney's brow unfurrowed as he listened and suddenly everything made sense. He'd been trying to use the fire to heat and strengthen the clay, when all along, he had just needed to form the earth!

That begged the question, though, how had he formed a half-melted flower pot a few months prior without blasting his face off again? Perhaps he'd used less fire alchemy and more earthen alchemy and the reason it melted was from the extreme heat...

Maybe.

"So, all this time I've just been using the wrong crystals!" he declared. "When I went to make ice, I tried to use a wind transmutation circle because I thought it would make the water colder, but I ended up just spraying myself in the face and nearly drowning on dry land."

Tryn nodded. "You've been over thinking it. Elements can

change and reform with the same alchemical counterpart. Not an adjacent one. You cannot form ice with wind and water, but you can create a water tornado. If you put your mind to it."

"Found that out the hard way," Rodney replied. "So, if I just try to use earth with earth, I should get this down?"

"Why don't you try again and see?" Tryn challenged.

Rodney furrowed his brow, concentrating as he pulled out his earth crystal. He took a breath and held the projection of the transmutation circle over the clay. Using his alchemy to form a flower pot, this time with the earth crystal, he managed a fully formed, unmelted clay planter with a hole in the bottom, perfectly rounded for draining the roots. It was shiny and perfect and he had done it!

"*Yes! Aw yeah! That's right*! I did it! I did it! Uh-huh! Oh-yeah!" Rodney did a little dance and had Tryn laughing as she watched him. She congratulated him and patted him on the back. He held up his hand for a high five and she looked at him curiously. Rather than explain, Rodney just high fives himself and continued his little dance until Tryn told him to get back to work.

CHAPTER 17
MISTRUST

The night shift classes were the roughest. The Dai-Nē had trained themselves to wake up two hours before dawn after a series of unfortunate events that lead them to fear over-sleeping ever again. When night came, their eyelids grew heavy, and when the stars disappeared from the sky, their eyes would pop open, wide awake and ready for whatever challenge to be presented to them for that day.

Night classes, however, threw off that entire schedule, and kept them yawning through the classes, falling asleep mid lecture, and being smacked on the head with a switch to keep them awake. Or water dumped over their head from a bucket.

Tonight, they whacked Rodney over the head several times to wake him back up, before they gave up and dumped a bucket of water on him. He shot up out of his seat and took a fighting stance to see what was attacking him. Tursanay calmed him down, Amara talking to him soothingly, before the teacher sighed and called an end to their lesson for the night. There was no point in teaching them further if they couldn't stay awake long enough to learn it anymore.

"Thank goodness," Rodney sighed with a yawn. "I'm so tired I could sleep for a week."

"We're not going to sleep just yet," Tursanay said as she made sure the teacher was out of earshot.

Rodney whined until she smacked him on the arm.

"I think we've made enough progress that we need to look up some information on our own."

"How do you plan to do this?" Soren asked.

"We're going to sneak back into the library once the teachers leave and grab some books to study."

"Why? We still have plenty of time to learn that stuff. They'll get to it eventually," Rodney said.

"No, they won't," Tursanay argued. "I found out they are hindering my training because they think I have a disadvantage by only having one arm. Imagine what they are hiding from the rest of us."

"I dunno, Tryn's pretty thorough in her teaching," Rodney said, scratching his chin.

He was getting a little stubble and needed to shave again. Come to think of it, his hair was getting a little long as well. Tursanay snapped his attention back to the present.

"She's not a part of the Council, is she?" Tursanay reminded him. "What are the alchemists in the Council teaching you?"

"Not that much," he admitted. "I've mastered the basics and they still demand I keep practicing things I've already got down pat."

"Exactly. They're hindering us because they think we can't handle it. But I think we can," Tursanay said with a flourish.

"What if it's something like 'master the basics until they're ingrained in you'?" Rodney said, but Tursanay shook her head.

"They barely let me brew an antidote potion that helps with allergic reactions. Let alone proper spells," Tursanay complained.

"Wait, so if they're hindering our learning, what is the point?" Amara said, not fully believing it could just be out of spite or something of the like. "What's their motive? To keep us subdued or something?"

"I dunno," Tursanay said. "Maybe!"

"Perhaps they do not want us learning more than they can perform themselves," Soren commented. "To keep their advantage over us."

"That seems like we're looking for trouble," Amara said, feeling like they were reaching. "I'm sure there's a perfectly normal explanation for why they're doing this."

"Think about it, A," Tursanay said, trying to reason with the mermaid before her. "If we became more powerful than them, what influence would they have over us? We could just walk all over them."

"Why wouldn't they want to build us up to the best we could be?" Amara argued. "That doesn't make any sense. My teachers are teaching me a lot of complicated things..."

"Well, yeah, you have the good teachers. I have the jerks," Tursanay replied, putting her hand on her hip in frustration. "At least your teachers will talk to us and show us stuff. My teachers are all stuffy old men that think they know it all and refuse to learn a different way to make it easier for me to learn. Do you know what my teacher was trying to drill into me today? A writing spell. When I could literally just pick up a pen and do it myself. You know why he was trying to teach me such a useless spell? Because he didn't think I could handle much else because of my missing arm."

"Maybe you misunderstood him?" Amara suggested sheepishly. "I'm sure he didn't mean it like that."

"No, he straight up said that he meant it like that," Tursanay replied. "They're not here to build us up, A. They're here to control us and teach us what they want us to know and I, for one, am sick of it."

Amara was quiet for a moment as she weighed these words. "I guess it wouldn't hurt to learn more stuff and surprise them with our ability to learn more than they expected..."

"I for one would love the chance to shove it in Sharrod's face that I can handle myself with one arm or none," Tursanay growled, setting her jaw.

"I do not see a problem with learning more," Soren agreed, looking over at Amara to see if that was okay with her.

When she gave a hesitant nod, he gave one to the others, and they all looked at Attalira, who'd been silent this whole time.

"What about you?" Tursanay demanded.

Attalira looked at them all, then shrugged. "I'm not going to stop you."

Tursanay grinned. "Let's go break into the library."

They had to pretend to go to bed and wait for the other Council members to trickle back to their respective houses before making their way to the library where all the history books and spell books and books on various types of powers were kept. Careful to avoid the squeaking boards on the floor, they trailed around the room, looking for any volume that stuck out to them.

Soren, in particular, found an interesting book that caught his eye. A book on breaking magical spells using spirit energy.

"It says here that using ether to invade the spell, you can break it down to its basic components and destroy it from the inside out," he read aloud for the others to hear.

"Dude, that's so cool!" Tursanay said. "You'd be like a spell hacker!"

"That would be really cool," Amara agreed, looking over his shoulder as he read.

"It also says how to tether one's soul to one's body when astral projecting to keep anything from entering one's body from the spirit world," Soren added.

"That sounds terrifying," Rodney said, considering that.

Tursanay found an advanced book on magical spells that looked rather complicated and grinned broadly.

"Oh, this baby is coming with me," she said, grinning to herself.

"You found a child?" Soren asked, confused, looking up from his book.

"Just a turn of phrase," Amara explained. "It just means she's really interested in the book."

"Oh," Soren said, looking a little less concerned.

Amara's eyes wandered the shelves near the top, her new found height abilities never getting old for her. Somewhere in the dust near the top, she found scrolls with special techniques from each elemental fighting style drawn into little diagrams.

"This is amazing!" she said, unfurling it gently. "It says here you can apply techniques from each element and use it for a different element. Like the breathing techniques in air bending can keep your inner fire going to warm you in cold climates."

"Nice!" Tursanay grinned. "I told you this was a good idea!"

Rodney found some books on how to be a traveling alchemist and have your ingredients at the ready without being bogged down with their weight, as well as ways to use the surrounding things in creative ways that allowed you to perform alchemy without using ingredients.

"Whoa," he said as he picked up a third volume. "Guys, look at this."

He opened the book and showed them the text and diagrams inside, but none of them understood the gibberish except for him. When Tursanay prompted him for what it was, he explained.

"It's how to transmute without crystals to produce a transmutation circle!" He flipped the page, and it showed a picture of hands with various circles tattooed on the palms and back of the hand. "Some people tattoo the main circles they use on their hands so that they can transmute without them!"

"That's cool," Tursanay said.

"You'd have to wear gloves all the time to hide your tattoos if we ever went back home," Amara hummed, thinking about it. "It would be a little impractical."

"Or I could do a mark concealment spell on him and it could hide them from plain sight," Tursanay reminded her.

"Does magic even work on that side of the veil?" Amara asked.

"Huh," Tursanay thought. "That's something we were

considering before, but never had time to try it out. We should ask about later."

"Well, it kind of does," Rodney said, scratching his head.

They looked at him.

"I mean, remember those creatures that chased us that Amara couldn't see because she didn't have her powers at the time?"

"Oh, yeah!" Tursanay remembered. "Whatever that was was definitely magical. Even if it was on that side of the veil."

"My thoughts exactly," Rodney agreed.

"What things?" Attalira asked, curious as she thumbed through a book on shapeshifting while using weapons.

"We'll have to catch you up sometime about what happened before we met you," Tursanay replied. "It was a wild ride, let me tell you."

"What did you find, Attalira?" Amara asked conversationally.

Attalira looked down at the book in her hand. "Just something on shapeshifting with weapons. I've never really used a weapon with shapeshifting. I've always made myself the weapon. Adding a weapon could increase my potency," she replied. "It's a thought anyhow."

"Taking things to the next level," Tursanay nodded in approval. "That's what we're here for."

"We should probably go before we get caught," Amara said.

"True," Tursanay said, checking over her shoulder out the window. Things were still clear of Council members. "Let's grab what we can and get out of here."

The other Dai-Nē followed her lead and grabbed as many books on the subjects they wanted and carefully made their way back to their house. They hid the books in their rooms with Amara and Tursanay's help to bury them beneath a floorboard.

Over the next few weeks, they practiced them in secret around each other to see if they could perform new things they'd learned. For a while they were out of their depth, but Tryn helped Rodney, proud of him for wanting to delve deeper into alchemy, as well as Amara surprising her own teachers at how easily she began taking to new techniques thanks to the various scrolls that taught her how to cross over techniques from each element.

However, the newfound curiosity of Soren and Tursanay about more complicated techniques did not please their teachers. The more they tried to get them to open up about the things they'd seen in the books of the library, the more they were yelled at and demanded of to know where they'd heard such dangerous spells. So, they set to work in secret to help each other. Especially since their powers technically opposed one another. Soren worked on breaking spells she created, and Tursanay tried to make more complicated ones he couldn't destroy. She got particularly good with barriers, almost to the point of frustrating Soren that he couldn't crack their base.

To Tursanay's credit, she'd added as many components to the spell as she could that still made it work, and she made good progress with it. The more complicated a spell she learned, the more Soren had trouble breaking them. Which only made him more determined than ever. It was a close bond the two created, breaking down and building up each other's powers, and Amara and Rodney were glad to see they were getting some kind of help to get stronger. Even if it was just each other.

Attalira, on the other hand, had taken to learning

weapons from General Eizo, who was a weapons master, and one of Soren's teachers. Soren was good at most fighting styles, being the Dai-Nē of Ether and spirit energy, but Attalira relied mostly on her shifting to keep her safe from his blows. And she was failing. General Eizo was an excellent fighter, and used to the shenanigans of shapeshifters, therefore very good at keeping her from being able to dodge most anything he threw at her. He taught her swords, spears, various forms of close range and long-range weapons and those that fell in between. He taught her how to fight a crowd of people versus a one-on-one fight with a powerful opponent. By the end of the day every day she was exhausted, more so than she'd ever been with the regular training. She took to shapeshifting like a fish to water - sometimes literally. But weaponry was her shortcoming. She was not as proficient as she wanted to be, and it frustrated her into fighting back harder.

The other Dai-Nē agreed to fight with her to help her out and to grow as a fighter and not get used to just one type of person's fighting style, and she liked the idea. They trained together, learning from her and she from them, and with each passing day they grew calluses on their hands and feet, making it easier to fight with them. They grew stronger by the day, and pretty soon the teachers were breaking up their fights, saying they were getting too dangerous and that someone might seriously get hurt if they continued the way they were going.

When they took to studying in secret, they'd sit around and share techniques with each other and exchanged with each other some things they'd learned in their own powers that might apply to one another's. That had been Amara's idea after seeing those scrolls. Perhaps there were things in each other's methods that could help them get stronger with every try.

"I don't see what part of shapeshifting could aid you," Attalira said to Amara. "You bend elements to your will, I bend myself."

"Show me how you transform from one shape to another," Amara replied. "I have an idea."

"Like what?" Attalira questioned.

"Let's start with something fun," Amara replied. "Something that's a challenge for me. Try shifting into a wolf or some other living creature."

Attalira got to her feet and stretched a little, rolling her head around in a circle as she considered what to change into. She took a moment, then shifted into an enormous snake, moving gracefully as she did so, stretching and reforming into the new shape with ease. Amara watched her carefully, and replicated her movements, getting up and stretching, then bending the water in the pitcher on the table into the same shape Attalira changed into, surprising the snake with an identical watery replica of herself. Amara then froze the water and moved the ice sculpture around as if it were a living thing. The grace and style it moved mimicked that of the snake before it.

"Try changing into something else," Amara said softly. Attalira then shifted with a twirl into a winged elk. Furrowing her brow as she watched, Amara stole more water from the pitcher as she reformed the ice the same way Attalira had moved. After a moment, the ice sculpture formed into a winged elk just like Attalira, and pawed the ground just as she did.

"Whoa," Rodney said, watching the ice move in awe. "A living ice sculpture! That's so cool!"

"I can make it fly too," Amara said. "Just not inside."

The elk lowered its head, and the ice mimicked it again. With a snort, Attalira changed back into herself and Amara grinned, mimicking her form with the ice.

"I'm getting a little faster at this," she said.

"I do not look like that," Attalira said, squinting at the reflection of her face. The ice mimicked her position and Attalira went straight again, casting a glare at Amara for continuing to reflect her movements.

"It's totally your twin!" Rodney laughed. "I can't tell you two apart!"

"The one that has no color is the fake Attalira," Soren supplied.

"He can tell them apart, Soren, he's just being facetious," Amara laughed, returning the water to the pitcher.

"Oh," Soren said. "That was good water bending none-the-less," he added.

"Thank you," Amara beamed.

Soren flushed at her smile and looked back down at the table.

"Who's next?"

"Ooh! Me, me!" Rodney said, getting to his feet as Attalira sat back down. They spent several hours trading ideas on how to work with each other's technique before the front door slid open to reveal Master Sharrod and Master Ryu standing before them right as Tursanay was creating a barrier she'd learned from the new spell book around Amara who was using a technique taught to her by Rodney to break out.

"What is the meaning of this?!" Master Sharrod demanded. "Where did you learn such a dangerous spell?"

"I made it up," Tursanay lied.

"Nonsense!" Master Sharrod growled. "I know about the missing books in the library. We are here to search for them!"

"I don't know what you're talking about," Tursanay replied firmly.

"She's lying," Master Ryu said. "Her aura is shifting colors."

"Don't read my aura without my permission!" Tursanay bristled.

"Don't read our books without our permission!" countered Master Sharrod. "You could have cut off her oxygen and killed her!"

"I know what I'm doing!" Tursanay argued. "I accounted for that!"

"You don't know what you are doing. You are just a child!" Master Sharrod snapped, barging past her and heading down the hallway. "Where are you keeping them?"

"Hey! Stay out of my personal stuff!" Tursanay balked as he entered her room. She followed and found him tearing apart her bed roll looking for the books she'd taken. "Stop it!" She formed a barrier around him and shoved it across the room, taking him down with it.

"You do *not* use magic against *me*, girl!" he hissed, getting to his feet.

The room grew dark, as if the sun itself was being blocked out. He growled a command and her barrier shook. He growled another, frustration flashing across his face, and the barrier shook again. Tursanay realized the barrier was the only thing between her and a butt kicking and scrambled to keep it steady. However, the third command shattered it like glass, and a sorcerous wind swept up the contents of her room. As he spoke, his layered voice commanded the words of power written for all to read to return to him.

As he called for the books, Tursanay noticed the floorboard giving way to the power of his command as they tried to return to their master. Casually, she stepped on the floorboard as if moving closer to cast another spell, and suddenly the wind pressure was blasting against her and knocking her back. Tursanay tried to command the wind to stop, but it muffled her voice and the command fell short. She desperately tried to throw up another barrier to defend herself, but Master Sharrod was much too strong.

Then an idea came to her. She was trying to bespell someone who was casting an impenetrable sorcerous wind, when in fact she should cast defensively on herself to give herself a leg to stand on. Throwing up a barrier around herself, the abrupt change in wind pressure almost made her fall forward. Able to breathe normally again as everything around her swelled and swirled in chaos, she formed her arm of light and took a boxing stance. She punched at the barrier and created a projectile on the other side to go flying towards Master Sharrod.

Surprised by the projectile, Master Sharrod had to dodge out of the way by throwing himself across the room to keep from getting hit by it. When she began to rapid-fire punch things at him, pushing him towards the door, he caught onto her scheme and began throwing a barrier up around himself to prevent it from hitting him at least directly. The swirling of her furniture seemed to cease as they fought between barriers and threw punches at one another that the other had to block or dodge because they were going to break the other's barrier if they didn't. Tursanay gave a twisting kick and knocked a powerful blast towards Master Sharrod that sent him flying back against the wall, knocking the breath out of him.

Suddenly cracks formed across Tursanay's barrier like

glass breaking, and she briefly wondered if she'd hit too hard against her own barrier, until she turned and looked to see Master Ryu with his hands on her barrier, a glow beneath his palm. He was using ether to hack into her magic; she realized. Throwing up a barrier that had stumped Soren, Tursanay barely saved herself from another blow from Master Sharrod before the outer barrier blew.

"Stop it! Can't you see I'm holding my own?" Tursanay yelled. "I'm learning something by doing this! Why can't you be happy about that?"

"You are learning to be a delinquent!" Master Sharrod barked. "I never should have left the library unlocked! I should have known that you would betray my trust and get into dangerous magic!"

"This isn't dangerous! It's protective!" Tursanay yelled. She was tired of being treated like a child. Tired of superficial magic. Tired of being treated like an invalid because of her arm. She'd gone her whole life without it and did just fine. Why was magic any different? Just because people were used to it being done two handed didn't mean she couldn't do it with one. She'd proven a lot of people wrong like that in her life. Her grandmothers had made sure of that.

'They'll feel sorry for you, Tursanay,' her g-ma had told her. 'Like you can't handle things on your own and like you should be sad for yourself because they don't see you as whole. But you are. And having only one arm won't stop you from punching them in the teeth.'

Tursanay, Masters Ryu and Sharrod all heard a crash as the other Dai-Nē came forward and stood between them. They weren't protecting Tursanay so much as they were backing her up. This fight was between all of them, not just Tursanay.

"Please, just hear us out," Amara tried to reason. "We're not trying to do anything dangerous, we're trying to further our learning."

"Then you have gone about it the wrong way," Master Ryu stated firmly. "If you wanted to learn more, you should have come to us first."

"I tried that!" Tursanay balked. "And he said he was hindering my learning because I only had one arm!" She gestured vehemently towards Master Sharrod.

"I never said that! You, child, couldn't even learn a writing spell correctly. How could I possibly ever believe you'd be ready for anything more?" Master Sharrod defended. "If you cannot learn the basics, then you are not ready for more advanced magic!"

"I'm tired of learning the same thing over and over. It's drilled into me! I understand them! Just let me learn something else for once! Something besides one handed spells!" Tursanay argued.

"Not until I deem you are ready for something other than the basics," Master Sharrod replied.

"I want a different opinion," Tursanay said firmly. "Someone who's not going to hold me back just because of some prejudice."

"And who, pray tell, do you wish to give this opinion?" Master Sharrod spat sardonically. He didn't really believe she was going to come up with a legitimate answer that he could agree on, and this fight would start all over again.

"Master Ross." Tursanay said the name so confidently, Master Sharrod opened his mouth to argue, then stopped.

"Master Ross?" he asked, taken aback. The look on his face made it look as if he wondered if there was some kind of trick here. Even the other Dai-Nē paused and looked at her, confused.

"I trust him," Tursanay replied, simply.

They all exchanged looks, but Master Sharrod nodded. "Master Ross it is," he said at last, straightening up. They all made their way out of Tursanay's room and out of the Dai-Nē house and down towards Master Ross's place.

Master Sharrod was the one to knock on the door and stand back as they waited for an answer.

Master Ross opened the door, took one look at them all, and said "No," before shutting the door again and disappearing inside.

Master Sharrod knocked again, but no answer came. When he huffed in frustration, Tursanay told him to 'step aside and watch this' and knocked more persistently, or rather, nonstop until Master Ross answered so forcefully and suddenly she almost clobbered him in the face when the door jerked open again.

"*What*?" he demanded.

"We need your opinion on a very important matter," began Master Sharrod.

But Ross cut him off again.

"Not interested," he clipped and shut the door again.

"Ross, they refuse to teach me anything other than the basics because they think I'm some kind of invalid!" Tursanay called.

"This child can't even perform a writing spell, and yet she wants to try more advanced magic!" Master Sharrod called.

"I know the basics!" Tursanay argued. "I just held my own against two Council members and he's just sour!"

The door opened back up to reveal a very perturbed Master Ross, who looked ready to go back to bed. He had some kind of drink in his hand that smelled of morning coffee, and despite being late in the afternoon, he looked like he'd only just risen sometime recently.

"It is the rest day. Why are you not letting me rest?" Ross demanded slowly and quietly. The tone was dangerous despite the soft voice he asked it in and Tursanay paled slightly. Perhaps this hadn't been such a good idea after all. Master Sharrod, however, didn't seem to notice. He continued to yell about delinquent children until spittle flew from his face. Ross held up a hand to silence him and Master Sharrod's eyebrows went up in shock and indignation. How dare he? the look said.

"If you do not lower your voice and speak normally, I will throw this scalding hot liquid into your face and rapidly heal you, leaving you with blistering scars for the rest of your life. Or until you find another healer that can undo that." Master Ross blinked slowly, a sign that his head was pounding and all this yelling was not doing him any good.

"We should come back at another time to discuss this," Tursanay said, realizing this would only end in disaster if they pushed him any farther.

"No. You said you wanted a second opinion. We are getting one. *Now!*" Master Sharrod demanded, stomping his foot with emphasis. "And don't you threaten me, Master Ross!"

"It wasn't a threat. It was a promise," Ross replied flatly.

Tursanay stepped back and ushered the others away from Master Sharrod, who was working up a rage towards Ross.

"I am your *senior*. You do *not* speak to me like that!" he growled.

"I will warn you," Ross said quietly. "One more time."

"And I will warn you I am not to be spoken to in such a

manner!" Master Sharrod yelled even louder. The shout that followed came with a resounding smack as Ross threw the scalding liquid in Sharrod's face and planted his palm directly into the other man's screaming maw. Rapidly healing the wounds as they formed, large bulbous blisters formed on his face and thick skin coated them before they could pop and deflate, leaving Master Sharrod's face bumpy and painful to the touch. He would need to dig through the layers of skin that covered the blisters to pop them again, or wait weeks for the pain and blisters to be absorbed back into his system. Regardless, his face would remain disfigured until someone could properly heal it. And it was extremely doubtful Master Ross would aid him in that endeavor.

The Dai-Nē stared in horror at what Master Ross had done and looked to Tursanay for what she wanted to do now. How could she trust someone that would do that to a fellow Council member? This man was insane. Master Sharrod held his face, gingerly, sobbing as he tried to ease the pain with a few spells he could mutter under his breath.

"Sorry for the intrusion," Tursanay said softly.

Those pale blue eyes focused on her, contemplating.

"We just needed you to weigh in on whether I could study advanced magic. Master Sharrod doesn't think I'm capable because of my arm. He also thinks I haven't mastered the basics, even though I feel like I could recite them in my sleep. I wanted to get a second opinion," she added, faltering slightly as she looked over at Master Sharrod. "But..."

Master Ross stared at her coldly for a long moment. So long, in fact, Tursanay squirmed under his harsh gaze. But then, just as she doubted herself, she let out a breath and squared her shoulders and met his gaze coolly. Master Ross squinted at her.

"Learn the basics until even he is satisfied," Ross began, jabbing a finger at Master Sharrod. Tursanay frowned, ready to protest, but then he added, "And study advanced spells to build from the basics. You'll need them soon enough."

"You will pay for this, Ross," Master Sharrod breathed, still unable to fully look at him directly. "I will make sure of it."

"Is that a threat or a promise?" Master Ross asked in the same conversational tone he'd been using.

No inflection, no dare in his voice. Just normal conversation.

Well... as normal as could be with Ross involved.

"We'll get out of your hair now," Tursanay said, shooing the others away from the porch. Never were a group of teenagers more than happy to oblige to leave somewhere than the Dai-Nē were at that moment. Even Attalira looked shaken by the turn of events. Master Sharrod growled something at Master Ross, who muttered something back before shutting the door behind him and leaving Master Sharrod to find his way back to another healer.

When they were far enough away to be out of earshot, the other Dai-Nē descended onto Tursanay about what they just witnessed. Lots of accusations of 'That man has lost his mind!' and 'How could you trust someone like that?' but Tursanay took it all in stride, waiting for them to finish. When they reached the porch, she stepped ahead of them and turned to face them from the top of the small set of steps.

"Look, I know what he did was insane," Tursanay said, cutting them all off. "But I still trust his opinion. He says what he's going to do and follows through even if it's something terrifyingly insane, like what just happened. I'm not making excuses for him. What he did was wrong. But I know what I know, and I don't care if you agree with me."

"Look, T," Rodney began. "I don't know if I can trust him because I don't know him like that. And after what I just saw, I don't think I ever want to be near him again when he's angry. But if you trust him, then... okay."

Tursanay opened her mouth to argue, but stopped. "Okay?" she asked, blinking.

Rodney nodded. "Okay."

"Wait, that's it?" Amara asked, taken aback.

Tursanay was as well.

"Yeah," Rodney said. "Different people can't always trust the same person. I can trust Tryn to have my back, but she's not someone that the rest of you like. But I'm not asking you to like her or trust her, because we have a unique relationship. We know how to work with each other's oddities when others don't. Just because I can't trust Ross, doesn't mean that Tursanay can't."

There was a small silence amongst the Dai-Nē.

"That is actually very wise," Soren said eventually. "I would not have seen it that way."

"Thank you," Tursanay said to Rodney. "For trusting in me, at least."

"Always, T," Rodney smiled.

With permission from Master Ross, the Dai-Nē went back inside and resumed their training scenarios where they had left off. They practiced until late before they were called away for food, then stopped for the night. When morning came, they went back to training as usual, Master Sharrod's face looking rather haggard, but much more healed. He was much more quiet than usual with Tursanay's lessons, but he said nothing more about the books and the extra training the Dai-Nē were doing in their free time.

After her last class of the day, Tursanay walked back to Master Ross's cabin and knocked on the door. When the door opened, Master Ross was holding another cup of coffee and glaring. Standing a respectful distance back, Tursanay held up her notebook and showed she had filled up most of it with information on the Council members. Master Ross raised his eyebrow and moved aside for her to enter, and she did so wordlessly.

They went over the information meticulously. Noting which were lies that had been told due to what Ross knew of them, and which were truths. Details of them, their ranks, their likes and dislikes, the history of how they got into the office of the Council of Dai-Nē. She had things on them, their families, how many siblings they had and what each of their jobs were. Information on some of their misters and mistresses from other Council members that liked to gossip; she had it. Stories of how they linked and what each Council member said of the other on how they truly got their status, it was in there. She had background information; stories from their childhoods, she had almost everything.

"What about their ages?" Master Ross asked, glancing through the pages filled with little tabs and notes everywhere. There were so many bookmarks with color schemed strings running through them.

Tursanay frowned, thinking. "I know Yasar is only in his thirties," she began. "But I'm not sure about the rest."

"Find out their ages," Ross said, taking a sip of his coffee.

"Will that be important later?" she asked, cocking an eyebrow.

"Any little detail can be important later," Master Ross

replied. "Never forget that. Always continue to ask questions and fill that notebook past stuffing of whatever you can find out."

"Okay," Tursanay nodded. She had a determined line on her brow. Finding out this information on the Council members had made her feel like a spy, but she also only trusted them so far because of Master Sharrod. When she was digging up information on them, she felt like she could understand them a little better, and have the knowledge of how to deal with them. Being given this mission had kept her satiated in knowledge gathering whilst learning magic. She wanted to know everything. She wanted to learn all there was to learn about the magic world and people around her. And she made that happen.

Tursanay took her book and went back to the Dai-Nē house, thoughts full of how to propose the question without seeming suspicious, as well as wondering what other information she could gather to help finish up the book.

CHAPTER 18
MADNESS

The air was chilly and the first signs of another fall were settling in around them. Leaves were changing color in the woods; the air was crisp and cool. And though the atmosphere should have been relaxing, the air felt displaced, as if something were off, but Amara couldn't place what. She sat on the front porch of their cabin and sipped at some tea she had made when a shrill scream broke the air. It was feral, clearly in agony, and bloodcurdling. It was seconds before the other Dai-Nē poked their head out the door to see what it was, and they exchanged silent looks.

"What was that?" asked Rodney.

"I don't know," Amara answered.

"It sounded like that scream from before," Tursanay noted. "I hope it's not another creature loose from the island."

"Did not Ross say they will come for the most powerful thing in the training grounds?" Soren asked.

"Do you think it'll come for us?" Attalira asked, stretching her fingers into sharp objects she could use to defend herself if necessary.

"It's not coming for you," came a familiar, usually sarcastic voice. This time, it was filled with disdain.

They turned to see Ross standing next to the cabin, leaning on his cane and watching the horizon. They turned to look at him and then exchanged looks again. This time, confused.

"What do you mean?" Tursanay asked.

"That's not the right question," Ross replied.

"What is it?" Tursanay said, adjusting to his teaching method quickly. He was trying to tell them something important that they needed to figure out for themselves. That's how Tursanay had told Amara he always taught their lessons when they were together. Especially his healing lessons. Those were the hardest to get through when she didn't know what to look for or to ask. But the more she studied, the better Tursanay was getting at figuring out what needed to be done to save whatever injured creature or Council member he brought to her next.

"That's the question you're looking for," Ross replied with a nod. He stamped his cane and hobbled over to meet them on the porch. He took a seat on the chair provided there and watched the camp in the distance. "What is it, indeed?"

"Did they not tell us it was a creature from the island in the lake?" Soren asked, following his gaze.

"Is it?" Ross said cryptically.

"It's something else, isn't it?" Tursanay replied.

"An interesting assumption. But what could it be?" Ross asked.

"Something the Council doesn't want us to know about,"

answered Tursanay. When Master Ross didn't respond, only tilted his chin towards the campgrounds, Tursanay got her confirmation.

"Something?" Rodney asked, watching a figure turn a corner and run straight for them. "Or someone?"

"Now that," Ross said, watching the figure get closer. "Is an excellent question."

The figure flailed wildly, screaming as it came towards them as if being devoured alive from the inside. It clutched and clawed at its head and face, staggering back and forth as if trying to regain its balance. There was a jaggedness to its movements that made it terrifying to watch. One minute it would take slow, deliberate steps, the next it would dash forward and race towards them as if finding what it was looking for at last, then slow again as if it had lost the scent. The screams and wails never ceased, save for it to take a breath. They were getting louder, shriller, more ear piercing as it grew closer. It had nothing stopping it from coming right up to them this time, but they could hear shouts in the distance as the Council members fought to catch up with it.

"That figure looks familiar," Tursanay said.

"Uh guys?" Rodney squeaked. "It's coming right for us. Shouldn't we be doing something?"

"Last time there was a barrier. Tursanay, do you think you can form one?" Soren asked quickly.

Tursanay cracked her knuckles by stretching out her inter-locked fingers of her regular hand and the hand of light. "Barriers are my specialty," she declared, forming the seal that would create said barrier. She spoke the word and a red barrier, much like the one that had encompassed them the night the first creature had been set loose, surrounded the

Dai-Nē cabin, protecting them. It threw everything into a red haze around them.

"Let's see if it holds," Ross said, watching the figure break into a run.

It slammed against the barrier and started beating and clawing at it directly in front of Ross, who stared at it nonplussed. He picked up his cane, standing again, and paced away from it, but the creature followed him wherever he went. When the Dai-Nē peeked over his shoulder to get a better look at who or what it was, there was a collective gasp.

"That is no creature," Soren said.

"It's Master Zhi!" Tursanay gasped.

Amara put her hand to her mouth. "What turned him into this?" she asked.

Suddenly, there was a wall of flame between them and the thing Master Zhi had turned into, and they watched as the flesh melted away from his face and the screams died abruptly. Amara let out a shout of horror and turned away, burying her face in the person's chest closest to her. She felt the arms go around her protectively, but that didn't stop her from shaking. Even through the barrier, they could feel the heat of the wall of flames intensely burning its way through the remains of Master Zhi and what he'd become. When the light died away and the flames no longer licked at the barrier surrounding the cabin, she turned back slowly to look over her shoulder to see nothing but a pile of smoldering ash lying before the porch.

"They killed him," she whispered. "Without so much as trying to help him. They just killed him!"

She buried her face back into Soren's shirt. When they took away the barrier away, they could see the Council members on the other side, gathering closer to their living quarters.

"Are you alright, Dai-Nē?" called Yasar.

At first, none of them could answer. No, they weren't alright. They just watched one of their favorite teachers murdered in cold blood after turning into some kind of crazed monster.

"What was that?" Tursanay demanded. They all wanted to know - why had they killed him without trying to heal him in the least?

"Another creature from the island, I'm afraid," said Master Ansari.

A strange look crossed Yasar's face, but he said nothing.

"Are you sure that's what it was?" Ross asked. "It sure looked awfully familiar."

"Then it was probably of the same species as the other," Master Ansari said pointedly.

"Is that so?" Ross hummed.

"You have not answered my question," Yasar stepped in. "Are you alright, Dai-Nē?"

The Dai-Nē exchanged looks. They'd caught the Council in a boldface lie, but could they call them out on it like this? No. They needed more information. Tursanay's face hardened, and she gave a nod to Rodney, who seemed to understand and nod back.

They would not let the Council know what they knew.

"We're just a bit shaken up," Tursanay replied, biting back what she really wanted to say.

"We are unharmed," confirmed Soren, still holding onto a quivering Amara.

"Good," Yasar said. "We will clean up the remains and

check the area of any more... creatures," Yasar said, looking at Master Ansari, who gave a brief nod.

When Master Ansari left, Yasar locked eyes with Ross, then glanced at the Dai-Nē. There was a hesitation there. Something he wanted to say, but seemed he had no choice but to stay silent. He opened his mouth as if to say it, anyway. Consequences be damned, but someone called his name, stopping him. Hesitantly, he turned and began calling after them.

"I don't like this," Attalira said quietly. "Something isn't right."

"Ross," Tursanay said. "We need to talk. Come inside with us."

"Don't tell me what to do," he said, marching over to the door and entering first. The Dai-Nē followed suit and shut the door behind them. Tursanay started putting up spell after spell and the others watched curiously until she finished and turned to face them.

"That should be all the ways they can eavesdrop on us," Tursanay said. "We can speak freely."

"Is that so?" Ross asked, and Tursanay hesitated.

"There are more ways?" she asked.

"There are shapeshifters that can turn into furniture and spy," Ross suggested.

"Oi," Attalira said. "I don't like what you're implying."

"You don't have to like it. It's the truth," Ross replied. "Have you checked all the furniture?"

"No, should we?" Rodney asked.

"I have a faster way to do this," Tursanay replied. "Real your true self!" she said, casting a spell that swept through the room. There was a moment where Attalira grunted in pain and she cycled through several colors, some unnatural, before she returned to her normal face.

"You could warn a person," she growled.

"And warn everyone else that could have been listening," replied Tursanay. "I couldn't risk that."

"Good spell use," Ross complimented.

"Thanks," Tursanay replied, a little out of breath. "Gotta work on my stamina, though."

"So, about what just happened," Amara said, bringing them back to the matter at hand.

"Right," Tursanay said. "I have a few questions. One, why are they trying to cover this up? What even is this that keeps happening? Two, you said they weren't coming after us," she said, turning to Ross. "What are they after?"

"Me," Ross replied, simply.

"Why you?" Rodney asked.

"I can't tell you that yet," Ross replied.

"Why not?" asked Tursanay, brow furrowing.

"Dude, you never tell us anything. You just sit there and ask questions and make us come to conclusions! Just spill already!" Rodney balked.

"You're spoon fed enough information daily. You are told what to think every day. By letting you form your own conclusions, you find the truth yourself. Not what someone else wants you to hear," Ross replied sharply.

"That's so frustrating, though!" Rodney complained. "What do you know about what's going on with the Council?"

"Or at least," Tursanay amended. "What can you tell us?"

"I can tell you that this Master Zhi was not the first one. There have been many Master Zhis. All with the same face."

"What, like, a clone?" Rodney asked, horrified but confused.

"Perhaps," Ross replied. "That's something you'll have to see for yourself before you decide."

"Why did he turn into that?" Amara asked.

"Sometimes growing older has its repercussions. More so for the Council members than anyone else," Ross replied.

He looked Tursanay in the eye

"That's why you said find out their ages," she said.

Amara looked up, shocked. Why was Tursanay gathering that kind of information on the Council members? Was she spying on them or something? Had Ross put her up to that? She made a mental note to ask later.

"Why?" Tursanay continued.

"I'll tell you this much. Something happens to them every three hundred years or so," Ross replied. "Sometimes it runs smoothly, sometimes it does not. What you saw was the aftermath of when it does not."

"What happens every three hundred years or so?" Rodney asked. "Wait... are you saying that all the Council members are three hundred years old?"

"Not all of them," Ross replied. "Some of them are young and new to the Council. Fresh blood. But when they reach a certain age, they'll change too. So has it always been with the Council. At least for those they choose to keep in their ranks."

"Are you three hundred years old?" Amara asked.

"No," Ross replied, locking eyes with her. There was a distant look there that caught her attention. "I am much, much older."

"How old?" Rodney asked quietly.

"I can't tell you that yet," he replied, earning a groan from the others.

"What can you tell us?" Rodney bristled.

"I can tell you that you need to find the last phoenix," Ross replied. "And I can tell you that you need to find out just what happened to the rest of them. The sooner you find the truth, the sooner you'll understand what's happening with the Council."

"Wait, I remember something about the last phoenix," Tursanay said. "During the ceremony where we got our powers, they said Asher was the last phoenix, and that they were planning to use him to power the training grounds for three days."

"But Asher died protecting us," Amara said softly. "The last phoenix is gone."

"Is that so?" Ross replied.

Tursanay's head shot up. "Asher is still alive?" she asked.

"Oh, no. Asher is still dead," Ross replied. "But when a phoenix dies, it comes back from the ashes."

"I don't understand. Wouldn't that mean he's still alive?" Rodney asked.

"When a phoenix dies an ash death, it comes back as a new person. Different face, different personality, different everything," Ross replied. "Except their memories. Those stay the same."

"Then how are we supposed to find them?" Amara asked, sounding defeated.

"Excellent question," Ross replied. "I'm sure you've heard of a library?"

"Yes..." Amara replied slowly.

"Then do your research," he replied.

Amara gave him a curt look, but he ignored it. The group was quiet for a moment, letting this new information sink in.

"Where do we find a library in this world?" Tursanay asked. "Outside of what they have in here."

"The largest one is in River Morn. South of the Delmar. You'll need to travel there when you get out of the Oheqia. It's also a military capital, much like the Alchemist government in Alhalanadria. They are very protective of the knowledge kept there," Ross answered.

"So, we find out information on the phoenix and how to find them, we find out what happened to the other phoenixes, then we locate the last phoenix and then what? Will they just give over the information about the Council?" Tursanay asked. "How do we know we can trust them?"

"That will be for you to decide," Ross replied. "Any information you get from someone is always going to be biased from their point of view. No one thinks themselves a villain in their own story."

"I know you said you don't want to feed us biased information and want us to find the truth out for ourselves, but can't you just tell us a bit about what you know and we still dig for information to see if it's true or not?" Amara asked.

"It doesn't work like that," Ross replied sarcastically. "You could find information and try to fit it to the things I tell you rather than finding the truth and fitting into the puzzle pieces you already have."

"That doesn't make sense," Amara tried to argue. "Why not just give us what we need to know?"

"Because I'm biased," Ross replied. "Extremely so regarding the Council. My words are just as poisonous as theirs are. Find your own answers. I won't give you any more until you come to me with the right questions."

And with that, he stood, making his way to the door

without so much as a backwards glance. He limped along, his cane in hand, and closed the door behind him.

Tursanay switched to sign language.

"We need to get to that library as soon as possible," she said.

"How are we going to do that? We're stuck in here for at least another year and a half if I'm keeping time right," Rodney signed back.

"I don't know, but for now we need to gather as much information as we can on the Council. Ask questions, take notes, learn about their lives. Which are the oldest, which are the youngest. And if what he said is true, which ones are clones and which ones are normal?"

"What do those gestures mean?" Attalira asked, watching them curiously.

"Oh," Tursanay said out loud. "Sorry, I forgot you weren't there for the lessons. It's sign language so we can communicate nonverbally. Rodney has trouble hearing without his hearing aids, so we learned it just in case something happens to them."

"Can you teach me?" she asked.

"Uh yeah," Tursanay replied, looking at the others. "I think we can all pitch in and catch you up to speed."

"What were you just speaking about?" Attalira asked.

"We'll tell you when we can sign it to you," Tursanay promised. "I'm going to be extra cautious about what we say out loud from now on. Even if it's just simple stuff. You guys should, too."

A week passed, and Master Zhi's absence didn't surprise any of the Dai-Nē. When questioned about his whereabouts, the Council dismissed it, claiming he was ill and couldn't be disturbed. They asked if they could visit him, but they vehemently turned down such a notion, saying it was an extremely contagious disease and they could not catch it and fall behind on their training. When at last that excuse lost its weight, they said he transferred out of the Oheqia and back to the Council's headquarters for proper care since they couldn't help him any more here.

The Dai-Nē exchanged looks. So, they were trying to cover this up. They were trying to hide the fact he'd caught some sort of madness and tried to attack Ross. Or tried to attack them. They were still unsure about that.

"I have a question," Tursanay said to their new teacher.

Nuri had taken up their history lesson for the day, and while she was curt, she seemed to give them some good information.

"I remember someone mentioning something about a phoenix when we were at the ceremony to get our powers. What does a phoenix look like and are there any in the Council?"

"There are no phoenixes left alive," she replied simply. "You do not have to worry about what they look like."

"Well, I'm still curious," Tursanay asked. "I've always had an interest in phoenixes. Can you tell us about them?"

Nuri sighed, setting down the book she'd been reading from. She paced a bit before the class and considered her words for a moment.

"Phoenixes look like any other person. Sometimes they could look like elves, sometimes they could look like wood nymphs, sometimes other races. It just depended on how they were reborn after an ash death. When they are in their people's form, they blend in with the world around them, save for their piercing eyes that match the colors of their flames. The colder the eye color, the hotter they burn and the more powerful they are. When they transform into their avian forms, they are large birds the size of an elf and their feathers became flames."

"That sounds beautiful," Tursanay breathed.

"And terrifying," Rodney agreed.

"What destroyed their race?" Amara asked.

"I had not been born yet when it occurred, but it is said that a disease swept through their kind and it prevented them from regenerating through an ash death. No one is sure how it began or spread, but it quickly wiped out their race, save for one who seemed to escape the aftermath. They have lived as the sole survivor for thousands of years."

"When you say ash death, how is that different from a regular death?" Tursanay asked curiously.

"When a phoenix died an ash death, they burned bright, covering themselves with their flames. This heals the injuries or old age they have succumbed to and turns them to ash, where they get reformed into their new persona."

"So every time they regenerate, they have a new face and a new personality?" Tursanay asked.

"I know they have a new face, but I have read nothing about their personality," Nuri replied. "I would have to have known one to answer that properly."

"Bummer," Rodney murmured.

"So were there phoenixes that died a non-ash death?" Amara asked.

"It was a rare occurrence until the disease that swept through them, killing them all, but yes. Occasionally, one died from unnatural causes. Usually because of a beheading or something similar where the flames could not heal them in time," Nuri replied.

"How long ago did their race get wiped out?" Amara asked.

"It has been many generations," Nuri replied. "Possibly eight to nine thousand years ago? I am uncertain of the date."

"They live that long?" Rodney exclaimed. Nuri fixed him with her icy blue stare.

"Phoenixes are... were... immortal," she replied. "They lived as long as their ash death regenerated them."

"Are there other immortal races?" Tursanay asked curiously.

"It is said that the Anunnakai are immortal," she replied. "Or at least, their life span is far greater than anything we can understand and measure."

"What are Anunnakai?" Amara asked.

"Star skinned people that were the original alchemists. They came to teach others of their ways - of alchemy. Because their blood contains the philosopher's stone, an Anunnakai can create something from nothing. Or rather, their blood hardens into a philosopher's stone. Other races must make an equivalent exchange of matter in order to complete alchemy," Nuri said.

"How can their blood be made of stone?" Rodney asked, curiosity piqued.

Nuri replied, "The philosopher's stone can take on various shapes. It is not limited to one. It can be a solid or a liquid. Some even speculate a gas, though few have could use one. It is also said that their blood is the only thing that can contain an Alkahest - the perfect solvent. Something that can dissolve through anything it touches."

"Wait, a perfect solvent," Tursanay said, glancing at the others. "Would it be able to dissolve, say, the veil between our worlds, maybe?"

"It can dissolve through anything, so it is possible," Nuri said. "Why do you ask?"

"I had a vision," Tursanay tried once again. "That there were holes being torn into the veil and that it was leeching the life out of the living cities. I was wondering if someone was using the solvent to breach the veil if we could fix it."

"A vision?" Nuri said, tilting her head. "But you are not-"

"The Dai-Nē of Sight. I know I've been through this. I still have visions from time to time!" Tursanay balked.

She really didn't want to go through this for the thousandth time.

"It's true," Amara agreed. "It's saved our lives before."

Nuri observed for a moment and shrugged. "Then I cannot argue. If you say you are having visions, then so be it."

"Oh, thank goodness someone finally listened!" Tursanay sighed with relief.

"So do you think that it's possible someone has created this Alkahest and is using it to deteriorate the veil?" Amara asked.

"I do not know," Nuri replied simply. "I have limited knowledge of this because I have yet to see an ill-living city."

"A living city reached Soren out to before we left Sendew. He said he didn't understand it at the time, but that there was a feeling of sorts. That it and the sister cities were ill and getting sicker by the day and that they were begging for help. Maybe there's something we can do to help them out in some way? Help heal them?" Amara added.

"You can take that up with the Council once you leave the

Oheqia," Nuri replied. "I'm sure they won't mind checking on this matter if the city itself reached out to you for help. That's what Dai-Nē are supposed to do after all: help those in need."

"My teachers wouldn't even listen when I said I had a vision," Tursanay sulked. "They refused to hear me out at all. You are the first person to listen to me besides my friends."

"Then don't start with the mention of your visions," Nuri said. "State that the living city reached you out to and you think you need to investigate what is going on in those areas. That is more believable and tangible to them than a Dai-Nē who is not supposed to be having visions, having them. But wait until you are out of the Oheqia before you bring it up so that you have time to be connected to the living city. Otherwise, they will think it a ruse since you have not brought it up in such a way sooner."

"Thank you," Tursanay said. "You've been one of the few people besides Master Zhi that have been forthcoming in information and actually listened to us."

A sad look crossed Nuri's face, but it was quickly wiped away. She only inclined her head in response and picked the book back up she'd set on the podium. She cleared her throat and began reading from it again, continuing their lesson they were on before all the questioning had begun.

The next time history class began, it was Yasar teaching them. He was just as forthcoming with information as Nuri had been, and the Dai-Nē finally felt like they were getting some pertinent knowledge at last. At least one side of it, they kept in mind. They asked similar questions they had with Nuri about phoenixes and Anunnakai and even about how old the Council members were.

"Their ages vary," Yasar replied. "Some like myself are

only in their late twenties and early thirties, others are over two hundred years old."

"Were any of them near three hundred years old?" Tursanay asked.

"I believe Master Zhi neared that age," Yasar replied.

"Was?" Tursanay piped up.

"Before he left the campgrounds," Yasar said quickly.

"Anyone else?" she prompted.

"Why are you so curious about this?" Yasar wondered out loud.

"I'm curious about everything, if you haven't noticed yet," Tursanay replied as an excuse.

"Curiosity is an excellent trait to have, though one must be careful not to ask the wrong questions in diplomatic situations. That could end badly for both sides," Yasar warned.

"Well, if I don't ask them now, how will I know what not to ask when the time comes?" Tursanay replied.

"Yeah, it's the reason we're taking this class and Attalira and Soren aren't," Amara agreed.

"We need to learn what customs and etiquette is normal for this world since we didn't grow up here," Tursanay nodded.

"I concede, I concede," Yasar laughed. "Alright, I'll answer your questions. There was one other that just turned three hundred a few months ago, actually, but I don't recall his name."

"Just the one, right? There aren't any more?" Tursanay pressed.

"There might be a few more amongst the older members. I'm not sure, maybe a dozen or so?" Yasar replied. "Why?"

Tursanay paled slightly. "N-No reason," she said, her voice suddenly going soft.

Suddenly she had no more questions at the moment, and was focused on the number of Council members that might devolve into the madness they'd seen Master Zhi do. The idea of fighting off that many of them - one at a time or all at once - was terrifying. How many faces that they saw every day would disappear? People they cared about? People that taught them new things about themselves every day?

"W-" Rodney began, but had to swallow to make his voice work. "When's the next person's birthday? We could celebrate it with them like we do in our world."

"If I'm not mistaken, there should be one in merely three days, come to think of it," Yasar commented. "Master Ryu, I believe."

"Three days?!" Rodney exclaimed, then caught himself. "That's.... that's not a lot of time to plan a party. We should, uh... we should get on with that. Right, guys?"

"I'm sure whatever you come up with will be a pleasant surprise," Yasar smiled. "After all, it's rarely we celebrate birthdays. Merely milestones. Three hundred is a milestone for most elves, since few live that long or much longer."

"Really?" Amara asked. "Why is that?"

"It is just the average lifespan of an elf," Yasar shrugged. "In the old stories, if you believe in such things, they got cursed out of their immortality somehow, but no one knows how."

The wheels in Tursanay's head were turning. She wanted to talk to Master Ross again and present a new theory. What if the old stories were true? What if they actually did get cursed? And if so, what if that was why they were devolving into madness? Perhaps there was more to these stories than Yasar thought. One way to tell would be to see if Master Ryu disappeared in three days, replaced by another 'creature from the island in the lake'. Then her theory would become more solid.

When the morning of the third day arrived, the three Dai-Nē were up early and waiting on the porch when Master Ross arrived on their doorstep. He limped towards them with a death glare on his face, not enjoying being on the receiving end of a summons yet again.

"Your message said to meet you here at the crack of dawn for something important," Ross said. "What do you want?" he demanded.

"We have a working theory about what is happening, but we need you here to prove it," Tursanay replied.

"Is that so? Where's your other two companions?" Ross asked. "Shouldn't they be in on this misery, then?"

"We haven't told them yet," Amara replied. "We want to make sure we're right before we set them on edge."

"Set them on-?" Ross began, but a scream rose in the air, followed by a shattering of glass and a loud slam.

"If we're right," Rodney said softly. "That's one of Soren's teachers."

"Master Ryu," Amara replied softly, watching the campgrounds for the first sign of movement.

Smoke began billowing upwards again, another fire started somewhere amongst the buildings.

"So, you think you've figured something out then?" Ross asked, arching an eyebrow.

"If he comes here and has gone mad like the others, then yes," Tursanay said. "If it's not him, then we might be a little off."

"Are you going to tell me your theory?" Ross questioned.

The three stood there silently, not giving him a reply, then it dawned on his face.

"You're using me as bait to lure it here to confirm your suspicions," he declared.

"Don't worry," Amara said. "We won't let it get in. We just need to confirm our theory."

"And if you're wrong?" Ross demanded.

Tursanay cracked her knuckles by stretching out her regular hand, and the hand of light, fingers interlaced. "Then we're going to have a lot of questions to ask you when this is through."

"Start explaining while we wait. How did you come to this conclusion?" Ross demanded, stepping onto the porch and turning to watch the campgrounds with them.

Smoke rose into the air, and shouts of surprise and shock sounded the alarm. Soon there were many voices trying to subdue whatever was causing the chaos, with little to no avail. Meanwhile, the screams of the individual wreaking havoc were getting more frantic and loud.

And closer.

"Yasar told us a story the other day that we think has more truth to it than the Council believes or at least is willing to let on," Amara began as Tursanay started setting up the barriers. "Of how elves and vampires and phoenixes used to be immortals, but after the phoenixes died out, the last remaining one cursed the other two races to only live three hundred years."

Ross looked over at her sharply, his pale blue eyes studying her carefully.

"When we asked who in the group was turning three hundred next, Master Ryu's name came up," she continued.

"Now, I don't know about you, but seeing as today is supposed to be his three hundredth birthday, and this is happening," she indicated the flames that grew in the distance. "I'd say there's at least some correlation. If it's Master Ryu, then this has something to do with them all turning three hundred this year."

"And if we're correct," Rodney added. "There's going to be at least a dozen more incidents."

In the distance, a figure appeared around the corner and began staggering towards them. First slow steps, then jagged, then quick paces like a racing heartbeat. When the figure grew close enough for them to make out, it hit the barrier full force and shook it.

It was Master Ryu.

"I forgot he deals with ether," Tursanay grunted. "His hits are going to be much more powerful."

She murmured the strengthening spell under her breath as she held her arms straight out as if holding the barrier up herself. When he struck again, a small crack formed along the barrier.

"No, no, no!"

"What can we do to help, T?" Rodney shouted over the sound of the barrier cracking.

The red glow between them and Master Ryu grew intense, a white light forming along the cracks.

"Use your alchemy!" she shouted back. "Make a secondary barrier! We have the confirmation. Now we just need to protect ourselves!"

Running forward between Tursanay and the barrier, Rodney grabbed a crystal and projected a transmutation circle onto the ground. From it erupted an earthen barrier that surrounded the cabin.

"I can strengthen that!" Amara said, swimming over and putting her hands against the additional barrier. Roots grew amidst the rocks and soil, lacing together to create a thorny, impenetrable wall. A shattering sound filled the air as above them the sight of the red barrier broke into shards and disappeared. Tursanay collapsed against the porch pillar and tried to catch her breath. The wall of earth and root shook beneath Amara's fingertips and an icy fear settled in her gut.

What if they weren't strong enough to keep him out?

"Where are those Council members?" Tursanay panted irritably. "They need to clean up their mess!"

As if on cue, the wailing of Master Ryu grew more intense, then abruptly stopped, and all fell silent. It was a long moment before a hole opened in the wall and Loki's head poked through.

"Is everyone alright?" he called.

"Yes," Amara said, then looked over at Tursanay. "You okay, T?"

She held up a thumb to indicate yes and focused on her breathing. That barrier had taken a lot out of her. She should have used a different kind. One that was better suited for ether attacks. But she had underestimated just how in control of his powers he would be in that state.

"You can take down the barriers," Loki instructed. "The creature has been subdued. Quick thinking and actions, everyone. Good job!"

"Thanks," Amara called. "We'll take it down once we catch our breath. We're fine otherwise!"

Loki gave a nod and went back through the hole that was quickly resealed by the roots that grew of their own accord.

"I should have used a compound barrier that would have

protected against ether as well," muttered Tursanay. "I wasn't thinking straight."

"You did good enough to keep us alive, and right now that's all I care about," Amara replied.

"No," Tursanay shook her head. "It wasn't good enough. Next time there might not be back up. I have to be ready for that."

"Instead of being hard on yourself," Rodney spoke up. "Why don't you try seeing it as an opportunity to improve? Switch tactics mid fight. Keep yourself and your enemies off kilter. They can't predict your next move if you don't know it yourself."

"That," Tursanay said. "Is probably the best piece of advice you've ever given me."

"It's the only piece of advice I've ever given you," Ross replied with a sniff.

"I shouldn't sit here and beat myself up, I should practice more," Tursanay said. "Being down on myself will get me nowhere, but doing something about it to change it will."

"Not to derail you on your epiphany," Amara interjected. "But we have a lot of questions to ask."

"Oh right," Tursanay remembered. She began setting up spells and barriers to prevent others from overhearing them outside of the porch area, and Rodney began to fidget and pace.

"Okay seriously though, why is it when these guys turn three hundred, they lose their minds and try to attack people and things around them? And why do they go for the strongest power source? And why is that power source you?" he asked in rapid succession.

"One question at a time," snapped Ross.

Rodney tried to make himself stop pacing by sitting on

one of the benches, but bounced his leg with anticipation as he waited for Ross to answer. The nervous energy coursing through his veins right now needed some kind of outlet.

"Firstly," Ross continued. "Do you remember what I told you about Master Zhi?"

"That he wasn't the first one, and that he was like a clone or something," Tursanay replied.

"Close, but not quite," Ross replied. "It's the same mind, same Zhi each time. It's the body that's new."

"So, what you're saying is they transfer the mind into a new body?" Amara asked. "Why?"

"Do you remember what you learned about the lifespan of those once considered immortal?" Ross countered.

"That they die when they're roughly three hundred years or so," Amara replied. "Again, why is that important?"

"Master Zhi and Master Ryu were exactly three hundred years old," Ross replied.

"So, what...?" Tursanay wondered out loud. "They have to transfer their minds into a new body before they turn three hundred or they die?"

"That's an interesting theory," Ross replied. "In fact, I'd say pretty spot on."

"But what does that have to do with the madness?" Amara asked.

"What does it have to do with the madness?" Ross repeated.

He looked at them expectantly.

"What if?" Rodney said, feeling an icy chill run down his spine at the thought. "What if something is going wrong when they try to go into a new body? Like a glitch that makes them go crazy? Like how in video games sometimes when you respawn, the game messes up and your character is floating around or almost naked or doing something weird or phasing through stuff?"

"We don't see them floating around and clipping through walls, Rodney," Tursanay began, but Ross cut her off.

"No, but you see them losing their minds on the exact day they get marked for death," he said. "Few people actually want to die. And if you found a way to cheat death, wouldn't you risk it even if it meant there was a slight chance you'd lose your mind?"

There was a long silence as the other two exchanged looks.

"So basically, they're glitching with this 'respawn madness' and losing their minds and attacking people," Rodney said, using air quotes. "But why are they going after the strongest power source?"

"Because it calls to them. If they can find something powerful enough to stop the madness, they'll do anything to get at it," Ross replied. "They hunger for it."

"You said there were no such things as zombies here!" Rodney hissed at Tursanay.

"Well, I was wrong, okay?" Tursanay hissed back. "But technically they aren't zombies, they're just clones gone mad."

"That's not much better!" Rodney squeaked.

"What's making them glitch now if things have gone smoothly in the past?" Amara asked. "Obviously they haven't had a problem with respawning before. What's changed?"

"I sabotaged them," answered Ross.

"You what?" squeaked Rodney, a bit more shrilly than he intended.

"Why?" asked Tursanay.

"I thought you were on the Council's side?" Amara said, confused. "Why would you sabotage them?"

"I'm not on anyone's side. I'm on my own side," Ross replied. "I have my reasons, and you needed answers."

"What are your reasons?" Tursanay asked directly.

She knew he wouldn't give the information unless you pried it out of him. He was like a dragon guarding a hoard with his information. The only ones allowed to see it or touch it were those with something of equal value. Ross dealt in the right questions and more information. You asked the right question, he'd give the right answer. But knowing what to ask when you had no idea what you needed to know was the hard part of dealing with his quirky trading method.

"That's not the right question," he replied.

Tursanay frowned. There was something right there she knew she should ask, but she couldn't for the life of her think of what it should be.

"What is the right question?" she tried.

"That's something you'll have to find out for yourself," Ross replied.

"Great," Rodney said, standing and pacing again. "Just great! On the one hand, we have Council members becoming zombies through respawn madness, and on the other hand we have someone who won't give us the answers we need unless we ask the right questions and he's been the one sabotaging them the whole time! And not to mention we still have to figure out how to fix the veil and the sick cities! We're running out of hands to juggle all this with guys!"

"Rodney breathe," Tursanay said. "You're going to hyperventilate."

He took a few calming breaths to ease his panic, but he kept pacing again. He couldn't fathom how they were going to manage all of this on their own, let alone how they were going to survive the training grounds with Council members dying off and going mad left and right.

"Can you like," Rodney began, looking at Ross. "Stop sabotaging them for a while so we can focus on training? That way, we don't have to have one more thing on our plate to worry about right now?"

"I've already set things in motion and they cannot be stopped," Ross replied simply.

"Why not?" Amara asked. "You're killing people!"

"It's no more than what they deserve for their crimes," Ross replied. "They've killed millions in their conquest for power. I'm only returning the favor."

"But doesn't that make you as bad as them?" Amara asked, appalled.

"I don't care," Ross replied. "I'm not here to look good in the eyes of others. I'm here to accomplish one thing."

"What is that?" Tursanay asked.

"I'm here to bring down the Council as we know it," Ross replied. He stared them down as they looked at him in horrified silence.

"But if you bring down the Council," Rodney said slowly. "What's going to happen to us?"

"That's why you need to focus on your training as much as possible," Ross replied. "This is to teach you how to survive on your own in a world you knew almost nothing about when you came here. Learn everything you can, train as hard as you can, find every way to win and survive. You're going to need every ounce of self-preservation you can glean from these trials. The Council is corrupt and I'm going to clean it out from the inside. Starting with those that think they can cheat death."

"I can't condone this," Amara said, shaking her head. "Killing for the sake of killing is wrong."

"I'm not killing just to kill them. I'm killing them for revenge. I am avenging my people, and there's nothing you can do to stop me."

"Revenge will eat you alive," Tursanay warned.

"Tell me," Ross said, standing to face her. "If they killed everyone you ever loved and knew, leaving you alone to rot in misery, would you not want to do the same?"

Tursanay didn't answer. She couldn't. She thought about her friends, her family, the kids at her school. If she lost everything, would she be able to just walk away?

"There are some in the Council I don't think have been corrupted yet," Tursanay said slowly. "Will you spare them?"

"I'm only after the ones responsible for the decision that killed my kind," Ross answered. "The young ones will be safe." Tursanay looked visibly relieved as her shoulders relaxed a bit.

"Then that's all I can ask," Tursanay replied softly.

"Tursanay!" Amara balked.

"It's all I can ask, Amara," she said, looking at her friend sadly. "If someone took you or Rodney or Soren away from me... you guys are all I have left. I can't say I wouldn't do the same, because I don't know what I would do. I honestly don't. But as long as he leaves the innocents out of this, I can't stand his way."

"This isn't right," Amara balked.

"If you had the chance to kill a serial killer, would you?" Tursanay asked.

Amara closed her mouth.

"That's not fair," she said. "Serial killers are deranged."

"They are heartless int heir selection of whom they let live and let die," Ross interjected. "I'm trying to keep them from killing any more that stand in their way."

Amara fell silent.

"I'm not looking for your approval if that helps you process how you feel," Ross said. "I'm in this for me and those I have lost. Nothing more."

Amara's frown deepened, but she said nothing. There was plotting behind her eyes, Tursanay could see, but what she was planning there was no telling.

"Break down the barriers before they try to see what's wrong," she answered, ignoring Ross. "We've had them up long enough."

CHAPTER 19
SURVIVAL

Tryn slid the door open to the Dai-Nē cabin with enough force to make it slam against the frame. Marching in, she looked around at the startled faces in the common room and set eyes on Rodney.

"You!" she declared, pointing at him. "Come with me. We are investigating the island in the lake."

The look of pure horror on Rodney's face was palpable as he dropped his spoon in his bowl of breakfast. The looks on the other Dai-Nē faces were a mixture of horror and confusion, as well as concern.

"There's no need for that," Tursanay balked. "Besides, we were told to stay away from the island because of the creatures that lived there."

"And yet they keep attacking the campgrounds. I think it's time to put a stop to that," Tryn declared. She placed her hands on her hips as if that had decided the matter, and Tursanay stood up.

"Then go by yourself," she said. "Why are you bringing Rodney into it?"

"Because he is my protégé, and this is an excellent learning experience for him," Tryn replied.

"Are you looking to get him killed?" Tursanay argued. "That island is dangerous, besides we think it's something else attacking the campgrounds, not the creatures from the island."

"Then going there is the best way to find out," Tryn replied. "By getting to the bottom of this, we can rule out if it is those creatures or something else, but either way, we need to get to the island."

"That's ridiculous! How does that make any sense?" Tursanay argued.

"Uh guys," Rodney tried to interject.

But the two didn't seem to hear him, arguing their points back and forth until finally he rose and slammed his hands on the table.

"GUYS!"

They stopped arguing and looked at him, surprised.

"It's fine, I'll go."

"What?!" Tursanay exclaimed. "Have you lost your mind?" She switched to sign language. "We know where the attacks are coming from. Why agree to this?"

"After that last attack, you made me realize, T. We need to get stronger," Rodney replied out loud. "If we're going to hold our own out there, then we need to at least be able to hold our own here. We aren't doing that yet. We're barely scraping by. And if going to that island makes me stronger, then it's worth it."

In sign he added, "Plus, I can see if she's on our side with sorting this out mess. We could use her help."

"Rodney..." Tursanay tried to reason, but she couldn't argue with him.

He was right. They were barely scraping by with all the training that they'd done and she herself had stated they needed to get stronger. She needed to get stronger. Think faster. More efficiently. They also needed any help they could get, and Tryn would be a powerful ally. But with them going off alone to the island, she couldn't help but worry. That and she hated having Tryn alone with Rodney to begin with. It just irked her considerably to have them working together and she couldn't place why.

"T, I gotta," Rodney said. "We've barely tapped into our full potential and I think this could help." He signed what he actually meant simultaneously. "We need her on our side and this little excursion will give me a chance to catch her up to speed and convince her to join us without the Council interfering."

"There has to be a better way," Tursanay signed back.

"If there is," Rodney signed. "I'll find it on the way over there."

Tursanay's shoulders bunched up anxiously. If he was determined to do this, then there was no stopping him. That and they really needed the extra hands-on deck.

"Just be careful, okay?" Amara said softly. "I can't lose anyone else."

"Promise," Rodney said with a small smile.

"Then it's decided!" Tryn said smugly, as if not having noticed most of the gestures they were making.

"There's gotta be a better way to get stronger than this, though," Tursanay tried again.

She truly didn't want to just give up like this, but she also didn't want to discourage him from going if that's what he truly wanted to do. It was a hard balance.

"Wish me luck, T," Rodney smiled. It didn't reach his eyes.

He looked at Tryn.

"I'll go get my things."

She gave him a nod, and he left the room. Tursanay shot a glare at Tryn, who didn't seem to be affected by it in the least, much to Tursanay's irritation. When Rodney came back through, she called his name and he paused in the doorway, looking back at her.

"Good luck," she said softly. He smiled and gave her a nod before turning and leaving with Tryn.

"I don't like this," Tursanay muttered as the door shut.

"None of us do, but we need to believe in him. He's doing something very brave right now," Amara said.

"He is correct in saying we are barely tapping into our full potential," Soren stated.

"Yeah, we need to up our game if we're going to get anywhere," Tursanay agreed, then looked down and Amara put her hand on Tursanay's shoulder.

"He'll be okay," she said softly. "He's got the world's best alchemist with him, after all," she teased.

Tursanay snorted. "The world's most vain alchemist, more like it."

Amara suppressed a giggle.

"What about you?" Attalira asked, taking a bite of some fruit she was munching on when the commotion had started. They'd all just finished eating breakfast when Tryn burst in. "How are you going to get stronger, Tursanay?"

"That's a good question. I'm going to see if some of the

other teachers will come at my barriers first because I want to strengthen them. I'm great against usual magical attacks, but I'm weak against other kinds like ether and whatnot, so I want to build on that. My spell work is okay, but I need to expand my knowledge of spells so I can use them when the time comes without having to think about it. The spells I have to prep. I want to have some on hand ready to go should the need arise, but I also want to have some ingredients on my belt to throw down and make something stronger if I need to. You know, I knew salt was really useful in our world, but who knew it had so many uses here? It's like a gold mine!" Tursanay rambled off.

"You could always have me try to break them or come at you," Attalira said. "As a starting point. I'm a pretty quick thinker when it comes to a fight, so I think you'd have your hands full with me first."

Tursanay grinned. "I do like a challenge."

"Then let's start in half an hour," Attalira said. "In the flatlands near the river. It'll be far enough away for them to concentrate," she added, pointing to Amara and Soren. "and close enough for us to use the different terrain that starts up in that area."

Tursanay agreed.

And so, for the next thirty minutes, Tursanay went through a list of spells, and went around the campgrounds gathering the ingredients to prepare those spells. The herbal magic was especially powerful here, and quite easy to assemble thanks to their garden. There were also some intangible ingredients, such as fear, hopelessness, intimidation, powerlessness, terror, worthlessness, despair, discouragement, and apprehension. Things that she could give to her opponent to weaken their attacks through self-doubt and overwhelming them; much like words of affirmation, just with the opposite effect.

She bottled them up and laced them into her belt, then made her way across the campgrounds and down towards the lake. She jogged the last leg of the mile to the lake and came to a gasping halt before Attalira, who was already there waiting on her.

"You're late," she informed her.

"I know," Tursanay breathed, trying to catch her breath. "Couldn't decide which spells to use. I think I'm set now, though."

"Good," she replied.

Attalira gave her no warning, attacking instantly, and knocking Tursanay to the ground. Sprawling on her back and dazed, Tursanay had to roll quickly to keep from having her face smashed in by the hoof of centaur Attalira, who had shifted into an instant before Tursanay could even think. She continued to roll, trying to remember the word she needed as Attalira tried to stomp her to death with her hooves. Tursanay threw her hand up and cast a barrier between her and Attalira, who kicked down on the barrier, trying to break it with all her strength. Thankfully, it held long enough for Tursanay to get her ground.

"You don't give much warning, do ya?" Tursanay said, casting a larger barrier around herself to give herself a dome of space to think in.

"If you could get the upper hand, why wouldn't you?" Attalira replied, giving a roundhouse kick to the barrier with her back hooves.

She let out a shout with the effort, knocking a solid crack into the barrier. Tursanay got to her feet and raised and lowered her hand in an arching motion, and a pillar of lavender smoke rose from the ground. She took a vial off her belt and threw it on the ground, shattering the glass, and green smoke rose, twisting and curling with the lavender. Tursanay took a boxing stance, punching through the smoke, and wave after wave of smoke formed into a fisted shape, lurching towards Attalira. The shapeshifter dodged the first two blows, but got hit with the third, knocking her back. She grabbed at her head with a yelp and sank to the ground.

"Hope you like a healthy dose of fear and intimidation," Tursanay said, punching twice more and sending a spinning kick the centaur's way.

Attalira dodge and flipped backwards, shifting into a vole and digging her way into the earth. In the tall grass around them, Tursanay lost sight of her, and it wasn't until she popped out of the ground, snake like, behind Tursanay that the other girl caught sight of her. Attalira clawed at Tursanay's face, narrowly missing her by an inch, and turned her momentum into a twisting roll that wrapped around Tursanay's midsection like a boa constrictor and dragged her to the ground in a heap of limbs and hair as they both scrabbled for a better grip on the other.

Tursanay grabbed another vial from her belt with her hand of light and bit the cork off the top. Attalira reached for her face to grab at the vial, but Tursanay held it aloft and bit down on Attalira's hand, drawing blood. The shapeshifter screamed, yanking her hand back, and Tursanay spit the blood into the vial and covered the top and shook it. Attalira's vision blurred as if someone had stuck her in a jar herself and started shaking it as hard as they could. She felt like her teeth were going to rattle out of her skull as she rolled away, releasing Tursanay and staggering on hands and knees, trying to get her bearings.

Tursanay stood, backing away and breathing hard, and cast another barrier between her and Attalira, this time with a floor that the other girl couldn't surpass. When the spell wore off within a few minutes, Attalira threw up on the ground and struggled to get to her feet. She looked at Tursanay, a darkness in her eyes that hadn't been there before.

"That was playing dirty," she breathed. "Blood magic isn't supposed to be used like that."

"Just because a knife isn't meant to be used as a back scratcher doesn't mean I can't use it that way. I just have to be really careful not to overdo it and get cut." Truth be told, the spell had rattled her some too because it had her saliva in it, but having Attalira's blood had made it much more potent on the shapeshifter. "Besides," she added. "Wasn't it you that said, if you could get the upper hand, why wouldn't you?"

Attalira looked shocked to have her own words thrown back at her in such a way, but she regarded Tursanay in a new light. "Okay, you want to play that way," she said, growing seven times larger than she was normally. "Then so be it."

She raised her foot and brought it down hard on the barrier, burying it into the dirt a good few inches with each kick. Tursanay held up her hand to keep the barrier in place, but with each stomp, she could feel Attalira getting the upper hand. She needed to do something, and she needed to do it quickly.

When Attalira's foot came down again, a crack formed along the top of the barrier, and Tursanay knew she couldn't hold on much longer. She took a step back, preparing to brace herself for the final blow, when she stepped on something. Looking down, she saw the glass shards from earlier and got an idea. Racing to the edge of the barrier, she placed her hands on it and changed its form from a dome to a spiked, jagged shape that pierced straight through Attalira's foot as she brought it down again. Attalira screamed and lurched back, limping.

She healed herself by reforming the skin into the proper shape on her foot and glared at Tursanay, who was already grabbing another vial from her belt and making a hole in the barrier so she could throw it at Attalira. Unable to dodge far enough away in time, the vial burst on the ground at her feet and the blast of power that came out of it choked her. She clawed at her throat, gasping for breath and coughing until she fell to her knees, then her hands, wheezing with each breath.

Tursanay brought down the barrier immediately and rushed over to her.

"Drink this! Drink this! Drink this!" she said in a rush, forcing something down Attalira's throat.

Suddenly her airways opened up again, and she coughed again, gasping.

"Were you trying to kill me?" Attalira demanded.

"It wasn't supposed to have that effect," Tursanay said. "That was just some patchouli to overwhelm your senses and make everything acute."

"I'm allergic to patchouli," Attalira said.

"Oh god," Tursanay said. "I'm so sorry! I had no idea!"

"What was that other thing you gave me?" Attalira asked.

"It's an antidote for most herbal potions. I always carry it just in case. I don't like using potions, but you never know when you'll come across someone that needs it," Tursanay answered.

"Why did you think to carry that?" she asked, confused. "If you don't like using poisons?"

"There's so many strange plants and things here

compared to where I'm from. I never know if one of us will have an allergic reaction to one, so I like to be prepared," Tursanay answered.

"Lucky for me then," Attalira said.

"Dai-Nē!" came a call from nearby. "Come and gather. We have a new training exercise for you."

"Maybe not as lucky as we hoped," Tursanay sighed.

Helping Attalira to her feet, the two of them met up with the other Dai-Nē in the campgrounds and looked out at the large group of Council members gathered there. Some wore sober expressions, others were blank faced, others still had a more serious look as they watched the group come forward.

"Where is Master Rodney?" Yasar asked.

The Dai-Nē exchanged looks.

"He went with Tryn to the island in the lake," Amara replied. "Weren't you supposed to know that?"

A murmur broke out amongst them, and Yasar wiped a nervous hand over his face.

"No," he said. "We did not know that." He cleared his throat. "That's fine. That'll count as his training scenario."

The murmurs died down.

"What scenario are you putting us through?" Tursanay asked slowly, walking down the hill a little closer to them.

Something about their expressions seemed off. Like this wasn't something they were looking forward to training them for, but was just required of them despite most of them disagreeing with it. Their shuffled gazes, clearing of throats and tense posture made Tursanay reluctant to hear them out.

Yasar rubbed the back of his neck and sighed. "You're going to be carted off to different parts of the training grounds and left there to survive in your assigned locations for a week. You must forage for food, water, and a living space. Survive, and you'll begin the next level of your training."

"Excuse me?" she balked, shoulders going rigid. "You can't just dump us out in the middle of nowhere and say 'good luck!' No one has taught us how to forage for food and water! We don't know what else is out here!"

"Many terrains exist in the Oheqia. You must learn to navigate each one in order to survive in the real world on your own, because you won't always be in a friendly place. You must learn to take care of yourselves," Master Loki said.

"This is stupid! Why can't we do that first?" Tursanay continued to balk. She didn't like this. Not one bit.

"Enough," Master Sharrod snapped. "I'm afraid it's already decided. You are to do this and in one week, a mirror will appear to bring you back to the training grounds for further training."

Tursanay closed her mouth and glared at Master Sharrod. There was when he returned it, but after a beat, he looked away. He muttered for them to get their things together and to be out in the yard in half an hour. The Dai-Nē slowly shuffled off to do as they were told, Tursanay the last one to join as she glared the entire Council down, ready for a fight. None of them would meet her eye.

Once they packed their things and filled their canteens with water from the river, they transported them one by one to a location in the Oheqia where they would spend the rest of their week.

Four days later.

· · ·

Having run out of water two days ago, Soren desperately searched for something, anything, that could quench his thirst. But the only thing he found in this desert was cacti and various lizards and strange birds and snakes. Very few of which had any kind of meat on their bones for him to eat, but he did as well as he could. It had been the shortage of water that was threatening to take him down, rather than the lack of food and shelter. He'd taken off his shirt and tied it around his head to keep the sun off his face for a bit, and stood in the shade of a large cactus, though it barely covered him. The heat was unbearable. It was a dry, dusty heat that made sand cling to the lining of your mouth and throat, making you cough and choke on the sand that was kicked up in the wind. There was nothing for miles. He'd been walking for days. There was no end to this desert in sight.

If only it would rain, he thought. Or one of these plants could yield water instead of stab him with their tiny, angry little thorns. If only he hadn't drunk so much water to begin with...

Tursanay wandered the forest curiously. Her first goal was finding shelter, then a food and water source. She didn't know what creatures lived in this forest, but with all the oak, pine, and birch trees surrounding her, she figured it shouldn't be too hard to find something to eat. Even if she had to hunt squirrels. She remembered going hunting with her dad when she was younger before he went MIA and she got sent to live with her grandmothers. She missed them dearly. Especially right now. They had always been so full of stories and wisdom that helped her out in unexpected ways, and always had enough food to spoil her with until she ate herself sick. One of them had been a fighter pilot in a war, the other a linguist trying to barter for peace on both sides. They'd met one day in the middle of a battle and hit it off ever since. It had been one of Tursanay's favorite stories to hear. They knew about survival and had taught her some things to remember. So, she knew a bit about surviving in the woods and what to expect living on her own; she just hoped she could apply what she could remember and last a week.

"Come on, Tursanay," she said to herself. "You got this."

"Tursanay?" a familiar voice asked. She turned toward the voice, surprised.

"Rodney?" she asked. "What are you doing here?"

Amara swam her way through the marshlands just above the water, not wanting to dip into the algae infested liquids. She'd seen something swimming just below the surface and while she needed to hunt for food, she was more concerned with her potential food hunting for her. Finding that snapping creatures were a thing in these waters, she had a bite on her fin to remind her to stay out of them. She'd ripped off a piece of her shirt to staunch the bleeding, but now it ached with every flick of her tail.

The moss hung heavy from the trees that stood in the swamp water, and every time she passed some and it brushed against her, it made her skin and scales itch. It was like there were a thousand tiny invisible bugs crawling on her and she couldn't stand it. There was no wind through these trees. Everything was stagnant. The water, the air, the rotting trunks of trees that were hollowed out and blackened with mold. The stench of it was strong in the air.

Something ahead of her caught her attention. A light in the distance.

"Hello?" she asked. "Who's there?"

The light flickered back and forth, beckoning her closer. It was as if someone were waving her down and trying to get her to come closer so they could see her. It was a mesmerizing glow in this dark and gloomy place, and for once she had a small hope that it was someone the Council had sent that could help her survive this miserable trek through the swamp.

Attalira made her way up the mountain pass, looking for a place to camp for the night. She was confident she would come out on top for this task and had no qualms about spending a week out here on her own. She wouldn't have to answer to the Council for a while, she wouldn't have to deal with the other Dai-Nē. It would just be her and the surrounding nature. The fresh air of the mountainside, the scent of pines in the air. The wet earth beneath her feet, freshly watered from the rain that had just passed. There was a peaceful atmosphere, and she could hear some deer running in the distance. It would be freeing to have some quiet time after all, she thought. Until the ground shook, and the sounds of a rock slide filled her ears.

She quickly grew to the size of a giant and tried to move away from the path of the landslide, but the path became slick with debris and rubble and it was hard to get a purchase on the ground because of the mud that coated her boots now. She fell onto her side, skidding down with the rubble towards the edge of the mountain pass she'd been traversing, and with it the side of the drop off that grew closer and closer.

Five days later.

Lying on the ground in the sun, Soren looked up at the circling vultures above him and smiled. Such pretty birds. Maybe they were friendly. Maybe they could show him where the liquid of life was. Did birds even drink water in the desert? He'd found some in a cactus and tried it. Now everything was wonderful. Reaching up to the sky, he drew the pattern they were flying in with his finger. Such pretty shapes. Such pretty patterns. The strange colors that emanated from the birds were a rainbow of echoing, bird shaped patterns that Soren tried to grasp with his hand but failed, them being too far away. Until he noticed his hand was making the same colors as he moved it back and forth.

"Oh," he breathed, waving his hand some more and watching the colorful echoed rainbow follow his movements. It was as if everything was moving in slow motion. His laughter echoed in his ears, high pitched and trilling with giggles as the birds above descended upon him.

Tursanay crawled across the ground, shaking her head and muttering to herself as she cried. "Don't sleep on the ground. Don't sleep on the ground, something will come for you. It's not who you think it is. It's not! It's not! Don't listen to it! Don't sleep in the trees, the trees don't like it. They throw you out when you fall asleep. There's no place to hide. Everything is alive. I hate this place. I just want to sleep, but if I sleep, I'm going to die. What do I do? Where do I go? This isn't fair. This isn't supposed to happen. We're supposed to be trained to be magical, not die in a forest that wants to eat me first-"

The crack of a branch caught her attention, and she gasped, stopping in her muttering. For a moment, there was no sound. Not a thing moved in the surrounding forest. Not a bird chirped, nor a squirrel chittered. No leaf swayed in the wind. Ice cold fear swam down her spine, her breathing becoming rapid and uneven. She tried to suppress a sob as she realized the thing she had been running from had found her again.

Looking into the water for food, Amara noticed something strange about her complexion. It was paler than before, almost sickly. Perhaps it was the lack of sunlight that came through the trees that made her look as pale as the dead things in the water. Amara swam through the air, looking for a nesting place to rest for the night, but there were few limbs that seemed safe enough to rest on away from the water with things that would bite and moss that made her skin itch. There were only trees for miles around and there was a still-ness that creeped into her nerves and made her question how things could live in this environment. Everything was stag-nant. Everything was still.

Everything was quiet. No sign of that help the Council had sent now.

The ground shook again, and Attalira's head popped up, looking around. There was a crashing sound, followed by another and another, and when she turned her head to look behind her, her eyes grew wide at the sight of a line of trees falling down right for her. Another landslide turned into a mudslide, this one taking the forest and making it into a hell scape. She flew out of her tree as fast as her wings could carry her, shifting into a falcon in midair. Breathing hard and bleeding, she struggled to get back into the air when another tree came crashing into hers and sent them both spiraling into the mud below.

She choked on the dirt that filled her beak and nostrils, and tried to remember how to shift without being able to breathe through it. She became a boulder, rolling with the terrain and crashing into things as the mud and rocks and trees and wind tossed her around, careless of where she landed. By the time she felt things slowing to a stop, there were layers upon layers of earth and debris settled over her, burying her in the avalanche.

The seventh day.

Soren woke with a start, coughing as he had inhaled some sand and looked around him to find an underground oasis of water inside of a cave. He must have fallen into it when he was wandering around the desert. There were stalactites glittering with beautiful gems and colorful arrays of rocks, but none of that seemed to matter to Soren. Racing to the edge, he ducked his entire head in the water and gulped it down until he couldn't hold his breath anymore and came up gasping for air.

The water was cool and magnificent against his burning

skin and he floated in the brink for a few moments before he gathered his wits about him and looked around. There were mushrooms growing around the edges of the cave, and Soren recognized them as the kind Nanako had used in soups and broths before. Making his way over, he ate probably a good dozen before he could slow down enough to make sure he'd have enough to last him a while. At least for the rest of the week. How many days had he been here? He wasn't sure. His time here was almost over, surely.

He took his shirt off his head and put it back on, wincing at the blisters on his skin rubbing against the fabric. At least this ordeal would end on a good note. He was definitely finishing out his week in this cave, away from the sun.

Tursanay built a shield up around her as the ice creature slashed and clawed at her. She pressed against the tree, holding out her arm to hold up the shield with all her strength. Carefully she stood with a grunt, her back scratching against the bark of the tree, and stared defiantly at the creature before her. Its eyes seemed to bore into her very soul and it let out a shrill cry as it clawed harder to get to her.

"Ignite!" she yelled, and a blaze lit up around the barrier, creating a wall of flame. The creature screamed, reeling backwards in pain, and retreated a bit. Tursanay instantly turned on heel and ran, keeping the barrier around her as she did so. Today was the day they'd take her back if she'd kept up with her days correctly.

From somewhere behind, she heard the whistle again and her breath hitched in her throat. She tripped as something soared over her in a rush and she pushed up off the ground to see the ice creature skid to a stop before her, then turn around and look her in the eye.

Amara blinked blearily as she took in her surroundings. Something was wrong. Something wrapped around her so that she could barely move. She was so weak. So tired.

Everything was quiet.

But there was a calming light that was soothing her. She didn't need to worry about anything else with the light there beckoning her back to sleep. There was such a presence about it that it even eased the pang of hunger in her belly and the ache of weariness in her bones. She could watch it forever.

But there were no fireflies about either. But who needed fireflies when there was this one great big light?

A strange noise filled the air as something with rather large needle-like teeth and black eyes appeared in her vision. But she still felt safe, calm, and warmed by the light despite the chill of the water against her skin. She watched it in almost a stupor as it edged closer, opening its mouth and letting out the noise again. Almost like a choking sound. When it opened its mouth wide, Amara suddenly snapped to her senses, realizing she'd fallen into the trap of the light. But when? How long had she been like this? She didn't remember falling prey to it...

Amara fought to free herself, but she was so weak she could barely lift her arms.

I don't have to lift my arms to breathe fire; she thought to herself, taking a deep breath and letting loose an inferno that sent the creature scurrying away with a scream. The blaze scorched her throat, but she didn't care. It got her the space she needed to think and try to escape the vines.

Finally, free of the vines, she swam upward and towards the canopy of trees and broke out of the swampland and into the open air. There, on the horizon, the sun was rising, warming her skin. She looked back down below and noticed the glint of light from the sun bouncing off a mirror resting at the treetops, as if waiting for her to find it. Relief rushed through her and she swam towards it.

Then the wail of the creature sounded behind her.

Attalira saw the mirror before she registered anything else. She ran for it for all she was worth, unable to shift any more from sheer exhaustion of trying to escape the fires around her and survive at the same time. It took every ounce of skill she had to stay alive in this mess, and now her freedom was just a few yards away. If she could just make it to the mirror, this nightmare would all be over.

The ground shook, causing her to stumble, and the mountain exploded again, sending ash and smoke into the air. She could feel the heat of the angry volcano at her back, rushing towards her in its semi liquid form of fire and molten rock. She just had to get to the mirror. She had to make it back to the campgrounds.

She was nearly there-

CHAPTER 20
PHOENIX

The week was over at last, and the group returned to the campgrounds looking haggard. They made their way back to the mirror that brought them there and called out to the campgrounds to bring them back. When they appeared one by one, the mirrors disappeared behind them so nothing else could get through. However, when they looked around, they witnessed a substantial amount of destruction. The smoldering remains of some buildings were lying in ruin before them.

There was a loud, angry, jeering crowd sounding off in the distance. They followed the sounds of the crowd and made their way to the source of their anger: a man shackled to the center of a stone circle that had a maze of ridges surrounding him. Once they made it through the crowd of Council members to see what was going on, they realized it was Master Ross in the center of the circle, staring down at the others without an ounce of fear in his cold, pale blue eyes.

"You're making a mistake," he called with a smile, lifting

his chin in defiance. "You fools have no idea what you are unleashing."

"You're killing us off one by one, Ross," called Council Member Ansari. "You are hereby tried for treason, and found guilty, and sentenced to death and burned alive!"

"No!" Amara gasped. "That's inhumane!" she called, but the sound of more jeers and calls of agreement drowned her voice out as they poured the burning hot liquid down the stone slope and into the maze of ridges below.

The fiery liquid circled around him slowly, inching closer to the lowest point in the stone maze, closer to Master Ross. Amara tried to rush forward to help him, but nearby Council members held her back when they realized what she was doing. Too weak to fight them, she struggled to throw a barrier of earth up around him, but Master Loki stopped her. He shook his head at her, sadly, as she looked on in horror.

As the crowd jeered, Ross' voice rose above them all, his eyes rolling back in his head, and the crowd fell silent as his words broke through to them.

"When one becomes two," he said loudly as the voices died down and listened. "And two becomes three, out of the third comes the fourth as one! The immortal bane will give rise to the reunion of the divided and destroy themselves in their greed. Those forgotten in the veil of time will come again, Rynon once again made whole. And with his ring, unite the kingdoms under one rule and reign for a thousand years!" he shouted.

"What do you mean by this, Ross?" demanded Master Ansari. "What nonsense are you spouting?"

"It is a prophecy," Master Ross replied. "A promise! The Council will fall and Rynon will rise again!" he shouted as the flames finally reached him and burst to life, consuming him.

Amara broke away from the Council members trying to cool the flames and direct them away from his body but a flash of light had her yelping in pain as the flames expanded rather than cooling and she pulled away and buried her face in Soren's chest, unable to watch it get worse despite her efforts.

Soren covered her with his arms as a shield between her and the horrific sight before them, and held onto her, wincing as she brushed against his blisters. Instead of screaming out in pain, Ross's laughter filled the air. It was merciless, cold, and eerie. He laughed until the flames consumed his flesh and the sound of it drifted away into nothingness, echoing in their minds, their jeers losing all manner of anger behind them, only to be replaced with fear.

The flames themselves grew bright, almost white, and all those standing around had to shield their eyes from the glow. When it finally died down, there was a silence to the crowd unlike any before.

What kind of man laughed as he was burned to death?

A scream rang out in the crowd as a Council member grabbed the sides of his head. Another followed suit and suddenly a dozen or so members were screaming in pain, grasping the sides of their heads and descending into the madness the previous members did. The screams went from someone being driven insane to that of a guttural sound that barreled from the chest and sounded as if they themselves were burning and melting in a fire. Those not consumed by madness covered their ears as the wail grew into a siren-like sound and filled the air with agony and despair.

"What's going on?" Rodney asked, walking up behind them. If they looked haggard, that was nothing compared to how Rodney looked after being alone on the island in the lake with Tryn for a month.

"They're going mad—one by one," Tursanay realized.

"Quickly!" Yasar declared to the Dai-Nē. "Put up your barriers and protect yourselves! We'll handle this!"

"No!" Tursanay called. "There's too many of them. We have to get out!"

As she spoke, the Council members, taken by the madness, attacked those around them, taking them to the ground and devouring their flesh. The sound was horrifying as screams rang out mixed with the growls of the mad. Drawing a symbol in the air, Tursanay shouted a word of binding and started isolating the mad Council members from the sane ones.

"Someone help me. I can't get them all!" she called.

Rodney jumped forward, realizing what she was doing, and used his alchemy to transmute the ground into pits beneath the feet of the mad and swallow them into a hole too steep and deep for them to climb out of.

Soren began fighting against those not occupied by the other two, hitting them in certain pressure points and making their limbs useless. They writhed angrily on the ground and Amara used her powers to grow plants up out of the ground, wrapping the fallen mad in a cocoon much like she had been in the marshlands.

Attalira couldn't shift any more, the exhaustion still clinging to her form, but she could move and push the wandering mad into the pits that opened up before them thanks to Rodney. She nearly fell in once, but Rodney grabbed her and pulled her back to safety. She gave him a nod of thanks and he returned it before they stood at the ready to take on any more mad Council members.

After finally containing the situation, Yasar made the order to destroy them and before the Dai-Nē could object, Nuri sent them all up in a blaze of fire and destroyed the remaining mad. The screams that filled the air were even more horrible than the descent into madness. The acrid scent of smoke and burning hair and flesh filled the air and choked them. Yasar created a wind that blew away the smell and he called to those around them to move away from the pits.

"Why didn't you give them a chance to be helped?" Amara demanded angrily.

"We have tried everything to help those who have gone mad in the past," Yasar said sadly. "But nothing helps. There is no saving them."

"You knew," Rodney accused. "You knew it wasn't creatures from the island in the lake and you lied to us."

Tursanay looked at him, then back at Yasar. Rodney's directness surprised Tursanay, but he said exactly what she was thinking. Yasar looked at the pit where the Council member who had spoken over him before burned. He'd been one of those gone mad. Master Ansari, Tursanay realized.

"He had no choice," Nuri said, stepping forward. "There is a hierarchy in the Council we have to follow. You do not undermine those above you in rank. When he spoke the lie, we had to follow his lead."

"Nuri," Yasar scolded.

"Yasar, you are stubborn if you are not loyal to a fault, but they deserve to know this much," Nuri argued. She looked at the Dai-Nē. "We know little about it ourselves, but we know that from time to time the older Council members can go mad."

"Nuri!" called an older member. One of obviously higher

rank than her, from her stiffening reaction. "Enough. That is not your information to give."

"Yes sir, sorry sir," she replied with a nod of the head and a fist crossed over her chest. She stepped back and fell silent. Obviously disagreeing with her silencer.

Master Sharrod stepped forward. "We will not speak of this matter anymore today. For now, we rest and recuperate. Tomorrow we will hold a ceremony for the fallen. After that, we will begin your training again. We have no time to waste. We only have a limited amount of time to get you trained to your full potential before the power supplying the Oheqia runs out."

"What does that matter anymore? People are dying and all you care about is training us?" Amara asked incredulously.

"They will be honored and not forgotten, but they would have wanted us to continue on in their absence," Master Sharrod replied.

"You don't know that!" she argued.

"Yes. I do. Now stop arguing about this and do as you are told, Dai-Nē," he warned.

"No," Tursanay, Amara, and Rodney said simultaneously. They exchanged surprised looks, but squared their shoulders in solidarity.

"We're through with this place," Tursanay said, her heart rate speeding up. She'd never defied someone on this level before. It was terrifying... and exhilarating. "We're leaving."

"I will go as well," Soren agreed, stepping forward beside Amara.

Master Sharrod turned red in the face. "You will do no such thing!"

"Bet," Tursanay said with a grim smile. Master Sharrod

growled a retort and took an offensive stance. Yasar stood between the Council members and Tursanay, surprising everyone in the vicinity.

"Yasar, what are you doing?" Master Sharrod demanded. "Get over here!"

"I cannot do that," Yasar replied, taking a defensive stance against the Council.

"You swore an oath to the Council!" growled Master Sharrod.

"I swore an oath to the Dai-Nē," corrected Yasar. "To protect them no matter what and to teach them to the best of my abilities. You are violating one of my oaths. I must stand between you."

"He's right," Nuri declared, coming to stand between them aside Yasar. "We swore to protect the Dai-Nē, not fight them. This is not what we signed up for."

"I'm with Nuri on this one," Nyx replied, coming forward cheerfully and standing beside the red-haired elf. "We will not fight them, we will protect them."

Another Council member, Anan, came forward - another one of Amara's teachers. She wanted to cry, receiving all their support. She and Yasar may have had some differences, but this was what mattered - actions over words. Tryn joined Rodney on the opposite side Tursanay was on, and gave them a nod, showing she was with them. For once, Tursanay was glad to have her there.

"Let's show them how a real alchemist gets things done," Tryn said, cracking her neck.

"Let's show them how the Dai-Nē gets things done," Tursanay agreed. "We are tired. Hungry. And angry. And we are not to be messed with."

"You do not want to make an enemy of the Council," Master Sharrod warned.

"You don't want to make an enemy of the Dai-Nē," Tryn retorted.

"You need us," Tursanay replied. "But we're not going along quietly anymore. You're going to respect us, and respect our wishes, just as we have respected yours this whole time."

"But your training is not finished!" Master Sharrod argued.

"It is for now. Tomorrow we hold a memorial service, and then we leave," Rodney said, standing straighter.

"This is ridiculous!" Master Sharrod argued still.

"Either we go peacefully, or we go with a fight. Either way, we're not staying here any longer than for us to get some food and rest," Tursanay agreed with Rodney.

"You're making a mistake," Master Sharrod growled.

"Then let us make it and learn from it," Soren added. "You cannot lead us by the hand forever. We must make our own path."

"But-!" Master Sharrod began again, but Yasar cut him off.

"No more arguing," he said. "Give them what they want or there will be more unnecessary bloodshed. We need to take care of the wounded and pack our things. I've had enough fighting for a lifetime."

And with that he went and made his way towards the campgrounds - that were mostly smoldering remains - with a sigh. Everyone seemed to drop their stances slowly and shuffle off to follow suit. Those that were wounded, Tursanay went and helped heal them, and those that could help brought the wounded back to the unscorched places in the campgrounds.

Food was immediately prepared and the Dai-Nē ate like their lives depended on it. Amara was still gaunt and pale, but the food seemed to put a little color back into her cheeks. She ate three helpings before she finally had had enough. Soren wasn't far behind with his two helpings, but the others picked at their food, not seeming to be really hungry.

"So that was the worst month of my entire life," Tursanay said quietly as the Dai-Nē sat and ate around the table.

There was a general nod of agreement and murmuring as they exchanged stories of what they went through. Soren seeming to have the most peaceful time of them all in the long run.

"So, what happened to you?" Tursanay asked, nudging Rodney.

He was silent for a long moment before shaking his head with a shudder. "It's still too close to relive right now. I don't want to talk about it."

"That just makes me more curious," Tursanay complained. Rodney was quiet for a moment, staring into his soup.

In a small voice, eyes a million miles away as he reflected on the events of the past month, he murmured, "I'm going to have nightmares about that place for the rest of my life."

Tursanay didn't pester him after that.

When it came time to go to bed, Tursanay was about to fall over from exhaustion from being up nearly a full twenty-four hours whilst having fought, healed, and run for her life all in that time span. But despite her exhaustion, she was still terrified of sleeping at night, lest the creature come and find her again. Walking out onto the front porch to look at the stars, she found Rodney sitting on the porch steps, a warm drink in his hands. Silently, she sat down beside him and let out a small sigh. They sat in silence for a while until Tursanay put her head on his shoulder.

"I can't sleep either," she murmured.

Rodney looked down at his cup and gave a small smile. "I kind of wonder if I'll ever be able to sleep again."

"We'll collapse from exhaustion at some point, I'm sure," Tursanay replied.

"Yeah," he said softly. His thumb rubbed over the side of his cup.

"Wanna keep each other company until then?" she suggested. "We can watch each other's backs."

"I'd appreciate that," he said quietly, laying his cheek on her head. "I'd appreciate that a lot."

The next morning arrived, and they held the ceremony for the fallen. Everyone had packed up what little remaining things they had left after the fires of the previous day, and gathered at the forefront of the training grounds where they had entered so long ago. The group stood before the doors, looking up at them with great foreboding, and Yasar was the first one to step forward and press his hand against the door, pulling it open with a great deal of effort. It creaked open slowly, pushing outward, and inside was a dark abyss.

Suddenly the world seemed to turn on its ear, everything a swirl of color and sound. The sound faded into a ringing noise that popped into their ears when the pressure became too much. The color swirled into nothingness and darkness consumed them. There was a moment where they were all conscious, then the next thing they knew, they were picking themselves up off the ground as if waking from a deep sleep. They were back outside the doors, the massive wooden structure closed behind them. The winged lionesses hissed, climbing down from their perches to stand before the group of people before the Oheqia.

"Why have you broken the pact?" they hissed in unison, their eyes glowing with the emphasis of their words.

"There were complications within," Yasar replied slowly, shaking his head and getting to his feet. The Dai-Nē and other Council members slowly stood, brushing themselves off. "Keep the remaining power as our apology for the inconvenience. We do not need it."

"You can't make that kind of offer, Yasar!" Master Sharrod argued.

"Offer accepted," the winged lionesses agreed. "Leave this place. Now."

"You can't just-" Master Sharrod began, but the winged lionesses had already jumped back up to their perch and returned to solid stone.

"It's time to make our way back, Master Sharrod," Yasar reminded him. "There's no need to fret over the tiny details."

"We could have used that power for something else! We still had a full day left!" Master Sharrod argued.

"And you would have had the Oheqia sealed from us forever for breaking the pact in doing so. I prevented this from happening by giving them the power," Yasar replied.

Master Sharrod fell silent after grumbling something under his breath, then turned and made his way to join the other Council members heading back towards the river where the dwarven ships were waiting for them. Surprised to see them back just under two days early, the dwarves scrambled to prepare the ships to bring them back down river to Delmar, but Tursanay pulled Yasar aside and asked to change their heading.

"We need to visit the library city," she said quietly. "We need to look up something that might help us with the sick cities."

"River Morn?" Yasar asked.

"Is that possible by ship?" she asked. "Or will there be other traveling involved?"

"It's south of Delmar by the river. Just a day's difference. We can make that trip, but what is this about cities being ill?" he asked.

"The cities contacted Soren in his sleep. They are calling out for help," she replied, not telling him just when they had contacted him like Nuri had mentioned.

"That is concerning," Yasar frowned. "We will make a stop in Delmar, but I will tell the dwarves to continue your journey on to River Morn."

"You won't come with us?" she asked.

"I'm afraid my recent dissent against the Council will subject to an investigation. Same as the others that stood with you. Only Tryn will be free of such as she is not of the Council," he answered. "As it is, keep it secret from the others that you are going to River Morn until you are well on your way. It is best for your path to be unhindered as much as possible if you are to help the cities. They are very important to this world. Please do what you can," he requested.

"We will," she nodded. "And Yasar?"

"Yes?" he asked.

"Thank you. For everything," she replied.

He gave a nod and made his way over to the dwarven captain to speak with him in private. It was three days on the river. This time, the journey was much smoother. No bandits attacking their ship. They made their way down to Delmar, and when the Council had cleared out and things settled, the Dai-Nē were snuck back onto the ship and they departed in the night, thanking the dwarves for their help.

When they reached River Morn the following afternoon, they took directions from the docking crew, and made their way through town. Soren stuck close, completely out of his element, and Rodney seemed to be the one that could point out landmarks mentioned by the crew easiest.

When they reached the center of the city, there was a large ash tree that towered over everything else. It was the largest tree they'd ever laid eyes on, being so big it could house a city inside. In fact, it partly did, as this was where the library was located. They were told by the signs on the wall—translated by Soren because the reading spell given to them had not lasted outside of the Oheqia—that there was a copy of every book written in this library.

Making their way inside, they requested to be taken to the history section and got brought down into the roots of the tree. There, a cellar-like place was carved into the wood. There were scrolls upon scrolls, books upon books, vials of spoken word sitting on shelves, and all manner of information that they could have possibly wanted.

"We're never going to find what we need here," Amara sighed.

"Don't give up so easily," Tursanay said, shouldering against her. "Think of all the things we can learn here. This is an amazing opportunity!"

"We need to focus on what we came here for first, then

worry about the extra later," Amara reminded her. "Or have you forgotten we snuck away from the Council and only have a day or so before they notice we're missing?"

"Oh right," Tursanay said, a bit deflated. She was itching to get her hands on some information about this world that they hadn't had access to yet, but Amara was right. They had to prioritize what they were looking for before they went down a rabbit hole. Sure, the ill cities were one thing, but they had a lot more things they needed to look up in a short amount of time. Like information on phoenixes and how to find the last one, as well as what happened to the other phoenixes. And not to mention the tearing of the veil.

"Is there something I can help you with?" came a quivering voice. They turned to see a hunched over man in a brown robe with a hood and scarf come hobbling up to them, carrying a book. His warm brown eyes observed them despite his dark brown, shoulder length hair falling around his face. They exchanged looks. Was this a librarian?

"Oh, actually we were looking for information on phoenixes," Tursanay chimed in. "Is there any way you can help us find the information, please? We'd be very grateful." She was laying the niceties on thick.

"Oh, of course. This way," he replied, hobbling past and making his way down an aisle. "Are you looking for anatomy, past lives, or history of the race?" he asked as they followed along.

"Oh well, actually a bit of all three," Tursanay replied. "But let's start with anatomy and history of the race. That might help us a little more right now."

"May I inquire what you need this information for?" the man asked.

"Just doing some research for a school project," Amara piped in before Tursanay could stammer out a response.

"Ah yes," the man said. "Then you have come to the right place. Here we are. This is the anatomy of phoenixes," he said, taking a large tome off the shelf above him. "And this," he said, going over to a different shelf and scanning through the scrolls there. He took out five or six and turned towards them, arms loaded. "is the history of their race. Everything is in here," he added. "The tree records all historical events as they happen."

"Perfect," Rodney breathed, relieved. No more guessing if they should believe something or not. Just straight facts.

"Is there anything else I can do for you?" the man asked curiously.

"Not right now," Rodney said, thanking him. "But we might ask you a few more questions later for another project. Is that okay?"

"Absolutely," the man said with a bow. "You can find me in the chambers on the west wing. I will be cataloging."

They thanked him again, and he set the materials they needed on a nearby table and left them to pour over them in peace. Once they'd all seated themselves around the table, Soren read through the materials, skimming through some, and pointing out important bits to the others.

"Look at this," he was saying. "It says a phoenix's power is determined by the brightness of their eyes. The paler the color, the stronger they are. Red eyes indicate a much younger phoenix, as pale blue indicates a very old phoenix." He skimmed a bit more. "Their reincarnation can be any age they choose or are predisposed to. If a phoenix dies a violent ash death, their next formation may be severely injured until their next reformation."

"What does it say about what happened to them in the past?" Tursanay asked. Soren searched through all the scrolls, then pulled out the tomes and began searching through them. He was quiet for a good ten minutes, reading over everything, but then he frowned.

"It doesn't say," he replied. "This is not the full history..."

"What the hell?" Tursanay swore. "Where's that librarian we saw earlier?"

"I'll see if I can find him," Rodney said. "Y'all keep looking over this stuff."

Soren nodded, and Rodney left to find the west wing chambers.

He passed shelves that were carved out of the tree themselves, and they crackled faintly of fireproof spells. The library had vaulted ceilings in most rooms with intricate carvings done throughout, and archways with living branches decorating them in an arc. Well-kept and thriving with life, the artificial light in the chandeliers seemed to feed them like the sun would. Rodney found the man, at last, pouring over a book and scribbling down notes. Walking up to his desk, he gave a polite smile.

"Hello, sir," he said. The astonished look on the man's face surprised Rodney. The look got quickly replaced with a polite and eager smile. He set his writing utensil down.

"Yes, Master...?" he began, asking for Rodney's name.

"Oh, uh Rodney," he supplied. "Just Rodney is fine," he added. Another look of surprise quickly covered up. Rodney wasn't sure what he'd said that would have made him feel surprised, but he hoped it wasn't something in the translation spell messing up. He didn't need to come across as rude to someone they needed help from.

"How may I help you, Ma-" he caught himself and cleared his throat. "Rodney?"

"We are trying to find out what happened when the phoenixes were wiped out, but that information isn't in the books you gave us," he said.

A measured look.

"That's because it's in the restricted section," he replied. "Only certain people may enter."

"Would a Dai-Nē be able to enter?" Rodney asked.

"Most certainly!" the man replied.

"Oh, great because-" Rodney began, but the librarian cut him off.

"If... they can produce their mark," he finished. He looked down his nose at Rodney pointedly, as if not believing he could produce such a mark.

Rodney sighed. Somewhere in the back of his mind, he knew this day would come, but he hoped it wouldn't be here in a library, of all places. Well, okay, he hoped it wouldn't be anywhere public of all places, but here he was.

Turning his back to the man, he took off his long robe, tossing it over his shoulder, then lifted his shirt in the back and showed the mark. It was a small, simple mark, made up of seven connected but not overlapping circles with his stone in the center of the circle. Each of the other Dai-Nē also had a stone in the center circle corresponding to their power.

"What are you doing?" the man asked, both curiously and hesitantly.

"Showing you my mark," Rodney replied. "Do I have to hike my pants down too? I can't tell."

Leaning over his table to get a better look, the man's face went from scrutiny to shock to horror. "Oh, goodness, I am so sorry Master Rodney! I had no idea you were a Dai-Nē!

Please forgive my arrogance in not using proper etiquette and referring to you familiarly!"

"Huh?" Rodney said, turning back around. "Oh no, don't worry about that," he said, realizing he meant the 'master' honorific. "I prefer to just be called Rodney anyhow. It's my name, after all."

"Oh, but your grace," the man began again.

"Just Rodney, please," he cringed.

"I couldn't possibly—" the man continued to fumble over himself.

"Please, it'd make me feel less awkward," Rodney replied.

The man hesitated.

"You are certain this would be beneficial to you?" he asked.

Rodney nodded. "Yes," he answered. "Same with my friends. We're all Dai-Nē, and we prefer to just be called by our names."

The man paled considerably. "You're... all... Dai-Nē?"

"Just keep that between us," Rodney said, trying to stop the inevitable onslaught of apologies brewing in the man's mind. "What's your name?" he asked.

"They call me Llog," the man replied.

"Log?" Rodney asked. "Like cata-logue? Or fallen tree log?"

"Um just... Llog," he replied hesitantly, unsure what Rodney meant. Perhaps something got lost in translation. Rodney dropped the subject.

"So Llog," he began again. "Can you show us the restricted section? We really need to look up that information."

"Oh! Of course," he replied. "Right this way!"

"Awesome," Rodney sighed with relief. "Thank you!"

"Of course, Mas- ah sir- uh- Rodney," Llog fumbled, trying to respect Rodney's wishes and remain polite at the same time. It was apparently rather difficult for him to find that balance on such short notice.

Gathering the other Dai-Nē, he led them through several corridors and down further into the roots of the tree. Here, he carried a lantern with him as he led them down into an area of low light.

"Why's it so dark down here?" Amara asked.

"The darkness preserves the writings longer," Llog answered. "They have protection spells on them, of course, but for good measure, we keep them in low light to help preserve their integrity."

"Oh cool," Amara replied.

"I've heard of them doing something like that with the dead sea scrolls back home," Tursanay said. "They're so old you can't take pictures of them because they are delicate."

"Thankfully, we don't need any pictures, we just need information," Amara replied as they reached a heavy door guarded by two men in armor. When they caught sight of the group, they held their spears at the ready, but Llog assured them all was well and that they had permission to enter the restricted area. They gave Llog a stern look, but pulled back their spears when he gave them a nod and a smile. They entered, one by one, and looked around.

There were shelves upon shelves of ancient scrolls and texts, tomes and vials of spoken word. The shelves here also looked to be carved out of the tree itself so there would be no movement or accidental tipping. When Soren entered the room, he had to hold on to the wall for support.

"You okay?" Amara asked, noticing his struggle.

"The heart of the city lies in this tree. Its voice is loud here.

It asks for help for its sister cities," Soren replied. "We must research what to do about the veil here as well."

"We will," Amara promised, rubbing his back. Tursanay had healed his blisters, and it wasn't as tender anymore.

Soren only nodded in response; the presence of the living city was much too heavy on him to respond verbally.

Making their way further into the roots, Llog led them to a shelf with special, glowing scrolls and pulled one out, examining it before replacing it gently and pulling out another. Several parchments later, he found the one he was searching for and turned towards them.

"These documents cannot leave this area. What you read here is to stay here and get replaced on the shelf once you are through with it," he instructed.

"No problem," Rodney nodded. "We don't need to go anywhere with it, we just need to know what it says."

"Then here you are," he said, handing him the scrolls.

They went down to a table that was seated in the center of the room and they began pouring over the scrolls, Soren reading some out loud and paraphrasing their contents. There were details of the hierarchy of phoenixes, details of their ash death and how it occurred, and the general politics of how the species interacted with other species. When it delved into their medical history, one particular passage caught their attention.

"In the years following the disease that ate away at the race of phoenix, one was reborn as a Dai-Nē. The once immortal elves, vampires, and phoenixes engaged in a war because of power imbalances, resulting in almost wiping out the phoenixes. When one remained, the Dai-Nē, a method of removing the power from the phoenix, was created using the ring of Rynon and a Pedestal of Power. They extracted the power of Dai-Nē from the phoenix without killing them by using the ring of Rynon. However, once the new generation of Dai-Nē received it, and that generation passed on, all the powers returned to the pedestal, awaiting their new vessels."

"Oh man," Tursanay muttered. "What Nanako said about the pedestal was true, then."

"Wait, there is more," Soren said, skimming over the next part. "According to this, before their power was stripped away, the phoenix cursed the elves and vampires with the loss of their immortality."

"Holy…" Rodney muttered under his breath. "So, you really can do that?"

"Apparently a Dai-Nē can. No wonder they're so revered," Tursanay muttered, running a hand through her hair.

"Or should we say feared?" Rodney agreed. "That librarian guy paled when he learned we were all Dai-Nē. Maybe we should keep that on the down low unless we need it to find out some specific information like we did with this."

"Good idea," Amara replied. "That and we don't want people trying to take advantage of us for it."

"Wait a minute," Tursanay began. "Blue eyes, much older than those in the Council, unbothered by flames, a vendetta against the Council… guys-" she turned and faced the others. "I think Ross was the last phoenix."

"Let's see, cryptic, likes to withhold certain bits of information until a later time but gets killed before he can give it out," Rodney listed off. "Matches up with Mr. Asher. That checks out."

Tursanay smacked him on the arm.

"What it's true!"

"It's my fault he's dead," Amara said, covering her mouth. "It's my fault they're all dead."

"Wait what?" Tursanay asked, doing a double take. "What do you mean?"

"I told them he was sabotaging the Council members because I thought it would help them stop dying, and they killed him and that triggered the madness and now several people are dead because of me."

"Hey, hey," Tursanay said, kneeling down to look at Amara as she sat down on the chair beside Soren and covered her face. "Thinking like that will only drive you insane. What you did, you did out of kindness, not malice." That didn't seem to cheer her up. "Listen," Tursanay tried again. "You can't control what happens in a chain of events that you may or may not have started. Don't spiral downward, worrying about the what ifs. You can't change the past, okay? You can only work towards a brighter future."

"She's right, A," Rodney agreed. "You can't do that to yourself. I know it's hard not to because of all we've been hit with recently, but it won't help you. It'll only hurt you. And I'm sorry, but nobody hurts my friends. Not even themselves," he added, earning a small smile from her despite the teary-eyed look she was getting.

"I just want one normal thing to happen to us. Is that too much to ask?" she muttered.

"Apparently," Rodney said.

"Oh, my god I'm an idiot," Tursanay said suddenly.

"T, we just talked to Amara about this literally seconds ago," Rodney began, but Tursanay shook her head.

"No listen," Tursanay said. "Phoenixes aren't hurt by fire. They're immune!"

"Okay...?" Rodney acknowledged, not seeing where this was going.

"Fire killed Ross and went out laughing!" Tursanay continued.

"Yeah, it was really creep-oh my god we're idiots," Rodney realized mid-sentence.

"Wait, if Ross was the last phoenix, that means he's not dead yet," Amara said, realizing too. "He didn't die after all!"

"See? There is a bright side to everything!" Rodney grinned.

"But now we have no idea what the last phoenix looks like and we're back to square one," Amara reminded him.

"Crap, you're right," Rodney said, shoulders sagging.

"How'd he get out of the training grounds without being noticed?" Amara asked.

"To be fair," Tursanay answered. "There was a lot of chaos going on."

"True," Rodney agreed. "They could have snuck out with the rest of us."

"Okay, so that's the mystery of the last phoenix partially solved. Let's see what we can learn about the veil between the worlds," Tursanay declared.

"Maybe we can find out how to help the living cities as well," Amara piped in, glancing at Soren, who gave a smile and a nod. A silent thank you for remembering and bringing up the living cities.

As if summoned, Llog came around the corner sheepishly rubbing his hands together and looking for all the world as if he were about to poke a hibernating bear.

"Is ah... is everything to your liking? Have you found the information you need? Or is there something else I can do for you?" he asked.

"Actually, we were wondering if you can help us find some information on the veil between the worlds," Amara said.

Llog smiled awkwardly and gave a small laugh. When the others didn't laugh with him, his voice trailed off until he realized they were serious. "But... the veil isn't real," he said. "That's just an old myth."

The Dai-Nē exchanged looks silently.

"Well, we would still appreciate any kind of information you have on it, if you don't mind," Amara said politely. "Mythological or not."

Llog hesitated. "What do you want with that information? You couldn't possibly-"

"Can you keep a secret, Llog?" Rodney asked. "Because what we are researching here can help a lot of people, but if the wrong person finds out about it, it could hinder that help."

Llog clamped his mouth shut for a long moment. "Y-Yes," he said, looking as if he'd rather run away than hear what Rodney was going to say next.

"What's your best kept secret then?" Tursanay challenged. "Prove we can trust you. What kind of things have people entrusted you with?"

"Lots of things," Llog answered. "But if I told you, they wouldn't be secret anymore."

Tursanay and Rodney exchanged a look.

"Good. Then we can count on you," Rodney grinned.

"Pardon? Oh—That was a test, wasn't it?" Llog asked.

"Just a little one," Tursanay shrugged. "More of a quiz, really."

"And you passed!" Rodney said, as if it was something to celebrate.

Llog didn't seem to know what to do with himself. Smile like they were or look terrified. He ended up with a terrified smile, and if his head shrunk back into his shoulders any more than it was, it would disappear into his robes entirely.

"We believe there to be holes in the veil, or weak points; where the life and magic is being drained out of the living cities, making them ill. We wish to repair these places in order to rehabilitate the cities and aid them in repairing them-selves," Soren said.

Llog's head seemed to reappear slowly from betwixt his shoulders as he stared them down cooly, brow furrowed in concentration. He stood up straighter than he had before and, for the first time, Rodney realized just how tall he was. His entire demeanor changed, and he was no longer a quivering librarian afraid of the Dai-Nē, but a formidable-looking figure standing before them.

"You're going against the Council, aren't you?" he asked, his voice no longer quivering but strong, steady, and deeper.

The looks of shock that spread across all the Dai-Nē's faces was unmistakable.

"That look confirms my suspicions. The living cities have been getting ill for some time now. Three have died further north. If something can be done about it, it's you lot that can do it."

"Whoa, hold up," Tursanay said. "Back up. What's with that complete change in personality? And how did you come to the conclusion we're going against the Council from that?"

He ducked back down to how he was before and his voice changed back to that quivering sound. "No one suspects a lowly librarian to be the head of the resistance. It makes it easier for me to read between the lines when people let their guards down around me."

"Head of the what now?" Amara said.

"Head of the resistance," he answered back in his strong, steady voice, standing back straight. "We've been trying to get the Council to do something about this problem for years. My home was one of those destroyed by this illness plaguing the living cities. They do nothing about it and dismiss it as a hoax. We've long suspected they may have something to do with it, but had no proof. And if the Dai-Nē are going behind their backs to fix it, then I say we just gained some powerful allies.

CHAPTER 21
BOUNTIES

There was a long period of silence, bordering on awkward. The group stared at Llog, not sure what they'd just seen and heard. A resistance? Against the Council? That Llog was the head of? The quivering librarian, who appeared upset when Rodney asked him to call him by his name instead of using the proper etiquette he was accustomed to?

"I'm sorry," Rodney said, blinking repeatedly. "The what now? Did I mishear that?" He kind of hoped that his hearing aids were going on the fritz because this was an entire can of worms he did not wish to open.

"No, no, he said resistance," Tursanay said, trying and failing to wipe the dumbfounded look off her face that she shared with Rodney. They were both staring at Llog as if he'd lost his mind, grown a second head, and pirouetted in front of them. "He definitely said resistance."

"So, we're not the only ones that mistrust them?" Rodney asked, earning a smack from Tursanay for admitting that out loud. He quickly recovered by adding, "I thought they were pretty well liked..."

"So they would have you believe," Llog scoffed. "There are those that believe the Council is doing what is best for the world, and there are a much greater number that have suffered at their hands for too many generations. Something must be done, and we seek that change. We are working with the Order of Rynon to enact it."

"The Order of Rynon," Tursanay murmured. "I've heard of that before. What can you tell us about it?"

"They seek to reestablish a connection with the other side of the veil, but we are having difficulty proving its existence to the public," Llog said.

"Oh, I don't think that's a good idea," Tursanay said quickly. "The other side is full of people that wouldn't understand what they were seeing. It would cause mass mayhem and planet wide panic. They would start a war without even realizing what they were doing, thinking it would be to protect themselves from strange creatures. There would be mass murder, and not to mention the other side is full of iron. It's a key component in a lot of things over there. Not only would it not be safe, but it would be toxic to your very beings."

"That is..." Llog began slowly. "How... how do you know so much about the other side of the veil?"

"We grew up there. Well, three of us did. These two grew up over here," Rodney replied, gesturing to Attalira and Soren. He supposed if they were spilling the beans about what it was like over there, there was no reason to not tell him that.

"What?" he almost exclaimed before he caught himself

and lowered his voice. "You grew up on the other side of the veil?"

"Yes," Amara said slowly. "Why?"

"Because you can teach us so much about it!" Llog said. "With the Dai-Nē having grown up over there and bearing the knowledge of what it is like, we can definitely convince the public that it is real!"

"Did you miss the part where I said it's unsafe and toxic to your kind?" Tursanay asked. "We learned in training that iron is harmful to magic and messes it up. And it's lethal to most species. People on the other side of the veil use iron and silver and gold in their daily lives. It wouldn't be a place you want to go."

Llog's shoulders seemed to drop a bit, the smile on his face faltering. "That is unfortunate. I suppose we will need to reconsider some of our standpoints."

"It's just too dangerous over there," Tursanay said, shaking her head. "Especially for magic kind."

"Then how did you survive? You have wings. She is of the mer-folk. Did you live in hiding your whole lives?" he asked.

"Honestly, there must have been some kind of disguise spell to hide our true forms because we didn't know we were magic kind until we arrived on this side of the veil and the spell broke," Amara replied. "It was rather upsetting to suddenly have a fin where there were once feet."

"I can imagine," Llog agreed. "So magic works across the veil?"

"Actually, I have a theory on that," Tursanay said. "We were told by the last phoenix that magic doesn't work on that side of the veil, but we had plenty of experience with magic in the days leading up to us coming here. I think there was a Dai-Nē involved with what was going on, but I can't prove it until I talk to the two remaining ones, or try magic on the other side of the veil whenever we get a chance to go home."

"You want to go back there?" Llog asked, confused. "I thought you said it was horrible."

"There are things we need to wrap up," Rodney replied. "We can't just disappear out of nowhere. There are people that will go looking for us. And if we return later, we don't want to have that hanging over our heads the whole time."

"Ah! I understand. Unfinished business," Llog replied with a nod.

"Speaking of the two remaining Dai-Nē," Amara interjected. "We need to find out why they ran away from the ceremony once they got their mark. I think we may need them to work with us if we're going to do something about the sick cities and the weak points in the veil."

"True," Tursanay said. "We should split up and look for them and continue our research. We need to have at least one person who can read on each team in case we come across something we need to translate, since the spell wore off when we left the Oheqia."

"I can handle that," Attalira said, taking a step to one side and splitting herself into two people. "I'm Atta," the first one said.

"And I'm Lira," said the second.

"We can split into two groups evenly this way," they said simultaneously.

"Sweet," Rodney commented. "So, who goes with who?"

"I will go with Amara to help locate the other Dai-Nē since I have some experience in this matter," Soren said. "I can scry to find them, and she and Atta can navigate."

"Right," Tursanay nodded. "Me, Rodney, and Lira can stay here and gather some more information."

"Perfect," Rodney agreed. "But let's get some lunch before we go our separate ways. I'm starving."

The others agreed and asked Llog where some good places to eat were. He directed them to a witch's brewery close to the library that he frequented. They parted ways for the moment, promising to return with more information about the Mortal World. When they arrived at the brewery, there were rich smells of food and drinks. A pleasant atmosphere of people chatting amicably, and the shop workers calling out orders and handing them out to their customers. There were booths where groups could sit or tables one could spread out more. With Amara's tail, they sat in the corner so she could be on the outside and not get stepped on by anyone walking past. There wasn't much of a crowd, but it was still a bustling little shop that had a lot of orders being delivered out of the window by delivery brooms overhead.

The witches at the counter dressed in black pointed hats and black dresses as a uniform. They had several cauldrons brewing potions they would add a dash of whatever they were brewing to drinks they made or sprinkle over food the prepared. A dash of luck here, a boost of inspiration there. The smells alone were enough to give one a rush of energy from all the concoctions brewing.

The shop itself had decorations of moons and cats, crystals, rosemary and lavender, most of which was scattered amongst common altar area with various statues. Here there was incense burning to cleanse the area and bring good feeling to the atmosphere.

"You know, that's still so weird to hear," Rodney said as they sat down at a booth together. "Calling home, the Mortal World and all."

"Well, remember, they'd give us a weird look for calling this place the Magic World too," Tursanay said.

"Well, it is," Rodney said, making a face. "Seriously, though - they have magic! Literally a world of magic and the fact they didn't call it the Magic World was a travesty."

"True, but try explaining Mortal World vs. Magical World to someone on the street back home. They'd think you'd lost your mind. It's no different here," Amara added.

"Fair," Rodney conceded. "It's still weird, though."

"We're being watched," Atta said quietly, not looking away from their table.

"Those three in the corner?" Tursanay asked. "I noticed that too."

She'd noticed the redhead's reaction when they first entered the brewery, and the other two that followed them in, taking a seat beside her. At first, she thought the reaction had been her recognizing the two men behind them, but after paying attention, she noticed they kept stealing glances their way and murmuring amongst themselves. The world hadn't heard of their reputation as Dai-Nē yet, so it couldn't be that. It had to be something else. But what?

"You know it's taking everything I have not to look in every corner right now," Rodney said, running a hand through his hair.

"Thank you for not just asking 'Where?' and then looking," Tursanay said.

"I think they're moving to block the exits," Amara said, watching them in her peripheral.

"We might not be getting our lunch today, Rodney," Tursanay apologized.

"Maaan," Rodney complained. "Why is it one thing after another?"

"Let's just make our way quietly out of here and not make a fuss. There's no reason—" Amara began, but the red-headed person in the corner suddenly appeared beside their table, cutting her off.

"So, we meet again," she said, looking down at them.

"We do?" Rodney asked, blinking in surprise.

"You escaped a week and a half ago, but you're surrounded now, and there's no getting out of here without a fight," she said. "You've got a bounty on your head the size of the seven cities, and I'm here to collect."

"There's like, what, three of you and five of us?" Tursanay said, grabbing hold of her drink, prepping for a fight. "What makes you so confident you can take us?"

"Guys," Amara began.

"I've seen what you five are capable of," the redhead laughed. "This will be a walk in the park."

"Guys," Amara tried again.

"We've been through Dai-Nē training, hun," Tursanay said. "We're not who we were a week and a half ago."

"Guys," Amara half whispered urgently.

"How much can you have learned in such a short time?" the bounty hunter asked. "I'm willing to call your bluff. About the training and about being a Dai-Nē."

"GUYS." Amara got everyone's attention then. She lowered her voice and pointed out the window. "The Council is here." There outside were several teachers huddled together and pointing out places for each of them to start searching. Two headed towards the library. Others, searching the shops and breweries.

Tursanay let out a curse. "It's too soon. We haven't gotten the information we need yet."

"I have an idea that'll make everyone happy," Rodney

declared, looking at the bounty hunter. "We'll go with you quietly."

"What?" demanded Tursanay, looking at him like he was crazy. There was no way she was going without a fight, the look said.

"As long as they can get us away from the Council without being seen, we can wait for them to leave and then come back and get the information we need. Meanwhile, they can turn us in for a bounty, skip town, then we can show our Dai-Nē marks as evidence of our pardon. It's a get out of jail free card," Rodney explained.

"I like you," the bounty hunter grinned. "I'd go along with that plan if I were you."

"But," Tursanay tried to argue, but couldn't find a counter plan. Her shoulders dropped with a sigh and she let go of her glass. "Okay, but you have to do this quickly. If we get spotted by the Council, the deal is off, and we're out of here. You get nothing."

"I like those odds," the bounty hunter replied. She signaled for her companions to join them and quickly explained the situation. As she gave out orders, the looks of confusion quickly transformed into focused gazes. One of them—the one with the short, mousy brown hair—dug into his bag and brought out a bottle of small orbs, much like the ones Soren had brought as a language spell. He tipped several into his hand and passed them out.

"This is a disguise spell. I use them for when I need to hide my face from a bounty," he explained.

"I don't need one," Atta and Lira said simultaneously, changing into an Aziza and a lizard, respectively. The lizard sat on the Aziza's shoulder and waited for the others to take their disguise orbs. Hesitantly, the remaining Dai-Nē took the pill sized orbs and with a glance at each other, and one back at the Council members roaming the streets, then each took them one by one and changed into different creatures.

Amara turned from a mermaid into a cynocephali, an ape bodied creature with a dog head; Rodney turned into a taniwha with red hair and a beard; Tursanay turned into a centaur; and Soren into a werewolf.

Led away out of the brewery, and getting a few odd looks, they went down a back alley and away from the major crowds. When the bustle of the city died away, they paused momentarily to make a plan of escape.

"We'll split into three groups. Two of you per one of us," the lead bounty hunter instructed. "That way there's less of a chance they'll find all of you in one go. Penjani, you take the werewolf and the cynocephali and go southwest." She looked at the black-haired bounty hunter with dark skin and he gave a nod. "Notah," she added to the mousy haired bounty hunter. "Take the taniwha and the centaur and go northwest. I'll take the Aziza and the lizard and go due west. We'll reconvene outside of the city's outskirts in the suburbs near the bank of the River of Stars."

"Understood," Notah said with a nod. "And if we run into trouble?"

"Well then, I'm sure our so-called Dai-Nē friends here can make use of themselves and cause a distraction," the lead bounty hunter said, eying the group as she did so.

The Dai-Nē looked between each other.

"I think we can come up with something," Tursanay said. "Remember Home Alone guys?"

"Oh, not bad, I was thinking Looney Tunes it," Rodney replied with an approving nod.

"Attalira's good at improvising, so she doesn't need to

rely on us, but you got an idea should something come up?" Tursanay checked with Amara.

"I'm thinking something along the lines of asking the city for help through Soren. I hear they can even rearrange streets to help us get away," Amara replied.

"Oh nice," Tursanay complemented. "Wouldn't have thought of that."

When they'd gone over the route they were taking, the bounty hunters ordered the Dai-Nē to let them tie their hands behind their backs so it would look like a legitimate capture rather than just walking in five people without restraints. Though they were hesitant at first, the Dai-Nē agreed and put on the restraints and let themselves get led through the streets, going their separate ways so as not to get caught. The bounty hunters talked with them amicably as they made their way through the streets.

"How long does this disguise spell last?" Tursanay asked.

"Only a few hours," the Notah replied. "By the end of the day, you'll be your normal selves again and capable of getting out of the dungeon."

"Wait if we're in disguise, how will they know we're the bounty that they're looking for?" Rodney asked, noting the obvious.

"They have ways to see through your disguise," Notah replied. "They'll check your faces only, so as long as none of you have a mark visible in that area, they'll not check for it."

"Good," Tursanay nodded. "That'll give us time to wait out the Council."

• • •

"So why are you running from the Council if you are Dai-Nē?" Penjani asked, glancing around as he led them around on a rope leash like a couple of dogs on a walk with their owner.

"Let's just say we need more information than they're willing to give us," Amara replied. "We've been through a lot since the day we got our powers, and honestly, I can't forgive some of their teaching methods, either."

Rodney shuddered. "At least you didn't have Tryn as a teacher."

"I probably would have tried to kill her," Tursanay replied.

"She's not so bad once I told her to stop that flirting mess," Rodney said.

"We probably should have told her we were coming here. She could have helped us research stuff," Soren suggested.

"No," Amara said a little too hastily.

As Tursanay said, "She's too loud and obnoxious."

The lead bounty hunter threw her head back and cackled. "This Tryn character sounds interesting. I'd love to meet her sometime."

"She's something alright," Attalira said.

. . .

"She can't help it," Amara said apologetically to Penjani. "Her personality is... forceful."

"And that's the kindest way you can put it," Tursanay muttered as they walked past an alley way down past some houses.

"Dai-Nē!" a Council member yelled behind them.

Rodney turned around to see the Councilman Sharrod wearing a strange pair of spectacles and pointing directly at them from down the street. Behind him were police officers of varying sizes. The largest towering over them shifted into a bear form and growled loudly, spittle flying from her lips. The sound echoed down the street, rattling their nerves and sending a shiver down their spines.

Turning on heel and running as fast as they could down the street, the group was jarred when a barrier formed at the end of the buildings, blocking their path and causing them to run into it at full speed. They fell in a tangled pile of limbs and bodies, and struggled to get back to their feet as the police made a formation and ran towards them.

Thinking quickly, Rodney dug into his pocket for a crystal and smashed it onto the ground, forcing the earth and cobblestone beneath their feet to shatter and erupt into spiked rocks, rushing towards the police, making the street difficult terrain. The police had to skid and roll to keep from impaling themselves on the spikes. While they traversed the rearranged street surface, the Dai-Nē and Penjani untangled themselves from each other and Tursanay set to work bringing down the barrier.

First she tried punching it, then she fired balls of decomposition magic at it, but it continued to absorb her magic. Turning to Rodney, she had an idea.

"It's magic absorption," she said. "You gotta hit it with alchemy." Looking back at the police struggling to get past the spikes, Tursanay felt the sweat trickling down her back.

"Stand back, everyone," Rodney said, getting out two more crystals. Folding his hands together, a sharp blast of wind focused on the barrier shot out from between his palms and sliced into the barrier, making a crack right down the center. Taking the first crystal, he put his hands against the ground and slammed the earth against the barrier. It pierced a hole through and crumpled instantly, leaving them an escape route. They crawled through just as the bear topped the final layer of spikes with a roar and ran for their lives.

"Do you think we lost them?" Amara panted, looking over her shoulder. As if in answer, Notah grabbed them and made them duck down behind the trash they huddled behind for cover. They were behind a business, so the dumpster available was large enough to conceal Amara's enormous form. Soren wasn't far behind her in size and the two of them squeezed and hunkered down as much as they could to stay out of sight as the group of police officers and the Council member rushed past.

"Soren," Amara said softly once they were far enough away. "Can the city help us lose them?"

"I will ask," he replied, his voice gravelly as a werewolf. Taking a steadying breath, Soren closed his eyes and placed his paws on the earth and concentrated. He showed images of the police in his mind and of them trying to flee. He recalled the conversations about trying to heal the living cities and a warmth rushed up his arms and into his chest. It was like the forest on a mid-spring day, with a gentle, constant breeze and the scent of apple blossoms in the air. The wellness of a city after a tough storm. Like seeing the patrons of the city take care and give back to their beloved home and treat it with kindness above all else. It was comfort, peace, hope. "The city hears us," he murmured. "She wants to help."

"There they are!" The Council member yelled a street away. It sounded like Master Lakshmi. They looked up to see a glimpse of their true forms running past the end of the alley and away from their current position. The police weren't far behind and the Lakshmi was pulling out a wand to concentrate a spell on their persons rather than a wide area effect.

When they disappeared around a building and the commotion died down, the three of them dared to ease out of their hiding spot. The Dai-Nē exchanged looks, and Notah whistled low.

"The city made an after image of you to throw them off?" he asked.

"It would appear so," Soren replied, the exhaustion showing in his voice. Talking to the cities, even for a short time, always wore on him.

"The city must really like you," he murmured. "I was expecting maybe a closed off alley to give us time to escape at most."

"They straight up Looney Tunes'd them," Amara added. The other two looked at her, confused, but Amara just said she'd explain once they were out of the danger zone.

•   •   •

Atta stepped away from the wall she pressed against and looked back down the street. There had been no sign of the Council members so far, and she wanted to keep it that way. But something was nagging at the back of her mind, like she was missing something. Like they were being watched, and she couldn't see from where. When she stepped away from the wall to look around the corner, something caught her eye in her peripheral. There was a figure forming on the wall. Before she could yell out a warning, the figure cupped its hand over her mouth and nose, making her let out a strangled noise.

The lead bounty hunter turned around in a whirl at the sound and saw Atta being dragged upwards and into the wall at their backs, kicking and struggling to get free. Changing into a half giant with rippling muscles, the bounty hunter grabbed a hold of Atta's legs and began pulling her away from the wall. The figure morphing out of the wall held on tightly, struggling with the bounty hunter in a tug-o-war with Atta's body. Shifting her upper half into that of a slick eel, she slipped right through the figure's arms and tumbled to the ground with the lead bounty hunter underneath her. They struggled to untangle themselves from each other as they got to their feet and looked around for the figure that had come out of the wall.

The bounty hunter took out a knife and slashed at the wall, only succeeding in catching the stone beneath her blade. The ground beneath them began rippling and undulating, making it difficult for them to stand. Both women and the lizard got caught in the mayhem and bounced around like dice in a cup, making it difficult for either of them to shift. The half giant was all flailing limbs, and the lizard bounced around in quite a bit of distress until it finally made its way back to Atta and re-morphed back into her leg to form one whole Attalira. Who was being bounced about and squished by a half giant who kept knocking the wind out of her when they would land, only to be tossed into the air again immediately.

"There!" yelled someone at the end of the alleyway. "He's holding them off. Arrest them!"

Panic settled into Attalira's gut as she realized it was the Council. She remembered the mudslide in the training grounds and tried to focus her senses into shifting into a gryffon. At first it was difficult, every change she made got knocked out of her by an elbow to the stomach or a knee to the face, when at last she jostled free of the half giant, she launched into the air. There she could breathe again, even if just for a split moment, and shifted into a gryffon in the shape of a lion head with feathered dragon wings, and what appeared to be a buffalo's hind end and the fore feet of an eagle's talons.

Attalira rolled in the air to gain some semblance of balance with her wings, and swooped down, grabbing the half giant in her claws before flying into the sky with her and over the buildings surrounding them.

"They're getting away!" the Council member yelled. "After them!"

Attalira chanced a look back over her shoulder to see something winged and horned rushing into the sky behind them. She yelled at the bounty hunter to change into something lighter and looked down to see her morphing into a winged, horned creature just like the one behind them. Attalira dropped her, letting her take flight beside her, and demanded to know what the plan was now.

"You're the distraction!" yelled the bounty hunter. "Distract them!"

Attalira swore under her breath and split into two gryphons, flying in two different directions. The bounty hunter followed the one that swerved right and the horned creature behind them faltered, trying to figure out which way to go. Deciding to go after the one that was alone, it struggled to catch back up, but was on Atta's tail in no time, swinging past buildings, flying low over people's heads, and dodging in and out of alleyways before Atta took a turn that it wasn't expecting, and morphed into a puddle of water where it didn't see. She waited until it flew past, paused in confusion, and took a high ground look around to see where she went. It turned in circles a few times, trying to get its bearings, but at last flew off in another direction with a curse, and left her to reform from the puddle to go back the way she had come in a brisk walk, disguised as an Aziza.

The other two were somewhere on the west side of town, having shaken off their disguises and followers alike, and changed back into their normal forms. When Atta finally caught up with them, the bounty hunter looked at Lira.

"I take it this is just you split into two, rather than two separate prisoners," she said, stating the obvious. She must have seen Attalira reform in the chaos.

"Quite astute you are," Attalira said, forming into one creature. "Then again, perhaps not, considering you chose the only person in our group without a bounty on their head."

"I figured since you threw your lot in with them, that you'd have at least something on you," the bounty hunter shrugged. "I'm usually good at spotting bounties."

"Karla!" Notah called, and the lead bounty hunter looked up to see them being waved down by the other two teams.

"You made it!" Karla called back. She motioned for Attalira to follow her and the two of them made their way to the other two groups, where Karla did a head count. "Everyone's here I see."

"Any trouble?" Notah asked.

"Nothing good distraction couldn't handle," Karla replied, ruffling Attalira's mane. The shapeshifter shook herself off, then transformed back into her normal form and shot Karla a dirty look. The lead bounty hunter only grinned and winked. "We best get going before they find us again," she added, looking over her shoulder.

Once again, they tied the Dai-Nē up, some of them having gotten out of their bonds in fleeing from the Council, and made their way west to the dungeon's headquarters where they would line up and get examined against wanted posters. They reached their destination within half an hour of walking and shuffled in one right after another in an odd little line up.

The man at the front counter gestured towards the waiting line, of which there were three others lined up to be seen, and they shuffled once more over to the line and stood in place. When it was finally their turn, they went one by one before a shoulder high screen that crackled and buzzed. It was just enough for them to show their faces and adjust to the height needed until they found the right spot to show the true form of the person in question. This both allowed them to make sure that there were no false identities trying to be snuck in, and make sure the person or persons in disguise were really who the bounty said they were.

"Match," called the centaur, comparing the faces to the wanted posters Karla had handed over. He said so with each of them as they passed through the identifying spell, and led them one by one to a holding cell where they would wait until the Council would get them. Except for Attalira, who was told she could go free. She winked at Karla and stuck out her tongue. Karla just shrugged as the others got taken away.

"That's that," Karla said as they were all locked in their cells. "Thank you for your patronage."

"Thank you for the disguise spells," Rodney returned.

"Name's Karla, by the way. This is Notah and Penjani," she introduced.

"Nice to meet you, Karla. I'm Amara," she said, then listed everyone in introductions. "Not that you'll remember who looked like what, probably once we turn back to our normal selves," she realized.

"Oh right," Rodney realized as he lowered his hand to indicate who he was when his name was called. "We look a little weird right now."

Karla grinned. "I have a better memory than you're giving me credit for, little mermaid," she winked.

"Good," Amara added. "Then you won't forget our bargain?"

Karla's grin etched into a toothy smile. It wasn't a pleasant look she gave the girl, but it wasn't evil - just icy. "I'll remember it alright, so long as you remember your part."

"Nooo problems there," Rodney said. "I'm not looking forward to running back into the Council later."

"Yeah first the Council, then this resistance pops up out of nowhere in the library of all places, then bounty hunters," Amara shook her head. "We've been out of training for a week and already my head is spinning."

"Did you say resistance?" Karla asked, frowning. "As in The Resistance?"

"Yeah, why?" Tursanay asked, narrowing her eyes at Karla.

"Who was your contact?" Karla asked.

"Why do you wanna know?" Tursanay persisted.

"Wait, library?" Karla swore under her breath. "Of course he would reveal himself to the worst choice of people imaginable."

"Hey," Rodney whined, offended.

"I don't mean-" Karla sighed and paused before she said the wrong thing. "What I mean is, he just gave a direct link to the Council of Dai-Nē - the very organization we're fighting against - information about who he was and jeopardized our entire mission."

"Oh," Rodney replied, understanding now.

"I'm going to kill my idiot brother," she said under her breath. She looked more livid than her voice was letting on. Her scowl was deepening and her foot began tapping in place. "What was he thinking?"

"That since we distrusted the Council, he could trust us too, I'm assuming," Tursanay said.

"Irresponsible!" she hissed. "Inconsiderate. Insane! He could have thrown everything away in the blink of an eye."

"To be fair, we have no idea what to even do with this information that there's a resistance," Rodney spoke up. "We're swamped with our own issues at the moment."

"Well, they are Council related," Tursanay said, looking at Rodney. "Maybe they'll have some information we can't find without help."

"Can we risk joining a faction knowing very little about them?" Amara asked.

"Can you risk not getting the information you're looking for?" Karla countered. "My brother is the information guardian at the heart of the living city. If there is something about the Council you want to know, he knows how to get a hold of that information. And with you being Dai-Nē, people will be more apt to believe the information you share than a group of rebels with a cause."

"She has a point," Tursanay said, looking at Amara, who pursed her lips in thought. "What we say from here on out has weight because of our title. We need to be careful who to trust."

"Hmmm," Amara hummed, her brow furrowing. "Let's call a truce for now and see how well we get along."

"I can work with that," Karla said. "Trust is something that is earned, not something that can be expected immediately," Karla said. Well, I'm off to collect my bounty," Karla said in parting. "I'll meet you back in the living city if you can get out of this. I need to have a word with my brother."

They bid her farewell and got strange looks from the other prisoners in their own cells.

"You sure are on good terms with your bounty hunter," one prisoner muttered.

"Isn't everybody?" Tursanay shrugged sarcastically.

When the spell finally wore off, the bounty hunters were long gone with their prize in hand, and the Dai-Nē were trying and failing to get the guard's attention. After about an hour of constant badgering, they had the entire prison block in an uproar to shut them up and the guards finally came to quiet down the ruckus.

"What do you want?" the guard demanded irritably.

"If we can prove we are Dai-Nē will you let us go?" Tursanay said, stepping forward.

"If you're Dai-Nē, then I'll eat my shoe," the guard snorted.

"I hope you like the taste of leather," she replied, rolling up her short sleeve and showing her mark on her shoulder of her missing arm. The guard squinted suspiciously and grabbed a truth revealing spell and held it over the mark. The mark stayed and shined vibrantly beneath the spell's light.

"I'll be damned," the guard swore. "My database must not be updated yet. How long have you had that mark?"

"A few days," she replied.

"That'll be it," he grumbled.

"Here's mine," Soren said, holding up his hand, followed by Amara sticking out her tongue. The guard looked at Rodney and huffed.

"Let me guess, you too?" he asked, unamused.

Rodney nodded.

"Where's your mark?"

Rodney sighed. Turning around, he hiked up his shirt and down his pants enough to show the guard his mark. The guard swore under his breath again. "I just got cheated out of a lot of money for you lot."

"We tried getting your attention before they got too far away," Amara shrugged. "But no one would come talk to us. So, we had to get annoying."

"Yeah, too annoying," the guard muttered, opening their cells. A riot of shouts and indignant responses rose from the other prisoners.

"What if I'm a Dai-Nē? I just ain't got my mark yet!" one yelled.

"Then you can wait for the Council to come get you and talk it out with them," the guard shouted back. "Now shut it, the lot of you!"

Leading them out of the cell area and back into the front where their release papers got signed, they were let free, their belongings given back to them. Once outside, they met back up with Attalira and talked out their plans.

"Soren," Tursanay began. "I'm going to construct a locating spell for you to find the other two Dai-Nē," she said, taking some things out of her bag. "It will lead you to them so you won't have to worry about getting lost."

"Once we get there, I'll know how to get us back so we don't have to worry about a return spell," Amara said, watching her work the spell together. She mixed a few ingredients together and whispered a word into the vial as she swirled it around. The bottle glowed, and she put a stopper on it, handing it to Soren.

"Good," Tursanay replied. "You, Soren, and Atta go work on finding them and making contact. Me, Rodney, and Lira are going to meet up with the bounty hunters to see about getting more information on the Council and hopefully the last phoenix and the veil."

"We can keep in contact with these," Soren said, pulling out two small compact mirrors. He handed one to Tursanay and opened the other. He ran his finger along the rim and spoke Tursanay's name. Her mirror flashed blue, and she opened it to see Soren's face looking back at her.

"Okay, that's cool," Tursanay grinned. "When did you get these?"

"When we were visiting with my cousin back before we got our powers. She said they might come in handy at some point if we ever had to split up, and she was right," Soren responded.

"Remind me to send your cousin a thank you gift," Tursanay said with a smile.

"I shall do so, though I do not believe she expected anything in return," Soren said.

"I know," Tursanay nodded. "But I still want to thank her for all she did for us."

"Be careful," Amara said, giving Tursanay a hug. She released her and did the same to Rodney. She looked at Lira and smiled. "Keep them safe for me."

An odd look passed over Lira's face, but she gave a nod.

"I will do my best," she replied.

And so, they parted ways.

CHAPTER 22
HUNTED

Standing before a large wooded area, Ilarys looked upwards and inwards, watching the giant elk pass by. They were the size of large buildings, their hoof marks in the dirt, large enough for her to lie in. Something pulled her forward into the woods, beckoning her closer.

She took a hesitant step and listened to the call of the will-o'-the-wisps leading her further down the game trail. The blue flames danced just outside of her field of vision, drawing her closer to what appeared to be a clearing in the woods. She stuck to the shadows, peering into the forest carefully, shadow-stepping as close as she could between the shade cast from the trees by the setting sun. When she was close as she could get without coming into the clearing itself, she stepped out of the shadow of a large sapling tree and peered around its trunk.

There, in the clearing, was a red-haired boy—one she recognized from Keir's vision from the inn they stayed in a couple of weeks ago. His rust-colored hair hung about his chin and was partially pulled back from his face in a topknot. His green shirt and brown pants hung about his frame loosely, as if made for a slightly larger person. When she took a step further into the clearing, she heard his voice murmuring something low.

He paused.

"She's here," he said.

He looked up directly at her and his startling green eyes caught her by surprise. He was a half elf; she realized. A young one at that. Not even a score old yet from the looks of him.

"Can you hear me?" he asked her.

"Yes," she heard her voice saying, though it didn't feel like her own. It was as if someone else had answered for her.

"Where are you?" he asked.

"In some woods," she answered. "I don't know."

"That is the construct I have created. Where are you located in the real world?" he asked.

"The real world?" she repeated, her brow furrowing. Something compelled her to speak, but her instincts were screaming to keep her mouth clamped shut.

"We are trying to find you," the boy said. "Where are you?"

"Why do you want to know?" she asked, her voice seeming to become hers again; no longer disconnected from herself.

"As I have stated, we are trying to find you," the boy repeated.

"We?" Ilarys noted.

"My friend and I are searching for you. We are Dai-Nē as well," the boy replied. "I am Soren," he added. "We must speak with you."

"The Dai-Nē that stayed with the Council?" she asked suspiciously.

"We have broken free of the Council, and we need your help," Soren stated. "Will you tell us where you are?"

"Where I am..." Ilarys tried to think, but something was clouding her thoughts. Something that made the hair on the back of her neck stand up.

"Please, there is not much time," he said warningly. "Tell us where you are before they find us."

"Found by whom?" she asked.

But even as she spoke, she heard the snarl from behind her. As she turned, the woercir slowly stalked out from behind the trees in dozens. Their fangs shone in the dim light of the setting sun; the wild look in their eyes focusing on her. They walked on their hind legs, crouching over and sniffing the air experimentally.

"Break the circle!" Soren cried as the creatures lunged for Ilarys. She took a step back into the clearing to get away from the woercir, and a sudden wave of nausea hit her. All the colors of the forest swirled around her into a haze and tumbled into a blur of nothingness.

Ilarys shot up in bed with a gasp and looked around, heavy pants filling the air with the panic she felt rising in her throat. Rolling over, she quickly grabbed a nearby trashcan and emptied the contents of her stomach into it as another wave of nausea swept through her.

"'Laris?" asked Aui'ani sleepily, but concerned. "Are you okay?"

"They're coming for us," she breathed between gasps.

"Who?" Aui'ani sat up, more on alert now.

"The Council," she said. "The Council is coming for us."

"If the Council is coming for us, we need to move away from the Order so they won't compromise our location," Keir said. "They have survived this long by staying out of their reach. We don't need to have a hundred of years of preparation ruined on our account."

Keir paced back and forth in the space that wasn't already allotted to the maps and luggage they had scattered throughout the room. There wasn't much space with the three of them gathered together, but he just couldn't stand still.

"The most disturbing part of the dream was the fact the boy didn't know how to ward properly. The woercir were on us in mere minutes. They almost cornered me until he shouted at someone to break the scrying circle."

"So they are with the Council," Aui'ani said slowly. "But no one has properly taught them how to ward?" Aui'ani said slowly. Something about that didn't make sense to her. She stated as such.

"They are Dai-Nē," Keir said with a shrug. "Perhaps they have had little training yet. It does take a while to become a fully realized Dai-Nē, and the ceremony was only a couple of weeks ago."

"You would think the Council would have taught them something like that first thing if they were going to use them to search for us," Aui'ani said, furrowing her brow.

"Whatever the reason, the fact still remains," Keir said bluntly. "We need to get away from the Order and keep it safe. If they try to scry for us again, they may come closer to finding our location."

"I just think there's something else going on here," Aui'ani argued.

"He's right," Ilarys said. "Even if there is something else going on, we need to protect the Order from being discovered by the Council."

"Did they say they were with the Council?" Aui'ani pressed. "Or did you assume?"

"Does it matter? If we end up meeting them, we need to control when and where they find us," Ilarys said, shaking her head. "And I have a feeling they won't give up until they do."

"I'm going with you," Aui'ani said. "I am a liaison after all."

"And you'll keep her out of trouble," Keir muttered, already moving to grab his go bag. He always kept one prepared in case they had to leave quickly and on short notice. It had become a habit after so many years of working with the Order. And with his sister.

"More like I'll keep you both out of trouble," Aui'ani said. "I know exactly how you two are together, and I'm not letting you mess this up because of your bickering."

"He starts it," Ilarys said, folding her arms over her chest indignantly.

"Do not," Keir bristled.

"Enough, you two," Aui'ani said, snapping her fingers to get their attention. "Get your things and meet me at the front entrance in twenty minutes. I'm going to inform the Head of the Order what's happening."

"Oh, I do not envy your job," Ilarys said with a shudder. Having to flee in the middle of the night was one thing, but having to wake up the Head of the Order and tell him they were fleeing in the middle of the night was not something she wished on anyone. The man was cranky at best when woken up, and one had to speak quickly and efficiently with a very good reason why he was being awakened to avoid his verbal wrath.

"Nor should you," Aui'ani agreed.

But that was what she was good at, Ilarys thought to herself. Aui'ani knew just how to command one's attention and hold it until she was finished speaking. The Head of the Order wouldn't have time to get angry with her there to deliver the information.

In twenty minutes' time, they gathered together at the entrance, bags slung over their shoulders, and headed out. They were traveling southeast towards River Morn, for a larger city would be easier to lose themselves in. It would take three days of various travel methods, but Keir was still iffy on using mirrors after their previous encounters with the Fae.

"I forgot just how difficult it was to travel with the two of you," Aui'ani said as they packed into a dirigible compartment.

"You can blame Keir and his superstitions for that," Ilarys said out of habit. "Though," she added before he could object. "I guess they're mine now, too." She pushed her hair back over her shoulder and scratched her head in frustration. "Why does everything have to be so complicated?"

"I hope we can get this settled soon," Aui'ani said, digging through her bag for her mirror. "The less we have to deal with right now, the better."

"I'm going to take a nap," Keir said. "Wake me when we get to our destination." Laying out on the seat provided, Keir used his bag as a pillow and drifted off to sleep quickly, still tired from being woken up by his sister much, much earlier that day.

"He can sleep anywhere," mumbled Ilarys jealously, watching him from across the way.

Waking up, Keir found himself in the middle of some unknown woods. Things were murky on the edges of his vision, and everything was oddly quiet. There were no usual sounds. No birds. No wind. No forest life. Just the creek of the pines that towered so high above, it was impossible to reach even their lowest branches. Their broad bases stood firm and steady, their rich scent in his nose.

The grass beneath his bare feet felt surreal. Soft, lush, much too green for having so little sunlight from above through the treetops. He glanced upward then, turning in a circle. There was a darkness the higher up he could see until the trees disappeared into a fog. Yet there was just enough light below for him to see what was around him. As if he were aglow, shedding light on his surroundings. He looked at his hands, but they didn't appear to be glowing. Yet there was no source of light that he could find.

He didn't even cast a shadow.

Where was he?

Looking to his right, something pulled him forward, deeper into the forest. Taking a tentative step, he followed the pull and approached a clearing. There, in its center, was the green eyed, red-haired boy from his vision. The one Ilarys had described as well.

Soren was it? He had spoken his name to Ilarys, but Keir had yet to hear it himself. He could only assume this was the same boy.

"Hello?" Soren called, not looking at Keir, but at the

surrounding forest. Stepping into the clearing, the other man spoke up.

"What do you want?" Keir called. "Why are you searching for us?"

He knew where he was now. This was the In Between. The place where spirits would gather when they were cursed to roam the world with unfinished business. When they had something preventing them from resting in peace or leaving this world entirely. Some said they turned into the horrible creatures called woercir and hunted any living being that wandered into their midst. Others said the woercir would devour the spirits that became trapped in the In Between for too long. Some believed if you found yourself in the In Between, and got caught by one and your soul devoured, you would never wake in the world of the living again.

This was why scrying and astral projecting was so dangerous and frowned upon. Without proper warding, one could be forever lost to the In Between.

Soren's eyes found his.

"We are attempting to contact you in order to locate and access you," Soren replied.

"Access us?" Keir said, wrinkling his nose in disgust. What did he mean by that? Use them? Use their powers? What did they want to use them for?

"We need some information and we need your help to get it," Soren continued. "We have little time in this place before the woercir come. Please, tell me where to find you, so we may discuss this further," Soren said urgently.

"You didn't ward properly again?" Keir balked, looking around. He felt a chill go up his spine. They were coming. He could hear movement in the forest now.

They were hunting them.

"Ward?" Soren asked, confused.

"You know how to scry, but you don't know what warding is? Child, you're going to get us both killed!" Keir scolded him.

"Please, just tell me where I can find you, so we may contact you again," Soren requested.

"No," he said, shaking his head. "Don't contact us again. It will only end in disaster at this rate."

"Please, we need to find-" Soren's voice cut off as his eyes flickered to something behind Keir. He turned and yelled over his shoulder. "Break the circle!"

"No, don't do it like tha-!" Keir began, but it was too late. A *whump* went through the air, spinning the world into a mesh of color and sending a sick feeling crawling into his stomach and up through his throat. When he thought he could take it no more, he sat up in his seat with a gasp, as if surfacing from underwater for fresh air at the last possible second. Rolling over and landing on the floor, he retched into the nearby trash can.

"Keir?"

A light came on in the compartment.

Keir groaned.

"They scryed for you this time, didn't they?" Ilarys said, frowning.

"That idiot child is going to get us killed. We need to set up a protection spell to keep him from being able to scry us," Keir muttered.

"I'll begin the preparations," Ilarys nodded, going to her bag to take out some essential items for the spell. Aui'ani brought Keir a canteen of water, which he accepted gratefully. She patted his shoulder and assisted him in getting to his feet once he was certain he had finished retching.

"He doesn't even know how to dismiss the spell properly," Keir said, taking a few deep breaths through his nose and letting them out his mouth. His stomach was still unsettled, but it was easing.

"I know. He just yells at someone to break the circle and it makes you so ill you can't function afterwards," Ilarys shook her head in dismay. "Whoever trained that child how to scry did a horrifying job."

"You keep calling him a child," Aui'ani said. "Just how young is he? He may have tried to teach himself with scrying being so frowned upon. It may have been his only option to use in order to find you."

"That's an even more horrifying thought," Ilarys said, measuring out some string.

"He seems like he's in his late teens? But he's a half elf, so I'm not sure if that is slow growth or actually that young. Though if he is Dai-Nē, it maybe he's just that young," Keir commented.

"So, you have five or six years on him at best?" Aui'ani said.

"Five or six years of more experience than him," Keir reminded her.

"True," she agreed.

"Alright, I've got the spell set up," Ilarys interjected. She glanced up at them. "He shouldn't be able to scry us again. At least not tonight or tomorrow. We can get clear of this area and make it even harder to find us."

"Good," Keir mumbled. "I need rest. How much longer until our destination?"

"Probably another few hours," Ilarys said. "The sun should rise soon."

The dirigible came to a stop in the primary station at Sumianis at mid-morning. Their stomachs rumbled irritably, desperately wanting food, and the trio stopped by a witch's brewery to get some baked goods and a warm meal. As they exited the brewery some time later with food and drink in hand, they made their way across town to buy a few spell ingredients, in case they needed to cast the protection spell again. Once they had all that they needed, they went deeper into the city and found an inn they could stay at for the night and deposited their things in their room. Heading down stairs to the common room, the trio sat at a table near the wall where they could monitor the patrons. Aui'ani volunteered to sit with her back to the room and watch out the windows as people passed by. She knew how antsy the other two were when it came to not having a solid wall against their backs.

Keir yawned. "I couldn't get back to sleep after that stupid scry dream."

"I'm surprised you could eat anything," Ilarys said. "When it happened to me, I was sick for the rest of the day."

"I've always had a tougher stomach than you, sister," Keir said, crossing his arms and yawning again.

"Oh, don't start," Ilarys rolled her eyes.

"Ilarys," Aui'ani said, frowning as she studied something on the wall behind the two of them. "What did you say the boy looked like from your dream?"

Ilarys and Keir blinked and twisted to look out the window to see if he was out there. When they didn't spot him, they looked back at Aui'ani and realized she wasn't looking out the window but at the wanted poster board behind them. She pointed, indicating a boy with green eyes and rust-colored red hair with a hefty bounty on his head. Keir stood and examined the posters closer. He pointed to three others.

"It's them," he said. "The others from my vision."

"They're all wanted for treason?" Ilarys murmured, standing and studying the posters herself. "What do you think they did that even a Dai-Nē would be wanted? Don't they get automatic pardons by the Council?"

"They should," Aui'ani murmured lowly. She glanced around, but no one was paying them any attention. The common room was mostly empty save for a few patrons drinking by the bar and a few others heading up to their rooms. "What if that's why they want to get in contact with us? Because they are on the run from the Council?"

"Should we talk to them?" Ilarys asked Keir slowly.

Something about this wasn't sitting right.

"I think we need to find out more about this before we contact them," Keir said, holding up his hand to show the Ring of Rynon.

"You brought that with you?" Ilarys hissed. "That was supposed to be left at the Order!" She pushed his hand down so no one else could see and made sure no one had caught sight of it.

"I think it's important we find out information on it and the only way we can do that is if we have it with us," he said. "This could be the key to finding out the Council's plans - like why they had this in the first place and what it can really do."

"It's dangerous to have it in the open like that," Ilarys hissed again.

"Relax. It's not like I'm going to lose it," Keir replied. "It'll be fine."

Ilarys rubbed her temples irritably, trying to make her idiot brother realize just what he'd done without alerting everyone around them to the same thing. The Ring of Rynon was something of extreme value, and as such, an object to be targeted by bounty hunters or thieves looking to score from the highest bidder.

"We should discuss this later," Aui'ani interjected. "What's done is done. Right now, we have to deal with much more pressing issues. Like the fact you two are being scryed by a child who doesn't know how to ward yet, and hunted by woercir because of him. A child that has committed treason against the Council."

"Not just one of them, but all of them," Ilarys said.

A small silence fell over them as they contemplated what to do with this information. Taking down the posters and tucking them away into her bag, Ilarys glanced around the common room again. If they had their pictures, she could do a reverse tracking spell on them and find them if they so desired. It was better to do the hunting than to be the hunted.

"I'm keeping these in case we decide to contact them," she said when Keir gave her an odd look.

"Good idea," Aui'ani said.

"So where are we going to get the information on the ring, anyhow?" Ilarys asked, changing the subject.

"I think we should go to River Morn to get information from the great library there," Keir said. "The tree records all the knowledge and important events of the world. We should be able to find something on the creation of the ring and what it does."

"That's actually not a bad idea," Ilarys said.

"You sound surprised," Keir complained, narrowing his

eyes and leaning away from Ilarys to get a better look at her, so his glare had the full effect he wanted it to.

"Don't start, you two," Aui'ani interjected before they could begin fighting again. All it took was one simple change in tone and they would bicker nonstop.

"So we go to River Morn, get the information on the ring, and while we're there, we can check the recent records to see what these kids did to have the Council put wanted posters out for them," Ilarys said.

"Oh, I didn't think of that," Keir said, surprised.

"That's why I'm here," Ilarys smiled. "To think of things you don't."

Keir opened his mouth to retort, but Aui'ani cut them off again.

"Let's get started heading that way. The sooner we get moving, the sooner we can get what we need."

With that, she took Ilarys by the hand and pulled her towards the stairs, where they would get their things from their room. Though they couldn't get their money back from the room for not using it, they made their way to the dirigible station and booked a flight to River Morn anyhow. They would have a pit stop in the Sarasul mountains, but after that it was a straight shot to River Morn. The trip would take two days to make, and the trio were not looking forward to it.

But none of them wanted to try the alternative of mirror travel right now, either.

When they arrived at the peak of Mt. Assesul, they stepped outside for some fresh air. The dirigible wouldn't leave for an hour and a half, so they had time to stretch their legs and make rounds at the dwarven shops in town. There were blacksmiths, jewelry makers, gardeners; some selling livestock and others fresh produce and other goods. The town was bustling despite its small size, and they seemed to do rather well for themselves.

Ilarys, however, made a noise of disgust. "I need to get away from the crowds for a bit." Then turned to Aui'ani with a pleading look on her face. "Walk with me?" she asked. She held out her hand and Aui'ani took it and they made their way towards the edges of town, where things were quieter. Keir stayed behind to look at some items of interest in a particular booth. When they arrived at a wooded area with no others wandering around, Ilarys let out a sigh of relief.

"You always were anxious in a crowd," Aui'ani teased.

"The noise just gets to me. And the lack of space to move around," she said. "Too many people."

Aui'ani kissed her on the cheek. "We'll soon be in a nice quiet library with little to no people around. You can relax with a good book and research to your heart's content."

Ilarys made a happy noise. "Now that sounds like heaven."

"We met in a library, remember?" Aui'ani grinned.

"How could I forget?" Ilarys smiled, lacing her fingers with Aui'ani's. "You were absolutely radiant and I was-"

A ripping sound filled the air and the two of them turned to see a blue portal open midair. The shocked looks that crossed their faces were nothing compared to the looks they gave the red-haired, green-eyed boy and yellow tailed mermaid that emerged from the portal. The two teenagers paused as they came face to face with the two women and hesitated. On the boy's shoulder, a small green lizard perched, but scrambled away upon seeing the other two women, and disappeared into the woods. The children did not seem to notice.

Aui'ani pushed Ilarys back and stood before her, taking

on a fighting stance. She planted her feet on the ground and grew into the size of a large ape with a dog's head. She let out a roar that made the other two lurch backwards a bit, nearly falling back into the portal.

"You stay away from her!" Aui'ani growled, her voice deep and guttural.

"Wait!" Amara said, holding up her hands in a gesture of peace. Behind her, the portal slowly closed. "We just want to talk!"

"As if I will believe that!" Aui'ani spat.

"Can you create a truth ring?" Amara asked Ilarys.

"What promise could I take from you that you wouldn't try to ambush me while I set it up?" Ilarys demanded. Amara thought for a moment, then turned to Soren.

"Do you trust me?" she asked.

"Yes," Soren replied without hesitation. She put her hands on his shoulders and kissed him on the cheek. The stunned look on his face was accentuated with a deep blush.

"Then trust I will be okay," Amara said, then quickly backed away from him and raised her hands above her head. Before Soren could react, between the two of them, a great earthen barrier rose and surrounded Soren, capping off at the top so he couldn't escape from above. It was a dome of earth and grassy clumps that encased the poor half elf in a shell of darkness. She held her hands above her head and turned around slowly to show she meant no harm. From behind her, the muffled shouts of Soren calling out her name were the only sounds between the two groups for a long moment.

"What are you doing?" Ilarys asked after a moment of strained silence.

"I'm surrendering myself to be questioned one on two, so

you have the advantage," Amara replied. "That barrier will only hold him for half an hour before he can punch through."

As if in confirmation, they heard the dull thuds begin to chip away at the inside of the barrier. Ilarys and Aui'ani exchanged looks.

"Don't move," Ilarys said, forming a circle around Amara in the grass with the string she'd bought earlier in Sumianis. She formed the broad circle, then stepped inside with Amara and recited the short spell to activate the truth ring and the string lit up and floated off the ground, surrounding them.

"Who are you?" Ilarys asked.

"My name is Amara, and I am the Dai-Nē of the Elements."

"Is that boy with you, Soren?" Aui'ani asked.

"Yes," Amara answered. "He is the Dai-Nē of Ether."

"Where are the other Dai-Nē?" Ilarys demanded.

"I don't remember the name of the city they are in, but they are gathering information on phoenixes, the veil, and the Council," she answered.

"Why?" Ilarys asked. Amara took a breath and let it out slowly, trying to figure out where to begin.

Keir tossed a coin to the merchant in the booth and pocketed the new dwarven-made sachet, mumbling something to himself about an Aziza child; when he turned and came face to face with a short, brown-haired girl with golden eyes, staring at him intently. Her eyes flickered down towards his hand that he just stuck in his pocket and back up to his face.

"Hello," he muttered out of reflex, taking a step back. It was a mumbled response as he tried to move around her, but she stood in his way purposefully. He looked at her in a new light.

"That's an interesting ring you have there," she said, her eyes going cat-slit.

"W-What?" Keir said, his stomach dropping like a stone. Who was this person? Could the Council have sent them? Or were they just a vagrant looking for a score? And why were they interested in his ring?

The ring.

"I'm going to have to ask you for it back," she said darkly.

"Back?" Keir's brow furrowed, then cleared almost instantly as he remembered her voice. "You're with the Council." It wasn't a question. A vision crossed his mind, and he heard the same voice from the room when they were raiding the Council for the ring.

"The Fae interfered, and the phoenix was there," a female voice replied. Her voice. *"What was I supposed to do? Fight all of them?"*

"You're fully fledged, why not?" the male voice spat back. "You should have been able to get at least one of them here!"

"I nearly had one of them, but he slipped through my teeth," she said. "But I did get the ring. That has to count for something!"

"It does," conceded the other voice. "It makes our plan that much easier. If we can convince them to combine their powers into one, we can transfer all of them at once to the new wielder."

His mind came back to the present within a blink of an eye and the girl lunged at him. He lurched backwards to get away, but as her hand swiped down, claws forming on the tips of her fingers, she ducked down and Keir caught sight of the mark of Dai-Nē on her chest: the barite stone in its center. Or rather, half of the pale blue stone. Half of it was missing.

"How did you find us?" Keir managed as he dodged

away, but the girl didn't answer. Instead, she shifted into a form of a large dog, almost wolf like, and growled. The commotion caused a few screams to ring out in the crowd as people parted for the two of them, dancing and weaving and dodging each other through the throng of people. Keir passed by a weapons booth and grabbed a large hammer that was almost too heavy for him to lift properly, and swung it at the creature. The hammer connected with her side and sent her flying with a yelp. The angry calls of the merchant in the booth had Keir throwing the hammer back into his shop and running for his life back towards the woods.

He had to find Ilarys and Aui'ani. They were his only hope of winning this fight.

"They all turned into those horrid creatures?" Ilarys asked, as she continued to interrogate Amara. The dull thuds of Soren's fists against the earthen barrier had not let up, and they were getting clearer and clearer as the minutes ticked by.

"Not all the Council members but many of them, yes," Amara replied. "The remaining helped subdue them and we demanded to be let out of the training grounds afterwards."

"And the phoenix?" Ilarys asked.

The Council burned him at the stake for his crimes against them. We believe him to still be alive because phoenixes are reborn from the ashes and we don't believe the Council knew he was a phoenix," Amara replied.

"So that's why you are searching for information on phoenixes," Ilarys said, leaning back on her heels, as things clicked into place and made more sense.

Amara nodded. "And the Council. We want to find out why things are happening like this and what started it all."

"I can tell you where to find some of it, but I'm afraid it's going to take some searching," Ilarys said. "The great library at River Morn in the great tree-"

"River Morn!" Amara's eyes lit up. "That's the name of the city! My friends are in the great library now, searching for what they can find. Someone is helping them as we speak."

"Then I hope you can trust them," Ilarys said. "Otherwise, news will get back to the Council and things could get much more complicated."

"He said he was the head of the resistance but honestly we didn't have the capacity to process that information," Amara replied, rubbing her temples. "We're already dealing with so much that adding a resistance to the mix was just going to send us overboard, so we accepted his help because we needed everything we could get a hold of."

"You met the head of the resistance against the Council?" Ilarys breathed. "He's so elusive I didn't think anyone had ever seen him outside of the resistance themselves."

"He's very unassuming. You wouldn't know it by looking at him honestly," Amara replied. "He acts all flinchy and unsure of himself, then when he thinks he can trust you, his entire demeanor changes into a serious, confident one and it's like two different people in one."

"That makes sense. No one would expect someone spineless to be running the resistance," Ilarys commented.

Somewhere behind them, they heard a snarl followed by a throaty yell, and Ilarys instantly went on alert.

"*Keir?*" she called, looking over her shoulder.

"Who's that?" Amara asked.

"My brother," she answered, brow furrowing as she tried

to pinpoint where the sound came from. "Something's wrong."

Then, just in the midst of the giant trees, she could see Keir running for all he was worth, a large canine behind him, snarling and all but foaming at the mouth. Aui'ani reared up on her hind legs and roared at the creature and ran towards Keir, who looked just as terrified of seeing her running towards him as he did the creature that was chasing him. As she approached him, he ducked under her grasp, and Aui'ani grabbed the canine and threw it into the trees. The creature bounced off a tree trunk with a yelp and spun away into the dirt as it tried to get its bearings.

A small limp, a shake of the head, and the creature was back on its feet.

"It's the coyote," Amara gasped in a small voice.

"Coyote?" Ilarys asked urgently.

"It tried to attack us before we came to the magic world," Amara explained. "To this world. It stole Rodney's ring. We think it was the ring of Rynon."

"The ring of-" Ilarys gasped. "Keir has that ring!"

"Wait, what?" Amara asked, suddenly looking at her in a new light. "Why do you have that ring?"

"KEIR!" Ilarys called, ignoring her question. "Aui'ani!" She couldn't leave the circle without breaking the enchantment and she needed more answers, but her family needed her help, too. The coyote jumped up and bit Aui'ani on the neck and Aui'ani grabbed at it, screaming in pain, and threw it off her again. Keir was hanging back, trying to figure out how to help, but this was a shifter fight, and there was no room for him.

"*Aui'ani!*" Ilarys yelled.

"We need to help her!" Amara said, putting her suspicion

aside for the moment. They needed the help of the other Dai-Nē, but what if the other Dai-Nē had been the ones to steal the ring in the first place? But neither of them could shapeshift… And the coyote was right there, attacking them. That meant they weren't with the coyote. But who was?

Flipping her fin and breaking the circle as she rushed out of it, Amara swam closer to the fight and looked for an opening. The two shifters were in a tangle of limbs and teeth as they roared at each other and snarled, clawing and biting. Amara swung her arms over her head twice, gathering the water from the plants around her and bled them dry to douse the two shifters with water. She startled them apart and began gathering the water up again in order to throw it at them once more. This time, she was planning to freeze it. The coyote shook itself and jumped back into the fight before Amara could react and bit down on the cynocephali's hand, drawing blood. Aui'ani let out a guttural roar of pain as she slung the coyote away and into a tree.

The coyote was back on its feet in seconds, growing to the size of an enormous horse and turning on the other shifter once more. Lunging for Aui'ani, the coyote pawed at her and slashed with its great claws, pounding its feet against her chest like it was digging in the earth. It tore at her flesh and pushed her back until she fell and the coyote was on her in seconds, biting down and shaking mouthfuls of skin and fur back and forth, as if trying to rip it from her body.

Ilarys screamed for Aui'ani as she fired a volley of shadowy orbs of power straight at the beast. It yelped, being pushed back from its prey, and that gave Aui'ani the chance to get back to her feet and shove the oversized coyote back, throwing punches at it as if her life depended on it. Which, at this point, it did.

"We have to stop them!" Keir shouted over the turmoil. But how? How could they stop this mess? There had to be a way to stop this.

Perhaps there was, he thought, considering the ring on his finger. The Fae had said that it switched powers around. Perhaps he could steal her Dai-Nē power and stop this fight all together. If the others had done it, couldn't he?

"Keir, what are you doing?!" Ilarys yelled as he ran back into the fray. He dodged and ducked, trying to figure out how to jump in, but the two shifters were going at it like beasts over a scrap of meat. Suddenly, the coyote shifted forms and stretched and bound the cynocephali with the form of a giant snake, and began squeezing the life out of Aui'ani. "NO!" Ilarys yelled, running towards them.

Keir took his chance and reached out, grabbing the snake by the tail. "Relinquish your power beast!" he growled under his breath, and suddenly a shock ran through his body, and the snake hissed in pain as it slowly shifted back into its human form, leaving Atta screaming as she crumpled to the ground and laid still.

"Atta?!" Amara gasped as she quickly swam over to the unmoving form of the girl at the feet of the other two. "What did you do?" Amara demanded. She felt for a pulse and her stomach dropped. Leaning forward, she tried to listen for any form of breath coming out of her. She shook her, calling her name, but the girl would not move. "You killed her!"

"She attacked me!" Keir defended himself angrily.

"She's with you?" Ilarys demanded, just as angry.

"I thought she was with Soren in the barrier!" Amara said, thoughts beginning to jumble and get confused. If Attalira was the coyote, then that meant...

"You attacked because you wanted the ring," Ilarys

accused. "That was your plan all along, wasn't it? To steal the ring back for the Council!"

"What? No! That's not true," Amara balked. "We're trying to keep it away from the Council!"

"As if I can believe another word you say," Ilarys spat. "Aui'ani, wrap around my arm. Keir," she said as Aui'ani transformed into a tiny snake and did as Ilarys asked. "Grab my hand and hold on."

"No, wait!" Amara said. "You can't just leave her here like this! Look what you've done!"

But as she watched, the three of them disappeared into the shadow of a tree and left her alone with the body of her friend and Soren, who was just beginning to escape the barrier.

CHAPTER 23
WAR

"Guys, I think I found something!" Rodney called, half standing from his spot on the bench where he'd been lazily skimming through some old documents, when something caught his eye. The librarian had seen their dilemma in reading and got them some reading spells. Tursanay and Lira made their way over to him, where they bent over the papers as Rodney shuffled them back in order and stamped them against the table to realign them. "Okay, look at this. It's almost like a diary of some sort. You might want to sit back down for this."

The other two did so along with him as he read out loud what was written in the pages.

7.4.9.32

A war has broken out. A secret war that will be the death of us all. The elves and the vampires have long memories and are malcontent with the way things are. They want to go back to the old ways when they had power and status. When the world feared them and bowed to their every whim. Absidee believes they are planning to wipe out all phoenixes, but there is no proof, though a sickness has been spreading through our ranks quickly. Very few survive once they contract it. There are few left to fight this war against the other two races.

The virus starts with a cooling of the flames. Veins appear, branching from the eyes, down the neck and into the arms. It turns the whites of the eyes bloody and the irises green. Like sea-soaked wood burning on a beach. It makes the ill feel cold. As if nothing could ever warm them again. Once the veins have reached the heart, it is too late. The inner fire extinguishes like a candle flame and the phoenix takes its last breath. No one knows how the spread is happening so quickly or how it began, but the Dai-Nē suspects the elves and vampires.

There is also a belief that the elves are searching for the ring of Rynon, but the reason behind their search remains unclear. Absidee thinks they are trying to use it to steal the power of Dai-Nē and distribute it to whom they please, but again, there is no proof. The phoenix are trying to convince them to turn away from this path, but many fear it is too late for reasoning. They do not heed outside voices, only their own council, and it will be the death of many.

Including their own.

3.11.17.32

The number of phoenixes left is dwindling swiftly. There are maybe a hundred left at most when there were hundreds of thousands before, at least. This pandemic has spread like wildfire, with no end in sight. They have gone from a powerful race to endangered in mere months. It is no longer believed this sickness was an accident.

Karen is doing some research to find the origin of this mess, and all eyes had fallen to the group of elves and vampires that banded together and called themselves the Acirassi Alliance. There are other races mixed in that believe in their cause, but they are the root. The Dai-Nē have discovered this and are fighting to find the cause and a cure as well.

If there is such a thing.

I have my doubts, but I also have faith in Absidee. She has the heart big enough and a mind brilliant enough to be the one that defeats this. I have to believe there will be a cure for this pandemic, or I will cease to exist myself.

I miss my family. I miss my friends and loved ones. The children never deserved this. They never should have been subjected to this. My siblings, their children. Gone. All of them. I've seen more death of my kind than I have seen birthed into this world now. It is a horror. It is a massacre. I am tired of the heartbreak. Tired of watching the fire fade from their eyes. Tired of watching the fear in the children's eyes as the veins appear on their parents, and the pain when the parents watch their child suffer the same fate.

It's not fair. It never was.

5.7.3.33

Kalen has been murdered before she could give us the information she found out, and there are only five remaining phoenixes left. One, a small child who has lost everything, just as I have. I want them to survive this, as if they were my own child. I have come to care for them dearly. But we cannot stay together. I sent the child away with Saeran to keep them safe, hoping they stay safe. I care for Saeran like a brother as well, even though he is not of my kind.

They have scattered the phoenixes to the corners of the world in order to keep them safe, but there is fear that it will not be the case. Things are progressing rapidly. The Order of Rynon has stepped forward to hide the remaining phoenix identities and locations, so that they can keep our race from going extinct. I still fear that the elves and vampires will find them in the end and destroy the remaining five. Absidee fears for my life. She will not stop crying when she thinks I cannot hear. No one can offer her any comfort, as there is none to give. I am in danger, and the only thing I can do is fight. If for nothing else, then for her.

2.9.23.33

I have survived another ash death. My memories are hazy at best, but my notes have brought me back up to speed. The elves and vampires have wiped out all the remaining phoenix but me. They found the child, and they killed them. I'm angry. Angry that they snuffed out the light of a child. Angry that I could do nothing to stop it. I'm hurt. Hurt that I promised they would be safe. Promised nothing bad would happen to them so long as I was alive and I failed them. And I'm scared. Scared that they will kill me if they find me. Scared of what they will do when they find out, I have the mark of Dai-Nē. I'm scared of what they will do to Absidee.

The dragons have taken up our cause and are going to help us fight this secret war that is about to be made public. We no longer wish to hide the fact this is, indeed, a war. I want my revenge for my people. Want to make them rue the day they ever thought they could do this and get away with it. I am scared, but I am angry. I'm going to get my revenge and it will haunt them for generations to come, for I have a plan. And if all else fails, I know what I can do to bring them down. Them, and all others like them.

1.10.18.33

They have discovered my mark, and know I am a Dai-Nē. They have made a public announcement calling for my head for the unfair advantage an immortal has to being a Dai-Nē. Claiming I will make a hierarchy under my rule, they are ruining my good name. They claim I will do everything they had set out to do, and are making me the villain of this war. Saeran is just as angry with them as I am, and has stood up on my account many times with Absidee. But even with the other Dai-Nē on my side, I fear the people will not listen.

In the three hours since I began this entry, I experienced betrayal of the highest kind. Saeran sold me out to the Acirassi Alliance. My best friend, the one whom, aside from Absidee, that I trusted with my life. Trusted with the life of the child. He has been working with them all along, selling them the location of the last remaining phoenixes and destroying the last of my kind. He will regret the day he did this to me. To Absidee. To my people. Of all those I am angry at, he has become the brightest beacon for my vengeance. If it is the last thing I do, I will hunt him down and rend him limb from limb. Let him taste the fire of a phoenix.

They have called together a council of elders, and claim

they will hunt me down if I do not turn myself in within a fortnight. I don't want to die, but I fear that will be my fate at this point. I have lost Saeran, and I have lost my people. If I lose Absidee, then nothing can bring me back from the edge.

There was a time when I would have fought for Saeran like I would have for her. But now I feel raw and empty inside. As if something stole my inner fire. I feel hollow. Cold. Like a shell of my former self. As if the sickness has found me at last. I keep looking at my reflection, expecting my eyes to turn green and bloody and for the veins to start forming, but I remain well.

Part of me wonders what I did to push Saeran away like this, but the other part of me thinks of his very name and feels enraged. I feel like my skin turns to flame and all my hatred burns into existence. I take flight when these times occur because I can't stand to be near others lest they betray me as well.

I pray Absidee never does. Then I will truly have lost everything. I am beginning to wonder if all this is worth it. If fighting this never-ending battle is just a useless cause or if there really is something worth fighting for here. They've taken everything else when it should have been me. It especially should have been me, and not the children. They never deserved that. None of my family deserved that. Why did I survive this far and none of them did? What's the point if there's no one left to fight for?

6.11.01.33

They have created a device that will take my power from me by force in order to remove my status as Dai-Nē, but I fear they may have something more nefarious planned. Though I can't say what. If they can create something that will take the powers of Dai-Nē away and seal it until I die an ash death and it can be passed to the next person, what more are they planning with this knowledge and how long have they had it? How did they come about it?

Probably Saeran. He has studied the Ring of Rynon more than any of us. He knows how it works, and has created a similar spell, no doubt, that can wrench the power from my body. Will I actually survive as they claim I will? I do not know. But I am turning myself in. I am tired of running.

During the ceremony, I get one last wish before they remove my power and force me to die an ash death. It is then I will get my revenge, for I fear they will try to prevent me from rising from the ashes again, and wipe out the last of my race from this world. It is the last chance I have to redeem my kind and get revenge for them.

The ceremony will take place one week from today.

6.11.19.33

So much has happened in the last day alone. I'm not even sure where to begin.

I survived without an ash death, but the fate of my friends and other Dai-Nē were not so lucky. When the other Dai-Nē heard I had agreed to the ceremony, they were furious. They did not think it was fair I should give up my power after having it for such a short time, or that our enemy was demanding it taken away whilst smearing my name. Nor was it fair that Saeran got to keep his powers despite his betrayal to the Dai-Nē and my kind.

The first day they were planning to go up against the elves and vampires before I knew what was happening. They had gathered their forces of dragons and Dai-Nē and began a march against our enemies. Only our enemies were ready for us. In the following days, our enemies wiped our allies to near extinction. I fought with two others and they used the Ring of Rynon to try to steal my power, nearly killing me. I only have wild magic left now, so I can only assume they stole the light and dark magic a piece, because each of them reacted the same way I did when the split occurred. There was a spark of light from the ring, and each of them yelled as if struck. I fell from my mount, and I thought for certain I was dead, my wing too injured to fly, but I was saved before hitting the ground far below. One of the others that fought me was not so lucky.

On the fourth day Éabha fell to the hands of the Elven army, despite being the strongest of all of us Dai-Nē. I lost all of my friends, those I would consider my family.

When the time came for the ceremony, I begged Absidee to let me go. I couldn't bear to lose her, too. It was time to put an end to this war that was killing everyone I loved. It was time to get my revenge on the people I hated the most in this world. To the one person I hated most.

I waited until they brought me before the pedestal, the device they had created to forcefully take my power from me, and they asked me if I had any last words. So, I cursed them. Cursed them with every ounce of power I had. Shortened their life spans to three hundred years, rather than the thousands they had experienced as immortals. I cursed them and their future generations to come; cursed their families, I cursed their children. I cursed everything about them and before they could force my mouth closed, my curse took effect almost immediately. Their anger was palpable, and I was pleased. I didn't care what they did to me after that.

Didn't care about my fate. I had achieved my goal, and I felt content.

But Absidee had other plans. Swooping in with a dragon, she ripped me away from their grasp and took me far away. How long we were flying, I don't know, for I passed out for most of it. When I awoke again, we had landed, and she was shaking me awake. She clutched a bone knife to her chest and told me she had found a way to hide where no one could find us. I asked where such a place could be and she said the Mortal World. I didn't believe her at first, because how could we ever get to such a place? But she was adamant and so I agreed with her we would leave in the morning. She wanted to go immediately, but I told her I needed to record what happened in my journals and hide them in the great library in River Morn. I didn't know if or when they would be useful, but this account needed to be told. As of now, I am finishing my story here.

If you are reading this, then I can only hope you are doing so to fight against these people and what they have done and most likely will continue to do. Please do not let them get all the powers of Dai-Nē in one place, and do not let them get the Ring of Rynon. Absidee somehow managed to steal the ring back in the altercation in Delmar, but we are going to hide it in the Mortal World, and pray they can never use it for evil again.

Rodney looked up from the papers and exchanged looks with the others. The air in the room had shifted with the weight of this knowledge and just what the words on the pages meant.

"They went to our world," he breathed.

"How are you certain?" Lira asked.

"The fact I had the ring was proof they made it," Rodney answered, looking at the scar on his hand where the coyote had bitten him.

"That's..." Tursanay began but fell short. She wasn't sure what to say.

Rodney nodded, as if he completely understood. "I know."

"What?" Lira asked, not following.

"I dunno," Tursanay said. "It just feels big that they had to escape to our world to live in peace. They had to leave behind everything they knew and lost everyone they loved."

"It feels weird when you know almost exactly how they felt," Rodney said, putting it into words. They fell silent, the weight of the story sinking into their minds.

A cry rang out behind Rodney, shattering the silence and causing him to jump and turn. Lira screamed in pain as she clutched at her sides and fell to her knees. A bright blue electrical current passed over her body, emanating from the Dai-Nē mark on her chest. The current turned to a black color and half of her mark went dark in the center where the blue stone was. She dropped to her knees, the straining of her voice as the pain ripped the noise from her throat ebbing as she ran out of breath. When the current finally ebbed away, she fell to the floor unconscious and lay there, unmoving.

Tursanay and Rodney rushed to her side to check for her breathing. It was shallow, but it was there, and it meant she was still alive. Llog came rushing into the room to see what the commotion was, and they instructed him to call for help. In moments it arrived and they took her to a healing house and was admitted promptly.

"What happened?" the nurse asked.

"She just..." Tursanay tried to think of how to describe it.

"started screaming, and this lightning came out of her Dai-Nē mark and-"

"She is Dai-Nē?" the nurse paled.

"Yeah, we all are. Why?" Rodney asked.

"I'm so sorry for speaking so frankly with you," the nurse tried to apologize with a bow.

"We don't care about that, we care about our friend," Tursanay dismissed irritably. "Is she going to be alright?"

"We will do everything in our power to see that she is well again," the nurse replied. "Please, describe to me as much as you can." And so, they did, and he turned and left quickly into the healing house and Tursanay let out a sigh of frustration.

"I don't like this," Tursanay began.

"Yeah, whatever happened just now is some serious-" Rodney began, but Tursanay shook her head.

"I don't mean- well, yeah, what happened with Attalira is bad, but have you noticed people fear the Dai-Nē? Llog acted scared when he first found out and now the nurse," she added with a gesture. "Couldn't even listen to a description of the accident without freaking out."

"Yeah - I mentioned that back in the library, remember?" Rodney said.

"Oh, yeah..." she recalled. Tursanay pressed her lips together in a thin line. She wanted to find out what was going on with that, but first they had more pressing matters to deal with.

"We have to call Soren and Amara," Tursanay said. "Ask if the same thing happened on their end and tell them what we found out."

"Right! And see if they found the other two Dai-Nē too," Rodney added, remembering their tasks.

Pulling out the mirror, she ran her finger along the surface and called out Soren's name. The mirror flashed with a blue light, much like that of the portals, and there was a long moment before Soren's face appeared on the other end, covered in dirt and sweat and a look of panic in his eye.

"Tursanay!" he called. "Is Lira alive?"

"What?" Tursanay stammered, not expecting the wild look and abrupt question. How had they known-? Something must have happened on their end, she realized. "Uh yes," she said, shaking her head and bringing her thoughts back into order. "she is, but she's badly injured. We took her to a healing house. They're helping her now. What happened?"

"Atta is dead," Soren informed them. "Also," he said, lowering his voice. "There is a chance we know who the coyote was that attacked us in the Mortal World."

"Who?" Tursanay asked, brows furrowing in anger. That beast had hurt Rodney and taken something very important from them. She was ready for some payback. "Did they kill Atta? What happened?"

Soren looked away from the mirror at someone she couldn't see. "Understood," he said to them, then turned back to Tursanay. "We need to convene and exchange information in person. We will bring back Atta and see if that can help Lira recuperate. Meanwhile, be leery of her. I fear there is more to her than we realized before."

"What do you mean?" Rodney asked, looking over Tursanay's shoulder.

"I can't explain now. I must go. We will meet with you back in River Morn," he said and closed the mirror, effectively cutting off their communication.

"I hate when he's cryptic," Tursanay huffed, shaking her

head. Though she, of all people, was used to cryptic communication from others. Ross included.

"I wonder what on earth happened," Rodney breathed.

"I dunno, but I want to get to the bottom of this," Tursanay murmured, biting her lip in thought.

It was some time before Soren, Amara, and the body of Atta were back at the healing house they'd taken Lira to. When they brought back the body and explained the situation, she was taken back with the other to see if it would help. Meanwhile, the others convened and exchanged information about what they had gone through and what they had found.

"So, you think she was the coyote?" Tursanay asked.

"I've been thinking about it," Amara whispered, making sure that no one could overhear them in the waiting room. "Soren said only Dai-Nē can cross the veil. We saw evidence of that when I didn't have my power and couldn't enter the portal."

Soren nodded. "I don't know about Dai-Nē enchanted people, but she turned into a coyote when she was fighting the other Dai-Nē."

"She attacked one of them? Why?" Rodney asked, frowning. "That doesn't seem like her..."

"Attacked or was attacked. We are uncertain how the sequence of events began," Soren added. "But I know those people had the Ring of Rynon and that makes me suspicious of them as well."

"Especially with what we found out in the library," Tursanay agreed.

"Do you know if they were vampires or elves?" Rodney asked. "No offense, Soren," he added.

"I do not take offense to this," Soren replied. "But I know

they are not elves. It was daylight, therefore I do not believe them to be of the vampiric species either."

"Do you think the council has something to do with all this?" Rodney asked.

"What do you mean?" Tursanay asked.

"Think about it," Rodney said. "A pedestal was created to take the power from the last phoenix. And now said pedestal has all the powers of Dai-Nē, including the split ones, and now the Ring of Rynon is out there being used by two of the Dai-Nē that now don't trust us because of our ties with the Council and the fact they got in a fight with Attalira. I just think there's something convenient about the Council having possession of the pedestal after all these years and the last phoenix telling us to be suspicious of vampires and elves and now the Council."

"Not all of them," Tursanay said, something dawning on her.

"What?" Rodney asked, confused. "Not all of who?"

"Not who, but what. They don't have all the powers, and I don't think they realize it," Tursanay replied. "Remember what the journal said about the phoenix only having wild magic left?"

"Right," Rodney agreed.

Amara gasped in realization.

"You know what this means, don't you?" Tursanay said.

"What?" asked Rodney curiously, looking between them.

"There's another Dai-Nē," the two girls answered simultaneously.

CHAPTER 24
FAE

"Augh," Keir groaned as Ilarys patched him up.

"Stop complaining," she snapped. "If you could go to a healer like a normal person, we wouldn't be in this mess."

"I don't trust healers. They just shorten your lifespan with their spells," Keir muttered. Ilarys turned to get another bandage and rolled her eyes at Aui'ani.

"And this doesn't shorten your lifespan?" she quipped. "Getting attacked by mongrels when I leave you alone for more than five minutes?" She slapped the bandage on his rib cage a little harder than she should have and Keir groaned again, this time weakly.

"Love," Aui'ani said. "Why don't you let me take over for a bit? You're only going to injure him further with your temper."

"I'm not upset!" she snapped and turned on Aui'ani. "And don't you dare move! You're more injured than he is!"

"I'll be fine," Aui'ani said. "Unlike your brother here, I don't mind seeing a healer."

"Suit yourself," Keir grumbled.

"Why were you being attacked by shapeshifter, Keir?" Aui'ani asked, trying to get back on topic. "What did you do?"

"Why do you assume I did something?" Keir balked, offended. "Ouch! Damn it, woman, I'll do it myself!" he said, snatching the bandage out of his sister's hand and giving her a look. Gingerly applying the patch to his remaining wound, he explained what had happened.

"So, you were just minding your own business, and she attacked you out of nowhere?" Aui'ani asked, skeptical.

"Yes! Why is that so hard to believe?" Keir demanded.

"You just have a way of pissing people off by opening your mouth, is all," Aui'ani replied. "Are you sure you didn't say something to her before she attacked?"

"No, I said 'hello'. She just mentioned something about my ring and then lunged," Keir replied.

"I told you it was a bad idea to have that thing on you," Ilarys said. "But you never listen to me, do you?"

"If I listened to you for everything, I would have been taken by the Fae years ago and you'd be an only sibling!" Keir snapped.

"Don't tempt me with fantasies, brother. I'll push you into a mirror myself," Ilarys replied.

"Well, it's not going to work now, they're on our side," Keir mocked irritably.

"Nyah, nyah, nyah—'They're on our side'," Ilarys mocked back in a whiny voice, crossing her arms.

"Ugh, don't you two ever stop?" Aui'ani sighed dramatically, flopping back on the bed and draping her arm over her face.

"How'd they even find us so quickly? I thought you set up a spell," Keir said.

"I set up a spell to keep them from scrying us. I didn't know they had a portal knife," Ilarys argued.

"A portal knife?" Keir said, turning around and looking at her. "Those actually exist?"

"Apparently," Ilarys said. "The boy had one carved of bone with a leather cord tied around a jeweled pommel. I got a good look at it just before Aui'ani shoved me out of the way."

"I thought it was just a weapon," Aui'ani replied. "I couldn't let some stranger attack you!"

Keir's thoughts suddenly flashed back to when they were infiltrating the Council and recalled a knife that looked just like that sitting on one of the many pedestals in the guarded room. He had wondered briefly why a bone knife was alongside the Ring of Rynon, wondering if it was from some extinct creature or just a part of some rich person's art collection, but now it made sense to see them together. What if that knife could...

"And I was supposed to watch one strangle you?" Ilarys countered, interrupting Keir's thoughts.

"I had it handled," Aui'ani sniffed.

"Oh yes, I could tell you had it handled when the giant snake constricted all your movements," Ilarys countered again. "Including your breathing."

"Alright," Keir said frankly, not wanting to listen to any more of their bickering. Standing and putting his shirt back on, he huffed. "I'm going to get some air. Aui'ani, calm her down. I've got to clear my head and figure out what our next move is."

"Shouldn't we decide that together?" Ilarys argued.

"You're in no mood to do that and my thoughts are too scrambled to deal with you right now. I'm going out, and" I'm going out, and when I get back, I'll tell you what I've come up with, alright?"

Ilarys huffed in reply and turned her head away. She didn't like admitting when he was right, especially when she was irritable with him.

"We'll discuss it then," Aui'ani agreed.

"Fine," Ilarys muttered. And with that Keir stepped outside and wandered down the streets of Sendew where they had retreated after hearing the other Dai-Nē were in the great library at River Morn. It was here he'd first seen the girl get taken by the Fae. Along the mirrored walls in the market-place in some back alley. He sighed to himself as he found himself retracing those steps and passing through the merchant tents to the alley where it had all started.

Out of the corner of his eye, he noticed his reflection turn to look at him and he glanced at it. The red eyes were back, but as he stared it turned to walk away, disappearing into the mirror space ahead of him. Furrowing his brow and looking around, Keir rubbed his goatee and made sure no one was paying him any attention. He moved forward, further into the alley and stood at the back before the apparition appeared again. This time, standing before him.

Have you considered our offer? the reflection asked.

Keir looked around and wet his lips. "A lot has been going on."

You have made a decision. It wasn't a guess.

How they could tell he wasn't sure. It had taken him ages to come to the decision. He had considered bringing Ilarys and Aui'ani in on this, but he couldn't risk them getting stuck in the Mortal World with him should he not be able to find a way back once the spell to fix the veil was activated. He was going to do this, and he was going to do it alone. That, and after taking the life of another Dai-Nē, he felt his power was too dangerous to stay around them anymore. He felt as if the new power was just as unstable as his own. As if he didn't quite have control over it or could only access certain parts of it. That something was off about it.

"I will accept your offer," he said quietly at last. "But I will need your help getting the key to my passage to the Mortal World."

What do you propose? the reflection asked.

"I'm going to steal a portal knife from the Council. One like the boy has. But the security will be much greater now and I will go alone," Keir said. "If I bring a mirror, will you trap the guards in the mirror but bring them no harm?"

The reflection went from smiling to a frown accented by a furrowed brow. *No harm?* It repeated with distaste.

Keir responded, "I will release them when I can release you. This is my condition. Including safe passage for me, my sister, Ilarys, and Aui'ani, wherever they or I go, and no harm comes to the guards you take in my fight."

There was a long moment of silence. *We can agree to this.*

"I have your word?" Keir prompted.

Yes, the reflection replied.

"Good," Keir nodded. "I will leave tonight."

We shall await your call, the reflection replied.

Keir struggled to carry the large mirror down the hallway where Aui'ani had taken them previously. It wasn't so much the weight of the mirror making things difficult, but the awkwardness of the shape and size to carry it. At least the frame had ridges he could hold on to as he maneuvered down the hallway unbothered, people assuming he was a maintenance man bringing in a new mirror to repair a cracked one. He'd been stopped only once to see if he needed any help, but he turned them down and quickly made his way further into the Council's headquarters.

Once he rounded the corner and saw the door he was looking for, he was glad for the backup he carried in his arms. Instead of two or three guards, there were five, and no telling how many there were inside as well. Grunting with the effort to bring the mirror in front of him so that the reflective side was facing the guards, he whispered something to the mirror under his breath and the colors in the reflection changed slightly to something a little off from what they were supposed to be. The guards watched him struggled down the hallway towards them stone faced and only spoke up when he didn't seem to turn down either hallway before him.

"Halt," the first guard said, stepping forward. "You may not enter here."

Keir set the mirror down for a moment, tall side up, and leaned it against his shoulder with a grunt. He let himself catch his breath for a moment before speaking up and clearing his throat.

"Is there any way I can get some help carrying this to the nearest transportation center?" he asked. "It's a little heavy."

"We cannot leave our post," the first guard replied stiffly. "You'll have to carry it on your own."

"It really is very heavy. I mean, look at it," Keir said, leaning it forward towards the guard. "Really, look at it."

The guard put his hand out to push the mirror away from his face, when suddenly his hand went through the surface and became stuck. He let out a curse and tried pulling away, pressing his other hand to the surface before that one sunk beneath the reflection as well and something began pulling him in. Before he could get out a word for help, the mirror sucked him in and startled the other men for a moment before they jumped into action. On the other side of the mirror, the first guard banged against the glass, calling for them to get him out. When one person tried to reach through to get him, the force pulled them inside as well, and a third guard attempted to yank them back out before becoming stuck and pulled in, too.

Keir picked up the mirror and used it like a shield to deflect a swing from one of the remaining two guards. And the man's hand went right into the surface and, with a yelp, went tumbling inward. The last and final guard tried to stand his ground by swinging his weapon at the mirror to try to break it, but the mirror swallowed that in as well and the guards inside had to dodge out of the way to keep from getting hit. Keir kicked out and backed the last guard against the wall and pressed the mirror against him, trapping him inside with the others.

From inside the room, there was a scuffle of feet as the commotion outside was heard dwindling into nothing, and the doors burst open, setting off an alarm to alert the entire palace to an intruder. Keir didn't hesitate. As the door swung open, he barreled through, holding the mirror in front of himself and catching nearly every guard there in the crossfire and knocking over one more. There were so many stuck in the mirror with one limb or another they couldn't all fit through the frame. He set the mirror on the ground, effectively trapping them on the floor, and ran for the bone knife sitting on the pedestal where he had last remembered seeing it.

Down the hallway, he could hear shouts of warning, commands being given out as the soldiers grew closer, and glanced at the knife, hoping this would work like he needed it to. If it didn't, well, he didn't want to think about that. Slashing it through the air and picturing the Mortal World in his mind as best he could, he watched as a shining blue portal opened up before him. His heart hammered in his chest as he wondered if this would work or if he was going somewhere where he'd never be seen or heard from again.

Casting one last look behind him and seeing the guards enter the room, he jumped through and disappeared.

"I can't contact him through the mirror and the locating spell just falls dormant when I try to activate it," Ilarys said, pacing. She bit her thumb in thought. "A location spell shouldn't do that. He has to be somewhere. Even if he was dead, it would locate his body. I don't understand!"

"Perhaps he got wards put up against finding spells," Aui'ani suggested, but Ilarys was shaking her head.

"The spell would have backfired if that were the case. It just goes dead as if he just never existed," she said.

"You don't think the Fae had anything to do with this, do you?" Aui'ani asks quietly. Ilarys froze. The only place they couldn't locate someone was in the in between or worse...

The Mortal World.

"I'm a fool," she hissed, moving straight to the mirror in their room. She banged against the glass, not caring who heard her. "Come here, you violent beasts, and tell me where my brother is!"

"Ilarys," Aui'ani tried to reason, but she wasn't listening. She beat on the mirror again and called out to the Fae and suddenly her reflection hissed. A feral sound that shook her to her core. She would have lurched backwards away from it if her anger hadn't kept her rooted to the spot. Her anger momentarily subsided, but when her reflection spoke, it gradually reignited.

Why do you summon us? it hissed.

"Where is Keir?" she demanded. "Where is my brother?"

He has crossed over, the reflection replied.

"Crossed over?" she repeated. "To where?"

The Mortal World.

"Did you take him there?" she demanded. "Steal him away?"

He went of his own accord, came the reply, *in exchange for safe passage for you and the one called Aui'ani.*

"That stupid, stupid man!" Ilarys growled. "Where is he now?"

In a fairy wrath, the reflection said. *He is safe. Disguised. No harm will come to him. As was our agreement.*

"That tells me nothing! Let me speak to him!" she demanded.

We cannot do this, the reflection denied her.

"Why not?" she snapped.

There is no magic here. You would not be seen or heard. Only watching through the In Between, the reflection replied. It turned away from her for a moment, as if listening to something. *We must go. There are others coming.*

"Others?" Ilarys asked. "What do you mean? What others?" But before she could get a reply, her reflection shimmered away and was slowly replaced by a normal one. "Come back here! What others?!" She cursed and slapped her hand against the mirror in irritation, cracking it. But the Fae were gone.

"What do we do?" Aui'ani asked softly.

"I need to find him. I need to talk some sense into him," Ilarys murmured. "He can't just go over there alone. How did he even get over there? The farthest the Fae have gotten is the In Between!"

"That girl," Aui'ani recalled. "The one called Amara. She mentioned she was from the Mortal World. Her and some of the other Dai-Nē. Perhaps they can help?"

"I don't trust them," Ilarys shook her head.

"I'm not asking you to trust them. I'm suggesting we come together under a mutual benefit. They, too, were looking to learn about the veil, weren't they?"

"True," Ilarys muttered, then cursed under her breath yet again. "I don't want to work with them... But I may have to. For Keir, that idiot."

"We all must do things we dislike for the ones we love from time to time," Aui'ani stood and took her hand, kissing it. "I will stay here and try to find you a way back in case the others will not let you use their portal knife. Hopefully Keir has found one of his own and you both will not be stranded."

"Hopefully," agreed Ilarys, clutching Aui'ani's hand to her chest. "I don't want to leave you, but I think it's best you don't get stuck over there as well."

"I knew you would," Aui'ani smiled.

"You know me too well," Ilarys said with a grim smile.

A small silence settled between them before Aui'ani broke it.

"So," she said. "Where do we begin?"

"With a location spell," Ilarys said, brow furrowing into concentration.

"Good. Now we need to find ourselves some Dai-Nē," Aui'ani declared.

Standing in the middle of a small library, Soren looked around, confused. There was a slightly open window that let in the light from outside, where a small pond with a fountain was trickling. It was a pleasant sound and gave the room a calming ambiance. There were tables stacked with books, a fire warming the hearth, and a familiar woman sitting in a chair in the corner with her legs crossed, hands resting in her lap. She had pulled her long, black hair into a braid that lay over her shoulder down to her knees. She was placid as she was stern looking.

"I assume you know where you are?" she asked after he had looked around for a long moment before laying eyes on her.

"You assume incorrectly," Soren replied. "I do not know of this place."

She tilted her chin to look down her nose at him. "Think carefully, Soren. You know who I am, though you may not know my name."

"How do you know mine?" he asked, brow furrowing. Then he seemed to place her face. "You are the Dai-Nē of Dark Magic. The woman I scryed for when-" A sudden dawning hit him and he looked around frantically. "We have been here too long. The woercir will be upon us any moment!"

"No, they will not," Ilarys said coldly. "Because I warded

this area so they may not enter. This is how you scry properly, boy."

"I do not understand," Soren said slowly. "How is this done?"

Ilarys rubbed her temple and sighed. "I do not wish to teach you the basics of scrying, but I will show you how to properly dismiss the spell before I go," she added with a curt look. "I have come here to talk to you about a much more pressing matter."

"I thought you no longer wished to speak with us," Soren replied. "Given that your brother had an altercation with one of our company that resulted in her partial death."

"Partial?" Ilarys looked up then. "So, she is still alive?"

"She is gravely injured and in the healing house. She had split herself into two people to aid in our search for information. You killed half of her," Soren explained.

"She attacked my brother," Ilarys said. "I do not take kindly to people that attack those I care about."

"Then why have you contacted me?" he asked.

"I would have contacted Amara, but she seemed more affected by the girl's death than you were," Ilarys replied. "I do not think she would have spoken with me."

"I am..." Soren hesitated. "Uncertain if we trust Attalira. A creature that she turned into when she was fighting your brother attacked us. It is my suspicion that it was her that attacked us and stole the ring of Rynon in the first place," he admitted.

Ilarys' eyebrows shot up. Was he really giving her this kind of information? "So, you have a traitor in your midst?" He must not be very bright, or at least was very trusting that people wouldn't use that kind of information against him. He would need to learn differently in this world of politics if he wanted to survive.

"It is possible," Soren agreed. "Though I had thought the same of you when you revealed you had the ring."

"We stole it from the council," Ilarys said. "Right before the ceremony, that gave us our powers."

Soren somehow looked both relieved and on edge at the same time. "Then we are right not to trust the council," he said after a moment's pause. "They must have sent the shapeshifter to attack us. And since only Dai-Nē can cross the veil, I fear it must have been Attalira that attacked us."

"Then I supposed we did you a favor of sorts," Ilarys replied. "Exposing your traitor for you." Soren gave her an odd look, so she continued. "I'd like to ask a favor in return. The reason I contacted you like this."

"What kind of favor?" Soren asked suspiciously.

"I believe my brother has ventured into the Mortal World, and fear for his safety. I know no way of getting there, save by you and your portal knife. And I know nothing of the terrain or people, whereas your friends grew up there and are familiar with it."

"What is your point?" Soren asked.

"I would like to propose a truce between us and work together to find my brother. I believe the Fae have coerced him into doing their bidding and I fear what may become of him."

"Why should we help you?" Soren replied. "You have given me no reason to trust your words."

"We know why the living cities are falling ill," Ilarys counter offered. This got Soren's attention. If she could give a little information to gain his trust, then she would. "There are weak points in the veil that are leeching the power from the cities and killing them. We believe the Fae have a spell that can replenish the veil and aid the living cities in healing again."

"At what cost?" Soren asked, still suspicious. "If they have such a spell, why have they not used it?"

"Because they are trying to cross the veil into our world," Ilarys explained. "They are dying off because of the iron and lack of magic in the Mortal World and have sought help in various places to find a way across. That is how they contacted my brother and I. They believed we were a key to escaping their torment."

"How so?" Soren asked, intrigued.

"We are Dai-Nē and can pass through the veil," she replied simply, returning his words to him to make things make sense.

"But they cannot," Soren surmised.

"Which is why they seek our help," Ilarys nodded.

Soren sighed. "I cannot agree to this." Ilarys stiffened, trying to hide the desperate emotion that ran through her veins from showing on her face, but then Soren continued. "First, I must contact my friends and convey this information to them. I do not know how they will wish to proceed."

"Understood," Ilarys said, a bit relieved he wasn't just shutting her down without consideration. "We will convene again tomorrow."

Soren gave a nod. Ilarys then drew a symbol in the air and spoke a word of dismissal, and in moments Soren was waking in his bed. No wave of nausea, no spinning colors, just his mind buzzing with this newfound information. He quickly committed the symbol to memory and rose to contact the other Dai-Nē. When they had all sleepily gathered together, Soren relayed the encounter he had, and all three of them sat up straighter.

"Wait, he went into the Mortal World?" Tursanay asked. "Is he crazy?"

"We gotta do damage control. If he uses his powers over there, things could get really bad really fast," Rodney said.

"Not that I'm eager to help a traitor find a murderer exactly," Amara began. "But you're right in that we need to stop him before word gets out about this place and scientists start trying to breach the veil like the Fae are."

"Oh, man, I didn't even think about that," Rodney said. "They would do so much damage."

"That being said, this thing about getting the Fae over here," Tursanay began. "How would we even do that? If only Dai-Nē can cross the veil?"

"It would be a good chance to test out our theory," Soren said. "To see if Dai-Nē enchanted things can cross the veil."

"True." Tursanay brightened at the thought. "I could cast a protection spell on each of them and-"

"But imagine what that would do to the economy and ecosystem of the magic world," Soren warned. "Introducing an entire new species to the world could be very detrimental to its existing system."

"That's true. We should start talking to various governments and see about how they can help introduce a new species into the general public," Tursanay agreed.

"It would be like both bringing in a new species and helping refugees escape a horrible situation," Rodney added. "I say we help wherever we can. I mean, it's what we're supposed to do as Dai-Nē anyhow."

"Agreed," Soren nodded.

"So, where do we start?" Tursanay asked.

"I can begin with speaking to the governments," Soren began. "You three said you had unfinished business in the other world, correct? You can take care of that amidst searching for Keir."

Tursanay breathed in with a hiss. "Oof, I didn't think about that."

"Oh no," Rodney groaned. "I have to remember dates of history again."

"We've been able to move about freely for so long. Going back to high school is going to seem like hell," Tursanay agreed.

"Oh shoot," Rodney realized. "How are we going to hide our marks?"

"I can do a concealment spell and they'll disappear," Tursanay dismissed. "No big deal."

"Thank goodness," Rodney sighed with relief. "I don't want to think of the flack I'll get for having a tramp stamp over summer break."

"Wow, it really has only been a summer, hasn't it?" Tursanay realized.

"This place has warped my sense of time," Amara groaned, rubbing her face.

"So," Tursanay said, slapping her hand against her knee. "Soren starts talking to the various governments and pleading our case, and we join up with the Dai-Nē of Dark Magic to find her brother. Are we all agreed?"

"I am," Rodney nodded.

"As am I," Soren agreed.

Amara nodded quietly.

"Then it's settled," Tursanay nodded. "Tomorrow, when she contacts you, tell her we'll help her."

"I still don't trust her," Amara said. "Even if she's the

reason we know about Attalira possibly being the one that attacked us. That doesn't make what her brother did right."

"Yeah, I'm a little iffy on that too," Rodney said. "Do we trust having her with us after all that?"

"Well, if they are telling the truth, Attalira attacked him first," Tursanay reasoned. "We can have them step into a truth spell and confirm that once we find him."

"There are a few things I want to ask him once that happens," Amara said flatly.

"We'll burn that bridge when we get to it," Rodney said. "Meanwhile, I need food."

"You and your stomach," Tursanay said, shaking her head while smiling.

"I will compile a list of governments to speak to in the meantime," Soren said.

"We should probably include the resistance," Amara suggested.

Rodney stood and stretched. "Whoever we include, that's going to be a lot of convincing if they don't even believe the Mortal World is real."

"True. I will try to contact the Fae as well and ask if they will aid me in my quest," Soren replied. "I can show them these people are real and will need our help."

"That might just work," Rodney agreed.

"Alright," Tursanay said, standing as well. "Meeting adjourned. Now my stomach is growling." Amara began to rise, but felt Soren grab her hand from behind, gently pressing his thumb into her palm.

"You guys go on ahead, I'm gonna come down in a minute," Amara replied.

"Race you to the kitchen," Rodney said, grinning at Tursanay.

"Oh, you're so on," she said, darting out the door.

"Hey no fair!" Rodney called after her, running out of the room.

Soren rose and stood alongside Amara, watching them go.

"Are you alright with this?" he asked her softly. "Working with them despite what happened?"

Amara looked down for a moment, then over at him. "I will be eventually. I just have to process things first," she said at last.

Soren nodded.

"Thank you for asking," she added, giving him a warm smile.

He returned it, and they shared a look.

"We should probably go downstairs and get something to eat as well," he said softly.

"Yeah," she agreed, squeezing his hand that still held onto hers. "Let's go."

CHAPTER 25
HOME

The library was warm and cozy; an inviting and relaxing atmosphere. Books lined shelves on every wall. There was a bay window with a cushioned seat overlooking a garden fountain trickling in the distance. The sounds of bird song wafted through the open window. There was a spiral staircase that led to a second level of books, and a desk in the center of the room. Books of all kinds, colors, and sizes stacked the tables. The light from the fireplace danced on the hearth as the fire crackled gently. The chair in the corner was empty this time, the woman not in her previous spot.

"Hello?" called Soren. The sound of a book snapping shut caught his attention, and he looked up on the balcony to see the Dai-Nē of Dark Magic descending the stairs slowly. When she reached the bottom, she set the book on the table nearby and folded her hands behind her back.

"So, you have come to a decision?" she asked. Her voice did not tremble or give away her hammering heartbeat.

"We have," Soren acknowledged. His answer gave nothing away, much to Ilarys's irritation.

She took a breath and let it out slowly. Was she going to pry this out of him? she wondered. "And your verdict?" she asked, looking away from him, preparing herself for said answer as she pretended to examine the books on the wall. If it was no, she would have to hunt them down and steal their bone knife herself, she had decided. She was much more skilled than these little brats, surely, with how little they knew of scrying, so it shouldn't be too difficult.

"We will aid you in finding your brother and helping the Fae escape the Mortal World," Soren said. She looked up, then, shocked. They had agreed to so much?

"I did not ask for your help on the latter," she said, obviously taken aback.

"We are Dai-Nē," Soren replied. "Helping refugees from the Mortal World into ours is our purpose. I am going to attempt to contact the Fae and speak with the governments to convince them to help us integrate them into our world carefully so that we do not upset the balance of life here."

"That... might actually work if you can show them the Fae exist and can convince them to help. But that's a big if," she replied. "I know someone who can help you. She has contacts in most governments, for she is a liaison for the Order of Rynon."

"That would be most helpful," Soren said, intrigued. "We also have a contact in the resistance that could help should the council turn us down."

"Good," she replied. "I fear they will be the hardest to convince."

"I feel as if they have been working with the Fae and

know of their plight, but having them admit it will be difficult," Soren said.

"Oh, I know they are working with the Fae. I heard it directly from the Fae myself, though I don't know what kind of dealings they have been up to. They refused to say," she said. "Saying it was between them and the council."

"Then perhaps the council is planning something," Soren said, thinking. "I dislike the idea of them working together with the Fae. It feels as if they are up to no good."

She snorted. "Aren't they always up to no good?"

"They are not wholly corrupted," Soren admitted slowly. "There are those that stood against the majority with us when we were training. I believe their intentions are much more pure than the others. Regrettably, their voices get drowned out because they are a minority.

"As is the way of their ruling," she grunted. "They never give a voice to the minority."

"As for the Fae, if what you say is true, I believe they have been trying everything to get over here, and that some of their actions stem from desperation rather than true malice," Soren said.

"I don't know them enough yet to agree to that statement, but I do agree they act out of desperation," she said. "That much is evident from the encounters I have had with them."

Soren nodded. "Since you have had so many encounters with them, is there a way you can contact them and introduce me so that we may work together to convince the alchemist government, the Council of Dai-Nē, and Kutawë to help in their integration? Most will not believe they exist without proof."

"I can do that," she said. "Though I do not look forward to it. Their encounters are... unsettling at best."

"What do you mean?" he asked.

"They use your own reflection to speak to you and it changes it slightly. Red eyes. Six of them. Two sets - one above and one below your own - make it eerie to see yourself presented in such a way."

"I see," Soren nodded. "That would be disconcerting the first time seeing it without warning."

"I once saw one rip open their chest to reveal a large gaping maw," she shuttered. "It was in the form of my brother. I still have nightmares."

"That sounds horrifying," Soren replied, looking concerned.

She nodded. "I don't recommend angering one," she added.

"Where do you wish to meet to begin this introduction and journey to the Mortal World?" Soren asked.

"Let us meet in the seven cities, in Yádnuwaith," she said. "With the bustle of the crowd, we won't be noticed in some back alley."

Soren gave a nod. "I will inform the others. Also, may I ask your name?"

"You may," she said, drawing the dismissal symbol in the air. "It's Ilarys," she said, and Soren woke up in his bed once again, her voice echoing in his ears.

The seven cities were all living cities that were connected by roads barely a few miles apart. In the center of them stood a tall tree, which was the tallest in the world. Its trunk was so broad it was a mile to make one revolution around it. Some mistook it for a lone mountain in the distance before the cities came into view.

The cities themselves did not center on trees like most living cities; instead, they grew from the roots of the tree in their center. There were seven main roots that sprouted out from around the tree and each of the cities were built in and around these roots. Glass buildings glittered in the sunlight, spreading rainbows across the trunk of the large Yádnuwaith as the sun made its trek through the sky. There were roads through the tree and along the branches, all lined with special lights that lit up with an ambient glow at night like fireflies.

The four Dai-Nē stepped off the dirigible and into the branches of the Yádnuwaith, looking around in awe. Amara pushed herself forward in a wheelchair that Rodney and Tursanay helped make her, and Tursanay had already placed the disguise spells on all of them to look like their normal human selves. Dai-Nē marks, fins, wings and all were gone.

"This is the biggest tree I've ever seen," Rodney breathed. "I didn't think it was possible for them to grow this big."

"The Yádnuwaith is said to be the oldest living tree in our world," Soren said.

"That's amazing," Rodney replied, still looking around in awe.

They made their way further into the city, following a location spell that would take them to Ilarys. They followed the twisting, winding roads and halls until they found her in a remote back alley where no one else was walking near.

Standing next to Ilarys was a woman with black hair down to her shoulders, a flat nose that suited her face nicely, and medium dark skin. Soren and Amara recognized her from their first encounter with Ilarys, though they had barely gotten a look at her before she had shifted into a cynocephali.

"This is Aui'ani," Ilarys introduced. "She is the Liaison of the Order of Rynon. She will help you in your quest to speak to the various governments."

"I'm Tursanay," she said. "This is Rodney, Amara, and Soren—you may know already."

The women nodded at each of them in turn.

"The shapeshifter is not amongst you?" Aui'ani asked darkly.

"Attalira is still unconscious in the healing house," Amara replied in the same tone.

Ilarys elbowed Aui'ani pointedly. Play nice, her facial expression said.

"We plan to interrogate her once she wakes up," Tursanay replied. "We have a lot of questions to ask her. One of which is why she attacked your brother. We want to get to the bottom of this, too."

"Good," Aui'ani said flatly. "I want to be there for that interrogation."

"Aui'ani," Ilarys warned. "Don't antagonize."

"Sorry," she apologized stiffly.

"Are you ready to do this?" Ilarys asked.

Soren gave a nod and looked at Amara. She hesitated, but gave a nod as well. Ilarys breathed out her nose, readying herself for the encounter. She knocked on the glass and called out to the Fae. And for a moment, nothing happened. Then she noted the slight change in color to the reflection of their surroundings. "It's okay," she said. "These are the Dai-Nē that are here to help you cross over into this world. We are working together to find a way."

Ilarys's reflection blinked its eyes once, then twice, the second time opening becoming a solid red. Rodney felt a shiver go up his spine at the sight of Ilarys turning to face them and her reflection facing them as well, even though her back was to it.

"These are the Fae," she said softly.

"Hello," Amara said softly, waving. The head tilted slightly downwards to look at Amara, then bared its teeth in a smile. It wasn't friendly. Amara fell silent, quickly putting her hand back down. Soren put a hand on her shoulder and took a step forward.

"We will find a way to save you all," he said. "One way or another, we will free you from the prison you inhabit."

Bold words, child, the reflection hissed without moving its lips. *A promise many have given us, but none have yet to prevail.*

"We are Dai-Nē," he replied firmly. "This is our purpose: to save magic kind and be a liaison between the worlds."

We shall see, the reflection replied skeptically.

"We need your help first, though," Tursanay said, stepping forward now as well. The reflection looked her up and down, as if sizing her up.

A bargain? it asked.

"Not... exactly," Tursanay said, furrowing her brow in confusion. "More like we need to prepare the people in this world for your arrival. So, we need you to show yourself when we call you and prove you exist to the people in this world. This way nothing upsets the balance of life here, because we've prepared for you to get here."

"It's so you will have a place here among the others and feel welcomed," Aui'ani added.

Tursanay nodded. "We want you to feel at home here, because after everything you've been through trying to escape the Mortal World, you deserve a home. Some place you can call your own."

We will not hope for much, the reflection replied, frowning.

We have fought alone thus far. We will find a way to cross whether you have prepared a place or not.

"Believe in us," Amara said, and the reflection looked at her again. "We are as determined as you are to make this happen."

The reflection studied her for a long moment, then looked away.

We will do as you ask, the reflection said at last. *But know this: should you break our trust, we will eat you first, little fish.*

Tursanay bristled, but before she could say anything in Amara's defense, the reflection turned and became Ilarys' again, with her back to the mirror and the colors back to their original shades. Aui'ani put a hand on Tursanay's shoulder and shook her head, telling her to stand down. Tursanay looked from her to the glass again, but realized the argument dying on her tongue was futile in the making.

"Wow," Rodney said at last. "That's going to give me nightmares."

"I can't believe they are so rude," Tursanay grumbled. "We're offering to help them! And they act like they could take or leave our help!"

Ilarys sighed. "They don't trust easily," she said, rubbing her temples. "They don't seem to like the idea of being put on public display."

"Well, I don't really blame them," Amara said, making Tursanay and Ilarys look at her curiously. "I mean, think about it. They've been in hiding since before the Veil was a thing. Do you know how long they've gotten used to blending in only for us to say, 'Hey! Put yourself on display so we can get people to notice you!'? It's a complete one eighty to what they're used to and has been ingrained in them for thousands of years. Would you trust someone who told you to do something against your very nature for a slim hope of escaping your life long torment?"

The others were silent, not having considered that.

"I mean," Rodney said, breaking the silence with a shrug. "She's got a point."

"I hate it when you use logic on me when I want to be mad," Tursanay complained.

"What can I say?" Amara replied, shrugging. "It's a talent."

"Yeah and annoying one," Tursanay teased with a smile on her face as she play shoved Amara's shoulder. Amara giggled at her as Ilarys cleared her throat.

"So, I suppose we take our leave now?" She didn't sound enthusiastic about it.

"I guess we gotta," Tursanay said, looking back at Soren. "Gonna miss ya, bud," she said, giving him a hug. "Take care of yourself, okay?"

"Indeed," Soren agreed. "You as well." When she pulled away, he turned to Rodney and held out his hand.

"Nah, man," Rodney said, shaking his head. "Imma hugger." He half grappled Soren in a hug, earning a half laugh from the half elf.

Soren checked over his shoulder to see if anyone was coming near the alley, then pulled out the bone knife and took a breath. Slashing it through the air, a portal opened up before them, shimmering a bright blue.

"We'll go first to make sure the coast is clear," Tursanay said, gesturing to herself and Rodney. "Then Ilarys can come through," she said. "Amara will take up the rear because we'll need to make sure there's nothing in the way of her rolling out of the portal."

"It should bring you back to your room where we first met," Soren said to Tursanay.

"Good," Tursanay said. "Alright guys, let's go. We have little time before this closes."

Rodney and Tursanay went through the portal, and after a few moments, Ilarys followed. Soren knelt down next to Amara when they were alone with Aui'ani and took her hand in his.

"Be safe," he said softly.

"You too," she replied.

Leaning forward, Soren kissed her gently, then pulled away. Amara's cheeks were thoroughly red, but there was a smile on her face. She bid him goodbye and reluctantly pulled away, turning to face the portal herself. Rolling through, she came out the other side to find the others waiting for her. Behind them, the portal slowly closed, leaving Soren and Aui'ani behind on one side, and the trio and Ilarys on the other side.

"There's been another act of treason," said a deep voice. "Another breech in the veil." It broke the silence in the small office space like the shattering of glass.

"When?" came the reply. The man stood with his back to the open door, where the guard knelt with the information.

"An hour ago," the guard replied. "In Yádnuwaith. Should we send the hunters, sir?"

"Not yet. Give them a day's head start," he replied.

"Sir?" the guard asked.

"Give them a false sense of security," he replied. "How is

the shape shifter?" he questioned. His voice sounded casually light, but it sent a chill down the guard's spine.

"Still unconscious," the guard replied. "Though the healers believe she should wake up soon."

"Good," he said. "We'll need her for this."

"Yes, sir," the guard said.

"Oh, and one more thing," he said. "When it's time to send the hunters, gather The Three."

"Sir?" the guard asked hesitantly.

"I'm not letting them get away this time," came the reply.

"Yes, sir," the guard replied. "I'll begin preparations immediately."

"Good," he said. "Dismissed."

And with that, the guard rose to his feet and made his way out quickly.

"Well," Amara said, relieved. "Looks like your theory was right. Dai-Nē spells hold up across the veil." She looked down at her legs, rather than the fin she'd become accustomed to, and patted them gingerly.

"I wonder if we can still use magic," Tursanay said. She drew a symbol in the air with her finger and whispered a word of magic and her arm of light appeared again. "Sweet!" she declared as she flexed her arm. "Imagine the looks on people's faces if I came to school with this baby."

"Remember, we can't use magic in front of others," Amara said, grinning.

"Yes, mom," Tursanay teased, releasing the spell.

"Oh man," Rodney said. "I can't believe we're back."

"Me either," Amara said, looking around. Their room was

in absolute chaos from when they left in such a hurry after the creatures had chased them out of the fire escape. That felt like ages ago, but it had barely been two months.

"Where do we go from here?" Ilarys asked.

"First, we need to get into clothes that will blend in," Rodney said.

"What is wrong with what I am wearing?" Ilarys asked.

"Yes," Rodney replied, gesturing to all of her.

"No one dresses like that around here unless they go to a convention to cosplay a character they like," Tursanay replied.

"Unless they what?" Ilarys asked, not recognizing some of those words. "Is my speech spell wearing off? I don't recognize some of those words."

"Oh shoot," Rodney realized. "How is anyone going to understand her? They'd have to eat the magic translator first."

"I have an idea," Tursanay said. "Can you make it so that others can understand you without taking a translation spell?"

"There is a spell, but it only works for short spurts," Ilarys replied. "A day or so at a time, maybe less?"

"That's perfect! You can recast it as you need it, just not in front of others," Tursanay replied.

"Wait, why didn't Soren just use that when he first met us?" Rodney asked. "It would have made things a lot easier."

"It's a magic spell. He's not a Dai-Nē of Magic. He can have it cast on him, but it would require a Dai-Nē for it to work over here, I am assuming," Ilarys said.

"Right," Tursanay nodded.

"Oh, that makes more sense," Rodney nodded.

"Okay, first things first. Rodney, take yourself to your

room and get changed. We'll give Ilarys some of our clothes to wear to help her blend in. Then we'll meet in the cafeteria. It's about time for lunch anyhow," Tursanay directed. Everyone gave a nod and set about doing what she'd said, and within half an hour's time, they were meeting up in the cafeteria for lunch. Ilarys wearing an outfit that was much more modern and simplistic than what she wore before, and the girls waved down Rodney, who was already in line getting something. The cafeteria had very few people in it, and there were plenty of places for them to sit.

After getting in line and getting their food, the group sat at a table and stared at each other for a moment. There was so much that had happened in this cafeteria before they became Dai-Nē and discovered a world of magic. There was so much that had changed them over the couple of weeks they had been gone. They weren't the same people they were when Asher had first met Amara here, just over a year ago. They weren't even the same people as they were when they last spoke to him before they traveled across the Veil. There was a long moment as they stared at each other and their food before breaking into giggles. Rodney was the first, and the girls looked up at him. He looked down at his mashed potatoes, then up at them and giggled again.

"Mashed potatoes," he whispered before giggling again. Tursanay's face cracked into a wide grin and she giggled, too. The sound was infectious and Amara followed not long after. They giggled until they laughed, and tears formed in the corners of their eyes. When at last Ilarys couldn't take being left out of the joke any longer, she huffed.

"What is so funny?" she asked.

"This," Tursanay said. "We've just gone on an amazing adventure that no one will ever know about, and now we're back in school in our normal lives like none of it ever happened."

"That doesn't sound funny, that sounds depressing," Ilarys replied.

"It is a little bit," Tursanay laughed. "But if we don't laugh, we'll probably cry."

"Oh, I am definitely going to cry later," Amara laughed.

"Same," Rodney agreed.

"You three are very strange," Ilarys said.

"That's fair," Rodney consented. As he looked out on the cafeteria, just taking it all in, something caught his eye that made the blood in his veins freeze. The laughter in his throat abruptly died as a lump of fear replaced it. There, walking past and not seeing any of them, was a tall man, dark brown skin, a bald head with a goatee, and piercing icy blue eyes.

It was Mr. Asher.

But Mr. Asher was dead.

"Guys," Rodney said cautiously. The laughter had died down, and they instantly went on alert at his tone and looked in the direction he was staring at. When the two girls' eyes fell on Asher, they widened in shock. "I think things just got a bit more complicated."

ABOUT THE AUTHOR

I. N. Knight is an emerging author of fantasy novels that take you on a fun ride from start to finish. As a fur-parent of a miniature zoo, they state if you find a typo, to blame the cats for climbing on the keyboard whilst trying avoiding the dogs. And that if you're ever in need of a laugh to join them on their Tumblr or Facebook page where you can find entertaining memes and story rantings to be shared.

Find all of their social media links at linktr.ee/inks.books